CRUMB
The Secret of the Riddle

Carol Worthey

Carol Worthey

Published by

WORTHGOLD PUBLISHING

17415 Mayerling St.
Granada Hills, CA 91344

Cover Artwork: "Crumb's Journey" by Carol Worthey
Copyright © 2014 Carol Worthey

Library of Congress Control Number: 2016pending
ISBN: 978-0-6927122-6-9
Printed in the United States of America

www.Worthgold.com

Carol Worthey

DEDICATION

Dedicated to my brilliant, loving and playful Father BERNARD KRIEGER SYMONDS whose short bedtime stories about a mischievous crumb kept three generations of children begging for "More Crumb, more Crumb!" In answer to that entreaty, it is my great pleasure and creative duty to present to those who treasure The Child Within: "MORE CRUMB!"

I would also like to thank my Husband Ray Korns for his constant affection, technical help and unshakable support in every way and assistance in preparing this manuscript for publication.

Carol Worthey

CONTENTS

Table of Contents

Prologue

Humble Beginnings

Legends have been known to start in the most humble of places. Heroes have been known to come from the most unlikely sources, often reluctant to take on the challenge. Nursery rhymes have been known to originate in petty protests or grand causes.

Fashions change as fast as the wind but the wind is a constant. Good and evil play out their struggle in a myriad of passing civilizations. Man and beast have cared for or fought with one another ever since fires were contained in caves.

Bread has been broken amongst weary companions on journeys ever since seeds were gathered or planted in soil. Riddles have opened or closed doors from the beginnings of time. We are echoes of all the old stories, we are promises still yet to come, and we sing to our young so they understand that some things will always be true.

Is it any wonder then that our story begins in a Kitchen?

Carol Worthey

Chapter One

The Heart of The Home

Crumb wasn't sure who his parents were but he knew Breadbox must be his Granddad. He had been born --- or so Breadbox told him -- one day during a hot summer spell when Toaster had discovered him at the bottom of the toast drawer, all round and light brown with just a hint of a little curly-cue on top.

"Yes," said Toaster, "there you were. I rescued you from a blob of melted butter on my tray that would have smeared all over you, and then I named you, right on the spot. You were a cute little tyke. All round and roly-poly."

Granddad chuckled, shaking his tin door up and down with mirth.

"Now you've grown a bit more fat and puffy," added Breadbox, "definitely more sturdy since we first found you. It's a good thing you've grown a bit. It's so much easier to see you as you roll around the counter now that you're bigger. You're not going to grow little bread-bumps for feet and hands for a couple more years. Watch out with all that rolling around you've been doing."

Breadbox paused. He knew that pauses sometimes speak louder than words.

"Crumb, honestly, could you please try to stay out of trouble? Your Granddad gets a bit worried from time to time. Just be sure you hide somewhere if that pesky cat or wagging dog come leaping up, looking for a snack."

Breadbox was always having to watch out for Crumb, who was very small indeed. Crumb had little idea how dangerous the Kitchen could be for a tiny morsel of bread.

"And watch out," warned Breadbox, "for the Family! They're only Human you know, they're not perfect, who is? Humans have the cozy idea that the Kitchen is the Heart of the Home, so they're always tramping in and out, messing with everything. The Family hasn't realized that it's OUR home, so they make a heap of trouble for us Kitchen Things!"

The dishes must have heard Breadbox because they began to rattle a bit on their shelves in total agreement with his wise caution or perhaps trembling in fear of the next broken dish.

"Humans! They sure do make it hard for us, Breadbox," said Toaster, clanging his bottom tray for a split-second, shuddering, until he realized that a Detective should never show a sign of fear. "They leave clues around all the time, but messes too."

Toaster fancied himself a descendant of Sherlock Holmes because he had been manufactured in London near Baker Street. (Now he lived with the Baker Family on Tempest Street.) He tried to act super-cool but he was kind of a hot-head at times. You could always tell, because Toaster's Light-Medium-Dark dial gave away his emotional state.

Trying to appear nonchalant and fearless, the dial whirled from its Dark setting over to Light and Toaster chuckled awkwardly, "I'm not scared of them, mind you, I just like to... keep a distance."

"Sure, that's smart," comforted Breadbox, knowing that Toaster didn't want to appear scared of anything.

Turning to Crumb, Breadbox repeated his advice to stay as far away from the Family, the maid, the cat and the dog as possible. Humans thought of the Kitchen as safe, secure, welcoming, the heart of the home. Little did they know how hazardous it could be.

"Sure, Granddad," said Crumb, leaning up against the tin door in a kind of a hug that only bread slices and breadboxes really know is a sign of utmost affection.

"Now, Crumb, I don't mind you exploring a bit, but please try to keep safe."

"I will, I will. I know JUST where to hide, Granddad."

"And where is that, you young whippersnapper?" Both Toaster and Breadbox had a good laugh at that.

"I'm not telling," said Crumb defiantly, "because if you laugh at me, I'm going to keep my secret hiding place to myself." Crumb was stubborn. Which was a good thing for a crumb to be, seeing that there were so many ways that getting soft or moist... or EATEN... could do him in.

"It's MY special hiding place and none of your BEESwax."

"I see," said Toaster, "you're cute but you're also fresh. Do you think you were baked today?"

"Let's give the boy a break," Breadbox advised. "He'll show us where it is in his own good time. Just be sure you get to that Special Place quickly, Crumb. We don't want to lose you."

Then he leaned over, whispering to Crumb, "Not good manners! 'None of your beeswax'? That's rude."

"Sorry, Toaster," apologized Crumb. He had learned to listen to his Granddad. ...Most of the time.

Breadbox was indeed wise, a sensible practical wisdom that commanded others in a gentle, relaxed sort of way, so that all the Kitchen Things listened to him. Since Granddad Breadbox was considered the most venerable object in the Kitchen, he had earned respect, even if begrudgingly.

Toaster gave it a moment of thought, "You're right. He'll show us where it is."

(Crumb would have to, because whenever the maid or cat or dog -- or worse yet, the Family -- came into the Kitchen, eventually or soon Crumb would have to hide and probably the round little morsel of bread would scurry into that Special Place he wasn't telling anybody about.)

"Gee, I was just teasing the pipsqueak," sighed Toaster. His knob spun around and then landed on the Light indication, which meant Toaster had to take Breadbox's advice with a light manner, not take it as a criticism of himself.

"No worries, guys, just kidding," Toaster half-chuckled awkwardly.

In truth, Crumb hoped that if he stalled long enough, he'd be able to figure out WHERE his special hiding place should be -- he actually hadn't found one yet -- he was just bluffing because he was a Big Boy now and didn't want to seem dumb. He'd figure out a good place some day. A place other than Breadbox to hide.

Meanwhile, he'd try to keep safe... but it was just too much fun to roll around the counters exploring the Kitchen. He'd hardly seen the half of it.

This used to worry Breadbox. Sure, there had been countless loaves of bread and certainly generations of crumbs left in his box over the years, but there was something he sensed about this particular little bread-ball. He'd housed many a piece of bread in all his years, so it didn't make sense. But when does something of the heart have to make perfect sense? Crumb was an orphan, maybe that was it.

All in all, Breadbox had a special feeling about Crumb, one that made him realize that even though he wasn't REALLY Crumb's Granddad, the boy had to have a family somehow. So he would be as much of a family to the little round breadcrumb as possible.

Seeing how mischievous and endlessly curious Crumb was, that would be a challenge. Breadbox was determined to guide and keep that little Crumb safe... somehow. Even in the Wilds of the Kitchen. Someday maybe he'd even teach him to read. There were traditions and knowledge to be passed on before old Breadbox ended up in a garage sale. Or a garbage can.

Breadbox knew he was an Endangered Species, an antique that the Mom in the Family had inherited from her Grandma Mildred. (Hardly anyone had a breadbox anymore.) But Breadbox felt it made him special -- that he had a mission to maintain a tradition: "Keep The Bread of Life Fresh!"

This was his Motto and his basic purpose. It was engraved on the inside-back of his tin door in one-inch letters, "Keep The Bread of Life Fresh!" Wanting to figure out what these letters meant, he had somehow managed to learn (as a fairly young Breadbox, long ago) how to read.

Yes, he was old in years, being well over one hundred, but he was sage (wise with experience) and in pretty good shape for his age, except for two things: His tin door squeaked uncomfortably (it needed oiling) and there was a gap between the "B" on his front door and the letters "READ." Breadbox figured that the gap was on purpose and entitled him to "B" ready to "read". He really knew his ABCs.

Everyone in the Kitchen looked up to old Breadbox. He was practical, learned, patient and kind, the perfect Granddad for a lonely orphan. And so he had taken Crumb under his wing (so to speak, although it was really through his tin door).

Inside Breadbox in a snug and cozy little corner in back was where Crumb made his little home and slept at night.

Breadbox's kind heart melted every time little Crumb, usually so jolly and daring, began to sniffle sometimes at night after tucking himself in with his thin sliver of a soft blanket made of leftover spongecake.

"Don't cry, young fella. Why you're growing bigger and stronger every week. Someday you'll be ready for me to teach you to read. That'll open up a whole new world for you. Why are you crying? It gets the spongecake all soggy and you better watch out, because you know that old expression, 'A soggy crumb is a sorry crumb.' "

"Thanks, Granddad. I know... but I feel so lonely sometimes. Where are my Mommy and Daddy, Breadbox? You never tell me! Why aren't they here? Was it my fault they left me? Didn't they love me? Are they... are they... Toast?" Crumb always gulped when he felt extra helpless.

You see, "You're Toast!" was the worst threat in the Kitchen, at least for all the Kitchen Things. The Family didn't seem to realize that the Kitchen Things felt that way and so they used Toaster all the time with nary a thought of anything being wrong.

Maybe that's what had happened to Crumb's parents... maybe they had become toast, eaten bite by bite. Toaster and Breadbox didn't really know what had happened to Crumb's folks, so they could never answer his questions about what had happened. It was getting harder and harder to dodge these outbursts or make up something that might comfort the tyke.

Worrying if he'd been responsible for Crumb's parents death, Toaster had developed a very guilty feeling, watching the Family placing fresh bread slices into him and listening to the crunch of toast as they munched away at the breakfast table.

So Toaster decided to make it hard for Humans to turn his Light-Medium-Dark dial all the way to the darkest position. He tried rusting that side of the dial where it said "Dark", but that didn't work. The Dad in the Family insisted on oiling it.

Try as he did to hide it, Toaster DID have a Dark Side. He always glanced at recipes starting at the bottom of the page so he'd know in advance how many servings it made. He never started with the ingredient list at the top. Underneath his shiny surface, he was afraid to make mistakes. And the last thing he tolerated was the threat "You're Toast!" It insulted him greatly.

Toaster masked his uncertainties by adopting a shrewd Detective exterior, pretending to be cool Sherlock Holmes with his analytical need to "crack the case" by catching the tiniest of clues. Below that seethed a deeply wounded Toaster, trying to turn his Dark Side into a light-hearted game of Cops and Robbers.

Nevertheless, since it was Toaster after all who had rescued baby Crumb from the sticky blob of melted butter, both Crumb and Breadbox considered him a real friend, even if he DID have a Dark Side.

"Aha! I gotcha this time, spill the beans... where's that hiding place, Crumb?"

"Toaster, I like you," said Crumb, "but you're nosy!"

"Elementary, my dear Crumbson."

Just then all chitchat ended. In came the maid Hortense but what was worse, she had the cat by the scruff of its neck.

When the cat was there, it was a House Rule (at least a Kitchen Rule) that no one uttered a word or moved. The maid was one thing -- she was always finding a loose piece of something to throw in the garbage or a fork or spoon to wash, and so all the Kitchen Things froze into position, but the cat -- that was serious!

Crumb froze where he was, stuck in a crack of grout in the white tile counter, right near the cutting board, hoping the maid or the cat wouldn't see him.

Nefertiti (for the cat was named after a regal, long-necked Queen from ancient Egypt) was proud of her lineage from the cat goddesses whose statues graced the inner chambers of royal pyramids. She had her own motto, "No matter what, I always land on my feet." Yes, Nefertiti was a survivor and believed that Humans didn't realize that cats had way more than "nine lives."

Like all cats, Nefertiti was psychic and independent and a sun-worshiper who loved to lounge on window sills.

Although most of the time she appeared to be a perfectly normal feline, there were two oddities about this particular cat that made her extra-specially scary to the Kitchen Things. For one thing, being an Egyptian Mau cat, Nefertiti belonged to the only cat breed whose fur was marked with spots, making her resemble a small leopard, not one to be treated lightly. Her gooseberry green eyes were rimmed in black like the eyes of Egyptian royalty, her forehead bore the markings of a sacred scarab, her voice, although melodious, was hypnotic -- she commanded fearful respect from all the Kitchen Things. Silence was absolutely vital when the cat came into the Kitchen.

The other weird thing about Nefertiti was that she had two speeds, On and Off. Nothing in between, it was either On or Off. When she was awake, she was either leaping, stretching, scratching, preening, kneading her paws, sunbathing, or purring every now and then, but generally on the move, constantly active and very fast. When she was Off, she lay there seeming to be in a trance, sometimes softly intoning something suspiciously like ancient Egyptian. The Family, Ken and Hazel Baker and their kids Johnny and Sally, all wondered about her moaning noises, but assumed she was just having a cat-dream, chasing a mouse or maybe a squirrel.

Little did they realize she WAS in a trance, reliving her glory days at the Pharaoh's palace, rubbing her velvet fur against the lotus-blossom base of a majestic gold and turquoise column or bathing in the perfumed pool under a peacock feather canopy.

Nefertiti had an indelible memory and had lived so many lives since ancient Egypt that her trances were full of odd foreign-sounding and ancient tongues.

The biggest concern Breadbox had was that this cat might stretch out her paws to knead, opening and closing her paws in a rhythmic pattern as ancient as cat-goddesses. For the danger was that maybe Nefertiti would do this right where Crumb was. Then little Crumb might get caught in the cat's paws and find himself blended and smashed into a nameless blob of dust, cat fur and food particles and lose his Crumb identity entirely. It was one thing to die but a worse death to lose one's unique personality, one's individual stamp.

Then, mused Breadbox in his reflective wisdom, *the body might continue like a zombie, soul-less, and what a shame that would be. Crumb has such a winning personality, plucky, funny, cute, obstinate but refreshing.* Or so Breadbox thought, chuckling at the mischievous ways of this smidgen of bread that had come into his life to tease and challenge him in his final years.

Crumb's parents --- whoever they were --- had once been kneaded by warm human hands into a plump mound of flour and yeast, covered with a cloth and left to rise before being baked. But kneaded a second time? *No!*, ruminated Breadbox. *It's one thing to be kneaded, and another thing to be kneaded too much... one time too many and there wouldn't be Crumb anymore.*

That was another reason Breadbox knew that when Crumb was ready, he had to be taught to read. No one could truly lose their unique identity if they could read books and gain the wisdom of the past, become more attuned to their present environment and get an idea how to make a better future. Reading made such a difference.

Why just the year before, when the Kitchen door was open so that he could see the front door, Breadbox had been very impressed with a neighbor-child down the street who had learned to read at a very young age. What a bright and enterprising young girl she was -- Breadbox mentioned her to Crumb, in hopes of inspiring him to want to read.

One weekend morning she had knocked on the front door of the Baker's home, carrying a bunch of library books in one hand and a sign-up sheet for a bake sale in the other. Dad had been home that morning and opened the door.

Zoe was her name, Zoe Baruti -- Dad had seen her father driving down Tempest Street every so often to get to work.

"Hi! What's your sign-up sheet for?" asked Ken Baker.

"I'm giving a bake-sale to raise money for stray animals and to help have some more no-kill shelters. Oh, you have a doggie! And a cat!"

Zoe had practically thrown herself at the pets.

"I have been begging my Dad to get me a puppy! I'm baking a German Chocolate cake, a bunch of brownies, making homemade lemonade with organic lemons and some of our raw honey. We keep bees, would you believe, isn't that GREAT!?!"

"Well, I see you are quite an accomplished baker! That's our last name, Baker. I'm Ken, and my kids Johnny and Sally are out at a Little League baseball game now with my wife, but maybe you'll meet them sometime! Say, put that stack of books down. I'll be glad to sign up for at least one cake or a batch of cookies. I'm sure Hazel -- she's my wife -- will bake you a cake of some kind, she's a fabulous cook."

"Great! Any kind will do, but please see if you don't mind, that it has organic pastry flour in it. I'm very particular about the kind of ingredients I use. All organic!"

"Wow, are you smart! Who taught you to bake? Your Mom?"

Zoe cast her long-lashed brown eyes down. "My Mommy died last year. I taught myself to cook. My Dad works long hours -- he's a research scientist at a big company -- so I started to read recipes so I could make him meals. I LOVE to cook! And read! I taught myself to read when I was four. I even read the dictionary."

"Let me sign my wife up for a cake. Any particular kind?"

"No, as long as it's made from wholesome stuff. Preferably no mixes, unless they're organic."

"Hazel cooks from scratch, scratching around the kitchen all the time, scratch, scratch.... She must be itchy." They both laughed at that.

"Say, what books are you reading now, Miss Zoe-from-down-the-street?" asked Ken Baker, glancing at the stack of books she had placed on the coffee table.

"BULLFINCH'S MYTHOLOGY -- I love fairy stories and myths -- and this is HOW TO CHOOSE THE RIGHT PUPPY FOR YOU, YOUNG CHEFS COOKING GUIDE, and OLIVER TWIST. Dickens is my favorite novelist."

"And you say you're seven? Maybe you should come around here and play with Johnny and Sally sometime."

"Will they let me play with their puppy-dog? And pet the kitty too?"

"Sure!... Ya know what?! I work for a hat company and we make all kinds of hats! I'm gonna get you a real Chef's Hat! Wait a minute, okay? I'll measure your head so it will fit you just right."

Dad opened the Kitchen door extra wide so Breadbox could see and hear everything even better than before. Rushing into the Kitchen Ken Baker fetched a tape measure from the sewing-equipment drawer. Zoe's corn-row braids took up some extra space but Ken was able to get her exact size figured out in no time.

The next week a box arrived at the front door of the Baruti's house. Inside, carefully puffed up with fluffy tissues, was a perfectly-sized Chef's Hat and a note that read, "From one Baker to another. -- Love, The Baker Family." This became one of Zoe's prize possessions, along with her karate outfit and ballet tutu.

For a while, despite that wonderful introduction, Zoe could only show up every so often at the Baker's house to play, because she was so busy with after-school lessons and cooking for her Dad. Still, Breadbox was fond of mentioning her to Crumb as an example of how Humans had their good side.

"When you get a Human-child who starts out with reading well and enjoying books, they usually turn out right, quite capable, social, interested in life and good to be around. So someday, Crumb, I hope to teach you how to read.... It makes a difference. Take these pets for example. They can't read and Humans keep on lording it over them because of that." (Little did Breadbox know that the cat could read Egyptian hieroglyphics from her days way back when.)

Breadbox didn't take much stock in the cat and gave Crumb a particularly strong warning about how the cat might knead him into nothingness.

"Watch out for that pesky cat, Crumb. Remember to stay away when she's in her On position. Watch her paws especially. She always ends up on those paws, even if she's jumped from the counter. And stay at a distance even if she's Off in one of those weird moaning-dreams of hers. She's up to something, I suspect."

"Yes, Granddad. I'll be careful."

No sooner had Crumb said that, than...

Chapter Two

Lessons

Just then the cat let out a furious "MeeOW!" Hortense the Maid was impatiently shoving yowling Nefertiti around by the scruff of her neck. How insulting (this was how a Mama Cat carried her babies). Cat-goddess as she felt she was, this treatment was a violation of the respect due all her sacred time-honored privileges. At this "OW", all the plates and pots on the shelves were trembling just so slightly, but fortunately not loud enough to be heard by the maid.

"I'll show you, you creepy fur-ball!"

Hortense wasn't one to fool around with when she was mad, but usually she was a cheerful soul, with a handy whistle that warned all the Kitchen Things that she was coming into their territory and might sweep some important stuff into the garbage. Tea-Pot had learned some wonderful tunes from her and imitated her whistle on many an occasion.

All the Kitchen Things (except Tea-Pot) nicknamed Hortense "Miss Demolition" and dreaded it every time she came in, whistle or no whistle. This time she was obviously at the end of her patience and threw the cat down. Nefertiti landed on all fours with a thud.

"Why you rascally cat, if I ever find you putting a dead mouse on my blanket -- you'll never get a dish of milk ever again, you hear?!"

Nefertiti looked up at Hortense, with a disappointed look in her big gooseberry green eyes, suddenly begging the maid for a touch of understanding. *Doesn't she know the mouse was meant as a love-offering?* thought the cat. Proud as Nefertiti was, she had chosen the maid as her special human friend so this anger and rejection hurt the cat to the marrow of her bones.

How she longed to tell Hortense that she, who was now a cranky maid in the Baker household, had once ruled as Pharaoh Hatshepsut, the wise woman-ruler of the eighteenth dynasty.

How the cat had loved to sit by Hatshepsut's throne, gently stroked by polished fingernails as priests chanted "Ma'at-ka-Ra -- may she live eternally." What transgressions across the path of many lifetimes had led this former Queen to be the one who emptied the cat-litter box?

It was no use. She cat-goddess had tried so often to show Humans the bigger picture: One lifetime? Not to Nefertiti.

She bowed her furry head, slumped her paws straight onto the linoleum floor and sighed. Hortense obviously didn't remember the ancient ways of cats, the sacred love-offerings on incense altars, the chants and trances of the priestesses of old. With a discouraged yawn, Nefertiti sank into her Off position, asleep right away.

"I've got better things to do than mess with you, Bad Cat! Great, take a nap. And don't you ever put a dead mouse on my blanket again!" Grabbing a dust rag, Hortense stomped out of the Kitchen in a huff.

But it wasn't chasing mice that Nefertiti was dreaming about.

She had gone back-back-back into the ancient past she remembered so well. In a split-second her deep psychic trance had begun, with its mumbling and its mysterious chanting sounds: "Ka, immortal life-force, you who are justified, maa-kheru, because you are true-of-voice, having been weighed in the balance and your soul found to be lighter than a feather, follow the river to the source, ankh, life midst death. It is I, Ubaste, Bastet, Goddess in Cat-form."

Her raspy tongue moved in the soft, mesmerizing tones of ancient Egyptian, sure that no one in the Kitchen would conjure up a clue of what was happening and think her just chasing another mouse in her dream.

"Thoth, mighty-in-knowledge of divine speech, inventor of spoken and written language, I offer you on this alabaster column my heart, which is immortal. Tell us, oh Thoth, lord of all scribes, how may I help Humankind, for so many of them are lost and know not."

Then as Nefertiti the cat-goddess stretched her regal neck upward, there in her trance vision appeared a Riddle inscribed in symbols and hieroglyphics emblazoned on a majestic palace wall in front of her. The bas-relief profiles of a Pharaoh and his Queen faced one another on thrones with calm dignity, then suddenly turned face-forward off the flat wall and nodded to the cat as if to say, "You will bring this Home."

As Nefertiti scanned the writing on the wall, all of a sudden the hieroglyphics morphed into the ABC of our modern English alphabet, revealing the translation of the Riddle. The Cat-Goddess smiled and instantly committed this timeless mystery to the vaults of her endless ability to remember. She could take this home, if only someone would LISTEN.

She had lived life after life wanting to make a difference in Human Affairs. Sure, she could always land on her feet, but Humans? Not very often. In fact, hardly ever. Here was a puzzle to be solved. From deep in the past, thousands and thousands of years ago had come a message, prophetic writing on the wall.

Was there a remedy embedded in these puzzling words that might prevent a future catastrophe? Would she be able to figure out its full meaning? Would she be able to share these instructions with others and summon some help?

Suddenly Nefertiti stiffened in her trance.

Compelling, enormous eyes (slanted like giant cat orbs) were staring down at her from above the hieroglyphic wall, two hollow cat eyes floating in an electric blue sky, glaring at her with fixed and fascinated intensity. The sudden appearance of these huge eyes made it harder and harder for her to concentrate on memorizing the writing on the wall. *Who is it that is spying on me?* she wondered. *Is it a giant cat?*

Nefertiti's chant began to grow louder and louder in her terror, making the words more distinct and audible in the Kitchen air.

Breadbox leaned a bit over the counter to overhear what Nefertiti was saying. Her moaning had taken on a familiar, broad accent -- amazingly, it had the nuance and flow of American English. The words were indistinct at first, but bit by bit as the cat became more terrorized by the huge cat-eyes looking at her, Breadbox began to make out bits and pieces of her incessant chant.

What was she saying? Why did it have a sing-song rhythm? Was this a magic spell? Was it a blessing or a curse? Breadbox had taken on the role of Protector. It was his duty to unravel this bunch of sounds.

Old Breadbox tensed his metal door and sides, tilting them closer to the very edge of the counter so he could hear Nefertiti better. What in the world was she saying? Bit by bit he leaned forward, mesmerized by the cat's moaning, his old metal joints squeaking in protest. Oops, too far! Breadbox had leaned forward so much that he was about to tumble off the tile ledge. The old codger stiffened straight back up and sighed a big sigh of relief.

To Breadbox's astonishment, this is what the cat was intoning:

> Where there's a will,
> you know there's a way!
> What looks like work
> can turn into play!
> When green is red
> and "N" turns to "D",
> A-B-C's the day!
>
> Learning to read
> plants a seed that is sound!
> Heed the signs
> and turn them around!
> "E"nunciate well
> and learn how it's spelled.
> A crumb will lead the way!
>
> No one's too small
> to follow a dream,
> and no dream's too big
> if it's straight from the heart!
> For life is in living
> and living's an art!
> Enjoy the journey today!

So hold on tight
to being taught,
for truth is a price
that can't be bought!
This Riddle will tell you:
It's real food for thought!

Hmmmm...., puzzled Breadbox, thinking to himself. *I'm not sure what all of this means. It's a Riddle alright. But one thing is clear, it's a sign that I need to teach Crumb to read.*

Then Breadbox, wise with years, sent a silent thought-message to the cat, *Repeat the Riddle. Repeat it, so I can learn it. Over and over. Please. I need to have this... now!*

The cat's tail curled in a figure eight (the sign of infinity) and then made the shape of an ankh (the symbol of "life") as if to acknowledge the Breadbox's wish, and began intoning the Riddle again:

Where there's a will,
you know there's a way!
What looks like work
can turn into play!
When green is red
and "N" turns to "D",
A-B-C's the day!

Learning to read
plants a seed that is sound!
Heed the signs
and turn them around!
"E"nunciate well
and learn how it's spelled.
A crumb will lead the way!

No one's too small
to follow a dream,
and no dream's too big
if it's straight from the heart!
For life is in living
and living's an art!
Enjoy the journey today!

So hold on tight
to being taught,
for truth is a price
that can't be bought!
This Riddle will tell you:
It's real food for thought!

Real food for thought? What did "When green is red and 'N' turns to 'D' " mean?

Breadbox listened intently and repeated each line. What especially appealed to Breadbox was one particular verse, because it was the only one that really made sense to him:

Learning to read
plants a seed that is sound!
Heed the signs
and turn them around!
"E"nunciate well
and learn how it's spelled.
A crumb will lead the way!

And so it began that Breadbox undertook to teach Crumb how to read. Breadbox had memorized the Riddle and could recite it -- after many repetitions (but silently to avoid detection) -- with fluid ease and yet with a growing apprehension that this was something prophetic that demanded he, Breadbox The Protector, pass it on, hopefully to the right Kitchen Thing.

He knew there was no way the Family would hear him out. One false sound in the open air and it wouldn't be a question of oiling his squeaky door, it would be the garbage or a garage sale or the confines of the musty, dusty garage, a kind of Purgatory for discarded objects. This would be psychic death for the old container, no more helping out to "Keep The Bread of Life Fresh."

But there it was, he HAD to take on the calling. Little Crumb was at risk of being crushed at every turn. Breadbox had always harbored a secret feeling that there was some Destiny waiting for this smidgen of somehow-sentient bread.

So he knew that as soon as he could, he would have to recite this Riddle to Crumb, maybe over and over. And the Riddle was telling him that "Crumb would lead the way" and needed to learn to read.

But there was one big problem:

Breadbox had long respected oral traditions, how ancient civilizations had known how to teach vast religious texts and instruction books to children or monks just by sound alone, by reciting over and over again until the words were sealed in their brains and gushed like waterfalls from their tongues.

But this might take forever with Crumb, and Breadbox as an enlightened teacher wasn't really fond of purely rote learning. Besides, he knew that the bread-ball wasn't going to tolerate long hours inside his box when he was always rushing off to explore.

This meant only one thing: Breadbox had to figure out some way to show Crumb the Riddle in writing. That was the only way Crumb would learn to read, by seeing it, not just by hearing it. Getting the Riddle in a written form was not such an easy thing -- Breadbox could read alright, but not having arms and fingers he had no way to write the Riddle down.

Then he had a bright idea. There happened to be but one other Kitchen Thing who knew how to read -- Sharpest Knife -- and being a knife, S.K. (as he was nicknamed) would be able to scratch out the verses on some convenient surface.

But where? Breadbox puzzled over this greatly.

Finally Breadbox decided that inside his roomy bread-container would be best, on the side and back walls. There Crumb wouldn't be distracted while he studied. More important: The Riddle needed to be kept away from prying eyes... for a while. It wasn't time to reveal it to anyone else. Not just yet.

Especially since Breadbox had no idea what most of it meant.

He was hoping he'd figure it out by sheer repetition or during a flash of insight, but the only thing that was clear to him was some indication that "a crumb would lead the way" and that reading would be an important skill. For exactly what? He had no concrete idea. In the meantime, he'd ask Sharpest Knife to help him out.

Sharpest Knife fancied himself an ancient scribe reincarnated into a debonair contemporary, a dashing but cool-headed literary fellow, a lexicon of wit. S.K. looked the part. He was slim, no-nonsense, and edged like the finest razor-blade. His steely, wise-aleck manner had been forged during his most terrifying experience.

Someone in the Family had closed him inside a recipe book and abandoned him in the Pantry for twenty-two miserable days. There he was, pinned between pages 95 and 96 of CUTTING EDGE RECIPES, stuck between "How to beat Egg Whites" and "Pineapple Upside Down Cake", while the Maid searched for the missing knife. Finally Hazel Baker had fancied making Pineapple Upside Down Cake for her husband Ken's birthday, and the recipe book had been opened and S.K. freed.

After that humbling entrapment, S.K. became fixated upon learning how to read. He thought it would save him from being "booked" or tossed into a carrot bin. Reading about French cuisine and books of Kitchen Tips developed S.K's cutting vocabulary and he delighted in quoting passages from recipes as if they were sage advice about how best to live: "Don't over-stir. Beat until fluffy" and "Can't cut it? Sharpen up!" were two of his favorites.

S.K. was cool, hardly ever showing any emotion, except when he was mincing onions.

So when Breadbox decided to ask Sharpest Knife to help him write the Riddle down, he knew it would be important to wait until all the onions in the storage bin had been properly sliced days earlier with no new onions purchased and all the onion juice (and tears) mopped up totally. (Sharpest Knife hated anyone to see him emotionally involved with his work.)

Finally the right day came and Breadbox approached the witty fellow, who looked insulted for a second.

"This is the price of being well-educated! Everybody thinks writing words down is as easy as reading them", Sharpest Knife complained with a snide swish of his thin cutting edge. "It takes extra knowhow to do that right."

"I agree, S.K. Reading is one thing, writing is a special skill! That's why I'm RELYING on you."

Breadbox knew how to get around even a sharp blade like S. K. with exactly the right words. Needless to say, S. K. began the task of writing each letter carefully inside Breadbox's interior walls. It probably hurt... but Breadbox maintained that it just tickled a bit. He didn't want to worry Crumb so he chuckled and squiggled around as the knife wrote the Riddle inside him. Every now and then, he'd say, "Oooo, it tickles!!"

While the engraving was going on, Breadbox discovered something interesting: It so happened that the Riddle had twenty-six lines (with one extra line for good luck) -- twenty-six lines, one for each letter from A to Z. When he realized this, Breadbox asked the knife to add an alphabet letter in front of each of the lines, slightly to the left. This would be useful in teaching Crumb the alphabet.

"Whadya think I am, Michelangelo?" quipped Sharpest Knife. (He had since read a book on THE ART OF CARVING.)

"Very funny, S.K. I'll tell ya what -- I'll ask Hortense not to use onions for a good long while. How about a month? -- Is that good enough for ya?"

"Not bad. That last onion had me choking. (Let's not go there.) I'll add the letters. You drive a tough bargain."

And so, with S.K.'s skilled work all the Riddle was memorialized inside Breadbox's roomy back and side walls. With the alphabet chart on the left, it looked like this:

A Where there's a will,
B you know there's a way!

C What looks like work
D can turn into play!
E When green is red
F and "N" turns to "D",
G A-B-C's the day!
H Learning to read
I plants a seed that is sound!
J Heed the signs
K and turn them around!
L "E"nunciate well
M and learn how it's spelled.
N A crumb will lead the way!
O No one's too small
P to follow a dream,
Q and no dream's too big
R if it's straight from the heart!
S For life is in living
T and living's an art!
U Enjoy the journey today!
V So hold on tight
W to being taught,
X for truth is a price
Y that can't be bought!
Z This Riddle will tell you:
It's real food for thought!

Breadbox decided that this was the very best method to teach Crumb how to read -- have Crumb repeat all the letters A through Z. Then recite the Riddle line by line, verse by verse.

"Why is this so important?" asked the little bread-morsel.

Breadbox sighed. He knew why, but that didn't mean that Crumb did. Slowly, he explained, "Life has its lessons. Learn THESE lessons first."

"If you say so, Granddad. But it looks hard."

"It will get easy after a while. The Riddle says 'What looks like work/can turn into play'!" Crumb liked that idea.

Breadbox noticed a stale lady-finger propped up in one corner of his box. It was stiff and dry but lightweight, so he gave that to Crumb as a pointer. Somehow managing to move the pointer to each letter, Crumb began learning his ABCs. Then Breadbox would recite the Riddle line by line and have Crumb repeat each line after him.

Soon Crumb was putting the letters together into syllables and then into words, reading the Riddle out loud and learning each verse by heart over and over again, until it felt like he could say it in his sleep it was so much a part of him.

Crumb had one particular verse that was his favorite:

> No one's too small
> to follow a dream,
> and no dream's too big
> if it's straight from the heart!
> For life is in living
> and living's an art!
> Enjoy the journey today!

After a few hours of this, Crumb told Breadbox, "This isn't as hard as I thought. But, Granddad, I can't stay here all day! I need to have some free time, I need to explore."

"Alright, but stay in the Kitchen and don't leave the counter!"

So Breadbox agreed to teach Crumb for only an hour a day. After twenty-six days Crumb knew his ABCs and most of the Riddle by heart.

"What does it mean, Granddad? I can't figure a bunch of this out. Just the part about being small and how it's okay as long as you dream big. Do you know what this stuff means?"

"Gotta admit, Crumb, I'm stumped. But I figure it will probably make sense some day." (Crumb wasn't used to seeing Breadbox stumped about anything.)

"One thing is for sure, you're the only breadcrumb in the world (as far as I know) who knows his ABCs! ....So do me a favor, pipsqueak, stay out of trouble, okay?"

"No one's gonna eat me, no one's gonna defeat me. I know my ABCs," said Crumb.

Somehow knowing how to read had taken on the character of an ancient amulet of protection and an accomplishment that certainly set Crumb apart from any loaves, slices or crumbs anywhere else. How he would use this skill, he had no idea. But it gave him panache, a certain specialness -- and that gave him confidence.

"Honestly Crumb, you have no idea what's out there!" cautioned Breadbox.

(*Sure*, thought Crumb, *but I'm dying to find out. Well, maybe not dying... just curious.*)

"I love you, Granddad," whispered Crumb.

"I know," said Breadbox. "I'm a bit fond of you myself. Now get some sleep. We've a whole lot of reading to do tomorrow."

After a pleasant nap, Crumb woke with a start. Someone was shifting the Breadbox around. His nice soft bed (next to a large slice of crispy day-old bread) was moving all around, banging back and forth from one end of the box to the other. *Is this what Humans call 'earthquake' or what?* wondered Crumb. He had heard the Family talking about that, and it had even scared THEM.

Humans! Did they even know how scary they made it for Kitchen Things, always breaking cups, throwing things away before their time, not letting anybody get any rest?

All of a sudden the tin door swung open and a plump, dimpled hand popped into Granddad's inside, searching around for that day-old slice. Crumb rolled over to the edge of the box, into the tippy-tippy corner in the back, on the right side, where a few of Crumb's little cousins had gathered, shivering from fright.

"Stay still, don't move," warned Crumb. "It's just the boy Johnny's hand. The Mom's hand is much bigger. We'll be safe."

"Oh, goodie, just the kind that makes the best French Toast, nice and dry," chirped the boy Johnny happily, pulling his hand out of the box with the day-old bread slice looking pale and frightened, as stiff as you'll ever see day-old bread look.

Breadbox's door was open for a second or two, and Crumb managed to gather enough air into his puffy roundness to let the slice know with a whisper, "It's not so bad, you get soaked into egg and milk, covered with maple syrup and then... and then... " Crumb didn't have the courage to tell Mr. Day-Old that slices of French Toast were eaten bite by bite.

Saucepan had tried to convince Crumb that ending up as a piece of French Toast was a piece of Heaven Come True, that French Toast was the Ultimate End for any decent piece of bread. (Even for a slice that was lazy and loafed around, implied Saucepan, who thought of Crumb as a lazy good-for-nothing round little brat.) Saucepan had a bad attitude sometimes. Crumb wasn't lazy, but sometimes he could sound like a brat.

Try as Saucepan did to paint a beautiful picture of the golden brown crustiness and inner moistness of a properly soaked and sautéed piece of French Toast drizzled with real maple syrup, Crumb was not convinced.

The legend of French Toast as Heaven Come True sounded almost too good to be true, so Crumb dreaded that fate, to be immersed in slimy egg and milk, dipped in rich syrup and doused with melted butter -- the very same melted butter that Toaster had saved him from when Crumb was born.

Crumb didn't dare think about the end result. It was... chomp, oh no, chomp, oh yes, chomp, chomp, swallowed, gone, vamoose, zilch, bye-bye-nice-to-know-ya!

The Breadbox door slammed shut, and Crumb and his tiny crumb-tidbits cousins banged into the corner, as Johnny, the nine-year-old boy of the family, plopped the box down on the counter. Crumb's cousins gathered round their Big Boy Cuz -- they looked up to him since he was much bigger and must know a thing or two about how to survive in the Wilds of the Kitchen.

The sound of Saucepan banging on the stove, the heavy fridge door slamming open and shut, and the fragrant smell and sizzle of butter, eggs and milk and poor Mr. Day-Old, resigned to his fate... or maybe happy that he was going to Heaven Come True at last, all that was making a big bunch of sounds and smells.

Crumb gulped. *Not me*, he thought, *I'll never get to be a piece of French Toast on its way to Heaven Come True. No one's gonna eat ME!*

Chapter Three

Explorations

Bit by bit Crumb was growing bigger until even the Cat or Dog noticed him every now and then but fortunately they were distracted from reaching a paw up to the counter. The counter was where Crumb knew he should stay --- Breadbox had warned him not to go anywhere else. So rolling here and there along the big tile counter, Crumb went exploring.

There were so many things to discover. What a giant world it was. To someone the size of a dot of bread, everything looked enormous! There were shelves and a stove, doors and windows, spice jars, the pantry and all kinds of Kitchen Things everywhere he looked. It was all so new and exciting! And because an orphan can feel very lonely sometimes, Crumb was spurred on by a hunger to find Friends.

One day Crumb bumped into Timer... literally. BUMP! Timer uttered an annoyed, "Hey, watch it." Timer kept time for when someone baked or broiled something in the oven. He loved to go beep-beep-beep when something in the oven was ready to be taken out. He prided himself on always being punctual but extremely jealous of wristwatches.

"They think they're so much better than us Timers. What snobs."

Secretly he envied their fancy dials and the fact that they had two hands, one big and one little. *I can do almost anything they can!*, boasted Timer to himself. But he certainly didn't have jewels, a wrist band or a phases-of-the-moon dial. That's why he was always warning, "Hey, watch it!" as if it would turn him into a glamorous wristwatch just by saying the word "watch."

But all in all, Timer was a good-hearted fellow, always ready to give someone at least five minutes, to chat, to smell a roast or batch of cookies in the oven and share a story or two about the good old days when sundials were in nearly every garden. Crumb and Timer became friends, good friends.

One day, as he rolled along the counter, Crumb nearly landed on Dish.

"Excuuuuuse me!" she said, raising one eyebrow. "I've just had my beauty bath and a rubdown with the dish-towel, and who do you think you ARE?!" Dish was a beauty alright with her porcelain skin and lovely painted fruit bowl in the middle of her flat round tummy. She had real gold around her rim and figured that fourteen-karat gold inlay gave her an edge. She knew she was pretty and delicate and very desirable, but boy could she dish it out. She had a way of making all the boy objects in the Kitchen feel like she was way too good for them, so they better buzz off.

The real truth was that Dish was afraid to be broken. Heartbreak was bad enough, but she could be in pieces in a second. Behind her come-hither-get-lost ways, Dish was scared of caring too deeply and being dropped.

"Who AM I? Can't you tell?" Crumb was spunky and not too happy about Dish's unfriendly manner. "I'm a crumb... Duh! I have one question for you. Don't you ever get tired of being so... so... uh... so beautiful?" Crumb had thought "snobby" and meant to say "stuck up", but looking at her sparkling porcelain surface had dazzled him for a moment.

"No, haven't gotten tired of it yet.... How nice of you to notice. I must say, crumb-face, you're more well-bred than most of the dudes around here."

"Well-bred? I'm a piece of bread, what do you expect?"

Seeing that Crumb wasn't going to kowtow to her cold ways, Dish promptly got a crush on the little fellow.

"Say, you're kinda cute!" This turn-around of attitude scared Crumb.

"Well, so long, Dish! Nice to meet ya!" and Crumb was on his way.

Day after day, as soon as his reading lesson was over inside Breadbox, Crumb rushed out in search of another Adventure. He was growing more round and roly-poly with handsome little bread-bumps on every part of his plump and jolly surface. They gave him traction, a fancy word meaning that the bumps acted like treads on a tire, so that he rarely slipped off the counter when he was rolling around. *Yo!* Crumb realized, *I'm getting bigger! I'm making new friends every day. And I'll admit I'm cute!* There was no denying he was cute. And mischievous.

Breadbox kept reminding him that it was important to watch out for the Family and the Pets, but sometimes he took wild chances. Then Breadbox would make his voice sound low and serious and remind Crumb that "Look-it, Crumb: Life has its lessons and they can come at ya. Take it one step at a time!" Crumb always nodded, but as soon as the reading lesson was over, off he went.

His confidence and his playful sense of daring had grown, encouraged by the Riddle line that said, "A crumb will lead the way!" It seemed like every day he was meeting new and different Kitchen Things. What a motley crew. Some of them were friendly, some weren't. But Crumb's derring-do attitude and playful friendliness usually broke down any resistance.

Even stocky, sturdy Rolling Pin (who liked to brag about how she had ended arguments between Mr. and Mrs. Baker when he came home late) became Crumb's buddy, promising never to pound Crumb into a pie crust. Still, Crumb wasn't completely free and easy around her (she had a hot temper when provoked) and felt better when Rolling Pin was in her drawer.

So Crumb rolled up and down the Kitchen counters whenever Humans or Pets were away, easing his loneliness and satisfying his endless curiosity by making new friends.

He was searching for something or someone but wasn't really sure who or what. Maybe hidden in the Riddle was the answer, but he still couldn't understand most of it, even though by now he knew all the verses by heart.

Whenever he recited the Riddle, certain words echoed inside him as if a huge unexplored cavern lay deep inside his tiny body, like a black hole sucking in secrets and vague memories. An internal windstorm seemed to blow images here and there until they disintegrated like puffs of smoke: A slamming door, socks flying around in a dryer, a feeling of being disoriented, a dread deep within that warned him not to remember too much. Every time he came to certain parts of the Riddle, some of the words rattled around that empty hole inside his core, right where his parents hugs might have filled the gap.

In fact, after a few months the Riddle began to annoy Crumb. A mystery is fun for a while, but it becomes wearisome if you can't uncover it. It was one thing to know that "a crumb will lead the way", but WHERE?

Despite these rumblings and echoes, Crumb decided it just wasn't time to look inward or to try to put puzzles together. After all, didn't the Riddle say "Life is in living/and living's an art"? He would LIVE, he would see, experience, explore and learn Life Lessons that way, wherever they led. He was a young sprout who had just turned five human-years old. It was the perfect time to discover new Kitchen Things, make friends and just plain have FUN!

However, every now and then a simple, pleasant spin around the counter to make new friends can turn into a hair-raising adventure....

One day Crumb followed the sound of a whistle, curious that it wasn't coming from the maid. There on the stove sat Tea-Pot, plump, content and whistling away, while eight tea bags danced in time to the tune. (No Human was in the Kitchen.) The entire tea-bag chorus line circled the Tea-Pot, lifting their tags on strings and swaying in time to the cheerful music, while skillfully keeping away from the burner-flame.

As they twirled and tango'd and formed a rhumba-line, Crumb was able to make out their names on the labels: Earl Grey, "Lapsang" Sue Chong, Herb Tease, Pepper Mint, Cam O'Mile, Jasmine Blend, Chai Spice and Ooo Long.

Suddenly Tea-Pot's whistle stopped. A final gasp of steam escaped from his lid and then no more steam came out. Oh no, he must be out of water, it must have all boiled away, but the stove's flame was still turned on. Tea Pot could be a hot-head but all the Kitchen Things valued him almost as much as Breadbox because he was steeped in ancient lore, could read tea leaves and was a great storyteller.

Now, if he was going to sit on the hot burner without any water inside, it wouldn't be long before his copper bottom would be scorched or maybe might begin to melt. Someone in the Family must have forgotten they turned him on!

The tea bags had stopped dancing and were racing around now, trying to turn off the flame but they were too floppy to be able to turn the knob.

Crumb rolled as fast as he could over to the stove. The counter touched the side of the stove but the stove-top was an inch higher than the counter. (To a Crumb an inch can be a big distance to jump.) Tea-Pot was beginning to gather big drops of sweat along his surface and his copper bottom was starting to glow a sickly hot coral-color — there was no time to waste.

Gathering his strength with every morsel of his body (but closing his eyes foolishly), Crumb leaped up toward the stove-top. Fortunately, all the tea bags had rushed over to the stove edge and had thrown their strings and labels over the side.

Crumb opened his eyes in mid-air — he wasn't going to make the stove-top but there were ropes and handles he could grab onto (the strings and tags looked like ropes and handles to him). Huffing and puffing, the tea bags had lined up tightly in a one-sided kind of tug-of-war pile and began to haul Crumb up the side of the stove.

Finally he was up the inch and on the stove top, fortunately far enough away from the burner not to get singed.

For a split second Crumb lay exhausted while the tea bags drew back their strings and labels, lying on top of each other in a pile, all limp from exertion. Sweat and fear were pouring down the sides of poor Tea-Pot, until the burner began to smoke threateningly as the sweat touched the flame. A small blast of fire burst out of the side of the burner, barely hitting poor Crumb but it was enough to energize him into action.

Rolling as fast as he could over to the burner-knob, Crumb began to push and push, harder and harder. The knob was stubborn. Finally the knob moved over to the off position. Crumb lay there gasping.

The flame sputtered to a stop. Tea-Pot's glowing, hot-pink bottom cooled, slowly turning back to solid copper dotted with black smoke-dust.

"That was too close...," Tea-Pot gasped. "I've got to cool down. You saved me! You and my wonderful tea bags! How can I thank all of you enough? I'll never forget this."

Then Tea-Pot opened his big black plastic lid, the one with the whistle hole in the middle, and yawned an enormous, long, wide and noisy yawn. A tea pot's lid doesn't usually open unless a Human is filling him with water, so this time Tea-Pot's yawn was extra wide and really something to see. (All yawns are catchy, you know.) After all their enormous efforts to save Tea-Pot, Crumb and all the tea bags began yawning away.

"Tea bags," said Tea-Pot, smothering another big yawn while he talked, "I'm knocked out from all this (yawn). You were so great when you helped Crumb. But it's time for some shut-eye. Storytelling can wait til tomorrow. Time to get back in your (*yawn*) boxes for a good night's sleep."

The tea bags waved their tags to say goodbye and slumped their weary way back into their little box-beds.

"Never expected you to be strong enough to move that knob! How the heck did you DO it?" exclaimed Tea-Pot while one last bit of sweat dripped down his side.

Crumb started to shrug (to tell you the truth, he was amazed himself) but instead decided to puff himself up so he could flex his crumb-muscles. Try as he did, his crumb-muscles soon gave out. He was just too tuckered out to bother about showing off at the moment.

In fact, Crumb began to yawn so much that he heard the tea-bags giggling inside their boxes. It was time to get some good rest. Crumb could hardly roll back to Breadbox without stopping every so often for breath.

Finally he reached home. Breadbox's door was closed tight. Crumb managed to wheeze out the magic words, "Sesame Bagel!" That was the usual signal for Breadbox to open his tin door to let Crumb in. The tin door swung open with a squeak. Crumb waddled in, bent over to one side, and plunked his exhausted bread-body onto his little bed.

The next day the whole Kitchen was buzzing with the news: Crumb saved Tea Pot!

"I'm glad you did it, my boy, and not a moment too soon. But don't let it go to your head, Crumb. Just so you know, you're the latest-greatest thing here in Kitchen-land... until something ELSE comes along. Just be sure to mention how the tea bags helped. And don't slip up!," advised Breadbox with understandable caution. He'd seen too many crumbs soak up the compliments until they were fools.

The next day after his lesson Crumb sauntered out onto the counter, all puffed up and looking around for admiration. Immediately Dish and Tea Pot, Rolling Pin and Timer began cheering and congratulating him.

He'd become a bit cocky, that was for sure, and wasn't taking his usual precautions. Looking around and nodding to his admirers, Crumb was not aware of the slippery dab of olive oil that lay just ahead on a counter tile. Breadbox's warning, "Don't slip up" reverberated in his mind as -- tumbling over and over as the Kitchen cabinets spun around -- down-down-down he fell. PLOP! Crumb landed on the floor.

"Oh no! Linoleum! LiNOleum, NO, NO, NO!" (As if saying "no" lots of times would make the floor turn into something else, like the safe counter he was used to.)

Now he was in trouble, for sure. How could he manage to get back up to his counter or into Breadbox in time to be safe again, before Hortense swept him up or the cat or dog made a snack out of him?

Timer waddled over to the edge of the counter to see what was wrong. "How long do you need?" said Timer.

"Give me five minutes," wheezed Crumb. "If I'm not back up on the counter by then, sound your beeper, and maybe that will get me some rescue-help. Or else I'll be in worse trouble. Let's shoot for five minutes, okay?"

"You got it, five minutes! You can DO it, Crumb!"

Every second seemed to last five times longer than usual... but all Crumb could do, because one of his sides was squished in, was to waddle back and forth painfully over to the refrigerator. Maybe he could hide under it if Hortense or Johnny or (oh NO!) Mrs. Baker came in to the Kitchen.

Now this particular refrigerator was named Coldylox. She tended to be protective but rather icy in personality, hardly the friendliest shelter in the Kitchen. But she had to do. It was all Crumb's strength could muster (drizzled as his bread bumps were with drops of slick olive oil) to get closer to her.

Hovering under the thin rubber bottom-edge of Coldylox, hoping he wouldn't be seen, Crumb edged his way in, toward the back wall. He could sense some of the refrigerator magnets shifting a bit from the friction. Coldylox protested, her electrical wiring shuddering louder than usual.

All of a terrible sudden who should come into the Kitchen but Hazel Baker. The dreaded Mom of the Family. From under the fridge, Crumb could see her bunny slippers, all pink and fluffy. Hazel was a neat freak, even Hortense wasn't as clean. Ken Baker was so tired of his wife's constant attention on cleanliness and neatness that he had hired Hortense to help her so he wouldn't have to hear about how hard she had to slave every day.

"Hhhmmph," Mom groaned as she bent to look at the bottom of the fridge. "I'll have to tell Hortense she missed a spot. Honestly, can't anyone keep this place clean but ME?"

Mom talked to herself a lot. Her kids kept to themselves, since she nagged them about their rooms being pigsties until they spent more time picking up their toys and crayons than playing with them.

Whenever Hazel passed a mirror, she felt compelled to glance at her attractive oval face and run her fingers through her wavy hair. Before she had settled on marriage, she'd been offered a bit part in a Hollywood movie and had brooded ever since that marriage and raising children had driven her away from her "big chance" at stardom. The superficial acting lessons in her home town had not really offered her an outlet for her strong emotions but instead had accustomed her to a histrionic set of mannerisms and pat phrases.

She wasn't always mean-spirited, but she played at being a Mother as if she were a puppet being held at a distance on a tight string. Oddly enough, Sally and her older brother had bonded because of this distance -- someone had to mother them, so they provided that for themselves.

Fortunately, Ken Baker was a hearty, outgoing fellow who adored his children, so they were guaranteed hugs and bedtime stories and trips to amusement parks every now and then. He had a talent for relaxing Hazel too.

The only problem was that his work took him away from the family sometimes for a week at a time. When he was home, you could always tell, because there were at least three men's hats on the hat rack. Ken Baker was a traveling salesman, selling hats in department stores all around the country. He had grown up seeing his Dad Marty wear a hat every time he left home. Marty would tip it to show respect for ladies and take his hat off when he came back home. Then --- because styles became more casual -- hats went out of style for a while. Now hats were slowly getting back in fashion. People were starting to consider that hats were practical, dashing, shielding one from the sun or adding warmth, keeping a bad hair-day or a bald head out of sight, and adding personality.

Ken had hats of every kind, from a top hat to a cowboy hat, from a straw boater to a beret, you name it. The kids would sneak into his closet sometimes to put on Dad's safari hat or his deerstalker (just like Sherlock Holmes had worn. Toaster craved having one just like that). Mom would find Sally and Johnny laughing in the closet and scold them. Her annoyance masked her loneliness -- seeing the children sporting Ken's hats made her miss him more than she wanted to admit.

When their Daddy came home from his sales trips, the kids got souvenirs from wherever he had been and funny anecdotes about train rides over steep mountain passes and local diners with weird concoctions and regional specialties: Johnny cakes and coffee milk in Rhode Island, grits and gravy in Tennessee, gumbo with okra in Naw'Leans.

Ken Baker was one thing, but Mom, quite another.

Maybe Crumb had picked the wrong place to hide -- Hazel Baker was guaranteed to go right for the fridge. Food was always a big subject for the whole family, and she was a great cook. It was her big hobby and best virtue -- once Humans tasted her pecan pie and fried chicken, they were likely to forgive her quirks.

Mind you, Crumb was not happy when she insisted on putting bread crumbs into her meatloaf. Often in his dreams at night suddenly her oval face would take on Alien Eyes as she chased little Crumb around the Kitchen holding Rolling Pin in her hands. Now she was heading toward the fridge where Crumb had hidden himself below the base. Would she see him there?

Her charm bracelet was clanging against the refrigerator handle, knocking a few magnets to the floor. Grand Ol' Opry magnet, Golden Gate Bridge, Mount Rushmore. (Ken always brought Hazel a new souvenir magnet from his trips and a charm for her charm bracelet like an Eiffel Tower or a little purse with a clasp that opened and closed.) He was loyal and didn't flirt while he was gone, but his patience wore thin when she nagged him. Still, they loved each other a lot -- sometimes affection comes in odd packages.

Crumb could see she had Rolling Pin in her other hand... this was looking grim. Crumb wasn't scared of any other Kitchen Things, not even Sharpest Knife, but Rolling Pin did give him pause. Rolling Pin used to gloat in her drawer every time she heard that Ken Baker was back in town. She was hoping the couple would have a spat. (You'd think it would be enough action for her just to roll out pie dough, but Kitchen Things get bored inside drawers and she was itching for trouble.)

For a moment Hazel moved away from the fridge to turn on the radio for her favorite program, "Sweet Sally Jones," as sorry a soap opera as you'll ever hear, overblown with sad tales of Sweet Sally falling in love with a bum or crashing her car or burning the toast.

Crumb froze. Burning the TOAST? That always made Crumb the most scared of all -- shudder -- burning the Toast was an unbearable horror. After all, wasn't "You're Toast!" the ultimate Kitchen threat?

As soon as the magnets tumbled to the floor Hazel was back at the refrigerator sensing that something was wrong. Her charm bracelet tinkled against the metal of the bottom part of the fridge as she bent over to peer down and pick up the magnets. Her apron covered her bunny slippers and (fortunately for Crumb) hid some of the fridge bottom, so she didn't see Crumb, who was trembling as he stumbled backwards on his soggy oil-slicked surface. Wouldn'tcha know, he rolled right into a pile of crusty bacon bits way in back, something that had avoided the broom for a long time.

All of a sudden Crumb almost squeezed into a tight ball! Oh NO! All the bacon bits were stuck to him and at the same time he could smell something else very scary. Cringing in terror, Crumb could make out the long whiskers of the family dog penetrating deep into the underside of the refrigerator.

Help, it was Whisk! That dog was so clumsy there was no telling if he'd signal to Mom that something was going on under the fridge. In fact, the sniffing sound coming from Whisk's big black trembling nose set up a dust storm under the fridge. The hard nails of his paws were reaching in, closer and closer, trying to snatch a piece of bacon from the floor.

If there's one thing that dogs love almost as much as Humans, it's bacon. Crumb was a roly-poly soggy bacon trap waiting to be licked and swallowed! What could he DO?

Chapter Four

Timing Is Everything

Crumb cringed away from the dog's paws, as the hot breath from the pooch's sniffing nose blew the breadbit back up against the greasy back wall. Just then Timer began to Beep-Beep-Beep, signaling that five minutes were up.

"What??" objected Hazel, scrunching up her apron and bending back up straight in a huff, puzzled. "Who set the Timer off? It's Hortense's day-off! Why do these things always happen to ME?" She flung her wrist to her forehead dramatically.

Timer to the rescue -- the distraction was enough to take Mom's attention off the refrigerator bottom. Whisk jumped up and put his big greasy paws on her apron, hoping to interest her in getting him that yummy bacon he was smelling.

"Get off me! Bad dog! Look what you've done. Now I have to throw this apron in the washer. What a mess!"

All Crumb could do was to breathe slowly or hold his breath. Mom dashed out of the Kitchen, followed by the dog.

A spoon had fallen from the stove top, unseen and unheard by the flustered woman in her rush to get out of the kitchen and get that apron clean. CLANG went the spoon landing next to an old pencil no one had seen, but Whisk had created such a ruckus jumping on Mom's apron that the spoon wasn't noticed in the slightest.

It was the first time ever that Crumb had seen Spoon. In a blinding second he was smitten --- dazzled by her beauty and grace. Spoon was a prized serving piece normally stored on a high-up shelf with the best crystal. She had come with a certificate of authenticity as a genuine antique from a chateau in France. Pure silver, curvy but polished and sophisticatedly embossed with fleurs-de-lis, she bore the patina of age and heritage with a grace that only comes from those who have served royalty at banquets.

Spoon had been around for a long, long time. In fact, she was fond of swearing that Marie Antoinette had never said, "Let them eat cake." No, it was "cupcakes"! Spoon remembered all those glorious cupcakes, with their fancy pink and white frosting-wigs sprinkled with chocolate bits and almond slivers piled high on top of moist cakes in lace cups. Those were the days! Before the Revolution.

Spoon had the worldly-wisdom of someone who has witnessed history and managed to survive. Why, she was three hundred and some odd years older than Breadbox but still gorgeous, curvy, every inch a lady --- five-year-old Crumb got a crush on her right away.

How could I have missed the sight of her for all this time? he wondered.

(That was how he felt, but truthfully, the top shelves where the crystal wine glasses and fancy bowls were kept were well out of his normal purview.)

As Timer watched from the counter edge, the punctual, precision-driven timing-machine felt very uncomfortable, squeamish in fact. No Timer enjoys the sensation that time has stopped still. He started to say "Watch it, Crumb!" but kept quiet in disbelief.

Because for Crumb, Time itself HAD stopped still. Smitten at first sight! In Crumb's universe (as big with wonder and hope as youthful imagination can make it) everything was in slow-motion, slowed down into the pace of eternity. The bread-ball felt the empty place inside him suddenly pounding as if a heart had entered to fill the hole and was beating slowly, telling him that he was indeed alive at last. *Spoon, how beautiful she is!* he marveled.

The next second he snapped back into a sense of Now and realized that he looked absolutely, embarrassingly ridiculous.

There he was all soaked and smeared with olive oil and covered with flakes of smelly dirty bacon. The hardened bacon bits covered him with a bacon-shield, bacon-armor and even an hilarious-looking bacon-helmet on top. Some Knight in Shining Armor! Not exactly how young love-sick Crumb wanted to be seen.... He skulked back into the far-back-edge of the fridge, hoping Spoon wouldn't see him.

But see him she did. Somehow the sight of this roly-poly bacon-splattered breadcrumb melted her reserve. Being a Lady, she had a caring and noble nature that had longed for some good company, something less formal than fine crystal.

Here was a tiny "knight" in distress. She was the damsel. The usual story (where the knight in shining armor rescues the damsel in distress) was in reverse -- HE was the one in trouble. Seeing this helpless ball of soggy bread somehow brought out all her maternal instincts.

"Who are you, mon petit? Do you need help?" she asked in a compassionate voice tinged with a subtle French accent.

Crumb blushed. He was too embarrassed to say anything so he shook his round bacon-coated armor a silent "no" and shrank farther back into the underbelly of the refrigerator. Seeing him back away from her turned her motherly voice into a more practical voice-of-reason.

"Come on, do you want me to help you or do you want the dog to eat you with his big tongue? Get closer so I can get you out of this! Hurry! Vitement!"

Spoon reached under Coldylox timidly at first, then struggled to push her handle farther in. Frustratingly, Spoon wasn't quite long enough to reach Crumb. Crumb could hear Timer repeating, "Hurry!"

What was worse, having this beauteous creature see him up close OR dying under the fridge?

It wasn't really a hard decision, so Crumb managed to push the bacon pieces from one side to the other until he rolled in an off-kilter path, bit by bit edging up closer to Spoon. All he could manage to say (with a gulp) was "Hi!" His voice cracked in the middle of that little word, because he was thinking at the same time, *Where have you been all my life?*

Spoon scooped him up in a flash. As soon as he landed on her silvery surface, almost all the bacon bits seemed to fly off him.

"Thank you," Crumb managed to gulp, remembering that ladies are impressed by gentlemanly manners.

"It's a bit too soon to say 'thanks', mon petit-pain," said Spoon with her tender French accent, pronouncing the word for bread ("le pain") like "pehhh". "We have to get you off this floor, back up to the counter where you can be safe."

Cleverly, Spoon managed to move over the smooth linoleum floor to the pencil that had lain for a long time hidden near the stove. Using the pencil as a lever, she twisted and turned back and forth until her long handle was positioned in a slant on top of the metal brace of the eraser tip. Next she maneuvered her handle until the round cup of her spoon-bowl (where Crumb was perched) was poised in the exact right position for a skillful trajectory. Heaving yet graceful even as she shifted, with one leap and turn, she tossed Crumb up --- up --- up --- like a soggy balloon with still enough light-weight flying power to land... to land... to land back on the counter!

"VOILÀ, c'est ÇA! There ya go!" Spoon spun a victory pirouette on her handle. She had always wanted to be a prima ballerina.

Crumb lay somewhat crumpled for a second, recovering on the counter, then leaned over the counter edge -- cautiously so as not to fall -- to wave a thank you to Spoon.

Too late. She was gone.

Sighing and blushing, the bread-ball rolled slowly back to his Breadbox home. "Sesame Croissant!" Crumb whispered. Breadbox shrugged, (which he managed to do by squeezing his side walls close-together a bit) as he opened his tin door.

"Huh? It's 'Sesame BAGEL', Crumb. You know that. What the heck happened to you? You look terrible!"

"As you told me, Granddad, 'A soggy crumb is a sorry crumb.' But as I just discovered all by myself... a lady is a lady."

Crumb's crush on Spoon was the talk of the Kitchen.

"Honestly, you'd think he would know she was around before the French Revolution," gossiped Dish, jealous of all the attention Spoon was getting. "Now he's plumb lost his head over someone at least three hundred years older. And those age-scratches of hers! My word!"

"I read some tea leaves the other day," offered Tea-Pot, "to see if there was any hope for romance between a five-year-old crumb and a very antiquated (well, let me call her 'seasoned') serving spoon. Nope, no chance! I adore Crumb -- after all he saved me -- but he wouldn't listen to reason."

"Don't cry over minced onions, I always say," said Sharpest Knife.

"What I can't understand," gossiped Toaster, "is that Crumb has always been very afraid of becoming French Toast. And here he is, with a crush on a piece of French history!"

"That's enough!" roared Breadbox, his tin door rattling with annoyance. "You all are taking advantage of this situation. Gossip never gets anybody anywhere, except into the trashcan!" That quieted everyone down right away.

But Crumb was so smitten he couldn't seem to do his daily lesson. He just lay there in a corner, hugging his

Ladyfinger pointer, as if it were Spoon. Breadbox had to do something!

"I'll see if Blender can fix this mess up. He's the most skillful diplomat I've ever seen. He can take a mashed up, crushed up mess and blend it into something that works. If he can't figure out a solution to this, I don't know WHAT we'll do. Blender, hey, Blender wake up!"

Blender whirled his cutting blades, suddenly brought into action by Breadbox's wakeup-call. After a brief discussion, Blender agreed to be Mediator. First he went to see Spoon to get a feel for how she felt.

Spoon was thoughtful but perplexed. "Quelle domage, this is terrible. I'm glad I saved him, but I could be his great-great-great-great-great-and-NOT-so-very-great Grandmère. I was born so many... (*Oh-là-là,* she realized in a split-second of silence, *a lady should never reveal her age!*) He's only FIVE?! Le pauvre, poor little chap."

Meanwhile, Crumb told Breadbox in secret he was going to ask Spoon to marry him. He even asked Breadbox to officiate at the wedding. Crumb had researched the ceremony and knew that it was customary to ask, "Does anyone object to this marriage? If so, speak or forever hold your peas." Crumb had consulted Saucepan who agreed that holding peas was a sacred duty, as objectionable as it sometimes was when the peas were overcooked or not seasoned correctly.

"Oh, Crumb, you are way outa line! You're too young to get married." (Breadbox decided not to bring up how old Spoon was. His declining years gave him wisdom and respect, but Spoon actually outdated him by a good two centuries.) "I've asked Blender to get with you and Spoon. You are missing your lessons over this."

"She won't even talk with me, Granddad! Okay, okay, if you think it might change things, I'll meet with Blender and... and HER," sighed the little fellow.

Blender, always the diplomat, sat Crumb and Spoon down for a face-to-face talk. As mediator he began the discussion with a suggestion, "Let's talk this over -- you might even find you can become friends!"

Spoon was all for this but Crumb thought it was impossible. A boy and a girl as friends?!

Spoon thought that friendship was a possibility but romance? No way!

"I remember when I had a crush on a handsome, dashing garlic press in the chateau kitchen many, many years ago," confessed Spoon. (Her face took on the misty veil of nostalgia.) "Now I am old, older than you can even imagine, Crumb, and I do understand. But... it won't work. It didn't work then.... Plus, I never liked garlic breath anyway."

"But... but I love you. I even learned to read and write French. Je t'aime. Je t'aime. Je pense donc je suis. I'm crazy about you. How do I know? I think, therefore I am. (That René Descartes was one smart fellow.)"

"Clever boy, I like you. I don't LOVE you, but I like you. I know what has happened -- I saved you, you're grateful, that's all. Find someone at least a hundred years closer to your own age." (Even someone as polished as Spoon indulged in a good wisecrack when the occasion required it.)

Both Blender and Spoon tried to stifle their amusement over that typical Gallic wit. But Crumb, Crumb was crestfallen.

He'd never known until that moment that he had some moisture locked inside, but here was a long tear squeezing out of his left eye. What could he do? Maybe this is what Breadbox had meant by Life Lessons.

Seeing that she had gravely hurt his feelings, Spoon took a napkin that lay nearby and gently wiped his tear.

Observing that some reconciliation was possible at that moment, Blender advised them both to think about becoming just friends. "It may take time but friendship is a rare gift," he said.

Both Spoon and Crumb looked at each other and small cracks of smiles broke from the corners of their mouths like little twigs blossoming in Springtime.

Blender's final advice was to let the circumstances of their meeting and the possibility of real friendship "sink in."

Crumb returned to his reading lessons to Breadbox's relief. To comfort himself during his love-struck recovery, Crumb began to concentrate on French Poetry. Spoon visited him often and found his recitations of Mallarmé poems and the famous "nose" passages from the play "Cyrano de Bergerac" quite delightful. It wasn't long before the two of them became fast friends.

Blender and Breadbox smiled to see this excellent outcome and a feeling of quiet relief pervaded the Kitchen for several peaceful days. (Maybe it was partially because the Family had taken the weekend off. Everything was much more relaxed.)

The following Monday young Sally Baker skipped into the Kitchen to fetch a banana and some cereal. Sally grabbed a banana, hurriedly peeled it and threw the peel down the drain but forgot to turn the disposal on. Down the drain plummeted the banana peel.

Then Johnny scampered in, grabbed a Day-Old piece of terrified bread out of Breadbox and started frying up some French Toast. This was too much for Crumb. He ran to his friend Spoon, shuddering.

"French Toast! I hate that stuff. It scares me to death. I'm sorry, I know you're French, but just imagine how it feels to be a crumb, watching that happen before your very eyes."

"And what is wrong with French Toast, pray tell?"

Spoon was deeply insulted, and the two began to bicker. Soon even the Tea Bags were awakened in their boxes, and Blender began to whirl his blades in protest, urging the two to "let your friendship sink in."

"Cyrano would not stand for this!" cried Spoon. "HE was a gentleman."

"Oh, do you suppose his nose was long enough to smell that as an insult," smirked Crumb. "I can say that in French if you want!" he added sarcastically.

"Vive la différence! We certainly ARE different, c'est la vie!" was Spoon's haughty response. She twirled away from him.

This spatting had to end.

Rolling Pin was getting ready in her drawer, anticipating a brawl. Tea-Pot was on the stove, simmering but getting hotter and hotter. Both Blender and Breadbox intervened and ordered the two of them, Spoon and Crumb, to talk one-on-one and work things out.

That night when the Kitchen Things had settled down for the night and Timer was snoring, Spoon and Crumb (recalling that Blender had suggested they let their friendship "sink in") decided to sit IN the sink and talk things out, where -- surrounded by stainless steel -- no one would hear what they had to say. It seemed like a good idea at the time.

While Spoon and Crumb were sitting in the sink discussing Crumb's fear of French Toast and Spoon's unyielding defense of all things French, all of sudden -- Oh NO! -- a big splash of tap water burst from the faucet right on top of Crumb.

Looking down at the two from the side of the sink, Sponge had been eaves-dropping, pretending to be asleep. Hearing the big splash, Sponge leaned over the edge, thinking she might jump down and soak up the water in time, but she'd dried off too much by the side of the sink to be any help.

Down, down, down Crumb went into the pipe, struggling to hold his crumb-face above the swirling water so he wouldn't drown, spinning and flailing as he fell lower and lower down the plumbing. The last instant he remembered was seeing Spoon racing to the mouth of the sink-hole, crying, "Help, Cruuuummmmmmb!" The water in the pipe made the sound of her silvery voice echo like the endless bong of a metal bowl being struck by a spoon, boooooonnnng!

Crumb lost consciousness after that. Blackness. Cold. Wet. Worried.

Chapter Five

A Soggy Crumb Is A Sorry Crumb

Falling and falling, lower and lower, Crumb became consumed by frustration: *Why did this have to happen right when Spoon and I were about to work out how to stop spatting? Now what's going to happen to me?*

The helpless sensation of falling was turning his grasp on reality into a whirlpool of fear as he fell lower and lower down the pipe. In his nightmare Crumb was spinning around and around, always out of reach of Spoon, who stood up on her handle looking down on him, laughing with haughty, sarcastic mockery at his soggy self. "What a little baby! A mere child!"

Then Dish had shown up in his nightmare, jealous of all the attention Crumb was giving to Spoon. "Age before beauty I guess! You flirt you. That floozy is past her prime. She's gonna give you the boot just like you rejected me! You're TOAST!" shrieked Dish.

When Crumb couldn't answer her, Dish pushed Spoon into the same spin as Crumb, and the two of them (Crumb and Spoon) spun away in Crumb's tumbling nightmare, circling in the swirling water farther and farther apart. Dish's laughter sounded just like the cackle of a witch.

Then Breadbox's frowning face peered down from the sinkhole at Crumb, scolding him with "I warned you Crumb but you wouldn't listen to me. 'A soggy crumb is a sorry crumb.' " Granddad's reprimand hurt the most of all.

Round and round Crumb churned and turned, his thoughts dizzy like a crazy pinwheel tossed angrily into wind-whipped surf.... Finally he began to realize what had happened and where he was.

YES! That's it, I'm in WATER, smelly water, the SEWER. How long will it be before I get so soggy that I break into a zillion pieces or — worse yet — so swollen and heavy that I fall to the bottom like a stone?

It seemed like forever but finally the pipe emptied the miserable tyke into the huge sewer with a splash that woke Crumb out of his nightmare. He found himself struggling, trying to get his dizzy eyes to focus on the damp walls of the sweaty, stinky sewer so he would not sink below the surface and drown. The stench was so heavy that Crumb almost went unconscious again. HELP, he tried to shout, but no one was there to rescue him and no sound came out of his mouth.

A crumb drowning is not a pretty sight.

Yucky sewer water was filling every bit of his spongy body. He was getting heavier and heavier and each time he tried to get to the surface, he went down into the sewer lower and lower. Poor Crumb! He WAS drowning!

Crumb's whole life seemed to pass by him in a flash.... His thoughts raced, *Born in the Toaster next to a blob of melted butter... Toaster rescuing me just in time... Wondering where my Mother and Father could be... Breadbox warning me to stay out of trouble... Humans, how they mess everything up... Nefertiti the cat in a trance intoning the Riddle... Inside Breadbox learning to read... Falling off the counter... Under the fridge covered in bacon bits... The Mom in the Family almost sees me there... Spoon looking beautiful... Sitting in the sink with her to talk things over... Oh no, a big splash from the faucet... I'm falling down, down, down the drain, HELP!*

Crumb suddenly jumped into an awareness of where he was and it wasn't good. *I'm filling up with water! I'm getting swollen and totally soggy and... Help! Help! Toast isn't supposed to be soggy, it's supposed to be crispy. Help... I'm TOAST!*

It seemed like an hour went by but Timer (if he'd been there) would have said, "Ten minutes, that's all -- I'll sound an alarm to let you know."

Terror can turn ten minutes into an hour.

Just as Crumb was so heavy with stinky water that he was about to burst or fall like a stone down to the slimy bottom of the sewer pipe, Crumb felt something wonderfully smooth and silky under him, lifting him up in a graceful curve above the water-surface -- it was a banana peel! In fact, as it turned out, it was the very same banana peel that young Sally Baker had carelessly thrown down into the sink.

"Whoa! Woweee! I'm not toast, phew! Where did you come from? Am I glad to see you!" Crumb had never felt so relieved in all his five years.

"They say you can slip on a banana peel, but we DO come in handy, don't we!" said Banana Peel, whose proper name was Happy.

"I'm so happy to see you!" uttered Crumb.

"Actually, I'm Happy. (Oh, don't worry, we'll straighten all this up when I get you back home.)"

"Back home?! Home?! How are you gonna get me back home? I miss Breadbox. And Toaster and Tea-Pot and even Dish. I need to see Spoon again, she's my best friend and I need to make up with her... we were working to let our friendship sink in and I took it too seriously and fell IN the sink. HOW are you going to get us back there?"

"Simple." (Happy didn't waste time worrying. That was how he had earned his name.)

"Simple?" said Crumb, shaking his head in disbelief. Then, finding that shaking helped get rid of the sewer scum, he continued to shake back and forth until most of the scum had spurted off him. He had always envied Sponge for her porosity and ability to absorb situations, now he was glad to be much drier. "Simple?"

"Yup."

"How?" It didn't make sense to Crumb that getting from the sewer all the way back home was going to be easy.

"I don't know how, but I know we'll make it back."

"Oh great," moaned Crumb, "you don't know how. Nice of you to be confident despite this little drawback of no Plan A or Plan B."

"Hey, I managed to save you so far. Don't be sarcastic! I just KNOW we'll get you back to the Kitchen. Everything will work out."

"Okay, okay. I better believe you. I don't have much choice."

"That's right. Where there's a will, there's a way." Crumb stared at the banana peel. The thought hit Crumb: *Could Happy have overheard the Riddle?*

They sailed on, banana boat and Crumb, following the current, hopeful to make it out of that stinky morass. Somehow.

All of a sudden a thick packet of paper that had been submerged under the sewer water blasted straight up as if it was a giant bubble and burst onto the slick surface of the water, creating a powerful wave that plunged the banana peel and Crumb down under the surface for a frightening second, then scooped them both UP directly onto the barge of its smooth paper surface.

These papers, sealed in plastic, were so tightly wound up layer after layer that they formed a relatively waterproof "boat." Much stronger than the banana peel by itself, this wrapped paper-stash bore some resemblance to a yacht. Sitting on the "deck", the curved banana peel suddenly took on the look and appeal of a lounge chair. On it an amazed round bread-morsel sat like a passenger waiting for a massage or a mint julep. (Unfortunately, the sewer didn't smell much like a mint julep.)

This was a much better conveyance, and Crumb began to hope that maybe, just maybe, they might make it out of the sewer.

The paper boat surged ahead... in the semi-darkness. A tiny pinprick of light moved back and forth as the boat swiftly journeyed on sewer-ripples that sloshed from one side to the other, nearly bounding the boat into the grimy sides of the sewer. Slowly the pinprick of light grew wider and wider and the stench of garbage got less and less as fresh air streamed into the pipe.

Whooosh, a final waterfall wave plunged the paper boat up, down and OUT! The yacht with its lounge chair of a banana peel and thrilled round "passenger" were suddenly gently afloat.

Crumb jolted upright. He could scarcely believe his eyes. What was THIS?

The swirling waters had stopped. The air had cleared. The paper boat with its banana peel lounge chair and astonished breadcrumb were adrift on a placid, wide riverway. On all sides lay a beautiful city, wharves, tall skyscrapers with patterned windows lit from within like winking eyes, park benches, trees, and a lofty sky above, with moonlight and twinkling stars.

Crumb felt huge and tiny all at the same time. He'd never imagined such a place existed, that Humans could make such wide and tall and exquisite places. The Kitchen had been his kingdom, his realm, and he had thought all the time while he was growing up that the Kitchen was all there was, a whole giant universe-entire. Now, seeing the city for the first time, Crumb knew, *THIS, this is what H-U-G-E really is!*

Instantly Crumb rushed to take his wonderment into new explorations: *All this time I thought the Kitchen was the World! I'm always getting into mischief, but the Kitchen is way too SMALL for someone adventurous like me! There are sooooo many things I could find and see and explore....*

Visions of glory and wild excitement grabbed him in their powerful grip:

Crumb saw himself blown up into a huge Crumb-Monster scaling a skyscraper like King Kong, with little, annoying moth-like planes buzzing around the summit to try to shoot him down. He was enormous, bulging muscles straining to grab ledges and balconies as he lumbered up the pinnacle. At the summit, he swayed menacingly from one side to the other, almost knocking gargoyles off the rooftop. Finally he managed to grab onto the slender radio transmitter, but the needle nearly broke in two. Crumb-Monster fought his vertigo, looking down at streams of cars as small as ants. *I like feeling big,* he thought, *but maybe not THIS big!*

Then, shrunk back to his normal miniature size, he imagined he was dodging a blaze of downtown traffic with thunder and lightning on all sides, cars and cabs screeching to a halt as they almost squashed him. Their car-paint shimmered in the neon-bright, rain-soaked streets -- hot pink, taxi yellow, flashing chrome, black rain. Crumb was caught in the stormy undertow, struggling to avoid a watery grate that threatened to pull him back down to the dreaded sewer. Just then a bus swerved to avoid an oncoming car, creating a giant splash that swept the exhausted breadlet onto the sidewalk. A second later an overstuffed pigeon landed on the pavement, spotting his favorite treat. Swaggering over to Crumb, the bird opened his beak to capture the tasty morsel. *Gotta get outa here,* thought Crumb. *Being too small is just as unsafe as being too big. Help!*

At that moment, he changed his perspective. Where would he be safe? Somewhere warm and dry, where he was just the right size. Crumb imagined himself at a side-walk café on a sunny afternoon, relaxed, dry and debonair. *This is much better*, he thought, seeing himself sipping from a miniature mug next to a glamorous, diamond-studded girl-crumb. He leaned toward his attractive date, lifting his drink to make a toast to the sunshine and the warmth of her smile. *TOAST? What was I thinking? No way!* Crumb began to tremble.

"Why are you shaking so much? Settle down," cautioned Happy. Crumb came to, back on his banana boat and paper-stash cruise ship.

Isn't there another reason I need to see the world out there? realized Crumb. *Somehow — out there — would I be able find my Mom and Dad? Maybe they're in this huge place, trapped.... Maybe they're dead. I have to take that chance, I have to find them....*

And just as he was about to say, "Happy, I need to get over to the river bank", one second later Crumb was overcome with a wave stronger than anything in the sewer, Homesickness.

All of a sudden Crumb remembered the feeling of being home. Home meant — not this glittering metropolis, nor even the wide evening sky above, nor the comfort of the silky banana peel and paper boat — home meant Kitchen, Breadbox, Toaster, Tea-Pot, Timer, Spoon and the driving need to solve the Riddle. Would he ever see his home again? How would he get back there? Crumb began to snort tiny little laughs out of desperation, then tears came. He forced himself to calm down.

The banana peel spoke softly, "Don't worry, little Crumb. We made it this far, we'll get home. Remember what I said, 'Where there's a will there's a way'!"

Crumb nodded. Maybe it was best to trust Happy than to doubt and be doomed.

All this while, the crescent moon was fading as glimmers of rainbow sunlight shimmered on the glass windows of the skyscrapers and dappled the waters of the riverscape. Bit by bit dawn came, and the paper boat with its precious cargo drifted more and more to the left side of the waterway, past the wharves, to the park where lacy benches of wrought iron began to sparkle in the early morning sun.

Crumb looked up. A huge hairy hand was reaching down to the water-edge to scoop up... to scoop up the paper boat with its banana peel. *Oh NO,* thought Crumb, *a Human!*

"Garbage!" said a gruff voice. "I'll throw it out. In that can over there."

"Wait!" said a softer voice. "Honey, through the plastic wrapping I can see something written. Maybe it's important. I can still make out some typing in smeared ink. Give it to me... please, honey! You never know...."

"Okay, okay, but if it's just junk, let me throw it out. Our city river needs to be kept clean."

"Good enough, thanks. Let me see, what does the top say in big letters?" The woman used her nails to tear off the plastic wrapping. In a flash, Happy sneaked inside the middle of the sticky papers, hoping her fingers wouldn't locate him. The slimy sewer water had fortunately glued Crumb in place.

"They're smeared a bit but... oh my goodness, listen to this! I can barely make it out... give me a second here. Yes! There's an "L", then an "A", an "S" -- you are not going to BELIEVE this, Henry!"

"What, Sylvia? Tell me!"

"It says, 'Last Will and Testament of...' It's a WILL! Whose will, Henry? This might be very important. We have to see if the papers say whose will! Some of it is washed away into ink blobs... Where's the last piece of paper?" She rifled through the soggy papers (missing Happy and Crumb) careful not to tear the wad so she could check out the last page for a signature.

"Hmmm... It says 'President Acme Hat Company'! It's the last will and testament of the President of a hat company. We have to find out where this person is, dead or alive, or get it to a relative, even if most of it is washed up and unreadable."

"You're right, Sylvia. What a sweetheart you are. (Inside of himself, Henry was really thinking, *This is all I need on a busy workday*.) Okay, okay, you and I will do our best to track this down."

Both these Humans were unaware that an amazed breadcrumb and a thrilled banana peel were trying not to cheer out-loud because it would have given themselves away inside the messy wad of paper. The irony of the situation suddenly hit Crumb, *Sometimes it's a big help to be small*. Right now it was handy, Crumb's saving grace.

Sylvia and Henry couldn't find any Acme Hat Company in the city records. But there was a hat salesman in town.

When Sylvia and Henry knocked on the front door, Johnny peeked out of the tiny round security window at two puzzled people with a wet stack of paper and an odd banana peel stuck in the middle of the stack, unnoticed.

"Mommmm," whined Johnny, running into the Kitchen.

Hazel was sitting in a chair, her head in her arms, weeping.

"What's wrong Mommy? There are two people outside. Should I let them in?"

Mom wiped her eyes with a clean dish towel. Clasped tightly in her hand was her favorite serving spoon.

"How did this get into the disposal? I'm so upset." She unfolded her hand and looked at the bent and twisted handle of the once-beautiful serving piece.

"I'll go to the door to see who this is, Johnny. Thanks." Mom wiped her nose and wet eyes, peered at her reflection in the dark microwave panel to make sure her hair was okay, straightened her face into a conservative pretense of a smile and walked to the door.

"Who is it?"

Behind the closed door, two strangers in decent clothes but slightly miffed at not being allowed in (and yet smiling blandly to assure this woman they were harmless) informed Mom about their find.

"Acme! Oh yes, my husband is their best salesman, come in."

Opening the door, she let the couple in and gestured to them to sit in the sofa across from the hat rack with its two hats, not three.

"My husband's out of town --- when he's home, there are always at least three hats on the stand."

"Do you know whose will this might be?"

Henry was about to pass the paper stack over to Mrs. Baker to inspect, when all of a sudden the banana peel fell to the floor. (Fortunately, Mom and the visitors didn't notice. They had their attention on the signature at the end.)

Crumb tumbled out onto the rug, unseen by the Humans. Nefertiti was lounging by the sunny window. Her tail curled into a figure-eight infinity sign when she spotted Crumb stuck in one of the loops of the rug. Crumb shrank back inside the thick carpet, hoping to hide from the cat.

"Go, roll home, GO!" Happy urged Crumb in the kind of whisper they use on the stage to reach the last row of seats -- he'd watched TV a few times when the Family ate banana-splits and picked up the skill of doing a "stage whisper." Happy was hidden under the sofa about a foot away from the sleeping dog and a long way from where Crumb was stuck in the carpet.

Suddenly the dog Whisk woke up from his nap, smelling the banana peel still a bit rancid from sewer water. Whisk didn't seem like the smartest pet, but that was just because he lumbered a bit when he walked. He was a rescue dog from a local shelter, devoted to his new family. The puppy had been abused by a former owner so that his spine bent a little. That gave him an awkward gait.

Two years ago Ken Baker had gone to the shelter to find a pet for his kids for Christmas. There was something in this particular puppy's eyes that attracted Dad right away. Devotion -- stifled by earlier mistreatment but still devotion -- gleamed in Whisk's brown eyes. All the doggies at the shelter, except this one, were yapping "Take me! Take me!", jumping up on the wiring of their cages, begging to be taken, tugging at Dad's heart. (*This is really tough*, thought Ken, *I can't take them all home*.) This one puppy was different. For some reason he sat still, calm, well-behaved with a hopeful dignity in his eyes. Whisk had found his Forever Home.

That first day in his new home Whisk sniffed every inch of the house and settled that night in the Kitchen in a big basket covered in clean rags with a ticking alarm clock to make him feel his Mother's heartbeat was there. It worked. He slept that night like never before. The doggie knew that he had only been one sad day away from death.

The next morning Ken had found the pooch passed out on the kitchen floor next to a fallen stainless steel whisk. It looked like the whisk had hit him on the head, because the puppy was dizzy and disoriented for days. Dad took advantage of this incident with the stainless steel whisk to name the puppy "Whisk."

Maybe the blow to his head had given the dog a mild concussion because after that morning Dad sometimes wondered if this dog, as devoted and cute as he was, had been a mistake. Whisk would tend to slip on the stairs. He'd sniff for minutes on end on walks so it made walking him very tedious. All in all he seemed a bit brain-dead. Dumb, in fact. But lovable.

With his lumbering gait and big grin, Whisk didn't seem like the Albert Einstein of Dogdom, but he was much more intelligent and capable than any Human suspected. For one thing, he had a nose smarter than Cyrano de Bergerac, that was certain.

So, on the morning when two strangers knocked on the door and Whisk had begun to sniff the scent of banana by the living-room sofa, Crumb (who had fallen only a few feet away from Happy) was terrified. The dog was twice as big as the cat and Crumb knew he still had a bit of bacon-aroma lingering on his bread-crevices, even with all the sewer scum that had been there. Bacon! What dog didn't love to munch and lick on bacon. Help!

Crumb shrank back into the heavy loops of the carpet, fearing that Whisk would snatch him up with his long pink tongue. He tried to roll over but got caught in the scratchy loops and couldn't move. He wouldn't have been able to budge anyway, he was so frozen with terror.

Whisk stood over the part of the carpet where Crumb was stuck, with his big black nose quivering as he smelled the still-soggy bread-ball. Long moist whiskers were spread like antennae over the rug, waving from side to side to absorb the scent of bread, banana, a hint of bacon and a lot of sewer.

Suddenly a whisker bent over Crumb and scooped him up onto its sticky thread. *Oh no,* thought Crumb. *I'm so close to the Kitchen — is this how I'm going to die? Is this one of Life's Lessons... that life and death can be so close they can meet in a whisker?*

All of a sudden he was being hoisted back Home --- to the Kitchen.

Whisk was actually bringing Crumb back to the Kitchen -- whether on purpose or by chance, Crumb wasn't sure. Crumb had never been so happy to feel linoleum beneath him, smooth and comforting and cool to the touch. He could make out a familiar sound... *What was it, WHO was it?* he wondered.

It was Spoon! She lay still on the counter where Mom had had her in her grasp a few minutes earlier. Stiff as if she were lying in a coffin, she was torn between gasping and weeping.

"Don't look at me, Crumb!"

"Spoon! I'm so happy to see you I could jump up to the counter and hug you bigtime, Best Buddy! What do you mean, 'don't look at me'?"

"I... I was trying to get you out.... I... I fell into the disposal.... I'm not beautiful like I used to be.... Hortense turned the disposal on.... She didn't realize I'd fallen in there.... I'm... I'm..." she sobbed.

"BEAUTIFUL! You are the sweetest, most gorgeous best friend in the world!"

"You mean? You mean you don't care if I'm... if I'm all bent and twisted? ...I'm not pretty anymore."

"Not so. You're beautiful. Inside and out."

Chapter Six

When Bonding, Watch for Cracks

Ken Baker contacted his boss Mr. Harry Ardmore Jr. the next day. Harry's father, the revered founder of the Acme Hat Company, had sadly died a year ago. A second official copy of the will -- personally signed -- had been tossed into the river by an angry distant relative who had failed to be mentioned as a beneficiary in the will. In his rage, the fellow had apparently forgotten to take off the plastic wrapper, thank goodness.

Harry Jr. had taken over the company and had inherited the bulk of the Estate... but the lost copy of the will had troubled his family for a whole year. The Ardmore Family decided to offer a substantial reward for anyone finding the lost will, in whatever state it was in, as long as it could be proved beyond a reasonable doubt to be the actual will.

A handwriting and forensic analyst was hired who determined (after methodical inspection of Harry Senior's uniquely characteristic flowing capital "H" and "A" and the highly slanted loops in the small "y" and "d") that indeed this was Harold Ardmore Senior's authentic signature and his Last Will and Testament.

The grateful President of Acme Hat Company rewarded Henry and Sylvia for finding the missing will and going to the trouble of locating his top-earning hat salesman Ken Baker. Ken got promoted to Vice-President of Marketing and Sales and his salary was doubled. (To tell the truth, it was a long-overdue promotion and salary hike. Ken's devotion to hats and to Acme was well-respected throughout the company and had turned the company's fortunes around several times. Sometimes serendipity ---

like the astonishing discovery of the plastic-wrapped document --- turns struggle into reward.)

Ken was able to join the Tennis Club he'd been longing to be part of for a few years, next to a Health Spa where Hazel could go get a massage while he played a good game or two. Tennis was his favorite game and suited his genial personality well. It was a gentleman's game, competitive but always -- well ALmost always -- involving good sportsmanship, even if Love was the lowest score. His tennis racket had lain too long in his closet. He'd have fun too in the Club house after a good singles or doubles game, wearing some of his snappy visors or maybe a sailor cap or a felt ascot golf-cap-- you never could tell when he'd make another customer for Acme.

Meanwhile, Hazel Baker had plenty of bucks to renovate her entire Kitchen. She had been begging him to do this for years.

Ken hoped he and his charming but difficult wife would get along better after that. Her sense of humor when she was in a good mood, her pretty face and cooking skills kept him loyal to her on his long sales trips. Now that he was Vice-President of Marketing and Sales, he could work from home rather than be on the road, spend time with his kids and reassure his lonely wife and get her more relaxed.

Ken counted on an age-old principle: A tough woman can be softened by prosperity -- little unexpected luxuries like chocolate-covered strawberries on a heart-shaped tray from the local gift basket company -- and well-timed compliments. Once Hazel was less worried about how the bills were going to be paid, some of her wrinkles seemed to fade, she looked radiant and his compliments could glow with sincerity rather than just be calculated moves. After all, no one could make a scrumptious meal just like Hazel. (Ken had to agree, the way to a man's heart was through his stomach.)

He invited the Baruti's over for supper every now and then, enjoying the fact that he had time to get to know his neighbors better now that he didn't have to be on the road half the time. Ken even helped Zoe's Dad find a wholesale outlet for bee-keeper helmets. He took the Doc to his tennis club a few times and taught him how to do backhand. Matt needed to get outside more, said Ken. "Do you think I need a tan?" joked the Doc.

The two fellows would tease each other then head home for a dinner that Hazel and Zoe had concocted together. Maybe a fresh Greek Salad with tangy olives and feta cheese, green peppers and thin-sliced red onions followed by creamy lemony-egg Avgolemono Soup and baklava for dessert, or Hungarian chicken paprikash with mushrooms and sour cream gravy over egg noodles and red cabbage with caraway seeds, cooked just right, and for dessert homemade apple strudel. Bonding was going on at the tennis court and around the dinner table, no doubt about it!

Zoe would bring along her Chef's Hat and her Mother's apron and help Sally and Johnny do the dishes after dinner. (Usually Hortense did the dishes, but when "company" was over for dinner, Hazel liked the kids to help out, especially when Zoe was over. Sally and Johnny needed to learn to help out and with the kids busy in the Kitchen, the grown ups could talk.) Once Zoe even brought some of her special coleslaw with lemongrass, raisins and diced fresh pineapple over to add to the table. Zoe and Mrs. Baker would talk "cooking" in the kitchen and exchange recipes. After a while, recipes were just a jumping off point for creativity in the kitchen. Sally and Johnny didn't feel left out and certainly didn't mind... who minds chewy cookies baking in the oven?

The Kitchen Things were always relieved to see Zoe helping out with the dishes after dinner because she was much more careful with the glasses and slippery dishes than the Baker kids were, and even Hortense broke a glass now and then. Breadbox always smiled extra wide when he saw Zoe, pointing her out to Crumb as his initial inspiration for wanting to teach him how to read. Crumb secretly resented the comparison a wee bit, because underneath all his spunk and derring-do was a hidden concern: Had his parents abandoned him because he wasn't all that special? Was he pretending to be smart?

Still, peeking out from Breadbox when his Granddad's tin door was slightly ajar, seeing Zoe by the sink with her cornrow braids poking out of her Chef's Hat as she carefully dried the dishes and made up stories for Sally and Johnny, how could he not admire her! She looked so sweet and had such a fun personality. Someday he'd have to meet her. Someday he'd prove to Breadbox that he was every bit as smart as Zoe.

All this while (despite Crumb's pep talks and sincere compliments) Spoon hid her twisted handle, self-conscious that her beauty had been tarnished. When the Kitchen Things heard that Dad's salary doubled, excited looks passed from one utensil and appliance to another. "They'll fix you, they'll fix you," offered Crumb, trying to get Spoon out of her gloom.

Fortunately, one of the first things Hazel did with her extra cash flow was to take Spoon to a top silversmith for repair and straightening. Spoon was thrilled. She had longed for a trip outside of the Kitchen, something to stir her recollections of formal gardens, chandeliers and lavish banquets. The modern city surroundings weren't at all as elegant as the chateau where she'd been born, but they were much more exciting than Kitchen shelves.

At Stein's Silversmith & Estate Jewelry Shop, Joseph Stein got excited when he saw her fleur-de-lis embossed handle so he leafed through a silverware pattern-book to find her heritage. The kindly old man was careful not to press her too hard or heat her unnecessarily. This was a rare antique with a silver pattern that might actually have served royalty at the palace of Versailles.

At last Spoon's handle was straight, the curves and bowl all in alignment, some of the bent fleur-de-lis re-embossed and restored. There was only one small mark at the base of her handle-leg which Spoon preferred to think of as her ankle when she pretended, later on, to tie ballet slippers or toe-shoes during her dance practice. Joseph polished her to a new sheen with a fragrant wool rag until she looked a mere two hundred years young instead of over three hundred and fifty -- what a facelift!

How Spoon wanted to thank this dear old man for taking a hundred and fifty years off her look, but as he was elderly she thought the shock of hearing silverware speaking aloud to him might be too much for his health. As it was, when Hazel came back to pick up Spoon, the silversmith informed her that Spoon was worth a lot. "A very rare antique," was how he put it. "I'll give you a discount because it's been such a pleasure fixing her as close to her original condition as I could. An honor, in fact." Hazel loved to hear that and Spoon beamed inside her special flannel, non-tarnishing covering-case.

After Ken did some budgeting, he figured that there was enough money now to give his wife the new Kitchen she had begged him for. The bids came in and they selected a crew. Hazel designed the space planning in the Kitchen herself, basing her design on the efficient Kitchen Work-Triangle of Stove-Sink-Refrigerator. (A *Triangle*, noted Nefertiti, *ah, the basic shape of the pyramids -- well, almost.* Pyramids, being three-dimensional structures rather than flat, were square at the base. Not bad space-planning, Nefertiti conceded.)

The outdated linoleum floor had to go. Crumb wasn't sorry a bit to see the thick, rubbery, inlaid black-and-white floor being ripped up and hauled away. Lino-no-NO-leum was how he felt about the floor after having fallen down from the counter. Ken and Hazel weighed the option of travertine stone against the foot-comfort of cork and decided (although cork would probably absorb the shock of fallen dishes and glassware) to opt for the stunning look of travertine.

Humans! Breadbox sighed to himself. *Always thinking of themselves first. Cork would have saved many a fallen glass or plate from breaking, but no!* Breadbox was disgruntled, but didn't dare to say a word out-loud. He didn't want to give away that Kitchen Things were ALIVE, talked amongst themselves whenever Humans and Pets weren't there, had feelings (especially when broken) and were a Community.

To Hazel's consternation the Kitchen renovation took four and a half months (not really a long time at all for such endeavors), estimates were exceeded (what else is new) and clouds of dust were mostly contained behind thick plastic flaps between the Kitchen and the rest of the house. Just as Crumb was developing an allergy to dust and wood chips, the workers were done, paid and gone. Finally all was resplendent, in a style that blended Contemporary and Fifties Retro.

Hazel kept all the best antiques and useful tools she treasured, giving them places of honor in her newly appointed Kitchen. Being a Foodie, she couldn't wait to cook her first meal in her brand new Kitchen. Ken, Johnny and Sally were so tired of delivery pizza and take-out food that they felt a new bond as a family, laughing and smiling round the table, munching Mom's meal of vegetable lasagna, finely chopped kale salad and gingerbread cake topped with homemade cinnamon applesauce.

Dad invited Dr. Matt and Zoe to join them. Zoe brought her cream of wild mushroom soup with snippets of fresh tarragon on top and a touch of grownup brandy stirred in for just a few minutes until the alcohol wore off. Everyone hardly said a word around the table, the food was so delicious. But giggles galore were heard from the Kitchen after the meal as the kids helped clean up the dishes.

For a few months Mom was in ecstasy and paraded around her renovated Kitchen with a new sense of warmth and confidence. She sent fancy invitations out and had a few parties for relatives and friends. Their "oohs" and "ahhs" satisfied her for a while and calmed her brooding about her "lost stardom." In fact, during those months, she hardly ever listened to "Sweet Sally Jones" on the radio anymore, because the soap opera did seem histrionic and predictably miserable.

The Kitchen Things were pleasantly surprised. Apparently Humans had the capacity to CHANGE. Hopefully Mom's new behavior would be a constant from then on out. Breadbox advised them to hope for that, but not put too much stock in this alteration, since once the Kitchen look was lackadaisically familiar she'd probably become grumpy again. Spoon, now repaired, had regained her confidence and playfully scolded old Breadbox a bit for being so pessimistic.

"I survived the French Revolution. I've seen Humans change for the better and change for the worse. But Breadbox, as wise as you usually are, wouldn't it be a better idea to give Mrs. Baker a chance?"

This was new -- hardly ever did any Kitchen Thing think of correcting the venerable wise-man of the Kitchen. Spoon herself was evolving and growing able to see a chink in the old container. Breadbox cautiously agreed. Spoon was probably right.

Still, Breadbox couldn't get himself to trust the Mom of the Family completely. He was an endangered species. How long would her affable mood continue?

The venerable fellow watched with sideways glances as Hazel busied herself surveying all her Kitchen utensils, pots, appliances and dishware to see what she needed, what she loved and what was expendable. The Kitchen Things held their breath -- who would go, who would stay? They tried to hide the garbage can where they thought they might be tossed, but it always got moved back in place. Who would end up being tossed away?

Mom spent a while deciding about Breadbox. Breadbox was getting old and his door squeaked no matter how many times Ken oiled it, but she decided to keep it anyway... for Grandma Mildred's sake. Toaster, Timer, Tea-Pot and Blender looked retro-cool, on their new polished granite and sturdy wood-block counters. Rolling Pin rested her temper in a beautifully-lined drawer, a sign that now Mom and Dad didn't need to argue anymore... well, hardly ever.

Usually Dish was stacked with other fancy platters... everyone agreed she had always been stacked... but Hazel considered her so beautiful that Dish was now featured upright on her very own mahogany plate-holder and displayed at the front of a special new glass-cabinet so that everyone could admire her. If a plate can be said to gloat, Dish was displaying not only her beauty but her sense of self-importance.

Adding to the new look in the Kitchen, Coldylox the Fridge got two coats of resilient blackboard paint (the latest rage) so that the Baker Family could write messages, menus and reminders to one another. (Little did they know that the three Kitchen Things that could read -- Crumb, Breadbox and Sharpest Knife -- would be privy to their plans.) The fridge magnets were moved to Coldylox's sides to make room for the blackboard. They felt rather shunted off to the side but stuck together as a group.

The Kitchen sparkled but there was something missing. Breadbox couldn't place his tin door on what exactly was going on, but he had a feeling something was up. At least Crumb was home now and Spoon was back in shape. What could go wrong?

***

The Bakers could now afford to eat out more often, even at the fanciest restaurants. It was quite noticeable how an influx of higher salary was an inducement to create a cheerier mood in the Baker's household. But every now and then Hazel would sulk and complain that no one wanted her home cooking anymore.

When that happened, Ken would contact Zoe right away to bring over her Chef's Hat and Mother's apron and entice Hazel to create another fabulous home-cooked meal together. The two of them would sit at the Kitchen table pouring over recipe books or use their imagination fashioning a delicious dinner or perhaps a yummy Sunday brunch: Eggs Benedict with homemade Hollandaise Sauce, fresh squeezed organic Orange Juice in fine crystal topped with sprigs of mint, fresh ground Viennese Coffee with whipped cream or --- in honor of Zoe's Dad --- piquant Ethiopian coffee with a wee touch of cinnamon added.

Zoe taught Hazel how to make one of her Mother's specialties, Organic grapefruit halves sprinkled with Cardamom and a touch of honey. Zoe warmed them in the oven under low heat for just a few short minutes to let the raw honey (taken out that very day from their bee hive) sink into the juicy segments but not ruin the enzyme content of the fresh honey, nature's sweet elixir from the bees.

Hazel began to hug her kids, realizing that they were her future and that she wanted them to be glad they had a Mother, unlike Zoe who would sometimes wipe a tear from her eye during their Cooking Expeditions remembering how many times a day she used to be enveloped in her Mom's arms. Hazel vowed to herself, *I can't replace Zoe's own Mother but I can do my best to fill that empty place in her heart.*

Hazel had always decided that intrinsically she herself was a self-centered, self-absorbed person -- now she began to notice kindness seeping into her soul like the warm honey on the grapefruit halves. It felt good.

On such a Sunday as the Brunch above took place, not everyone was content.

Crumb hid in the farthest corner of Breadbox during the food preparations gathering his little breadcrumb cousins about him, praying that the English Muffins plunked into Breadbox for a while wouldn't press onto him before they were removed to be toasted for the Eggs Benedict muffin-platform.

Toaster refused to speak to Crumb for days after that, so insulted was he that Crumb didn't allow the muffins to be crisped without shuddering and making a big fuss. "Elementary, my dear Crumbson" was out of his vocabulary for a while and he decided that Crumb was acting too persnickety. The Detective's dial was set on Dark and he was determined to observe the breadcrumb with stealthy eyes.

Nevertheless, this was a time of renovation and renewal and the Humans and Kitchen Things had taken on a downright jolly air. Ken was smart to ask Zoe and Matt over. The kids were getting hugs from Mom now. And Hazel was cheery to have everyone licking their lips and complimenting her and Zoe about what a world-class, five-star brunch they'd enjoyed in their own home.

She and Zoe had bonded. Foodies are like that (unless they despise each other, as any sous-Chef in a fancy restaurant will tell you).

Zoe gave Hazel a calm respect -- she knew she really did need Hazel's added expertise to show her exactly how to crack and separate eggs in a snap without those annoying little eggshells falling in, and how to beat egg whites from soft moist clouds to stiff hilltops when she darted a wooden spoon into them. Big and Little Chefs they were, finding new pleasure in the creativity of cooking. Soon they stopped using recipe books and started to think of making one of their own -- BAKER AND BARUTI, maybe it would lead to a TV show of their own someday!

And so Hazel, relieved that her husband could work from home (except when it came time for Hat Conventions) and finding companionship with Zoe, contented herself once again with brightening all her favorite things in her new Kitchen.

Spoon was polished and placed delicately on a handmade doily where she could practice her ballet steps, First Position, Second Position (rather hard with only one "foot", but she pretended). Spoon discovered soon that she could imagine her lace doily to be a spotlight glowing below her twirling handle. It wasn't long before she began to make tutus out of practically any material left on the counter. There was that convenient Kitchen drawer full of sewing equipment, needles, thread and little patches of cloth. Plastic bags made her sweat too much during her ballet bar exercises, but anything else was possible. She had become a fashionista, recalling her days with the royal court and its embroidered damask gowns and high wigs for the ladies-in-waiting (as high as the cupcake frosting Marie Antoinette had so favored) and velvet vests and lace cuffs for the male courtiers.

To help Spoon practice her ballet routines, Crumb managed to turn the radio dial to the Classical Station and hovered near the edge of the counter mesmerized by Spoon's pirouettes, pliés and arabesques. Hazel Baker came into the Kitchen one day and found the dial changed from the "Sweet Sally Jones" station to "Magnificent Music of The Ages." She and the kids began to listen to stirring and sensitive symphonies, concertos and sonatas and for variety, fun jazz and rock-and-roll stations too. The music began to close the distance between Hazel and her kids with the healing beauty of timeless music.

Crumb was changed too in his exploration-approach to the Kitchen. After his ordeal in the sewer, Crumb decided to avoid the sink area as a general rule, but reassured Sponge that he was fond of her and wasn't rejecting the sink because of her. (Breadbox had told him that Sponge had tried to mop up the excess water to save him.) So he cultivated a new friendship with her. Sponge fascinated him because she had two very different personalities, dry or wet, and had the uncanny ability to absorb information on first hearing. This impressed the breadcrumb because it had taken him over three weeks to learn his ABCs.

Being jealous and possessive, Scrubber decided that Sponge had a nerve trying to be heroic, it was Scrubber's job to show his grit, not hers. So he turned his rough side away from Sponge and smugly declared, "Tough! I could care less." Crumb was learning to choose his friends and didn't care either --- Scrubber was bothersome and smelled like old grease.

Another change in Crumb was that he lightened up about French Toast --- he really didn't want to offend Spoon anymore. So he decided to just let Day-Old slices become French Toast and not make a big fuss about warning them. These Day-Old pieces didn't seem to believe any harm could come to them anyway. They felt they'd loafed enough and wouldn't mind some sizzling action for a change. Maybe French Toast wasn't such a bad fate after all. (*Come to think of it*, thought Crumb, *anything sounds better with a French accent.*)

Not long after the Kitchen renovation was complete, Crumb and Spoon shared a celebration picnic one fine afternoon, delicately munching tidbits of French Brie on top of thin slivers of Pippin apples. (Naturally, no rolls were served --- that would have offended the bread-morsel.) Crumb had been practicing his French accent and read a beautiful poem by Verlaine out-loud to her.

> Il pleure dans mon coeur
> Comme il pleut sur la ville.
>
> It weeps in my heart
> Like it rains on the town....

Spoon beamed and shared some anecdotes about her long history as they sat laughing and chatting.

"Tell me Spoon, what is the most important moment in history you ever personally witnessed?"

"Oh, mon ami, I was there when the most important invention in human history took place!"

"The WHEEL!??! I didn't think you were THAT old!"

"No, no," laughed Spoon, "the most wonderful invention of all time -- I witnessed in the kitchen of my chateau."

"What was it?"

"The invention of ICE CREAM! Chocolate, Fresh Peach, Coffee, Pistachio, Rocky Road!"

"Rocky Road? That was created way back then? I thought it was a relatively modern flavor," exclaimed the bread-ball.

"Oh my goodness, Crumb, you have never experienced travel in a stagecoach --- Rocky Road was a way of life back then, let me tell you. I barely survived being bumped up and down inside a picnic basket in those days, but fortunately I'm still here."

"And how glad I am of that, Spoon. The greatest invention in history? Ice Cream, of COURSE! Yes, yes, that is DEFINITELY the most important invention in all of history!"

That night Crumb in his Breadbox and Spoon on her doily up with the crystal glasses slept with contented smiles on their faces.

Hazel didn't mind Ken's snoring quite as much, and Sally and Johnny hugged their teddy bears more tightly than ever.

Doc Baruti noticed an old wound beginning to heal. And Zoe felt that she'd found an extended family.

Ample change can create a lot of renewal. But when you bond, watch for cracks.

***

Unfortunately, Breadbox had estimated the situation correctly. After a hiatus from crabbiness, Mom found occasion to storm into the Kitchen one day, nagging Hortense the maid and kicking the cat out of the way. Nefertiti glared. Most of the Kitchen appliances, utensils, dishes, pots and pans had assembled on the counter, awaiting a special Fashion Show organized by Spoon and Crumb which was just about to start any minute from then. Little did the Humans know.

"You're fired. The Kitchen is an absolute mess! ...Okay, okay, I won't fire you, but this is your last chance!"

All the pots, pans, utensils and appliances froze right where they were. Spoon nearly fainted but Crumb held her up.

Mom looked around the Kitchen, trying to find something else to complain about to Hortense.

"What's this piece of dark brown blob on the counter?" (It was Crumb in a roasted sesame seed tuxedo -- he was studying the famous fashion-design house and perfumery House of Channel-Five to please Spoon.

Roasted black sesame seeds seemed like the perfect idea at the time. *Oh great! My tux is coming undone!* he groaned to himself.)

"And what is my favorite fancy napkin doing draped around my good serving spoon?" (It was Spoon all dressed up in a lacy gown for a fashion show.) *Well, is she worried more about her fancy-dancy napkin or ME? I was just about to strut down the runway!* protested Spoon.

Mom continued her tirade. "I thought I told you to put all the pots and pans away -- Look at this mess! Can't anything get done right around here without ME? Clean all this up right now, Hortense! I'm tired of having to do YOUR WORK!"

"Well, I try to whistle and be patient and do my work, but I'm tired of having to hear YOU! I've had enough! I QUIT!"

With that, Hortense and Mom and the cat bound out of the Kitchen, chasing each other in a mad fury.

"Humans!" sighed Breadbox. "When will they ever learn? Maybe never, but it's a good thing they need us. Maybe they need us more than they THINK." He paused considering what to do next and realizing all was quiet, grinned as he opened his big tin door.

"We're safe now -- Miss Demolition just quit! Now all we have to worry about is Mrs. Baker. Hey Crumb, how about a lesson in French history? Say, you two sure look fancy!"

Toaster was so relieved his tray banged up and down, Blender whirled his blades, Timer proclaimed "Perfect timing!" and even Coldylox smiled so wide from one edge of her to the other that the refrigerator magnets on her sides almost fell off.

However, there was one creature who wasn't celebrating.

The cat had lost her favorite Human-of-choice, the maid. There would be no catnip treats, no sitting on Hortense's blanket, no one who reminded Nefertiti of Queen Hatshepsut back in the lotus-blossom Palace, no one who made her purr half as much as Hortense.

That night as soon as the Humans were in bed, Nefertiti crept into the kitchen with downcast eyes and slumped across the travertine floor, suddenly in her Off position, moaning in her trance, even trembling in her sleep. She seemed to be reliving something very terrifying. Her tail curled into all kinds of odd symbols, looping and twisting in anxiety.

Breadbox couldn't make out what she was saying. It wasn't English, and Spoon swore it had no resemblance to either old or modern French. Tea-Pot felt it might be ancient Egyptian or perhaps late Sumerian but he'd never heard such strange sounds before. Hoping to help, Tea-Pot read some tea leaves and concluded, "A journey. The stars are aligned."

Breadbox shook his head. He was much too practical to believe in such guesswork or magic. Crumb rolled close to the edge of the counter near the cat to listen as best he could.

"Ka-poonga-TONGa! MoogaNISHa, ablatoo-vaLOONias, skrumTOOPa, oonu oonu, ka-poonga-TONGa, naptra kalapoom-PINee, moogaNISHa, oonu oonu, ka-poonga-TONGa...."

Nerfertiti's chanting was incomprehensible but totally compelling, hypnotic, and very troubling. In fact, it made Crumb dizzy.

Spinning off-balance as he made his way back to Breadbox, Crumb almost fell off the counter on top of the cat, but managed to get back to Breadbox and gasp, "Sesame... Sesame... I beg you, open up... Bagel." Breadbox opened his door and let Crumb in.

Disturbed by the moaning and struggles Nefertiti was going through, Crumb fell into a fitful sleep inside Breadbox's reassuring inside.

As Crumb closed his eyes, he caught the engraving of the Riddle on the side and back walls. With each strange word the cat intoned, the words began to glow as if lit from within, but there was no source of light whatsoever to explain this eerie glow.

Breadbox was itching as the Riddle words began to glow one by one, triggered somehow by the mysterious chanting of the cat. "What's happening? I'm uncomfortable. Itchy..."

Crumb didn't answer. He was fast asleep, deep in a strange dream, immersed in it, taken over by it, back down-down-down, swept into that inner cavern at his core, that black hole of emptiness and echoes that he had tried so hard to put aside by looking outward and exploring during the daytime.

Now he was consumed by vivid and compelling visions in a fitful dream-state, haunting images that seemed unreal and yet strangely hyper-real, more real than everyday life.

In Crumb's dream he could feel echoes of a huge windstorm outside, rattling the Kitchen windows, howling at the back door. The cat and dog had raced into the kitchen to check out what was causing all this noise. Crumb was too scared to move. Spoon was shaking against the crystal glasses on the top shelf as they spilled onto the baseboard and rumbled up against the glass cabinet door which fortunately held tight. Crumb called out to her but it was too noisy in the Kitchen for her to hear him. A thought echoed through the tumult like the moan of a ghost, *This is only a dream, but it seems so real. What a storm!*

Suddenly the back door blasted open and a gale storm swirled and roared into the kitchen.

Chapter Seven

Windstorm on Tempest

Crumb was lifted in the tornado-like spirals of the windstorm, sucked as if an air-vacuum had grabbed onto him. The dog stumbled onto his clumsy feet, howling, racing around the Kitchen, whiskers moving almost as fast as helicopter blades. Crumb flew into a wad of those whiskers and stuck there, clinging to the antennae. Nefertiti was hovering in mid-air, stretched out like a flying carpet with her arms and legs stiff in front and back of her like starched fringe. The wind-torrent began to buffet the cat-carpet up and down -- her pale eyes were glowing like radioactive coals.

In a flash all three, Nefertiti and Whisk with Crumb on his whiskers, were pulled out of the open door, outside the Kitchen into the backyard. A street sign was shaking in the wind. A massive light from above pulsed on the sign, revealing and then hiding what it said: Tempest Street.

The grass was standing up straight, pulled taut from above. For a second Crumb spotted a little honeybee floating in a pool of spectral neon-green light above the crop circle that had just been made in the lawn -- a Happy Face imprinted in the grass!

Crumb fought the wind to look upward into the blinding light. A UFO was hovering about a hundred yards above the roof of the house. *This must be a dream, only a dream*, he thought to himself. *I'm only dreaming, right?* Crumb felt his eyes freeze in disbelief. (He'd never been in the backyard before, but he never expected it to look like this.) The tornado-windstorm had shifted upward to its source, the alien spacecraft, which suddenly turned invisible, cloaked for security.

Just then, a bubbly sensation seized Crumb as if he were turning into foam and evaporating into an ocean of air.

The next thing Crumb knew he was inside the spaceship, still stuck on Whisk's long antenna. All four, Crumb, dog, cat and that honeybee that Crumb had spotted just a second ago, all four of them were being greeted by a troop of fifty Aliens, standing there in ten neat rows of five each.

Nefertiti recognized their eyes right away. They were slanted cat's eyes, hollow but hypnotic, the same eyes that had looked down at her when she was reading the Riddle on the ancient wall during her trance state. *Were these Aliens spying on me then?*, she wondered, *or were they possibly sending me the Riddle?* There was no way to tell. Below the riveting eyes were identical Happy Face smiles. The eyes said one thing, the smiles another.

"Greetings Earth Pets! Have a Nice Day... er, Evening!"

Dog, cat, Crumb and the little bee froze.

Am I dreaming this? wondered Crumb. *This can't be real. What if it IS? Is this really happening right NOW in real time? Or am I remembering something that already happened? Is this just a nightmare? Where the heck AM I?*

Time and Space had collapsed into a tangled mass of string-theory fibers all stuck together, knotted and tight, winding around Crumb like a crushing net, keeping him THERE in this scary spaceship when all he wanted to do was to return to his nice safe bed in Breadbox.

Try as he did to decide it wasn't really happening, there he was, in the UFO staring at fifty weird Happy Faces, trying not to be seen. *Maybe they won't see me here in this big dog-whisker!*

"Greetings, Earth Pets!" The Aliens were talking in monotone, exactly in synchronization. The dog, the cat, the bee and Crumb were so terrified they couldn't move, but their eyes darted around, trying to sneak glances at each other to see who had been captured.

"Our universal translator is working. One Voice, One Thought, One Purpose! One Size Fits All!"

"WHY have you brought us here?" Nefertiti found herself (with the help of the universal translator) talking in Alien tongue, which sounded exactly like English to the Dog, Crumb and Bee:

"Ka-poonga-TONGa! MoogaNISHa, ablatoo-vaLOONias, skrumTOOPa, oonu oonu, ka-poonga-TONGa, naptra kalapoom-PINee, moogaNISHa, oonu oonu, ka-poonga-TONGa...." The cat was affronted. What Whisk, Crumb and the bee heard was, "How DARE you! Why have you torn us from our safe places on Earth? What a nerve! Send us back right NOW!"

The Happy Faces just smiled their bland smiles, except that those innocuous smiles grew a bit wider. The Aliens recognized their own guttural language being spoken by the cat. How pleased they seemed to be that her speaking-in-tongues was being converted by their universal translator so that everyone there would understand the exact same thing at the same time... and thus there would be no uncomfortable dissent. That would be intolerable.

These Aliens were obviously consumed with Unity, with everyone sharing the very same thought at the exact same time. Dissent was completely foreign to them. It was beyond their ken to notice differences, to perceive anything other than complete agreement. These Happy Faces spoke with One Voice, they shared One Thought, and apparently they were motivated by One Purpose of some kind. What that Purpose was, none of the four abducted creatures could even guess.

Unable to spot any differences, this long habit of Sameness made the Aliens appear ridiculously dumb in effect, despite their technical wizardry of space travel and machine-control. Their inbred compulsion to crush dissent also made them malleable to suggestions from those who could detect differences and thus were brighter, more alive, more perceptive.

Perhaps, wondered the bee, *they're under some hypnotic command, long since forgotten. WHY did they capture us and bring us here? Maybe they can be manipulated....*

Concentrating on their own unified thoughts and behavior, the Aliens failed to notice the different terror reactions of the four. The bee froze in place with his wings stiff as darts, the cat glared defiantly, Crumb trembled (stuck as he was on the bouncing tight-rope of a long dog-whisker) and the dog crashed to the floor with his front paws crossed over his eyes, nearly crushing Crumb in the process.

The Aliens droned on. "We are all of One Voice, One Thought, One Purpose, but... it's been quite a few parsecs and about a hundred-thousand light years since we left our nice uniform bland world. After all this time, we may all be of One Voice, One Thought and One Purpose, but we are ALL in agreement about... in agreement about..." They paused to nod, exactly in unison motion.

"Agreement about WHAT?" demanded Nefertiti, absolutely disgusted with having been beamed up without her lofty permission. *I've been guessing something like this would happen for a while*, thought the cat. *Why did it surprise me? Getting lifted up here was all too FAST, that's how it took me unawares. Back in Egypt, things took their time, dynasties lasted for thousands of years, sand wore down the Sphinx over untold centuries. Now everything is hyped-up, way too fast for me, it whizzes by and then it's gone. Flavor-of-the-month, and it always tastes like tuna. Whatever happened to a nice l-o-n-g cat-nap on a sunny window ledge....*

The Happy Faces complied with Nefertiti's "Agreement about WHAT?", explaining why they'd brought the Four up to their ship.

"You see, we are very, very BORED with One Size Fits All. It was fine for a few hundred thousand years. Then we spotted Earth! You are a planet of Oddballs, never agreeing. We wanted to find out what makes Earthlings and their Pets such... such... what's the word for this? Such interesting IndiVIDuals!"

The Happy Faces laughed a scratchy kind of monotone snigger. "Hee-hee-hee." The very concept of "individuality" must have been a huge joke to them in the first place.

"We come to you as Friends -- see our Happy Faces. We promise not to harm you."

"Yeah sure, 'Have a Nice Day'! I've heard THAT before!" muttered Whisk sarcastically, growling Alien language with a bark-accent, although it sounded like English in his ears and to all the other Abductees. "Some friends! Who is your leader? Take us to your leader!"

As soon as Whisk had moved his mouth, Crumb fell off his whiskers and plunged down to the floor. *Help!* he thought, *Now they'll see me. They look hungry, don't they! Am I ever going to get home to Breadbox and Spoon?*

"Leader?! What's THAT? We are One Voice, One Thought, One Purpose, One Size Fits All!"

"You mean," Whisk exclaimed, "you don't really have a leader?"

Crumb was dumbfounded. *This must be a dream, a group with no leader? I'm only dreaming, right? Maybe not....* The next instant, he spun back into the dream-scene, pulled in by the very unreality of it.

The Aliens answered in a total monotone, "Why have a leader when all of us agree with everything anyone else in our group thinks?"

Whisk and Nefertiti looked at each other and shook their heads in bewilderment. All their lives they had been accustomed to being either top-dog, runt of the litter or somewhere in-between. They were used to being boss or being bossed around, bred to a pecking-order laid into their very bones and blood.

"No, we don't need a leader," asserted the Happy Faces. "We do what everyone wants and no one objects. It makes life easier than arguing. But, after all this time, it's B-O-R-I-N-G. We are bored, bored, bored. One Voice, One Thought, One Purpose — You'd think it would be great, wouldn't you."

Crumb, Nefertiti, Whisk and the bee looked at each other in disagreement. It didn't sound great to them. The Fifty Happy Faces continued.

"After all these light years and parsecs of instant agreement and accord, our Purpose NOW is this: To find out how we can stop being so BORED." They paused exactly in synchronization.

"We brought you here for a reason. We need to examine you to find out how and why you are so interestingly indiVIDual." All four captives exchanged furtive glances. What did this "examination" mean? Would it hurt? Would they ever get back home?

I have no hive-home, no family left, what's going to happen to me? realized the bee, shaking his little golden tail in frustration. Acting on the impulse of the moment...

To everybody's astonishment, the little bee spoke up, suddenly compelled to reveal his brilliance and his dilemma. Perhaps he thought it might be a bargaining-point to get him out of there. Perhaps he was showing off. The other three looked at him as if he'd just spurted a bottle of ketchup all over himself. What was this tiny bee thinking? He burst out with it:

"Perfect! I'm glad to help. I am an expert in the ways of Humankind. They are a troubled but ennobled species, burdened by their inability to create a stable social order (like my bee colony) toward the goal of survival and the gift of sweet honey."

Shut up, thought Nefertiti. *Huh?* thought Whisk. *Who IS this bee?* thought Crumb. If the bee tuned in to these protest-thoughts, he certainly was disregarding them.

He rattled on, loving the sound of his own poetic imagery: "Mankind's very inability to interact in unity has given them freedom, individuality, artistic sensitivity, a taste of greatness, a curiosity to know.... and sad to say, an occasional evil and depraved dictator or criminal. (We won't go there.) I miss the hive, but ever since I've been on my own without them, I don't miss the hive mentality anymore. Between the bee colony and the innovative diversity of man, I hope there is BALANCE."

The bee stopped, fluttering and equalizing his wings to demonstrate what he meant by "balance". All of a sudden, he blushed and his yellow and black velvety surface turned orange for a second he was so embarrassed. He had given too much and way too soon, right after meeting these strange creatures. *Was it so important*, the self-critical thought hit him, *for me to appear to be the brightest newcomer here? Have I been taken in by these Aliens' seeming naiveté?*

The bee made a firm decision to be more cautious in the future, more reserved and clever. To cover his dismay, he quickly suggested, "Ask me anything. But first, before you examine us, show us around your wonderful ship. I know it's boring, but it's not boring to US."

"Yes! What an excellent idea!" Then the Fifty chanted in a monotone the very same thing that the bee had said, "Show-us-around-your-wonderful-ship."

A split-second later, all Fifty had snapped back to a sense of the Present and asked in a more welcoming voice, "What would you like to see first?"

The Bee and Crumb exchanged subtle smiles of amazement. Nefertiti was still glaring defiantly, the dog was still plunked down on the floor, looking up with as skeptical a look as a dog can muster.

These "One Size Fits All" Aliens were not exactly hard to handle. At least it appeared that way. They were so used to agreeing with one another that anything voiced was probably fine and dandy with them or hypnotically absorbed by them to be an order.

Nevertheless, the bee (an especially perceptive fellow) began to suspect that there was more to these "One Size Fits All" Aliens than their seeming simplicity. Their actions were bland, but conflict was written on their faces -- haunted hollow eyes above and innocuous smiles below, the conflicted makeup of creatures stuck in unquestioning Unity while obsessing over how dead-bored they were. The bee didn't trust them but decided that they probably could be manipulated if he was clever enough. So he repeated "Show us around your wonderful ship." The Aliens sprang into instant agreement.

"We have two very special Experiment Rooms. One of them is completely Off-Limits at the present time. Would you like to see the other?"

"Yes," said the little bee, "show us around. No examinations yet." The idea of an alien lazer nano-probe was horrifying to all four newcomers to the ship.

"One Voice, One Thought, One Purpose agrees. Come this way!"

So saying all the four Alien Abductees moved forward past curved walls of diamond glass.

"How is this ship constructed? Will you tell us?" asked Crumb, admiring the shimmering, graceful curves of the corridors. Curiosity was always getting the better of his common sense.

"Yes, oh Tiny Ball of the Staff of Life" (for that is what they named Crumb) "but we cannot share the exact chemical construct, we too have our secrets -- mankind is not ready, after what the Buzzing Wizard" (for that is what they called the bee) "has told us. But this we can mention: The One Voice, One Thought, One Purpose civilization was able to formulate -- millennia ago, mind you -- a wonderful construction material for our space explorations, a bone-like material that is less dense than water but as strong as mega-steel and able to be coated inside with this bendable diamond glass. Perhaps your Earth scientists will be able to discover the molecular construct of this and manufacture it in the future to make ships that can follow us... we trust, in FRIENDship."

Thus revealing only the most rudimentary data about the ship's structural makeup, the Fifty Happy Face Aliens -- marching in neat rows same step at the same time -- guided the Four into a Turbo-Lift. After a second of anti-gravity, the door to the lift opened in front of an endless-seeming sparkling corridor. Whisk, Nefertiti, Crumb and Bee found themselves in front of a huge electric-eye door, followed by fifty Same Ones. Fifty smiling faces beamed with pride. It was now their chance to brag.

"This," said the Fifty, "is our Alien Gene Pool." The vast door went transparent. "Enter." said the Fifty.

An Olympic-sized swimming pool lay before the Four. Doing laps, splashing, diving, laughing and cavorting in the warm preserving liquid were dozens and dozens of... JEANS.

All the jeans were blue and faded, all the jeans were the exact same size, all the jeans had alien eyes near the waistband and a funny curved zipper below for the mouth. All the jeans were smiling that Happy Face Smile.

Around the pool sunning on lounge chairs were more jeans, sipping glasses of preserving liquid from straws.

"But... but... they look so HAPPY!" sputtered Nefertiti.

"Of course!" monotoned the Fifty. "They're DESIGNER jeans."

"Okay," said the little bee, "Is this what you mean by One Size Fits All?"

"Yes, our Jean Pool guarantees that no one will grow up DIFFerent!"

Cat, dog, bee and breadcrumb looked at each other in astonishment and -- perhaps scared by all this uniformity or beginning to be bored with it themselves -- said (in one voice, mind you), "This isn't what we expected."

"What's the other Experiment Room?" asked the bee. The uniformity of talking in synchronization shook the four of them up. Both Crumb and the bee had the same thought simultaneously, *Are WE being affected by Alien Lifestyle?*

"That is Top Secret!" All Fifty shook their heads back and forth. "Sorry, Earth Pets, strictly forbidden."

"Top Secret, eh?" said the bee. He was all a-flutter with excitement. *How can I convince them to let us see this Top Secret Experiment Room?* he pondered.

He piped up with, "What if we each tell you one SECRET in exchange for you showing us what this Top Secret place is, okay?"

Again, the bee had gone too far -- one SECRET? One secret EACH? Nefertiti shook her head, Whisk growled, Crumb turned pale, but the bee had his way.

"Secrets? That doesn't sound boring. Okay. One Voice, One Thought, One Purpose has decided: You tell us One Secret Each... first. Then if we LIKE your secrets, we will show you our second Top Secret Experiment Room! Start telling!"

Nefertiti went first, wanting to get this unpleasant duty over with as fast as possible. "Humans just see me as a pet and so this IS a secret: I've lived one lifetime after the other, from the temples of Ancient Egypt where I was a Goddess, up until now and I can read the Past and foretell the Future. Humans say 'Cats have Nine Lives'. If they only KNEW. So I keep it a secret!"

The Fifty nodded all at the same time, "Good secret! Plus you have slanted eyes just like us. Maybe we share a common ancestor. I'll tell ya what --- One Voice, One Thought, One Purpose has just decided to give you a special power! We find you INteresting... " There was a significant pause and then the One Size Fits All bunch continued. "Well, we DID for a second, anyway. And that is worth granting you a special power. If we like the other secrets, we may decide to give you ALL special powers."

SPECIAL POWERS?! The cat, the bee, the dog and Crumb shot that thought back-and-forth like a toy-ball they were playing with, each one catching the ball-thought perfectly and tossing it around to savor the thought-transference and test it. *No missed catches. We can read each others' thoughts*, the Four realized in a flash. *That will come in handy!*

The next thought they bounced around was this: *Don't let on. Don't tell the Happy Faces we can share thoughts. That will be our REAL secret.* All four almost started to laugh it was so hilarious, keeping this a secret while the Aliens were asking for secrets. Crumb started to chuckle out-loud but disguised it as a cough.

Hmmm... thought Nefertiti. *I'm really getting hungry. Maybe these Happy Face guys can fork over something to stave off my stomach-pangs. They just said they're gonna give me special powers. Maybe this is the right time to ask for a treat.* Crumb tried to kick that food-thought out of the way but he was too late. Nefertiti was already doing her best to look gorgeous and graceful, lifting her head so the Aliens could see her gooseberry green eyes with that intense begging look she'd practiced to perfection.

"By the way, I'm awfully fond of salmon in cream sauce. Do you happen to have any?"

"What's THAT?" The Aliens for once split up into odd movements, turning in every direction to look at each other, breaking their exactly-the-same straight-ahead posture since they were so puzzled. This was the first time that they had made any gestures that weren't exactly the same.

Nefertiti responded, "Salmon in cream sauce? My favorite thing to eat."

"EAT? What's THAT?" The Happy Faces went blank for a second, their eyes all of a sudden spinning around, in synchronized circles of course. Their eyes then glazed over and finally resumed their "normal" look and proclaimed, "We live forever too, like you, Earth Pet. We don't know what this thing you call 'thaman in queem thawth' is, never heard of it.... but we promised to give you special powers. We'll give you at least one."

Crumb and all the other Abducted Ones tried to act nonchalant. Crumb had to hold in his desire to sigh or jump up and down. *What a relief,* he gasped inwardly. *They don't eat!*

"Let's move on to other secrets, this is getting BORING," inserted the bee, cleverly deflecting interest away from food and eating. Apparently, these Aliens really didn't eat. At all. No WONder they were bored.

"And what is YOUR secret, Dog?" the One-Size-Fits-All Happy Faces asked.

"My secret?" The dog paused, tossed his head to one side and then piped up. "I'm not really stupid. My Family loves me but sometimes they think I'm just not all that bright. In their minds my supposed dumbness GIVES me the ability to love them (since they consider they are flawed in their own minds), so they call it my 'Unconditional Love'. Yup, I have that pureness they so seek. I give them 'unconditional love' with a glad heart, but I'm smarter than they think I am." Whisk realized he would have to enumerate his abilities to be more convincing.

"I can hear sounds they can't hear. I can smell layers of odors and separate them into each smell and follow that particular smell for miles and miles until I find where it came from. I can pick up their thought-pictures. I can cheer them up. I can tell when they're coming home even when they're miles away. I can lick their little paper cuts, and the enzymes in my tongue will help heal them. Some of my kin, like Huskies, are vocal enough to speak their language, at least a few words here and there. We have learned all kinds of helpful jobs, like herding and pulling, and we even entertain them. We save them in avalanches and sniff for bombs so planes won't get blown up. We take THEM on walks so they don't become Couch Potatoes. Our proudest accomplishment: We have taught Humans the power of PLAY! So that's my secret, I'm not dumb, I'm smart! I'm a DOG and proud OF it!"

Whisk would have been the first to admit that this wasn't really much of a big "secret" that he'd divulged (his fear of being considered dumb) –– but he couldn't really think of a deep dark secret. Dogs have never been terribly clever at hiding their feelings and that's part of their winsome appeal. When they're hanging out a car window on a ride, their smiles are so gloriously blissful that anyone can see their sheer pleasure in sniffing and feeling the breeze blow through their fur. There's no secret that dogs relish how open they are, just as much as they love running in an open field.

Still, Whisk had a funny feeling that his "secret" wouldn't be enough to convince the Aliens to give him his very own special powers, so he suddenly got a bright idea. Whisk made them an offer. "Say, speaking of my power to hear sounds above the range of Human hearing, how would you like to hear some of those sounds?" At the same time he was thinking, *No food or treats here? I can't wait to get outa this place. Maybe if I do this, they'll let me go.*

The Aliens nodded. Whisk began to whimper, higher and higher in pitch until the crystalline walls of the spaceship began to vibrate in sympathy. This made Whisk's nose shake and his whiskers began to take on the appearance of mere ripples in the air, almost invisible. For a terrifying second the outer-space metals in the walls began to fade in and out of visibility. As soon as that happened, Whisk stopped whimpering.

Gads, thought Nefertiti, *Dogs! What good would it be to have the walls disintegrate? We could all have been killed!*

"Okay, okay! We get it!" the Aliens screeched in a high-pitched monotone. Their voices then lowered to normal pitch. "Sounds that can disintegrate matter or carry messages that Humans can't hear, pretty handy. If that is really your secret, we can use it! We'll give you special powers too."

Whisk didn't look particularly happy. His tail fell between his legs and he lowered his head. He had gone too far, so anxious to please these strangers or so hopeful to get home, that he had almost blown the spaceship to smithereens or given away a secret that could be used against Earth People.

I'm smart, but sometimes I do dumb things, he admitted to himself. He hoped no one would pick up that thought -- it was a failing too intimate to be revealed. There are secrets and there are SEcrets -- some of them lie in layers so deep that they seem to disappear as soon as they are noticed and go buried back beneath the easy surface of things because it's just too painful to admit them to oneself.

Whisk looked around to see -- the breadcrumb, cat and bee were immersed in their own thoughts and hadn't picked up his admission that sometimes, even as smart and capable as he was, he did dumb things.

Phew, the pooch thought, and lifted his tail a bit. *How was I to know the diamond-crystals in the walls would vibrate too?* Whisk sent that excuse and apology around to the other three and began to wag his tail slowly, just slowly enough to look innocent of any evil intentions to destroy the UFO.

The little bee caught Whisk's apology-excuse and jumped in to ensure that the Aliens wouldn't be alarmed and arrest them all as Secret Agents of Destruction or some such threat.

"You do plan to return us back to the planet, right?" the bee blurted out. Special powers or not, he wanted to make sure the Aliens intended to return them to Earth. Hopefully right away.

"Yes, WHEN we return you to your planet." *An interesting way of putting that,* thought the bee, *they're not saying WHEN they'll return us, just that they WILL. I hope they don't plan to hold us here indefinitely. Maybe these Happy Faces aren't as dumb as they look. What secret can I give them that will be safe for me to divulge?*

"What's your secret, little... Tiny Ball of the Staff of Life?" *Phew, I'm not next,* thought the bee, *that gives me time to think of something.*

Crumb burst out in a goofy awkward smile, trying to disguise how flustered he was, but his worried brow gave him away. His answer began all wrong.

Crumb was over his head. He felt so nervous that he didn't think things out. He grabbed the first thought-thread that showed up without realizing he could hang himself on that same thread. He blurted it out, pretending confidence with a false smile.

"Yes, I am what is called a 'crumb', in fact, that's my name, Crumb. I'm a very small but extremely clever and cute piece of bread that has fallen off the main loaf or bread-slice somehow. Technically, my scientific name is Panis Frustum ('bread piece' in Latin, an old Earth language). Humans think that I am quite important because they consider bread the staff of life, essential nourishment -- you see Humans and Animals DO eat on my planet." (The thought hit him like a lightning bolt: *Oops -- why did I mention eating? What a DUMBee! I've gotten in over my head now. I better get out of this one fast. I'll make it sound complex and scholarly. Anything to take their attention off the subject of... gulp... eating.*)

So thinking, Crumb followed, in a snobby, professorial tone of voice, "Over the course of our Earth-history, Humans have developed a ritual of breaking bread together. Just breaking it, that's all. Into pieces. Taking the crust off first. There's a whole science to this, you see. Then Humans just put them on altars and look at the pieces." (He was lying, he didn't want them to know that "breaking bread together" means sharing food.) "Part of Earth religion, you know. You wouldn't want to copy that and alter their indigenous culture, their Home Ways, of COURSE. That would alter your Prime Meat Directive."

He continued, his voice becoming more professorial: "After years of study, I have found out that the very word 'companion' comes from the sacred idea of breaking bread on a journey. Um... um... Oh yes! Humans use the bread pieces as convenient milestones so they can re-trace their steps when they want to journey back Home. Legendary heroes Hansel and Gretel found this very handy."

By now Crumb felt the same feeling he had experienced when he was drowning, OVER HIS HEAD! He realized with shocked embarrassment that he might have inadvertently introduced these Alien creatures to the concept of eating, to the very UNboring delight of cooking and munching food (after they had spent millennia never EVer having eaten ANYTHING). Then to his horror, he began envisioning himself being eaten.

He backtracked quickly, his voice rising in pitch as his terror came in on him like sewer waves, "Some of us crumbs are held SACRED. We're special. I'm one of those very special Revered Religious Relics known as..." (Crumb searched for a good word but he was too scared now to think of anything except) "BREADCRUMBS!"

"Very impressive," said the monotones. "What's your first name again?"

"Name's Crumb, that's me!"

"You are highly indiVIDual, Crumb. Is that your secret, that you are sacred? Doesn't everyone on the planet worship you already? It must be Common Knowledge on Earth. How can that be a secret? Crumb, we promise not to tell Earthlings, or else they may feel you revealed Mystical Religious Doctrines. Don't be afraid to share a REAL SECRET with us. So... What IS your real secret?"

Hmmmm... thought the bee. *These One-Thoughts can be pretty shrewd when they want to be.* He nudged the breadcrumb to come up with something more conventional and hopefully, closer to the truth.

Crumb answered with a tone of voice calculated to sound more matter-of-fact and sincere. He wanted to go back Home, special powers or not. He would HAVE to give them a genuine secret. That was why Crumb revealed something to these Strangers that he had not even wanted to admit to himself:

"My secret is... well, it is... Alright, here's the skinny: I'm an orphan, that means I have no Mother or Father, no Jean Pool in a sense, if you follow my drift." Crumb paused to swallow a lump of emotion. "My secret is I don't really know WHY I'm here. I don't just mean here on this Ship, I mean, I don't know what my Voice, my Thought, my Purpose is yet. Maybe it's to find my parents. I'm just not sure why I'm here."

"That's very sad," said the Fifty and for the first time their Happy Face smiles turned upside-down, all at the same time. Fifty Frowns.

"But very INteresting." The frowns reversed and became Happy Face smiles again.

"We like your secret. Maybe you can learn from us and get One Voice, One Thought, One Purpose! It's boring but..."

"Oh," said Crumb, "I have another secret: I can't STAND being bored for even one second. So sorry."

"Well, we like your first secret and understand your second secret so we'll give you Special Powers too."

"What? What powers?" asked Crumb, leaning toward the Happy Faces with intensity. (There was that curiosity again, like a chain pulling him in before he could think things out.) But this "curiosity" was what most impressed the Happy Faces. They had been bored for so long that the whole idea of wondering about anything, or having the fixated pull of curiosity was a point of strength to them, a distinguishing factor, something they were able to recognize as distinctive.

"You may not know why you are here but you possess strong individuALity and strength of character. What you need -- being so tiny and at risk of being crushed, despite your sacred status -- is STRENGTH, muscular strength, stamina and flexibility!" The Fifty Happy Faces looked at each other eagerly. "We'll give you, little bread-thing, physical strength!"

"I like it, good job!" shouted Crumb puffing himself up for a second and examining what he hoped would turn out to be his new muscles. (It was too soon. The Aliens had not endowed him with strength yet.) Not long ago he'd begun to sprout little arms and tiny bread-bump feet. Now, he squeezed his little arm and watched a puny hint of a muscle pop out! *How cool is this?!* he reveled, lying to himself that his skinny arm was now muscle-bound.

" 'No one's too small to follow a dream' and now I'm going to be strong enough to see that dream through... whatEVER it is." (Crumb's face turned puzzled momentarily.) *What dream? I haven't a clue what it is... AM I dreaming?*

A split-second picture flashed to his mind: A stubborn knob on the stove, a flame, copper turning hot-pink, a sense of strength he never knew he had, then he jolted back out of that uncomfortable, nervous sensation of urgency. *Is this dream in the spaceship really a flashback? Is that how I was strong enough to save Tea-Pot?* He wasn't sure and decided not to look too deeply.

Then he was back in the dream, excited to receive his reward of strength and squeeze his new muscles. *If this is a dream, I don't WANT to wake up!*

Next thought grabbed him like a lasso: *Am I in a Time-Warp?* Time had become all jumbled, like a bunch of string the cat had been playing with, all tangled, threads knotted together, loose ends, where was he? Suddenly he untangled one thought that stood out from the rest: *Woops! I almost got the Aliens interested in eating!* Maybe the bee could cover for him. He shot a message over to the bee: *Distract them, pleeeze!*

The bee looked at Crumb -- he got the message. "Now that that's done, we're almost ready for you to return us to our planet," prompted the bee. *I spoke too soon,* he thought. *When will I learn?*

Chapter Eight

The Sting of Death
and The Sacred Cloth

All Fifty turned at once to the little yellow-and-black buzzing fellow and said, "Now, YOUR secret." The bee had prepared his answer.

"I'm an endangered species. I was born in a hive and knew my purpose. I was to serve our Queen and build a beautiful honeycomb formed from six-sided wax figures."

"You know about HEXAGONS?!" remarked the Fifty all at once.

"Yes, of course. We specialize in those. We are nature's original Architects. Everything was working fine, right on schedule since I don't know when. Then recently... suddenly we were bringing back pollen from sick flowers and getting stuck to some yucky sprayed-on something-or-other. I escaped from my hive just in time but not in time to save all my family and friends. The whole hive... I lost them all. I'm the only one left."

"You lost your family? What went wrong? Why were you the only one left?" asked the Fifty.

"I don't know. I wish I did. Now my purpose is to tell Humans what happened to me and stop this from happening again to my kind."

The sound of Fifty Frown-Faces crying all at the same time sounded like fifty ambulances roaring to an emergency ward. (The idea of "losing" your family and being the only one "left", that was real to them and completely horrible, since the Group was everything to them.)

Then just as fast as the group-crying had happened, the frowns turned upside down into Happy Face smiles again and all fifty One-Size-Fits-All said, "You have the BEST secret of all! It's so FAScinating. We aren't BORED anymore."

(There was a telling pause.) "Uh-oh, we spoke too soon.... how boring is THAT? ... now we're BORED again. Oh well. Okay, you'll get special powers too, Little Buzzing One!"

"And then you'll return us to our planet!" the bee slipped in once again.

"We always do what we promise. Yes. It makes us predictable, but it's our best quality. All four of you have revealed your secrets and earned what's next. We will now take you to our second Top Secret Experiment Room!"

"What about the powers you were going to give me?" said the bee nervously.

"Little Buzzing Wizard, you will get those. We have something special planned for you." (That's what the bee was afraid of.)

"Special? Will it hurt?" asked the bee.

"Nothing hurts if you use it well. You'll receive your powers in the Examination Room after we take you to see something Top Secret."

The bee replied, "Hmmmm... 'Nothing hurts if you use it well.' It doesn't always work that way. There are things that sting when they are used well. Like my STINGer. If I use it and bite someone to save myself or my friends, I die."

The One-Size-Fits-All were squirming all at the same time in the same directions. Dying was totally out of their range of understanding. All of them asked, "What is meant by... 'die'?"

The One-Size-Fits-All began to moan all at once. (They had guessed what 'dying' was.)

"We live on and on and on and it's so... BORing after a while. It was okay for the first million light-years but we can't ever grow old. No pain, no gain, no nothing that is different, no dying, no living, just existing, how BORing."

The Aliens looked concerned. "...Are we BORing you?"

The Four nodded up and down a unanimous "yes." Then realizing they might be insulting their hosts, the cat, dog, Crumb and bee changed direction of their heads (in synchronization) and shook their heads "No."

"Maybe we can take the sting out of stinging someone, Buzzing One... in case you need to protect yourself. We can fix your stinger so it won't kill you. But that trick will only work ONCE. You have only one stinger, so keep that in reserve, okay?"

"Good! Agreed. I can sure use that power. Along with whatever else you've hinted at... I guess. So let's go up to the Top Secret place!"

"This way.... " intoned the Aliens.

Up-up-up the Fifty and the Four went in the Turbo-Lift. The transport door opened to reveal a mammoth double-door emblazoned with a huge sign. Crumb could read the letters on the door as they morphed from Outer-Space-writing to English:

"BUREAU OF SOX RESEARCH"

Below that was a notice: "Security Check-Point: No Entry without Special Authorization."

The gigantic, nearly three-stories-tall double door opened slowly as if protecting the contents within by screening each entity passing through the door. It scanned every new person with a purple lazer probe, then when satisfied that they were okay to enter, issued each a badge which instantaneously materialized on their skin, fur or outfit. As the Four entered, they were completely astounded.

I'm only dreaming, this can't be real, the reverie echoed in Crumb's consciousness for a split-second, but the sight before him was so completely riveting, he zoomed back full-force from his introspective thoughts to the spectacle before him.

Hovering hundreds of feet above the floor --- floating in air as if they were coma victims trapped in hypnotic deep-sleep -- were single tennis socks, single argyle socks, single sleep-socks, single knit socks, single dress-up socks and a few isolated silk stockings. Behind these floating apparitions rose an imposing, gargantuan wooden bureau, five-stories tall, looming above them --- a giant dresser with drawers half open, drawer-bins stacked one on top of the other from which dangled loose socks of all description. The loose socks dangled over the edges of the drawers like wiped-out dog tongues, waving slightly up and down as if exhausted and out-of-breath.

"They tire out so quickly, we have to replace them at every opportunity," chanted the Happy Face bunch.

"Yes," interjected the bee, "but why are they HERE? What is the experiment?"

"Since we never die and we don't have to procreate, we want to find out how these things PAIR UP. What is it that makes them decide they belong in pairs? How do they find their Mate? That's why we're conducting this SOX research."

Suddenly the Four looked up. One very loud sock was clinging to the ceiling attempting to sing "How Dry I Am." His second line was "Fresh from the Dryer." A long wooden pole was stretched horizontally across the entire Research Facility from one wall to the opposite wall, way up there close to the ceiling. Socks were hanging from it hiccuping or spinning around the pole.

"What's that up there, that pole?" asked Whisk.

"Oh that? The socks can't seem to find their Mate, it's a Singles Bar. They get desperate sometimes and hang out there hoping to meet and Pair Up. We've been researching which opening lines work and which are losers."

"I see. We're familiar with that on our Planet," uttered the bee, stifling a chuckle.

"So this," said the dog to all the other three, "is where the MISSING SOCKS GO!! Wait until I tell Humans about this! They'll finally admit how smart I am!"

The One-Size-Fits-All group droned on: "Dryers are the greatest invention, in our way of thinking. Aiding and abetting our craving to Alien-Abduct just one sock, one sock ONLY out of every pair on Earth! It is our one indulgence, our one hobby!"

How much like Human research this was, thought the bee, *collecting, gathering, hoarding — pieces of data, bits of information, unrelated tidbits, sorting them, naming them, listing them, so it all looks good on paper — just a bunch of busy-work without coming to ANY useful conclusion. And no useful product. All run by committees like the Same Ones here. Ugh.*

The Aliens noticed that the bee looked very bored. So it was time to go. The Fifty One-Size-Fits-All took the Four out of the Bureau of Sox Research down to a lower deck next to the Bridge where there was a large Examination Room. Buttons in neon green flashed back and forth next to purple lazer beams zapping out of screen displays on consoles encircling the outer rim of the Examination Room. A few Happy Faces were sitting at flight-controls but there was absolutely NO Captain's Chair. (They didn't have a leader, the Four reminded themselves.) However, there were two Examination Tables with straps and one very big tufted chair that sparkled on and off. At the front end of the room was an enormous viewing window looking out into space. (Earth was not even there in the window, sadly, noted the bee and Crumb.)

Although all Four were terrified, three of them found that they were painlessly given Special Powers after a light scan was passed over their bodies.

The dog was empowered with whiskers even faster than before, so lightning fast in motion that they could act instantly like the most powerful dog whistle ever known. Humans would not be able to hear it but Whisk would be able to call dogs from far and near. This also guaranteed that Whisk would be In Charge, Top Dog, known by all breeds within a certain wide radius. He was even endowed with a ritualistic name, "The One The Only." Boy, was he smart now! He would be Top Dog.

"You," said the Fifty, "are a Dog-Whiskerer now. Use your power well. ...Just not here on our ship. Our diamond walls can't take another demonstration."

Whisk began to strut around.

The cat was given the power to transcend time at any moment it was needed. Having lived lifetime after lifetime with quite excellent recall, she would now be able to transport herself bodily, with her entire feline form fully materialized and all her faculties of perception, directly into the past or into the future. She could also stay quite aware in the Present in order to warn her companions of any imminent danger or to advise them on the wisest path to take.

"How is this done?" asked the bee, stunned that the cat was going to get such a phenomenal power and hoping that he'd inherit some of this ability himself if he just understood it better.

The Aliens briefly explained that Time Travel involved going from the normal three dimensions of height-width-and-depth into a very pliable fourth dimension of Time that was extended across numerous Vortex Rings and hung together on multiple cosmic strings.

"This sounds complex. I kind of get it, but I'm not sure," admitted the cat, nervous that she might disintegrate if she didn't really understand the workings of Time Travel. "Do you mind going into a bit more detail.... The idea of materializing my body safely all around these so-called 'Vortex Rings' sounds a bit extreme. Is there any way you can give me a clearer picture how this works?"

The Aliens showed Nefertiti something she could see and touch that might explain how the Space-Time Continuum worked -- it was one of their special fabrics with a texture similar to velvet. The black cloth shimmered as if it were covered with actual stars and galaxies. It was also extremely pliable with dense threads that had elastic properties.

"This is our special upholstery fabric for our Knowledge Chair."

"Knowledge Chair?" The bee got intensely excited about that and flew close to the fabric to inspect it. His brusk action violated their set of Good Alien Manners. This cloth was more than upholstery fabric, it was Sacred.

"Please! Be patient, Buzzing One," cautioned the Fifty. Their hollow eyes grew bigger and the bee backed off, suddenly afraid that he had offended them.

"We will let you know more about that... later. IF we like your secret." The bee flew back near Whisk and hid for a second behind the dog's tail. The dog was scratching behind his ear with a paw, puzzled about all this Time-Travel stuff and what it had to do with practical things like where the fire hydrants were and how to locate a good place to dig for bones.

Turning to Nefertiti, the Aliens began stretching and contracting the sparkling fabric before her eyes. The cat's tail began to curl at the thought of Time-Travel. This was something she instinctively understood, having lived so many lifetimes and having remarkable recall of the past.

Not wanting any more Bee interruptions, the Fifty spoke softly all of one voice to the regal looking cat, gathering around her. They were divulging part of their Sacred Doctrine of the Universe. They explained to the cat, "The sparkles on our special cloth are neuron-sensors just like those in your brain. In a sense, it's alive, but it has no Individual Personal Consciousness the way you Four fascinating IndiVIDuals have -- our Noble Ancestors invented this cloth many millennia ago. You may touch it." They handed the cloth to Nefertiti.

As Nefertiti gently kneaded her paws on the fabric, the cloth stretched and contracted. When the fabric's threads pulled more and more apart, it was like the Expanding Universe. When she let the fabric contract, then folds and ripples appeared in the cloth. In this way, Nefertiti saw that the interlocking "threads" of time and space sometimes stretched and expanded and sometimes contracted and formed rippling waves like folds in the cloth.

Nefertiti thanked the Fifty and handed the cloth back to the front row of Aliens. The two Happy Faces at opposite ends of the first row began to stretch the cloth, pull it wide and tight. Then the Alien in the middle of the row threw a little ball into the center of the outstretched fabric.

"See how the ball falls into the middle of the fabric," all Fifty continued to explain with soft voices, so the information would be imparted privately to the cat. "The weight of the ball has made the stretchy fabric fall downward in the center where the ball landed. The cloth gets lower with the impact of the mass-weight of the ball --- this is how Gravity works."

The bee had strained to overhear this explanation of the Space-Time-Continuum, the strings that held it together and the mysterious force called Gravity. The dog couldn't have cared less. He was thinking, *Don't these nuts have any treats at all? I'm thirsty too.*

"Fascinating!" exclaimed the bee. "Your cloth-demonstration makes it much easier to understand. I hope you don't mind my following this explanation. It might save my hive some day." The Aliens nodded that it was fine.

"I don't get it," said Whisk, rubbing his tummy where a hunger pang was beginning to make him feel uncomfortable. "What does this have to do with life as we know it?" The Aliens said nothing, probably because they were hypnotically asking themselves the very same question that the dog had posed.

Crumb kept quiet, even though he wanted to play with the fabric and jump into the middle of it after the ball --- it looked like fun. The mischievous breadcrumb was nearly always ready for play but at the moment, he was still too scared to ask the Aliens for permission to jump into the cloth.

"Can I have a piece of this cloth?" asked the cat.

"No, we cannot give you our Sacred Cloth. But do you understand how the Space-Time Continuum works now?"

"Yes. Gravity. Strings of Time and Space, pulsing with Matter and Energy. I understand," the cat intoned.

"Well... maybe not totally, but I understand this well enough now to be able to leap into the Future and return to the Past. What worries me is this: Are you sure I'll be able to return in one piece, intact, not a piece of my fur missing, with all my Personality there, to the ever-moving Present? It's constantly shifting, you know." All Fifty Aliens nodded.

"We are sure. You, oh Fur-Creature-Pet, have slanted eyes like us. We consider you a possible Offspring of a branch from our Genetic Line, even if you don't wear Jeans, so we certainly don't want to harm you." Nefertiti purred.

"I get it," piped up the bee, bragging again, "String theory! Multiple universes. Cosmic Inflation and Gravitational Waves."

This time the Fifty Happy Faces didn't seem to mind his interruption and stretched their innocuous smiles even wider to hear that the Little Buzzing One seemed to have a brilliant grasp of their Time-Travel mechanics. Then returning to the cat, they pronounced, "Nefertiti, you once were a Goddess, now you are one again. Mistress of Time, use your power well."

"Mistress of Time, that's me! Much obliged, Ancestor Race," purred the cat, curling her tail. (She wasn't sure that earth-cats and these Aliens were related but it was probably highly in her favor to agree with that idea.)

Crumb had waited too long. He wasn't sure if he trusted these Happy Faces but he couldn't stand the suspense any longer.

"What is my special power? Is it my turn now?" cried Crumb as loud as he could. (He was concerned that the Aliens wouldn't hear him, being so small, and then he wouldn't get his Muscles.)

"We have thought about that carefully. You are a complex IndiVIDual -- we found you fascinating for an entire minute and half. How about this? You will know your Voice, Thought and Purpose. And you are now as Strong in Body as you are in Character." A purple lazer beam was waved over the breadcrumb. Crumb was happy to find out it didn't hurt. He beamed.

"I'm little but I'm strong. When will I find out my Sacred Purpose?"

"We don't know. Only you will know. But you will have your three helpers there... and maybe they can call for a few others to help. USE THE RIDDLE, CRUMB!"

"Use the Riddle... that sounds familiar...," muttered the puzzled bread-ball. Suddenly he felt more connected to the Riddle than ever, but he could feel a disturbance in it. (Or was it really a disturbance inside himSELF? There wasn't time to answer that, so he plowed on.)

"I wonder if you'll answer one question..." said Crumb. "Did you GIVE us this Riddle? Where did it come from?"

"That is part of the Riddle itSELF. Some mysteries are better left unanswered. All we can say is that 'we simply are UNABLE to answer that at this time' -- we got that phrase from some of your Politicians on Earth. But what we CAN tell you is this, USE the Riddle. USE it!"

"Use the Riddle, Crumb" echoed in his resolve. *Am I dreaming this?* thought Crumb. *Is this a dream, a dream, a dream?*

As soon as the cat, the dog and Crumb had been endowed with their special powers, the bee pretended it wasn't his turn. All he wanted to do was to get back to the planet in one piece. He now had a better understanding of the Space-Time Continuum. He knew these One-Size-Fits-All were bored-stiff. He knew that not having a leader and not eating food were two reasons for their abysmal monotony. He wanted nothing more to do with these BORING blokes. He had learned enough -- or so he thought -- it was time to go.

Maybe they'll skip me. I HOPE. I better not say anything right now.

He looked down at the floor pretending to be invisible, hoping they'd get so bored that they'd just forget him. He knew he had already been much too brash and outspoken for his own good. He had even violated their Good Manners Code of Conduct by buzzing close to their sacred cloth without their permission.

What was worse, the bee had a scary suspicion that these Aliens had a unique (and maybe devious) plan for him. Would whatever-they-were-going-to-do hurt? Would they hold him prisoner? Would he be left mindless? Or dead? The Fifty turned all at once to the bee with a special intensity, their hollow black eyes sizzling into an electric indigo blue.

"And now for you, Brilliant Buzzer. You know how to make something called a 'hive' from a six-sided shape. We consider that the strongest shape in the Universe. You are very intelligent. Resourceful. Inventive. And that is not boring to us. (At least it wasn't a minute ago.)"

With that, fifty pairs of eyes switched from vibrant indigo blue back to hollow blackness. Bored or whatever, they knew what their Plan was for the bee, so they droned on. The bee felt his thorax tighten and his wings stiffen.

"For you we will give you the sum total of Human Knowledge... well, maybe we've skipped a few places but it will definitely be a lot of Knowledge, everything that we've been able to upload off your planet's electronic machines and that insect-like web that circles the planet. This will take probably an hour, maybe two, but you will be the smartest indiVIDual on Earth! Your friends can stay in a comfortable Conference Room in soft chairs and relax."

Then realizing they had forgotten one last thing, the Aliens added, "We will also deactivate your killer-stinger-mechanism so if you have to sting someone to defend yourself, it won't kill you. But remember, use it once and use it wisely."

That didn't sound so bad. In fact, it sounded too good to be true. Was it?

"Wow!" said the bee, "Are you kidding?" Oops, the Aliens smiles turned into frowns again -- they were insulted for a split second. This sounded like Dissent. Intolerable dissent.

"How excellent a gift!" the bee offered to soothe matters. "I'm very grateful." This satisfied the Aliens and their smiles turned right-side-up. Then the bee noticed concerned frowns on his three companions.

"Don't be jealous -- dog, cat or crumb." Dog, cat and crumb did look crestfallen. They all wanted to be the smartest.

"I'm smart," said Whisk the dog.

"I'm intuitive and smart," said Nefertiti.

"I'm strong in character, I can read, I'm the smartest crumb in the world. And I'm incredibly strong, flexible, and able to lift stuff.... Why look at these muscles!" Crumb popped a mini-mountain of a muscle out of his tiny arm.

All three spoke simultaneously, "We're smart. We're ALL smart! And we're good-looking too." *Are we being affected by the Alien lifestyle and beginning to talk exactly the same words at the same time? We better get out of here soon,* thought Crumb.

"Don't be jealous," urged the bee trying to placate the others. "I'll share as much of this with you as we need, once Crumb finds out WHY we're here and WHAT we need to do on Earth."

Apparently these boring One-Size-Fits-All had not only been abducting Humans, they had been intent on extracting information: Knowledge, wisdom, lies, certainties, pastimes, trivia and trends --- whatever these impoverished Aliens could find. Privacy was no more, now information was Inter-Stellar.

"Did you know that the word 'utopia' is Greek for 'nowhere'?" offered the Aliens. "And that it's illegal in Detroit, Michigan to chain an alligator to a fire hydrant?" (Whisk thought, *I'm never going to that city and peeing on one of those contraptions.*)

The bee filed that under Odd Human Behavior: Subsection Trivia and hoped the Knowledge he would get would surpass what he had just heard. It was time to find out.

Whisk, Nefertiti and Crumb were ushered into a Conference Room next to the Bridge. "You can make yourselves comfortable here. It's the Little Buzzing Wizard's turn to get his gifts. Don't worry, he will be just fine. It should take about an hour. Two at the most."

The other three looked around the Conference Room. A long curved table, comfortable gray swivel chairs, a small box on one side with glasses of preserving fluid, the same "drink" that the Jeans had been sipping. *No thanks!* thought Whisk. *No water, I guess.* At the far end of the room, an observation window looked into the Examination Room they had just left. The three nervously went to the window.

Their shared thoughts zipped back and forth between them so fast the three felt that they were condensing time itself. *What are they going to do to the bee? Why can't any of us be in there with him? Will the Aliens hurt him? Will he live through this? How long will it take? What IS it that'll make him so much smarter than us? Will the Happy Faces be upset if they know we're spying on them? Heck, there's a window in this room, why can't we look! Should we sit down so the Aliens don't see us at the window? Why can't we get this Knowledge stuff? What's so special about the bee anyway?*

All these questions were bouncing around, zooming in thought-transference from one to the other.

Am I dreaming this? This is such a strange thing happening. Is this a dream, a dream, a dream?

This disturbing question once again echoed in Crumb's mind, making him toss and turn. *Tossing and turning? Am I in BED, dreaming? Get back, get back, don't wake up now! I have to find out what happens NEXT!* Quickly jumping his attention back to the Examination

Room on the UFO, Crumb re-assumed his viewpoint at the Conference Room window, looking intently into the Examination Room along with the cat and dog.

A few of the Happy Face Aliens in light gray uniforms were pointing out an enormous and impressive chair -- this must be, the three figured, the special Knowledge Chair the Fifty had alluded to earlier. It was covered with the same black and flexible Sacred Cloth that they had used to explain the Space-Time Continuum to the cat. The tiny bee was lifted gently and carried across the Examination Room and placed in the center of the shimmering seat. He was so tiny in this huge chair that the three had to squint to find him at first.

There he is! spotted Nefertiti, alerting the other two to the bee's location in the exact center of the chair, up against the tufted back, his wings spread gently on either side, his eyes alert. Crumb strained to see him and then finally zeroed in on his tiny form. Whisk's nose was twitching, but the wall and window of the Conference Room blocked his ability to smell what was going on.

The Buzzing One was indeed dwarfed by the Knowledge Chair which had apparently been built for a Human-size person, even a rather hefty Human.

Without a doubt, thought Nefertiti, *many an Abducted Earthling has sat in this very chair.*

I think you're right, Nefertiti -- it's not built for bee-size, that's for sure. What do you think, does our bee-friend need our help? thought the dog, always loyal and willing to come to the rescue.

That's a scary looking chair, even though it looks soft. I'm glad I'm not in it. But so far, so good, Whisk. I think our friend is fine, thought Crumb.

The Knowledge Chair was elegantly tufted with this remarkable non-terrestrial material. As soon as the bee was placed in the center of the seat, the cloth seemed to come alive as if electrified. The sensitive network of neuro-sensors lit up in rapid-fire patterns like neurons being zapped. Lines with tiny dots of iridescent colors suddenly turned transparent or black and opaque and then iridescent again. Sparkling dots of color or mini-areas of blackness and transparency raced all over the chair. The patterns seemed random but appeared to be designed to function as thought-and-image transmitters in pre-arranged sequences coordinated with the images programmed to flash on the screen in front of the bee.

The Aliens had used great care not to crush the bee's wings or any part of his body. *Good, looks like they're being gentle with our new friend,* Crumb thought. Whisk and Nefertiti picked up the thought and nodded. All of a sudden the One-Size-Fits-All Happy Faces inside the Examination Room nodded too and Crumb, Whisk and Nefertiti were afraid that they had been spotted at the window. But it was just a non-verbal instruction to the two Aliens in gray uniforms to attach a thin band to the top of the bee's head area.

Oh, no, thought Whisk stiff with nervous tension, *are they going to hypnotize our buzzing buddy? I hope not.* The cat and breadcrumb shared that concern and all three hovered on the very bottom of the window, hiding from the Aliens in the Examination Room. But the bee looked calm and confident.

In fact, as soon as the little bee sat in the chair, he seemed willingly transfixed, but extra alert, not hypnotized or asleep in the least. It was as if the neuro-sensors in the chair had AWAKENED him, energized him, made him eager to see what would appear on the screen in front of him.

The three Aliens shot a purple lazer beam into a large rectangular flatscreen about five feet in front of where the bee sat. Flashes faster than lightning began. The Knowledge-Flashing Machine was turned away from view so that the only thing Nefertiti, Whisk and Crumb could see was that the bee was in his Knowledge Chair, his eyes growing wider, taking in whatever-it-was that was being flashed into his mind's perception-receiver and memory bank.

The three could not see anything the bee was seeing. *Maybe that's safer for us*, Nefertiti shared as a comforting thought to her two friends.

Suddenly Crumb, Nefertiti and Whisk had to turn away. The strobe effect was overwhelming. Flashes zipped around the chair and in the air between the bee and the screen -- flashes nearly as fast as the speed of light, or so it seemed.

All three returned to their comfortable chairs and sat around the Conference Table staring at each other, silent, waiting, wondering what was happening. Soon all three were fast asleep.

Emerging from the Knowledge Chair and flashing Knowledge-Screen, the honeybee felt as if he'd aged a million years. But Time was an illusion -- he hadn't aged in the least. Indeed, he glowed. Knowledge had taken him on Time's Journey and he was energized. Ready for the Mission with his True Companions.

He was escorted to the Conference Room. All three of his friends were asleep. Crumb was snoring gently. The bee tapped each one gently to awaken them. They opened their eyes. The bee! He was fine! He looked good, even great actually! They stared at him. He took the opportunity to address them with a grand announcement.

"Companions! Don't call me Ishmael," he said, in a deep throaty rhetorical voice, "Call me WILL! I am Will!"

"We will, Will!" agreed all the other Three, echoed in unison by the Fifty.

"Now it's time to return us to our planet!" ordered Will. The Fifty were ready to comply. "Agreed."

The Fifty began to bid goodbye to the Four, reminding each one of the powers they had been endowed with: "Use the Riddle, Crumb! Be Mistress of Time, Cat! Know when to be the Dog-Whiskerer, four-footed fellow! And where there's Will, you will all find the way!"

Suddenly the Fifty Happy-Face One-Size-Fits-All Aliens looked concerned and puzzled. They went over a mental checklist to try to figure out what they were leaving out:

"Haven't we forgotten something? ...What have we forgotten?

* We beamed you up. ---Done.
* We showed you around. ---Did that.
* We found out your Secrets. ---Check.
* We examined you. ---Sure did.
* We gave you powers. ---Yup."

The Happy Faces continued to be puzzled.

"There's something ELSE we should do." (They paused for a second and then burst into bigger smiles.) "OH! We almost forgot, silly us, there IS one thing we FORGOT. We must make you forget US!"

"That's forgiveable, 'forgive and forget'," said Will, trying to take advantage of their lapse in memory and not particularly wanting to be sent home with blank mind and no memories.

"Can't we re-negotiate that part?" inquired Will with a persuasive tone of voice. "I've never been fond of a blank mind and short-term memory loss."

"But we must make you forGET us. Forget about this Alien Abduction, forget how bored we are, forget how BORing we are, just forGET it!" The last words "Forget it, forget it, forget it" resonated into a mind-well as deep as an outer-space worm-hole.

With that forgetter command, Whisk and Crumb blocked out almost all memory of their abduction. They spun around for a few seconds, quite dizzy with their eyes totally blank.

Not all the Four Companions followed the Alien's Forgetter Command. Two of the Four had indelible recall of every single bit of the Alien Abduction. Nefertiti being Mistress of Time could always return to this incident and as for Will, he was much too smart now to forget. Nefertiti winked at Will -- they were not blank or dizzy in the least.

Whisk's eyes were dull, he was stumbling around more than usual, his tail was between his legs, his ears were flopping, his tongue was hanging out. He had forgotten about the Abduction.

With that, all Four were beamed back to the Happy-Face Crop Circle in the Family's backyard. Whappp! Crumb landed with a painful thump back in the garden behind the Baker's home, right where this dream -- or nightmare -- had begun. He lay there unconscious for a second.... As he struggled to come to, he felt like he was drowning again, like he'd felt in the sewer months ago, swirling back and forth, struggling for breath. The grassy sensation under him was turning into a spongecake texture, then going back to grass blades.

The grass nodded as the spaceship blew across the late night sky, disappearing in a micro-second, flashing a tiny burst of light as effervescent as a twinkling star as it left the black sky. Tall blades of grass waved over the left eye of the Crop Circle Happy Face, making the eye seem to wink goodbye to the Alien ship.

Am I dreaming this? thought Crumb. *What just happened? Where AM I?*

The solidity of earth, the weight of Crumb's body because of gravity, and the soft woven texture of grass made physical sensation palpable: Reality felt tactile. Returning to the planet was a Touching Experience in every sense of the phrase. Reality meant the weight of mass, the movement of Time and Things, it was not weightless. Dreams were immaterial but they possessed the immediacy of Thought.

Am I dreaming? Dreaming, dreaming, dreaming? Crumb heard the murmur of this reverie sounding in his sleepy ears but just for a second decided not to believe that he WAS dreaming. The abduction -- IF it had really happened or would happen in the future -- was certainly more spectacularly REAL than anything Crumb had ever experienced before. How could he be just a sleeping Crumb tossing and turning in a Breadbox, covered in a spongecake blanket, experiencing a nightmare fantasy when bits of dew on grass were all around him? It didn't make any sense. He vowed never to forget this experience!

Forget, forget, forget... Crumb found himself repeating. The glittery diamond walls, the tufted chair, the jean pool, the socks in comas... Comas, comas, blackness, nothingness. *WHAT AM I SUPPOSED TO REMEMBER, WHAT AM I SUPPOSED TO FORGET?* Forces like swirling whirlpools were shifting him in time and tossing him back and forth from one place to another. Picture-memories popped to view then vanished. Strange guttural words were avoiding his understanding. Haunting echoes began reverberating in the hollow pit of emptiness that he hid in the center of his lonely self. Amnesia.

Crumb and Whisk lay on the smiley mouth of the Crop Circle, dazed and dizzy. Nefertiti and Will smiled knowingly at each other and Will buzzed over to the cat's ears and whispered, "As Alien Abductions go, that wasn't all that bad." The cat's tail curled into an Infinity sign in acknowledgement.

All Four, two who had forgotten and two who remembered it all, waited until the sun rose in the sky.

Suddenly the image of the Smiley crop circle began to spin, with Whisk, Crumb, Will and Nefertiti twirling round and round and the grassy plot of grass blowing like a symbol of disorientation. What was happening?

Slowly as the dawn rose pink and promising, something dawned on Crumb. *Where am I?* he thought. *Where am I really? I can't sit this one out, I HAVE to find out.*

He opened one eye. Then closed it. He opened the other eye, then both were open, staring at the Riddle engraved inside Breadbox's wall.

He wasn't outside on the grass, he was in his bed inside cozy Breadbox. He was half-asleep but just beginning to feel the sunlight poking its way through the thin edges along the sides of Breadbox's tin door. His bedclothes were all tossed into a heap including his spongecake blanket. THIS was real. Crumb felt for the tactile reality and weight of his bed and his soft blanket, the sight and smell of bread, the welcome familiarity of it, the fact that Time ticked away in reasonable doses, not in flashes of micro-mini-nano-seconds. He yawned. He needed to doze a bit longer. He needed to know where he was, when it was -- WHY didn't matter as much anymore as long as Time and Place were back to normal.

Crumb took a long time to get up that morning, watching the yellow sunlight and shadows grow and flicker inside the shelter of his cozy Home.

Once he was ready to face the day, he realized that yes, this had been a wild dream, maybe partly a nightmare. And yet a sneaky suspicion pulled at him.

Crumb began to think it might have really happened. That would mean that the cat and the dog WEREN'T terrifying anymore, they were his FRIENDS. They were his Companions. If true, they all had special powers. But could that be the case? He'd try to ask the cat. He lay in bed seeing if he really could pop his muscles out. Yes, he had mounds of muscle power in each arm! He better put his strength to the test later that day after he got up, but not so daringly that he got Breadbox all worried and bothered.

And the biggest mystery of all: *I've never, ever met this mysterious brilliant bee? Where is he? This just doesn't make any sense. A bee? The smartest thing on Earth?*

That alone was enough to pull in doubts. There was no Bee in the kitchen, at least as far as he knew. *The Bee... what was his name again? Oh, yes, Will....* He'd never seen a bee coming into the Kitchen. He'd heard little Zoe, the neighbor girl, talking about bees, but he'd never seen one, and certainly not the smartest thing on Earth.

And the dog, well, Crumb wasn't really sure he trusted that lumbering fool quite yet. Unless, unless, the dog, cat, bee and he had REALLY been Alien-Abducted.

He better not tell Breadbox quite yet, until he actually knew for certain one way or the other: *Was the dream a flashback to an actual event or not? Was it a portent of things to come?* Breadbox was protective and practical and might think Crumb was off his rocker. This was one secret he hoped he could keep. Telling his Granddad could wait, until HE was sure himself.

Try as Crumb did to be casual that morning as Breadbox coached him through the Riddle for the umpteenth time, something felt different. The Riddle made more sense, at least in part. He finally understood "Where there's a will, you know there's a way."

If that dream was right, the line had been misspelled. It should have been engraved to read "Where there's Will (in other words, drop the "a" and make the "w" a capital letter) you know there's a way!"

Don't rush to conclusions, Crumb cautioned himself. *There's no bee in this kitchen. Zoe talks about how she keeps bees sometimes but that is 'neither here nor there.' There seems to be plenty of honey in the pantry — Endangered species, really? Maybe it was just a bad dream. I better go see that cat.... not too up-close-and-personal yet. She might start kneading too close to me. But let's see if Nefertiti remembers any of this or not.*

After his lesson, Crumb ventured out of the box and strolled around the counter looking for the cat. He HAD to find that cat.

Chapter Nine

Food for Thought

Nefertiti was nowhere to be found. Not in the Kitchen. Not in the Pantry. Soon the Family started looking. Not in the living-room. Not near her kitty litter. They put out catnip toys. They put out a lovely dish of milk. Nope. She didn't appear, as she normally would have. Not upstairs. Nowhere. *Oh no!* thought Crumb. What was he to do now?

Once the Family realized that she was missing, Sally and Johnny walked around the neighborhood carrying little bags of catnip and Nefertiti's favorite toy, saying, "Here, kitty, kitty, here kitty!" Dad posted flyers with a photo of Nefertiti he had taken a while back, nailing it into all the telephone poles in the neighborhood from Tempest Street to a tall one on Crossroads Avenue.

Hazel confessed she had kicked the cat a few times. She offered to bake cookies by the dozens for anyone who found the family cat and returned her. Johnny and Sally cried themselves to sleep. Crumb thought, *Wow, Humans really have strong feelings, don't they! And I hope they find her, or else I'll never find out the truth!*

Crumb hardly slept that night, praying that Nefertiti would show up. Something else was odd: He could hardly get to sleep, flashing on bits of memories: A wind-storm, an open door, crumpled grass in a strangely familiar pattern, a hum of monotone voices mouthing incomprehensible words. Ka-poonga-TONGa? He HAD to find that cat! Was his dream real or not?

The next morning, Zoe Baruti showed up at the Baker's front door. She was gingerly carrying a very dirty, flustered Nefertiti.

A year had passed since the bake sale. By this time, Zoe's face was less round and more mature. A whole year had flown by, full of dinners together, of times around the stove, of Sunday Brunches and jokes at the sink helping the kids wash the dishes. The Baker place was almost like her own home. Maybe more special. (For some reason, it was always easier washing dishes in somebody ELSE'S house rather than dealing with the cruddy dishes in one's own sink.) Zoe had carried lots of platters or cooking supplies over to the Bakers, but she'd never had a handful like Nefertiti -- filthy, furious and fatigued.

The Bakers squealed when they saw the missing cat. Thank you, thank you, they all took turns in saying, hugging their dear neighbor.

Zoe explained that she had NOT been able to bathe the cat. She'd tried but the cat MeeOW'd loud and started to scratch her, which Nefertiti had never done before. *Something strange has happened to Nefertiti*, mused Zoe, *but I can't place what it is. The cat is not herself.*

How had she captured Nefertiti? the Bakers asked. She and her Dad had heard Sally and Johnny going down the street crying "Here Kitty-Kitty" and so they looked down the street, by their front door and in the backyard. There in the back of their house, they had found the cat rubbing her sides against the empty bee-hive, desperate to find something.

Nefertiti sure looked like she was searching for something. What? -- no one had a clue. The cat, who had always in the past welcomed the Baruti's with purrs and nuzzling, ran away the instant Zoe and Matt tried to grab hold of her. Nefertiti was disoriented and, unlike her usual silky fur that was kept clean by her neat little tongue, here was a hardly recognizable bundle of frayed fur covered in an odd mix of grass pieces. Zoe knew she'd have to clean her off before bringing her back to the Baker's. Nefertiti tried to hide for some reason but eventually the cat got hungry enough to approach a dish of raw cream that Zoe put out. However Nefertiti refused to let Zoe bathe her. She had clawed on top of Zoe's skirt, ripping a hole in it.

So here was the eight-year-old at the front door, holding a very wet, very dirty, very grumpy cat.

Sally and Johnny let Zoe in, the cat plunged down and ran under the living-room couch, her eyes glowing like neon even in the bright light of day. Zoe went to wash her hands off for a second. Meanwhile, Hazel, true to her promise, started to mix a big batch of fresh chocolate chip cookies in a bowl and also Ken's favorite, coconut-raisin-oatmeal bars.

Sally and Johnny were so happy to get their cat back safe that all three of the kids began to play together, laughing and tickling one another and telling stories about rescue dogs and missing cats. Then for some reason Zoe's mood changed and a shadow of sadness came over her.

"Mom always wanted a puppy. I miss her a lot. She used to hug me lots every day." A thin rim of moisture glazed her eyes. Sally and Johnny exchanged quick looks but said nothing. *What a sweet mom Zoe had! Lots of hugs every day.* (Their Mom Hazel had softened of late and was giving them a hug or two every day, but "sweet" didn't quite describe Hazel, except for the desserts she loved to make.) A momentary look passed between the siblings, and they shared a thought: *Maybe we haven't been giving our Mom a chance. We can hug HER too. After all, she's baking us cookies right now.*

"My Dad Matt, you know how great he is. Really nice, really smart. (Except he won't get me a puppy yet.) Oh well -- he's taught me a lot about science, he loves my cooking and makes sure I get to go to all those classes, and I know he loves me forever-and-ever-and-a-day." Sally and Johnny nodded.

"But, if you can keep a secret you two, I'm worried about him. Dad has been working way too hard, every night up late, not getting enough sleep and... this may sound strange, but yesterday he told me that he hopes that someday the company he works for... how did he put it?... someday his boss won't 'buy his patents out from under him'.... Then Dad says, we'll be rich. And maybe then I can get my very own puppy and maybe a kitten too, though I hope she won't put up a fight like Nefertiti did today. Most of the time cats keep themselves clean all by themselves."

"Rich is good," commented Johnny. "I want to be rich too."

"Well, it's not everything. I'd give all the money in the world if I could get my Mom back. But... "

Both Sally and Johnny reached over to give Zoe a hug.

"You two are the BEST! Would you like some of our raw organic honey? We have jars and jars of it. Still."

"Yummm. Speaking of yummm, those cookies our Mom is baking sure smell good. Let's go get some!" All three kids trotted off to the Kitchen to sample the chocolate chip cookies cooling on wax paper.

Meanwhile, Nefertiti was getting a bath from Dad and not enjoying it too much. Ken was outside with her in the back yard, using the hose but holding on to the squealing and squirming feline. Bit by bit the Egyptian Mau spots on her fur were beginning to reappear as the dirt and grass pieces washed off.

All of a sudden he dropped Nefertiti.

"What the heck??" Ken exclaimed, grabbing her back into his grasp and wrapping her in an old towel to dry her off. Nefertiti looked like a crazed half-leopard, half-lioness with her fur sticking up in a messy mane about her infuriated face.

"What is THAT??" Dad uttered. "First I better take you back in." Dad hauled the wet and furious cat back into the kitchen and petted her to soothe her a bit.

"Um... I hate to bother you, honey, but... there's something awfully weird that I... oh, you'll think I'm nuts...."

"Whadya mean, I KNOW you're nuts! That's why we hooked up in the first place," joked Hazel. She wasn't bad when she was in a good mood. "What is it, Ken?"

Somehow Mom had softened up a bit and was more patient after realizing that kicking the cat might have lost Nefertiti for good and that the maid had quit on account of her badgering. So she was milder these days... *just like Sweet Sally Jones would be after a near-disaster*, she thought.

"There's something you HAVE to see. Or else you won't believe me. Put down that spatula for a second. The cookies are out of the oven now. Let them cool. Maybe I'm hallucinating."

"Oh, lordee, what is it now? First the cat gets lost, now this, whatever it is." Mom was still needing some practice to perfect her new gentle persona. After all the fuss and bother about the missing cat, she didn't want any more emergencies.

"Come," said Dad.

Hazel and Ken Baker opened the Kitchen door. All the Kitchen Things were watching, wondering what was going on. Crumb held his breath.

"Who made this?" Mom let out a scream! There on her backyard lawn easily seen but a bit overgrown was... a Happy Face!

A crop circle right there. The grass had been carved low to form the outside circle of the head, cut amid the taller blades with great precision. The smile was formed by lines of carefully mashed-down and skillfully interwoven grass, and the eyes... the eyes were almond shaped slanted ALIEN eyes!

Mom fainted. As Dad bent to gently wake his wife, Nefertiti fell into a trance inside the kitchen. "Ka-poonga-TONGa!"

Crumb leaned up against Breadbox, almost fainting himself.

It was true! The dog, the cat, he himself and some bee out there who was super-smart had all been Alien-Abducted!

***

"What do you want for breakfast, Sweetpea?" said Doctor Matt. "I'm making YOU breakfast for a change!"

"Sweetpea" was his favorite nickname for Zoe. Her given name meant "life" in Greek, and Matt counted on her to infuse his day with a boost of vitality -- he needed that when he was working such late hours on his research. Matt's lean and competent brown hands opened the cupboard and the fridge to see what options were available.

"I have organic heritage cereal, fertile eggs, some homemade cottage cheese, strawberry yogurt, raw milk and bananas."

Zoe pouted her "Let me see now, what will it be" face and said, "Cereal! With sliced bananas. It's not just the taste, I love reading cereal boxes. I'm addicted to reading, I guess."

Both Doc Matt Baruti and Sweetpea chuckled over that.

"Well, you're a straight-A student, so I'm happy!"

"But Dad, how is that latest research going? -- You haven't told me and I thought you were all excited about it."

"I am, I am. It's complicated, honey. You'd make a good scientist yourself, with that curiosity you have."

Matt Baruti (his African name was Matsimela Baruti, the first name meaning "roots", the last name, "educator") had come to America as a teenager, sent by an uncle to get Matt to a country where food was more easily available and educational possibilities abounded.

A few years after his arrival in the US, nearly all his family died of starvation or poisoned food, his uncle, aunt, mother, father and two sisters... all gone. Only one older brother survived. They wrote to each other every now and then but the brother was too set in his ways to want to come to a new country.

The worst thing you could do to insult and upset this brilliant scientist was to make a joke about one single rice kernel getting stuck in an Ethiopian's skinny throat. Not funny when you've lost almost all your family.

He'd met Zoe's Mom Natalie at the University. Natalie's slender grace, her skin as pale and translucent as fine porcelain, her warm, caring, exuberant personality attracted him right away. They had instant rapport.

After a few months they bucked racial prejudice and got married under a tree on the campus, so much in love that everyone who met them had to cheer them on. It was a love so palpable that the two of them thought nothing would ever get in the way.

While Natalie studied Marine Biology and sang in the University choir, Matt majored in Botany, Genetic Chemistry and Philosophy all at the same time. Natalie's family was wealthy but Matt insisted on working at a health food store part-time to pay his tuition. Soon he got a full scholarship and then earned his Masters in Global Agricultural Sustainability and his PhD in Molecular Research.

When Zoe was born, it was the happiest time in his life and in Natalie's. They moved from the University town to the big city, and Matt had to choose between three job offers. The best salary and an opportunity to do research that might help end starvation and famines was with

AlliedGreene Corporation. Their house was only about ten minutes away.

Everything was working out perfectly, love in the family, a good income, fun and hugs and wonderful times together.

Then when Zoe was six, Natalie had come down with bone cancer. It was odd because they had been careful to eat natural foods. Mercifully, it was only a short time of suffering before she died.

Matt was devastated. He would have to be both Mother and Father to his little girl but that was a challenge that warmed his empty heart. Every day that went by he thought of the love of his life. He could never even conceive of dating. His resolve to feed the world nutritious food became an obsession, not only because Natalie's deathbed request was that he follow his mission, but also because hard work and long hours took his mind off the emptiness of loss.

Zoe had been her mother's jewel. The six-year-old was grief-stricken and brooded for weeks, alone in her room, tossing her toys around angrily. Finally her Dad had talked with her and convinced her that her Mom's death was not her fault and that Mom would want her to be happy. After that, Zoe donned her Mother's apron and learned how to cook.

Sometimes she cried reading her Mom's recipe book and seeing a bit of blood on some of the pages, where a knife had cut her Mom's finger. She would think back to the day her Mother left her.

Natalie's last words had been, "Take care of each other. I love you both so. Don't give up your mission, Matt.

Help your Dad, Sweetpea, and believe in yourself. I...
I'm..." She couldn't get the last words out. Zoe and Matt
had bent down over her bony chest and wept for what
seemed like an eternity. The room glowed golden. She
was gone.

It was Matt Baruti's passionate commitment to
research food sources so that famines would be a footnote
in history books or forgotten in times of plenty. His
Ethiopian roots were deep in the soil and his very name
seemed prophetic, "Roots Educator." He had been delving
into DNA and evolving some brilliant methods for
improving productivity, especially in light of his Farming
Methods research.

Raising bees was his second passion. Zoe asked
for a child's protective bee suit, gloves and face helmet,
and Matt and Zoe tended the bees with loving care. It
wasn't just about the delicious raw honey they took from
the hive. Bees were amazing creatures. When they
surrounded Zoe, she could feel their passion to pollinate
flowers, fruits and vegetables, to protect and worship their
Queen. The honey they produced was as sweet on her
tongue as the recollection of her Mother's eyes.

Then one day, after school, she had gone out to
the garden and all the bees were lying on the ground like
miniature victims of war. For a whole day Zoe wept. She
vowed to do something about this slaughter.

It hit her Dad almost as hard. It was a second
death, a senseless and disturbing one.

Doctor Baruti was very troubled about the use of
pesticides (particularly those known as neonicotinoids) and
sprays that seemed to be causing sudden hive death,
known formally as Colony Collapse Disorder.

He had even gone to the CEO of AlliedGreene about this, but wasn't able to get in to see him for some reason. The boss' hawk-nosed, beady-eyed secretary Ms. Scoop had said, "Mr. O'Greene is very sorry. But he is going to the Dentist and then on vacation for a week." She paused as if deciding whether to add something or not. "Can you make another appointment?"

But there was a reason Matt Baruti didn't make another appointment, not just then.

***

Dr. Baruti needed time, a lot of time. Would he get it?

He had -- by sheer surprise one late night at the Lab -- discovered a molecular indicator, an unusual genetic marker that had significant potential to be developed into a remarkably organic seed, totally resistant to disease and pests. It had been overlooked by anyone he knew about. In order to avoid any animals being tested on this (the neglect and cruelty of animal testing was absolutely abhorrent to Matt), it would take at least ten years of hard and thorough research, painstaking care, copious notes, inventive methods and absolute secrecy so as not to pirate this into something destructive, non-organic, dangerous to ecological systems and to human consumption.

Careful documentation of every step was vital. One false move or a premature announcement would ruin the chances for research. It was just too early to make any announcements, even too early to hint at something.

Plus, the CEO had bought Matt out of two preceding patents -- at a time when Natalie's medical costs were adding up drastically. Telling the CEO about this potential product might tempt his Boss to destroy any hope for owning his own patent, if that were even possible. But money was NOT Matt's motivation.

Still, he had to be practical too -- he had a bright child to send to college at some point, and the money might be a form of justice after losing two patents... provided he could patent this. There was never any guarantee of gaining a patent, but he didn't want the CEO to get wind of his latest findings.

So Doc Baruti worked after hours with the doors closed to the lab. Locked in fact. No one, not even Zoe, had a clue what he thought he'd noticed or what he thought might come of it. Each night before leaving work, he'd carefully seal that day's documentation inside a large safe he kept hidden in his private office, manipulating the lock with a complex secret combination known only to him.

Despite his long hours, somehow he managed to be both Mom and Dad to his darling girl -- she had a spunky sense of humor and kept him on his toes. He was always amazed that Zoe, all of eight now, had a tasty dinner waiting for him when he came home. Soups, homemade bread, chili, salads, even desserts and fresh lemonade, his favorite. As for his father-role, he had learned to braid cornrows in time for the school bus. He found a trusted friend to drop her off at Ballet Class, Karate Class, and Piano Lessons but he always managed to pick her up on time himself --- it was a pleasure to hear her instructors tell him about Zoe's progress. His biggest regret was that Natalie wouldn't see how this amazing child was developing. Becoming her own person.

She was almost ready for toe shoes, she'd earned a Brown Belt, she played Beethoven's Für Elise quite well for an eight-year-old, and she was a born investigative scientist, curious about everything, not accepting opinions but searching for validity.

Now she had two friends her own age a few houses down the block. This was good, because she had encountered some snobby kids at her private school.

Her Dad had told her, "It's their problem. You are more than your body anyway, you are more than the color of your skin, so wear it with pride." Natalie had been blue-blood, her ancestors had come over "on the boat." What did it matter anyway, it was who you were NOW, what you made of your life and gave to others.

So there she was, Zoe and her bowl of organic heritage cereal plumb-full of banana slices and drenched in fresh raw milk, reading her cereal box in between looking out the window at what once had been their beautiful, thriving hive.

"Dad, listen to this. It says here that there is no genetically modified anything in this cereal. Thank goodness. I think that's what might have killed Mom." (Matt winced a bit.)

"We always thought we were eating all-natural stuff but 'natural' is a no-no-word today," Zoe added. "Companies lie about being 'natural' all the time. You have to do research to make sure you're eating what's really good for you, and not believe labels that lie."

"I know, I know, Zoe. Right you are." He began to think out-loud to himself. "Hmmmm, I hope I make a difference in what people eat, but maybe it won't happen in my lifetime. I hope you'll carry the banner when I'm..."

Matt stopped mid-sentence, hoping Zoe hadn't heard him say that last part. Zoe was reading the cereal box with full concentration.

Good thing she hadn't heard what he had started to say. It wasn't just that he had alluded to the fact that someday he wouldn't be around. He hated to enforce his brilliant daughter to be a scientist just like him. He would be glad if she chose that profession, certainly, but he wanted her to know that the world was open to her, that she could be or do whatever she decided. She had so many talents and interests. Matt sighed in relief that she had missed what he'd started to say.

Zoe sensed something stirring in her Dad's mind. She tossed her head to look especially cute, putting her chin on her hand.

"Daaaddeee..." Zoe adopted a special tone of voice whenever she said "Daddy" instead of her usual "Dad."

"What is it now?" Matt was used to this tactic and preparing himself to hear a pleading request of some sort.

"Well, I wish I could have a dog. Sally and Johnny have Whisk and Nefertiti. Can we pleeeeze get a puppy? Pretty-please with cherries on top? I'll take care of it. I promise."

"Not now. Maybe. Someday. I'm too busy to walk it and I don't like the idea of you walking around the neighborhood by yourself with a puppy."

"Oh, Daddy, you're being over-protective. I'm almost a black-belt."

"And you're pretty good as a beggar-for-a-puppy too!"

Chapter Ten

Spelling Bee

Once Crumb realized that the Crop Circle proved that all Four had been abducted, a meeting was in order. He was no longer scared by the dog or the cat. The only one missing was Will the bee.

Whisk was still galumphing around, with his careless paws. Sometimes he would go to Breadbox's open door and stand there sniffing.

Even though Crumb wasn't scared of the dog anymore and considered him a friend, seeing his black nose up close was very scary –- Whisk's nose looked like an Alien face. The nostrils were slanted and hollow and looked just like alien eyes, the doggie lips were upturned in a goofy Happy Face smile. Was Whisk dumb or was he just hiding his new Powers in a rough-and-tumble, clumsy way? Crumb knew he'd have to find out from Whisk himself. It was no use just guessing.

After her initial disorientation, Nefertiti resumed her usual feline serenity. On the surface it seemed like she hadn't changed much. She was either On or Off, as in the past but there were subtle differences. Every now and then she yelped at Mom, angry that Hazel had made Hortense so upset that she had quit. She had lost Queen Hatshepsut once. Twice was too much.

But there was one very noticeable change in Nefertiti. Sometimes the cat would go missing for half-a-day or longer and the Baker kids, afraid that Nefertiti was lost again, would search high and low for her. Crumb wondered if she was "visiting" some ancient time and place or taking a quantum leap into the future, returning just in time for dinner.

On the surface nothing really seemed much different in the Kitchen, but everything was altered in invisible, subtle, penetrating ways. The Riddle was still almost as puzzling as ever but Crumb knew that there were clues and directions hidden in it. He had to make sure that all Four (even the missing bee, once he was found) were One Voice, One Thought, One Purpose as to what they now had to do. Whatever it was.

Where was Will? If they were going to be successful in completing their Mission, they certainly would need the Smartest Thing in the World. In fact, Crumb was hoping that Will would decipher the Riddle so he could know exactly what it was all about.

For several days Crumb made his rounds on the Kitchen counter scouting for Will, but there was no bee in sight. Crumb was beginning to worry and doubts began creeping back that maybe his dream really HAD been just a dream. He remembered Breadbox telling him, "There are times when you can't predict what's in store and it just hits you, Crumb. Life Lessons don't come as easily as ordering a meal at a restaurant. I always say it's best to 'Know before you go' but still be prepared for the unexpected."

Then of all things Sally and Zoe (without intending to do so) made it a lot easier to locate the missing bee. Crumb heard them in the living-room one afternoon trying on Ken's hats, putting them back on the hat rack and giggling. They began practicing their spelling, working from a "Spelling Can Be Fun" workbook -- "Pneumonia", "hysterical", "stationery" (as in paper supplies, not "stationary" as in "not moving"). Crumb recalled the Riddle had mentioned "E-nunciate well and learn how it's spelled," so maybe this was going to help the Cause... whatever it was. Crumb strolled over on the counter near the door that opened into the living-room to listen more carefully, putting on a casual air because he'd have to walk by Toaster.

"I'm good at spelling but I get so nervous when I'm called on," confessed Sally. "My whole school is counting on me."

"Oh don't worry, you'll be great at the Spelling Bee. I won it last year. I'll go over all the words in the book. You'll do fine. Okay, spell 'basin'."

"B-A-C-I-N."

"Nope, it's not "c", it's "s" in the middle. It's the easy words that get ya, believe you me! Try it again, Sally."

Crumb took in a breath and stopped dead in his tracks in front of Toaster. A Spelling Bee!

Toaster cocked an eye up. His dial was clearly turned to Dark and this time he wasn't trying to move it to another setting.

Toaster said in a sneaky tone of voice, "Where were you going, Crumb? And why did you stop like that?"

Ooo, Toaster could make Crumb so mad that he could hardly answer. He started to say "None of your beeswax" but the words stuck inside of him. Even mentioning beeswax might act as a clue and point to Crumb's search for Will.

"Off to see Blender and Spoon, that's all. I forgot my miniature French phrase book and suddenly realized I'd have to go back to Breadbox to get it," Crumb lied. To make his lie appear truthful, Crumb now had reverse his path and trudge back to Breadbox.

"Sesame Honey Bagel!"

Breadbox squeaked open his door, while looking puzzled at Crumb. "Why did you put 'honey' on the bagel, I mean 'honey' in front of the word 'bagel', when you know it's Sesame Bagel? Don't fix it if it ain't broke!" quipped the wise old codger.

"Sorry, Honey!... uh, I mean Sorry, Granddad." (*Oops*, thought Crumb, *maybe that'll make Breadbox think I'm still pining for Spoon. No WAY! I just can't stop thinking about Will. I HAVE to find him!*)

Back inside the cozy box, Crumb sat forlorn, wishing he had done what he had originally set out to do, go closer to where Zoe and Sally were practicing for the Spelling Bee just in case Will would come by. There was one good thing though -- now Crumb was beginning to understand the meaning of one more part of the Riddle, "learn how it's spelled."

Breadbox soon was fast asleep, snoring loudly, and Crumb sat on his bed brooding a bit, deciding he better just stay put and not wake his Granddad up. Suddenly he heard a buzzing whirring sound.

It was Will! The bee flew once around the Kitchen to see if he could find Crumb but not seeing him, he began to head into the living-room just as he heard the girls practicing for the Spelling Bee. Will knew all the words in all the dictionaries of every major language on Earth and wanted to help Zoe and Sally out, but something told him that that might not be a smart idea. For a moment he hovered at the door separating the Kitchen from the Living-room, trying to decide where to go.

There was more at stake than winning a spelling bee. Although he'd been raised by Zoe back at the hive and was quite fond of her, he was the only surviving bee. If she saw him she might try to detain him (by capturing him in a jar) to find out how and why he had lived through what had killed every other bee including the Queen. He couldn't risk that.

Even with all his knowledge he wasn't sure himself why he'd survived. He guessed that it was because he had a Purpose to fulfill. The Hive's Voice and Thoughts were demolished but Purpose had gained intensity. Will's anguish had turned into a fire inside him that made Purpose burn more strongly than ever. He was determined to help save other hives from what had happened to his.

The girls had finished practicing for the spelling bee and Zoe stood at the front door saying goodbye to Sally.

Instead of going into the living-room, Will decided to search more thoroughly back in the Kitchen. Where was Crumb?

Will spotted an old-fashioned container that said "B-READ" on the top and figured that was as good a place as any to find a breadcrumb. For a few seconds the bee hovered outside the tin door fluttering his wings, trying to signal to Crumb (if he happened to be inside) that he was there.

Sitting on his little bed Crumb caught a fleeting glimpse of familiar yellow and black stripes through a tiny crack on the side of Breadbox's door. He didn't want to wake his Granddad but he had to take the risk. A split-second before Will was about to fly away to look elsewhere, Crumb nudged the door open. In flew the bee who sat next to Crumb and quieted his buzzing.

I'm so happy to see you, I missed you. I was worried we'd never meet up! Crumb shot the thought over to the bee. Will understood, *Same here.*

Surrounded by the gentle shadows inside the cozy breadbox, sudden warmth filled the two of them as if they were outside illuminated by sunshine. The two looked at each other, spellbound with a mutual feeling of recognition and surprise. The last shreds of doubt vanished from Crumb -- the Abduction had really happened. Finally they were face to face, feeling like they were old friends and new friends all at the same time, like twins reunited. (In fact, they did look a bit like mismatched twins. They were almost the same size, with the bee just slightly bigger than Crumb.) After a few seconds basking in the joy of finding one another, they broke from the intensity of the welcome, both realizing that they had something important to do. Now.

"I have a job for you, Will. Please get the cat and the dog over here for a Conference. I need to know what they know and what they don't know about this little trip to the UFO. Maybe we can all figure out the Riddle. Think of it as an intelligence test. 'Intelligence' in both senses of the word: Kind of like spy work and smarten up time!"

"Sure." There wasn't any time to waste. Will flew over to the tin door, gave it a shove, and off he went.

The shove woke Breadbox. "What's happening?" asked the old fellow sensing something was going on.

"Oh nothing, Granddad, but would you keep your door open? It's getting a bit hot in here," the little bread-ball fibbed but then realized, *Maybe that's not really so far from the truth. Seeing Will again made me feel all warm inside.* Breadbox kept his door open, but fell back asleep and began snoring so loudly that the tin door fluttered up and down a bit with each booming snore-breath.

A few minutes later Whisk and Nefertiti showed up escorted by the bee. Whisk stuck his big nose up to the open-door and again Crumb could not get over how much like an Alien Happy Face his nose looked, all except for his extra-long whiskers. The same almond-shaped slanted hollow eyes (his big nostrils) and goofy smile.

Nefertiti looked in to the box just to be sure no mouse was inside. If there had been, you could be sure it wouldn't be alive for long. Seeing no prey, she purred hello.

"It's good to be together again. We are Four, they were Fifty, but we got back," said Nefertiti.

Breadbox's loud snoring was the perfect cover — none of the Kitchen Things were privy to what was being said. Tea-Pot, Timer and all the other Kitchen Things wouldn't have moved or spoken anyway, since they were still terrified of the cat and dog. Even Toaster was too scared to intrude, but did keep opening one eye from time to time, suspicious of why the pets were looking in at Breadbox's open door. He figured maybe someone in the Family had forgotten to close the tin door and the dog and cat were taking advantage of that, searching for a snack.

The meeting began. "Do you have special powers, Cat?" whispered Crumb.

"I always had, bread-piece. But now they are enhanced. I can quantum-leap into the future and I can return — in body and mind, every little furry hair of me — to any place and time in the past. I can sense things in the Present very well. I'm extremely useful."

"Very cool," said Crumb.

"Do you remember, Dog, being abducted?"

"Yup. At first I didn't remember a thing. Then a smell from that place came back to me. All those socks... phew, most of them needed washing."

Will and Crumb had a quiet chuckle about that.

"Well, Whisk, do you have special powers?"

"Sure do. If I want to or need to, I can spin my antennae so fast that the high-up tones (and mind you, those Humans can't hear any of it) will summon dogs from all over the city! Guaranteed."

Crumb decided to confide in Whisk. (After all, if they were going to be real friends and carry out a Mission, being up-front with each other would be the best policy.)

"I have to say, earlier today you scared me, Dog Whiskerer, when you stuck your nose up to the Breadbox opening!" admitted Crumb to Whisk. "Your nostrils look a lot like those hollow Alien eyes!"

"That's the idea, bread-let. Who knows, maybe that'll come in handy." Whisk hinted at powers that might prove helpful.

"Sounds good," Crumb agreed.

"Now, Will -- I have a very important question for you. Do you remember all the knowledge that was given to you on the UFO? Is it all available to you in a micro-second?"

"Definitely. Would you like to know about the 'Ontology of St. Thomas Aquinas'? Or the structure of the bone mass of a herring and why it resembles herringbone tweed? How about what Dark Matter is? Just ask!"

"Most impressive, Will. What would you say is the Ultimate Question of the Universe?"

"That's easy. '2 Bee or not 2 Bee, that is the question!' "

"Sounds right to me. You're good to go! Only problem is... WHERE are we going and WHAT are we in search of??"

"The Riddle will tell us, you've known that all along, Crumb." The cat and dog nodded at Will's pronouncement.

"But the Riddle," moaned Crumb, "(and sorry to have to word it this way, but it fits) is riddled with mysterious phrases that I can't make head or tails of." The cat and dog nodded their heads and wagged their tails at the reference to their handy nods and wagging tails.

"Help us, Will! Help us solve the Riddle so we can KNOW before we GO! If --- after this conference --- we find out where we're going and why, then it must be our calling!" At that, the cat and dog added purring and tail-wagging just to show the bee how much confidence they had in Will's genius.

"Okay, okay. This must be my Ultimate Test. I must confess from the get-go that this riddle makes about as much sense to me as who or what caused the Big Bang!" sighed the bee. "We should all pray I get it right. But thanks, guys, for your confidence in me. The best I can do is to try my best!"

"The Best that the Smartest Thing on this planet can manage to do should be kind of good, wouldn't you say?" Crumb noted with a steady look at Will that said, "You can do it."

"Yeah, but I hope there's no time limit on my intelligence and fund of useful information."

"No, no way," said Nefertiti. "I've looked into the future and you continue to be as smart as you are now, well... actually smarter. It's exponential intelligence, growing all the time."

"You saw where we're going?" Crumb leaned closer to the cat. "Where was it? And why were we there?"

"In the future: I saw a big building, a bunch of dogs and a whole lotta wind, but what this building is, why the dogs are there and why it's so windy, I have no clue. Maybe I should try to materialize myself into this future time. But I haven't tried that trick yet and I'm (frankly) a bit nervous about doing it right away."

"No worries, you don't have to go there," comforted Whisk. Crumb and Will concurred.

"Let Will check the Riddle out," offered the dog. "I think he can find out all the specifics we need. And with my nose and whiskers, we're gonna do this..." he paused, "whatever it is."

"Okay, I'll do my best to decipher it. Give me some time alone. Inside Breadbox so I can see the Riddle laid out in writing. And don't wake Granddad. Even though his snoring is distracting, I have tremendous powers of concentration. It's just not the right time for anyone else to be 'brought in', so let him sleep."

Crumb climbed up on one of Whisk's sticky whiskers, Nefertiti landed on all fours as she always did, and the Three went off to the living-room. It was Crumb's second time there but the first time (after being rescued from the sewer) had been scary. He thought to himself, *As long as I don't get caught in the carpet loops again, all is well. I'm among friends now.*

Two hours later, Will came flying in to the living-room.

"I've got it! I've figured it out!" Will proclaimed. Inside, he was thinking, *Spoke too soon. All of it? You wish.* (But right now it wasn't the time to confess that to the others.) "Let's get back to the Kitchen. Once we're safe, I'll explain it and then we have a LOT of work to do." Crumb could see the fever of excitement that Will was in. The bee continued.

"This is BIG! This is important to all four of us. In fact, this is important to everyone and everything here on Earth. I can't lay it out in a sentence or two. I need a blackboard, a piece of chalk, a light on in the kitchen but a night when all the Kitchen Things won't be snooping around. This is TOP SECRET! And I'm not talking about loose socks." (Will was referring to the Top Secret Bureau of Sox Research.)

Crumb pointed to the blackboard paint on Coldylox's surface. Will looked at the fridge blackboard where Hazel had scrawled "Oil change SUV. Hat Convention. Pack kids stuff. Leave Thursday 5 p.m. - Visit Zoo/Sunday. Give Zoe keys. Back Sunday night." Will smiled and the plan was begun. The Family was going away for the weekend and the Four would be able to use the blackboard to lay out their plan... whatever it was.

"How can we be sure that the Kitchen Things will be tired enough not to interrupt us while you are laying out the plan?" asked Whisk. Crumb, Will and Nefertiti turned their heads right away to look at Whisk -- that was exactly the right question to ask. The dog WAS smart, brilliant in fact!

Will figured out the solution right away. "Here's the deal -- the Baker's will be out of town leaving this afternoon and gone all weekend. It's the perfect time for a Kitchen Party! Tonight. It'll be 'Saturday Night on Thursday Evening'. Saucepan banging, Tea-Pot whistling, Dish showing off, even Rolling Pin at the door to function as Bouncer.... A PARTY! Once they're all tuckered out and fast asleep, you cat and you dog sneak back into the Kitchen for a de-briefing. (You know the rest of the Kitchen Things are still scared of you so you are NOT invited to this shindig, okay?) We'll meet up after the party."

"We can sit this one out," offered Whisk. The cat agreed.

Will smiled and nodded a thanks and continued with his strategic plan: "Once everyone is fast asleep that should allow me to sit you three down, QUIETLY mind you, and I'll take the chalk and use the blackboard on the fridge to walk you through the Riddle, line by line. There are still a few points I don't get. I'm counting on the answers to show up while this whole thing is rolling out... I sure hope so."

"What about Coldylox? We have to erase her first. And then write. The chalk might tickle. And then she'd know something was going on," said Crumb, concerned for the security of the plan.

"You are right. Erasing her is no problem. But writing on her, hmmmm... Maybe the blackboard paint on top of her original enamel has anesthetized the fridge?" figured Will. "If so, she wouldn't feel a thing. I can run a preliminary test to see about that. If she feels my soft wings on her tummy, then we'll have to swear her to secrecy for a price and bond her for ten thousand magnets to keep our secret."

"Good idea," piped up Crumb. "You mean if she gives us away, she has to give up her own magnets and manage to find a ton of other magnets too and turn 'em all over to us? Ten thousand?"

"That's the price. I think that will scare her enough to keep her big mouth shut. Let's hope the blackboard paint has dulled her sensations enough that we don't have to clue her in to our plans at ALL," advised Will.

"So you'll find out if she's de-sensitized, right, Will?" asked Nefertiti. "Then after the big shindig in the Kitchen, with all the Kitchen Things knocked out, Whisk and I join you for a debriefing, right?"

"That's the plan."

"My fur is standing on end!" exclaimed Nefertiti. "Tell me something to keep me from exploding and not looking too far into the future, Will!"

"All I can tell you is this: The Riddle IS the plan, the purpose, and... I hope... the way." Will looked very serious.

"The way?" asked Crumb, probing for more information.

"The way to WIN!"

Chapter Eleven

Party with A Purpose

Since the Humans would be out of the house for days, it was a snap to interest the entire Kitchen in a party. They hadn't had one in a long time. There was tension in the air, most of them had sensed it, and a party would help diffuse that. So they all got together and did a little planning and this became the Best Party Ever in the Kitchen's history, the talk for years afterwards!

It began with a bang, literally! All the Pots and Pans and Wooden Spoon mallets announced the great celebration in a pounding beat that set the shelves bouncing.

Blender stepped in and took a whirl as Ringmaster announcing every act, working the crowd up to a pitch of excitement as everyone took a turn creating a fantastic show. His black lid with its pour-and-stir tube on top made the perfect Ringmaster's Hat and he sported a jolly red-white-and-blue straw for his Ringmaster's baton. *For once,* thought the long-suffering Mediator, *everyone is finally gonna pay attention to me and LISTEN to what I say!* If he couldn't quiet the crowd down fast enough, Blender figured his rubber stopper might do the trick.

Tea-Pot had prepared for the festivities by downing enough water to whistle a bunch of snippets from Broadway tunes. The tea bags did the limbo bending their flexible bodies under Sharpest Knife's straight but razer-edged blade. Muscle-man Can Opener and flexible Spatula performed acrobatic tricks that had the crowd cheering.

Soon Crumb's little breadcrumb cousins began begging Granddad Breadbox to let them do something, so he opened his big door flat to makc a stage. Out came the tiny breadcrumb cousins like a bunch of kindergarten cuties, singing "Ode to Joy": La-la-la-la-la-la-la-la.... Sponge and Scrubber almost fell into the sink giggling and everyone agreed they were the most adorable toddlers ever seen in those parts.

All this merriment wasn't sitting too well with a few of the Kitchen Things. Toaster found himself heating up and getting suspicious that something was up, so he and Rolling Pin were checking out the doors. (Rolling Pin was taking her responsibility as Bouncer quite seriously in case the Bakers showed up early from their weekend trip.) All their suspicions laid to rest, Toaster and Rolling Pin decided to join in the fun but keep an eye out for trouble just in case.

Then Ringmaster Blender, skilled at sensing when a change of pace might work best, turned his speed-dial setting down from Crush to Chop. Everyone needed to settle down for a bit so the change of mood was welcome. Accordingly, Spoon pirouetted ballet with a lovely tutu of fine orange mesh she'd found in the tangerine bin. Not to be undone, Dish followed that with a sensuous Belly Dance where she somehow was able to make her fruit bowl tummy appear to move up and down!

The Spice and Herb Jars were all a-titter with excitement because they had planned something never before seen or heard in the Wilds of the Kitchen: Wearing their various native folk costumes, decked in ribbons and embroidery, multi-colored skirts and pantaloons of all kinds, they joined in a grand International Chorus, all their voices blending, rendering folksongs from their native lands!

Cinnamon and Cloves from Sri Lanka and India, Cardamom from Guatemala, Tarragon from France, Thyme from Poland, Ginger from Nigeria, Dill from England,

Paprika from Hungary, Rosemary from Morocco, Mint from Egypt and Coriander from Romania -- what a delicious sonority, what harmony among the nations. Happy the Banana Peel kept them all together as Conductor, keeping the beat with surprising musicality.

It brought tears to old Breadbox's eyes to see this kind of unity among the diverse youth of the Kitchen! *If only the world outside*, he thought, *could flavor their lives with this kind of understanding.* Blender as Ringmaster led the crowd in a long ovation.

Changing the mood of the evening, Saucepan revealed his flair for one-liners. His impeccable sense of timing and spicy innuendos proved to be quite hilarious. That spurred the Pots and Pans to start up again and the noise was getting so loud that Rolling Pin was afraid a neighbor might call the police.

Breadbox had provided some of the best seats in the house but finally closed his door, making sure all of Crumb's tiny breadcrumb cousins were safely tucked in their beds. All this banging had tired him out and he fell asleep, snoring away.

In deference to Breadbox, Timer got everybody's attention and announced, "Fantastic fun everybody! An evening to remember. But it's time to end the festivities, folks. Enjoy your rest-time and thanks for all the talent and great entertainment! Ringmaster, take it away!" Blender stepped into the center of the counter and with a grand tip of his Black Lid-Hat, announced, "Party's OVER!"

Suddenly Crumb got a clever idea. Before Sponge went back to the sink to go to sleep, he approached her and asked if she would just take a minute so they could work up a magic act for the next party. Crumb called it "The Disappearing Act." She needed to be reassured that he wouldn't saw her in half or anything quite so life-threatening. Scrubber glowered at the two of them as Crumb splashed a bit of water on Sponge and lifted her up in his muscle-bound little arms, delicately sweeping her across the refrigerator door in broad strokes. Hazel's reminders were gone.

"Perfect! You're the loveliest Magician's Assistant I could wish for, Sponge. We'll do this 'Disappearing Act' the very next party! *(yawn)* I guess it's time to sleep now. Thanks!"

"Oh, Crumb, you're so strong!" sighed Sponge.

"Get over here right now!" ordered Scrubber, turning his rough side to Crumb like a threat. "I'm your manager. I'll get you the entertainment gigs, not him." The jealous fellow pulled Sponge over by his side. Soon the two of them were yawning and fast asleep.

With that, all the Kitchen Things returned to their shelves and drawers and places on the counter, tiptoeing memories through a lagoon of sleepy unconsciousness, utterly worn out from hours of playful and raucous partying.

Carefully waiting for enough time to make sure all the Kitchen Things were fast asleep, Crumb and Will approached the blackboard on the fridge. Will had pre-tested the sensitivity level of Coldylox's surface. Apparently, the paint had numbed her exterior sufficiently for Will to write on her surface without waking her up.

Moonlight sifted through the window curtains as soft and white as powdered sugar, frosting the dreams of sparkling glassware and glinting on stainless steel. Lamplight from the street gathered in a pool that floated across the blackboard like a spotlight waiting for one last curtain call. Intense quiet filled the Kitchen. The only sounds were occasional murmurs from a few spices, dreaming of their homelands and completely tuckered out after their choir performance. Breadbox slumbered without snoring, which happened only when he was plumb exhausted and revisiting an ancient memory or two. Even the tea bags nestled in their boxes without a sound. It was time. Crumb signaled to the dog and cat to return to the Kitchen -- they entered stealthily on silent paws.

Crumb positioned a small piece of chalk in Will's mouth and jaw so that it fit snug and tight. With a delicate touch Will began to copy the Riddle. After each line he left room for notes to clarify the meaning hidden in the words. He speculated there were double meanings in some of the lines, but the problem was that these double meanings might not become apparent until the Four of them were actively mid-mission. Essentially, Will had a reasonable idea of what the Riddle laid out, as far as preparing and executing the plan. But a complete grasp of every nuance of the Riddle? No. Not in the least.

So Will took his time writing each line, trying to figure out how he could go over what DID make sense, while indicating gently that he had no clue about some of the wording. He certainly didn't want to discourage anyone, but part of his hesitation was that he felt the burden of being labeled "the smartest thing on the planet." *Shouldn't I be able to decipher this?* he fretted. *Why is the full meaning eluding me? It's embarrassing and counter-productive.* Meanwhile suspense became palpable, as if a thick vapor of dry ice were gathering around Coldylox. Finally Crumb could stand it no longer.

"What's it all about? What IS the mission? Why have we been chosen?" Crumb was frustrated, chaffing at the bit. Nefertiti and Whisk crept in closer, completely absorbed in their curiosity and need to know.

Will quietly said that he would reveal all this but that "we have to take this one step at a time. Bear with me."

As soon as Will said the word "bear", Coldylox stirred and her electrical wiring began to groan for a moment. (Memories of her iconic ancestor, who had visited three bears long ago and eaten porridge, broken a chair and slept in the wrong bed had been stimulated by that word.)

"Look," uttered Will, "apparently I can't use that word. Let's proceed and please don't interrupt. If you have questions, hold them until the end. Do I have your agreement?"

They nodded, sobered by the sudden possibility that Coldylox might awaken and find out what they were up to.

With an exceedingly gentle touch of the chalk, Will finished copying out the Riddle. (He had already committed it to memory in a single glance.) Then he began his clarification of each line:

" 'Where there's a will/you know there's a way' – Seems to me there are two meanings for this: 1) Keep focused and don't doubt yourself and you will find a way to make what you want, happen, and 2) I am Will who will lead you to victory (...I hope)."

Crumb, Whisk and Nefertiti nodded but caught the "I hope" at the end and looked at each other with mixed reactions. Will went on.

"Next two lines: 'What looks like work/can turn into play' -- That's easy to see. It means: Keep it light, don't get serious and heavy about this. More is accomplished by a playful attitude than by worry or struggling because that's too negative to work well."

Crumb smiled, "Yeah, makes sense to me. Work can become play if you make it that way. (Say, that rhymes!) Continue, Will!"

"Alright. Next line: 'When green is red'... Now here's where this gets tricky...," admitted Will.

He was trying his best not to show any discouragement. "I'm guessing on this one. Pure speculation but my calculations after assessing the rest of the riddle lead me to interpret this as... as... and I hope this is right..." (He was stalling for time.)

At this point Crumb blurted out, "What?? What does it MEAN? I hope we're not totally going on GUESSWORK here!"

"Shhhhh" said Nefertiti. "The Riddle isn't done yet, let Will explain. And don't wake anybody up!"

"Sorry," apologized Crumb with a whisper.

"As far as I can see," continued Will, "this Riddle has lots of double meanings and, I mySELF am sorry to be a wee bit stumped every now and then. Some of this is very obvious and some is open to a couple of inter-pretations. Every now and then guess work is the best I can do. My feeling (as your Advisor and Strategic Planner... Crumb being your Project Head) is that we're going to have to go on our Intuition and on our Best Guesses while we're actually ON the mission."

Crumb, Whisk and Nefertiti stared at Will, dumbfounded. Will didn't waste a second. He didn't want any comments right now and just barreled through the next instructions.

"It will be crucial to keep your eyes and ears open... open for ANYthing. Nefertiti, we will probably want to call on you to check out the future at points where this is getting especially tough, so stay on your toes. Whisk, we may need you to summon help. Crumb and I are going to have to TRAVEL ALONE."

Crumb's eyes got almost as big as his whole face. He began to shake. Will had to point ahead to the verse about "No one's too small to follow a dream."

"Let's go back to where we were. Please BEAR UP under this pressure. ...Oops." Coldylox began to stir a bit after hearing the word "bear" again and her magnets were rattling.

Line by line, in hushed voice, Will laid out his certainties and his speculations about the meaning of each line. The Riddle wasn't all there -- Will knew they'd have to figure it out "in transit", as he termed it. But slowly a plan began to emerge, like a map that seems to lead in a certain direction but has holes and rips in it at odd places.

"Well, that's the gist of it," whispered Will. "Tomorrow, when the sun is rising and before all these tuckered-out Partygoers wake up, we'll head out of the house. Meantime, get some rest. We'll need lots of energy. You two furry-folks, go back to the living-room to get some shut-eye. You can stay close to the Kitchen entrance but keep a certain distance, in case any Kitchen Thing wakes up. You still scare them, you know." Whisk and Nefertiti nodded but didn't leave, sensing that Will had something more to say.

"Crumb, you are my biggest worry right now," the bee revealed. (Whisk and Nefertiti rotated their ears to be able to hear better.) Will continued. "I wish I could tell you how to relax and get some sleep, Crumb, because you are going to need every ounce of that strength they gave you. In case you can't sleep, wake me up. I got with Cam O'Mile and worked up some tea to help you sleep better. In the meantime, do your best."

"Listen," Crumb said. (He objected to Will pointing out that he was Will's biggest worry in front of the others.) "YOU better get some rest too, Smarty-pants. I thought you had all of this Riddle figured out, but now you tell me you're gonna have to fly with ME on your back and we're stuck with figuring out some of this 'in transit.' I hope we're not gonna be flying by the seat of our pants on this one."

"You don't wear pants," said Will. "Now get some sleep, everyone."

The mood was not exactly like a party. All Four knew they were in for a tough day ahead.

Will dismissed them with a crisp, "Debriefing Over!"

Chapter Twelve

If Ya Can't Take It, Don't Dish It Out

Zoe got up that Friday morning early to make her Dad some scrambled eggs.

"These are delicious, honey.... I mean, Sweetpea." (The very word "honey" reminded him too much of the bee colony that was gone.)

"Glad you like 'em." Zoe's countenance took on an intense glow. "Dad, about the hive, this is the way I look at it: When something happens, it's best to see it for what it is. Honey is a GOOD thing.... Glad we still have a bunch of jars left."

"You're right, Zoe. (Matt thought, *She reminds me so much of her mother, so practical, so wise all at the same time.*) Now, are you ready for the school bus to pick you up?"

"Yup. Ready as I'll ever be." She had on a brand new outfit --- a teal green vest over a new blouse, a flower-print skirt and silk ribbons tying her braids --- and was hoping it might get her a more warm reception from her classmates than she usually got.

"You look great. Let me walk you outside." (Matt always waited for the bus with his daughter. Over-protective, some said. It didn't matter. Zoe was his whole life.) "I hope I'm home early today. I'm tired."

"That would be good, Dad. Too many late nights at the lab and you'll run out of steam."

"Right again." He reached to hand her her lunch-box.

The two of them went outside. It was a beautiful sunny day with puffy clouds in a vivid blue sky. Zoe spotted the Baker's dog sprinting out of the yard, barking his head off. It wasn't the time to ask her Dad again for a puppy. She was fond of Whisk, but he could be so rambunctious at times. When she got a puppy, she'd be sure to take it to Puppy Training right away.

Just then the school bus turned onto Tempest Street and rolled up to the Baruti's house. Zoe hugged her Dad and stepped inside the bus. Dad was lost in thought, as if transfixed on the sidewalk. Then he pulled his attention back onto Zoe who sat by the window. A blond-haired boy had moved across the aisle to a different seat, leaving her all alone on the bench. Zoe was used to this. She looked down at her new outfit and sighed. *Whisk*, she thought, *shut up, it's too early in the morning for all your barking.*

But something else was bothering her, something she couldn't put her finger on. Her Dad seemed troubled -- he had his attention stuck on something. Mustering a smile, Zoe waved goodbye and the bus trundled down the street. She'd make him his favorite meal tonight, stuffed peppers and rice with baked apples for dessert.

Matt went back in the house, grabbed his jacket and laptop and headed for the car. He'd get to work early today and that might give him the chance to get home a bit sooner than usual. He rubbed his eyes... they hurt.

There was that dog again, Whisk, the Baker's galumphy mutt, his usually floppy ears pointing up like traffic cones at an accident, dashing down the street directly toward him with his eyes glazed and his tongue hanging out.

Whisk screeched to a halt inches from the doctor. His keen nose began sniffing. (Nope, the dog sensed, the Baruti's didn't have a dog. Not in their house.) For a second the dog bent with his hot breath right over Doc's shoes and took a second sniff on the cuff of the doctor's pants: Something chemical, similar to the vinegar the dog whiffed in the Kitchen or that acrid smell at the vet's.

Matt reached down to pet Whisk, happy that he had stopped barking. Maybe some day he'd get Zoe the puppy she was always begging him for -- they'd go to a pound and rescue a pooch and maybe even a kitten.

The quiet moment didn't last too long. Whisk leaped up, stretching his legs and chest to put his big paws on the Doctor's collarbone, desperate to get his attention. He WAS a Doctor wasn't he? That's who was needed right now, a Doctor!

There was an emergency in the Kitchen! A broken plate, a trapped friend, a failed early morning plan. A betrayal.

Matt scolded the dog gently.

"Hey, not now, down, down! You're awfully friendly, Pooch. Just don't get my clothes dirty with your paws. Down! Down!" Whisk started licking the doctor's chin. That was too much. Matt pushed Whisk off him. "Down!"

Yes, thought Whisk, *this is what I've been trying to convey to you. Down, down, Dish fell down. She's in pieces, maybe dead, certainly wounded. Will might be hurt too, he'd been trapped under the plate for a while. We need a Doctor!* When would Humans understand that non-verbal thoughts could be transmitted by dogs and cats? No use! The man was walking to his car. When would Humans listen?

Whisk slumped and ran back home limping, going over in his image-picture-mind what had transpired just a few minutes ago -- Pandemonium! It had all started... well, Nefertiti and he had been snoozing in the living-room per Will's instructions when all of a sudden, a commotion woke them up.

Dish hadn't been asleep when Will was giving the Debriefing to the Four! She pretended to be asleep, kept her eyes closed, but her ears open. Like a spy she had done a seductive belly-dance at the Party that night and now she was eavesdropping to get information for the enemy, although she had no idea who the enemy was.

After the secret meeting had reached its conclusion, Dish peeked out from her cabinet window and watched Crumb erase the mysterious symbols off the blackboard surface of the fridge. Dish brooded and fumed, *How can this tiny crumb be so strong? He's actually carrying a big blackboard eraser, what muscles he has! He's getting more handsome the bigger he grows. Why does he prefer Spoon to me? He was even flirting with Sponge earlier, making her his Magician's Assistant!"* Desire and jealousy struggled inside her. She had once wanted him, now she hated him.

Of all the nerve to exclude her from this secret meeting! The sheer audacity of Will to throw those peculiar words into her sneaky ears -- the Riddle made little sense to her and confused her so much that she was shaking on her plate-holder. Somehow she enlisted S.K.'s help to open her cabinet door with his sharp edge. Then the exhausted knife went back to sleep without a clue why she had insisted that he pry open the cabinet door.

Maybe Trivet, used to calming hot platters down, could have served to cool her off, but he was stored in the pantry far away. Now she was hot with fury. How could she stop what the bee and Crumb were up to? Crumb had rejected her and here he was going to be the Project Head?! It wasn't fair. She'd been left out. She'd show them!

When the first rays of sun hit the Kitchen counters, Will had awakened, eager to rouse the others and get going. Dish was perched upright on her mahogany plate-holder but the easel was a little off-balance. Dish was leaning forward against the partially open cabinet door.

Flying around to check out the area, Will spotted her sneaky eyes suddenly peering at him over her fruit bowl tummy. Sensing that she had been eavesdropping, he began to fly near the half-open glass door. Had she just opened her eyes for a second or was she really wide-awake during the debriefing? It was vital that no one, not even Breadbox, know about the mission. Not at this point anyway.

Suddenly Dish spotted the crafty little bee fluttering directly in front of her face. She'd show him! Just as Will came toward her, she tilted forward off of her plate-holder, flattened out on top of the shelf and turned upside down, right on top of the bee. Captured!

Will was TRAPPED! Crumb woke up with a jolt! He could hear the bee buzzing, but it sounded more like a distant lawn mower down the block than Will's hearty, close-up buzzzzz.

Something was dampening the sound. Where was Will?

Whisk ran in and heard the commotion and sized up the situation instantly. Pushing the overturned plate to free Will, Whisk miscalculated his effort and pushed just a hair too much.

Dish plummeted off her shelf, past the open cabinet door and crashed to the floor. She was in pieces, her heart finally broken... dashed into bits... but only by her own jealousy and spite! The cat was in a trance moaning an ancient chant as if she were a priestess gathering remnants of a soul to place in a funerary jar: "Ma'at-ka-Ra -- may she live eternally."

Crumb began to shout, "Dish! How COULD you? You spied on us." Then changing his tone and quieting his voice so as not to wake anyone up he whispered, "Oh no, Dish, I'm so sorry you're broken! Don't DIE!" (Crumb felt torn in two by the conflict between friendship and betrayal.) For a few seconds the shards of porcelain that had once been her rim whimpered as they lay shattered on the travertine floor, then no sound at all.

The only piece of Dish that had stayed more or less intact was the large middle section with the fruit bowl in the center. Sadly that circular part wasn't even whimpering, it was unconscious, eyes closed, edges frayed and splintered, perhaps dead. Crumb couldn't help but think, *If only the Family had chosen cork for their new flooring.*

At that point Whisk ran outside to fetch the Doctor.

What an unruly but lovable pooch, thought Matt. *But I just don't have time for him right now.* He turned his key to open the car door and plopped in the driver's seat, flipping the radio on for the morning commuter traffic report. Look at what time it was - Darn! He'd intended to get to work early so he could come home at a decent hour and handle his growing exhaustion. Then right at Crossroads Avenue, where a train track and Culvert Pass met, the Train-Crossing warning gate cranked down in front of the line of cars and a long freight train chugged by, erasing five more minutes from his early morning start. He could feel his pulse jerking with impatience.

Waiting at the train crossing, Matt's mind kept on jumping between two very different things: The appointment he needed to have with his pompous boss, and that excitable dog down the street. There was something in the pooch's nervous energy that troubled him. *Why did Whisk have such glazed, frightened eyes?* Had Matt abandoned the dog when someone was in trouble inside the house? No, he knew the Bakers were out of town for the weekend, because they had entrusted their house key to Zoe and asked her to feed the animals, take the dog for walks and water the plants for them.

Enough of that! His logical mind pushed his intuition to the side. He better not let any more distractions grab him. Turning off Crossroads Avenue and making his way to the next red light intersection he stopped, began rubbing his eyes again and missed when the light turned green. The car behind him was honking. Matt forced himself to focus on his driving and continued through the green light, but his attention kept on flipping between the anxious dog and the CEO.

How was he going to tell that forceful, money-hungry butterball of a boss about the genetic marker he'd seen without having the boss get over-stimulated to rush it to market? He didn't trust that Marketing Dude, what was his name? Something-or-other Fripple. That beady-eyed

Vice President of Marketing had a smile that could freeze a penguin out of his tux, a face that should have been in the dictionary under the word "smarmy" -- it was fake, overdone and self-serving. (Matt shivered every time he pictured it.)

Doc Baruti and Mr. VP Marketing Fripple had once been stuck in the company elevator for ten minutes until Security had contacted the elevator repair company. It was one of the longest ten minutes of Matt's life. Not because of the stuck elevator. Because of Fripple.

Farts are not a polite subject of conversation, but Fripple had insisted on talking about them, apologizing for them, discussing how baked beans and pizza weren't a good combination and... presenting "samples" of his topic-of-choice that permeated the stale air of the box they were stuck in. Most unpleasant.

What if this Marketing vulture got a hold of even a whiff (it seemed appropriate as an analogy) of Baruti's research?! Fripple would undoubtedly rush it to market before the proper research was done. The CEO used to frequent bars with this creepy guy, and Fripple had his ear at any and all times. Matt had heard they went to high school together and neither of them had made the football team. Was that an excuse for bonding? Apparently, this something-or-other Fripple had even been his boss's Best Man at his wedding.

If Fripple had been to my wedding, the Doc thought to himself, *I'd wonder if the champagne would be poisoned.*

So he'd have to side-step Fripple and somehow get his boss to want to keep this creep out of the prospects.

All Doc wanted to do was to get his boss's agreement (in writing... he realized) to allow the Experiment to continue for as many years as it might take. No, he wouldn't tell him it might be ten years. He was a scientist, not a negotiator. No one else was privy to his nighttime research. No one could be trusted, not really. Not even his Lab Assistant Harvey Singerman.

Matt's assistant Harvey was very bright, easy to get along with, but what an awkward twenty-something geek. His cowlick was uncontrollable and his horned-rimmed glasses had lenses that resembled a kid's play microscope, he was that near-sighted. Harvey's one saving grace was his kind heart and good intentions. That was how Matt separated his circle of friends from acquaintances he kept at a distance -- good intentions or harmful ones. Harvey was all about helping others, but he hadn't learned how to help himself.

Maybe it was because he lived with his Mom who was always getting after him to find a suitable young lady and settle down and have grandkids for her. Finally, he nervously started asking girls out, the more unattractive the better so he didn't look half-bad sitting next to them. Lacking self-esteem, Harvey also figured that since they were not exactly beauty contestants, they wouldn't say no when he asked them for a date. On top of that, Harvey sometimes was awfully absent-minded and Matt figured his assistant would probably end up single and a chemistry professor someday.

But knowing about loneliness from having lost Natalie, the Doc was encouraging him to get more of an idea about the world than being stuck in the four walls of the lab.

So Harvey had started asking his boss about how he could meet girls without hanging out at single bars and did Matt think his shirt looked cool enough and did he have garlic on his breath. (That was going too far.) The young fellow had even arranged with his boss to leave work a bit early every day so he could shower and shave for a date or hang out at a local bookstore. That suited the Doc just fine.

Leaving early, Harvey didn't have a clue about what Dr. Baruti was doing at night. All the documentation and digital records and other paraphernalia were all securely sealed in a bulky fireproof safe hidden behind large charts and boxes at the back of a locked closet in his office. Matt Baruti had a complex combination encoded into the massive lock on the safe — a code so clever, thought the scientist, that he liked to pretend that it might have taken the famous Enigma machine of World War II weeks to solve it. This appealed to the scientist's master-mind mentality and his brilliance with mathematics, probability and codes. *No one's going to rush my research to judgment,* emphasized the Doctor to himself, *or steal it from under my nose!*

In fact, sometimes it took more time for the Doc to clean up and hide his findings for that day than to find the "findings" in the first place. He kept his desktop free of papers and his office neat. Utmost secrecy was required and he didn't even want the night cleanup crew to get curious.

Matt encouraged his assistant to ask girls out, so Harvey left about twenty minutes early every workday and assumed his boss left work a few minutes after he did, at normal closing time. Especially since he knew Dr. Matt had a young daughter to take care of and was devoted to her.

Meantime Matt had actually arranged for a trusted friend to pick Zoe up from school and drop her off at her Karate, piano or ballet class. Devoted Dad that he was, no matter how busy he was, he always made sure he was on time to pick her up afterwards and bring her home. While she cooked dinner, he'd go back to the Lab for an hour or two, then arrive home for a late dinner. At this rate, Zoe was becoming an expert at crock-pot stews or soups -- they'd be hot and ready whenever he came home. He always wanted to spend time with her or help her with her homework if she needed it, but lately he was getting home so late that he'd tiptoe into her bedroom, tuck the blanket around her neck, whisper "I love you, Sweetpea" and fall into his own bed exhausted. Someday he hoped it would all be worth it.

This schedule was wearing him out. He was a forthright person, straight-forward, not easy on himself at all if he felt dishonest. Now here he was, deceiving his assistant and keeping secrets from his boss. And from his closest friend, Zoe.

One thing for sure, Dr. Matt Baruti would have to be as clever as he'd ever been when he finally made that appointment.

How could he introduce this subject to his rotund, self-serving boss without making it seem enticingly lucrative, while at the same time pointing out some attractive possibilities in the future so that he could gain his boss's okay to conduct the research to completion? Matt summarized the situation this way, *To sell but not to over-sell, that's the dilemma.* For here was a potential goldmine as well as an organic miracle, the possibility of developing (after research) a robust organic seed impervious to pests so no insecticide would be needed.

This was tricky. He'd have to reveal just a bit of his findings and hypothesis, not all of it. He'd have to be matter-of-fact but persuasive. And all the time, underneath his low-key casual manner, he would feel his wife's last breath on his conscience and the image of dead bees like murdered angels on his lawn.

Preparation was key. It made him less nervous to try to be organized and neat, so he started to work up an actual flow-chart for his presentation. On the left side of the paper he drew little flow-chart boxes where he could write simple words like "No" and "Are you kidding?" to represent doubts from his boss. On the right side he drew boxes for positive responses, "Wow" and "Start!" In the middle he started a column for bland or conservative things his boss might say but decided to erase it. It didn't work to sit on the fence. It was "yes" or "no" or nothing.

The doubt boxes were filling up faster, flowing one to the other down to an angry "You're Fired!" Then he found a subtle line of how to word the box-to-box flow of logic. He wrote in clever enticements that (he hoped) would convince Mr. O'Greene to give him an "Okay. Go ahead."

The trouble was that Logic and Emotion were not joining up. He cared too much but had to sound like it was all purely sensible and good business at the same time. He knew he wouldn't succeed by trying to appeal to his boss's altruistic, caring, ecologically-motivated side --- there WAS no side like that! Pure greed. Covered over by hypocrisy.

On top of that, he couldn't keep sneaking in and out of the lab at night for much longer. He was getting exhausted and he knew Zoe was aware of that. It was one thing to care desperately that his research would add up to something the world really needed, and another thing to worry that he was upsetting his darling girl. The world-view tugged at the big muscles in his heart, the home-scene pulsed through every corpuscle in his body.

He had gone to his own doctor and his blood pressure was high. This had never happened before. He didn't have the heart to discuss this with Zoe. He would have to change his schedule as soon as possible.

Arriving at AlliedGreene Corporation, Matt pulled in to the company parking lot, swallowed hard and walked through the huge facility's revolving door. On the right of the lobby next to a wilted palm was the CEO's office. *How come they can't afford a fresh-looking plant?* he wondered. *The boss is filthy rich. Maybe it's the stale air in the building, something not quite healthy in the air.* He'd put some fresh water in the poor thing when he got a chance and open up a window in his office when he got up there. Then the doctor scolded himself for getting distracted again. *Focus,* he ordered himself, *focus!*

He'd have to make an appointment with Ms. Scoop, who always intimidated him with her hawk-like face and chilly manner. Yessss? she'd say. He'd put on his lab coat first, to look more official.

"May I help you, Dr. Baruti?" Her hawk beak was lifted ever so slightly to the side, revealing a tight bun and lowered eyes. He didn't trust people who never looked him in the eye. Fripple was like that too.

"Um, yeah, I need to make an appointment with Mr. O'Greene today or maybe Monday. Today if possible, please." Matt's hand went into his pocket nervously, where his flow-chart lay crumpled up.

"Well, he won't be available for hours. He's in a meeting with the Marketing Head." She turned her ergonometric chair in a sudden commanding manner, facing Matt like a Chinese dog statue guarding the Forbidden City. "Closed doors, I'm afraid. He's not even accepting any calls.... But I'll ask him when he can meet with you, as soon as he opens the door. Will Monday do?"

"Fine, I guess. But... today would be better. In the afternoon if possible." The crumpled flow-chart seemed to be sending messages up his arm, through his veins into his pounding heart, telling him, *It's too soon. You're not prepared. Put it off until the middle of next week.*

In the other pocket on the other side of his lab coat, he could feel his key to the closet (where the safe was hidden) jingling against his normal laboratory key. His hand was shaking, so he inserted it awkwardly into that pocket.

Now he was standing there like a schoolboy in front of the principal's office, both hands in his pockets, staring at a sign just above Ms. Scoop's tight bun. It said: "Feeding The World, One Bite at A Time." The company's trademarked slogan. Fripple had no idea about genocidal starvation. *Some marketing gimmick,* thought Matt. *One bite at a time? Maybe that vulture is planning to take one bite at a time out of the company's profits.*

"He's in there with Fripple?" Matt's nostrils curled up in disgust.

"Yes, strictly confidential. I can't knock on the door. You'll just have to wait."

"No problem." Matt put on his best casual air. It wouldn't do to try to ingratiate himself with Ms. Scoop. Her beak, her tight shoulders, her glassy eyes resembled something in a taxidermist's display case. She had worked for the CEO for eighteen years, ever since he graduated as a gawky kid from the mail-room and clawed his way up the ranks. Now the boss had to order super-sized office chairs to accommodate his massive, greasy frame. Still, it was her mission to keep his privacy sacred and her salary secret. There were too many young buxom girls wanting her cushy job.

"Ta-ta," Matt said, walking out the door into the hallway. *Ta-ta?*, the astounded scientist asked himself. *What's gotten into me to say such an eccentric goodbye? It's sarcastic, that's what, and a bit snobby sounding. Good! It's about time you stood up for yourself, Matsimela Baruti!* he said, giving himself a pep-talk.

He better get back to the lab upstairs and bury himself in his standard everyday work because... *I'm losing it*, he thought to himself. *I've never said "Ta-ta" in my entire life up to now.* Maybe he could rehearse his presentation over lunch and fill in more square boxes in his flow-chart. He didn't have much time. It was this afternoon or Monday.

Ms. Scoop had done her secretarial duty: Behind the bastion of the heavy wooden door, Iago Fripple was leaning over Gordon M.'s ulcer-shaped desk, whispering in his boss's ear. The thick lips of the CEO were spread in a rapacious smile. His hazel eyes had taken on the luster of gold coins. He was practically drooling.

"Yes, yes, we'll corner the market. I like your product name and slogan: 'Impervious: Seed for All Seasons.' Baruti doesn't need to know. We've got his formula. I'll start production right away. It tested fine for pest-resistance. Who needs to belabor this?"

Both Iago and Gordon M. began chortling the kind of ghastly belly-ripples that anyone listening would have taken for corpses raised from the dead.

When Matt Baruti got to the lab, he saw Harvey inspecting the calibration waveform simulator.

"Hi there, Harvey! Sorry I'm late. A train crossing took forever. How was last night?"

"Oh, don't ask. She left me to go to the ladies room at the restaurant and never came back to the table. I'm never gonna find a broad who'll appreciate me for who I am!"

"That's not true, Harvey Singerman. You're a terrific guy, all heart, and once some gal gets used to your style, you have a certain... a certain..."

"Don't work too hard, Boss. You'll think of something soon. Speaking of working too hard, were you up here late last night? There are ruffled papers all over your desk when I poked my head in to your office to see if you were in. Looked a bit strange. Just saying...."

"Ruffled papers? I never leave papers out overnight, and..." (The hair on the back of Matt Baruti's neck was starting to stand up.) "I like my paperwork stacked neatly in the desk."

In mid-sentence, Matt started to turn around and walk -- as slowly as he could without risking suspicion -- toward his private office.

Harvey hadn't wanted to scare his boss. "Ruffled papers"? Some understatement. It was a mess! Papers were thrown on the floor, ripped up in the wastebasket, the photo of Zoe was turned upside down, his favorite coffee mug was overturned in a small puddle of two-day-old caffeine.

Whoever had come in was looking for something and didn't care if their search was obvious or not. *Why didn't they care to clean it up? OH MY GOD! Maybe they'd found what they were looking for and it didn't matter if they left a mess. Maybe they had been interrupted.* Questions and conclusions raced through Matt's mind.

Rushing over to the closet where he kept his safe, he unlocked the closet door. Oddly someone had decided to lock the closet up again but... but... Matt Baruti's high blood pressure was about to explode into heart-attack zone -- The safe was GONE!!!

Speculations hurtled through the scientist's mind: Fripple was downstairs bending O'Greene's ear behind closed doors. What if he had stolen the safe? What if he had cracked the code and gotten in? (*Impossible*, thought the Doctor.) What if the bulky combination lock had been sawed off or exploded off? Who would have been able to get the key to his closet duplicated or a master key?

Who had suspected about his secret researches enough to do this? A vague image flashed into his mind then faded: *A shadowy figure lurking around a corner as I've locked up the lab at night, the flicker of someone spying on me* -- he'd dismissed these at the time as fearful projections of his exhausted imagination. As paranoia and lack of sleep.

Matt Baruti's heart was racing. His head was spinning. Harvey found him bent over the desk. His forehead had landed an inch away from the coffee spill.

"Doc, Doc, are you okay? What's going on here?"

Matt came to, although everything seemed to spin around in his office.

"Nothing, Harvey." Matt was really thinking, *Yeah sure, nothing. How do you spell 'betrayal'?*

"Doc, smile. Give me a smile."

"You gotta be kidding. What's there to smile about?"

"No, really," Harvey said with quiet determination. (The ends of Matt's tight lips pursed into a phony smile for a second then dissolved into a pout.)

"Doc, put your hands up! Stick'em up!"

"HARVEY!! You're not arresting me, are you?"

"No way, these are ways to check if you've had a stroke. Thank goodness, you're fine."

"Had me worried there for a minute.....," gasped the Doc.

He wasn't about to give away that this wasn't just about rumpled papers on his desk. It was ludicrous to entertain the idea that his gawky assistant might have master-planned this heist. But still it was worth asking.

"You didn't have anything to do with this... this mess in here, did you?"

"B-o-s-s, I never come in here. You're usually out there by the particle analyzer or Bunsen burners anyway, so why would I come in here and mess up some papers on your desk? Anyway, you were still here when I left. Had another date. What a loser -- all she could say was "like" after every other word, jeesh. I should have stayed home and caught a basketball game."

Harvey was innocent. Matt knew it.

Maybe the safe hadn't been cracked open -- maybe it was still on the premises and he could recover it. His heart was still racing, and his blood pressure -- he didn't even want to think about how high it might be. Slowing his breath, he took a minute to figure out his next step. He set the overturned coffee mug upright and began to wipe up the spill on his desk.

"Want a coffee?" he asked Harvey with a matter-of-fact tone of voice. It wouldn't do to reveal any of what had really happened.

"No thanks."

"Well, I'll run down to the cafeteria. Hungry. And I can sure use some bootblack."

Harvey chuckled as he sat at the digital microscope. Doc Baruti was alright, a very good boss to work for, fun, low-key (well, usually... he'd almost passed out a few minutes ago) and very brilliant.

Matt walked across the hall to the elevators, measuring his steps to keep himself from racing.

Once in the elevator, when he found he was alone, he leaned against the fake marble on the back wall. How could this have happened? Who had the safe?

His first thought was Fripple, second thought was the CEO.

Matt had always found that his first thought tended to be the right one. *Maybe they're bedfellows together, that makes more sense. Fripple & O'Greene — it has a nasty aftertaste.*

As soon as the elevator arrived at the bottom floor and the door opened, Matt lost all sense of propriety or subterfuge -- he raced to the CEO's office, not caring who saw him.

Ms. Scoop was bending over a file cabinet inserting folders.

Matt didn't let his feet, his mind, his heart or anything stop him -- flying past her desk, he reached for the door handle of Mr. O'Greene's executive office. It was locked!

"Need to see you! Now! It's Dr. Baruti! Open this door! Urgent!"

Behind the door: Mumbling... coughing... fast words spoken in a panic... anything but coming to the door to open it.

"Doctor BaRUTi, you'll have to WAIT! I'm in a private conference." The CEO's bombastic voice bellowed from the door. Someone was snickering in the background... Fripple.

"Private conference? Oh yeah? Not any more." Matt began to beat down the door first with his shoulder, arm and the whole side of his torso, then he turned and blasted the door with his fists. The door wasn't budging.

"WHAT is so URgent?" The boss was screaming. "Glenda! Call Security and get this crazed FORMER employee of this company OFF the premises!"

Chapter Thirteen

Betrayal

Matt could feel his heart pumping what seemed like tar, squeezing the tar from the dark recesses of his ravaged hopes. The sign "Feeding the World" was stretching and bending before his eyes as the floor leered up at him and smacked him in the forehead. Down for the count. For a second he saw his body lying there then he bounded back into his head.

Glenda Scoop had called the Company Infirmary, not Security. (Maybe ol' Ms. Hawkeye had a kind streak after all, maybe she was trying to protect the company or her boss.) Matt was flat on the floor, gripping his left arm, struggling for breath, trying to focus on his shoes that kept on turning into multiple images as if he were dancing in slow-motion. From behind the locked door, something heavy with scratchy corners was being pulled out of the way. The safe!

Matt was fighting a panicky feeling. Was he going to lose it -- leave Zoe with no one to care for her? --- leave the safe and its findings in the wrong hands? Never before had he felt such a searing bolt of betrayal. It felt like lightning was burning his life to a crisp.

There was a tight feeling in his chest for a second --- *Oh, not a heart attack!* Not on top of the theft of his life's work!

Then as if a calm had overtaken him, Matt remembered Zoe's words: "*When something happens, it's best to see it for what it is.*" She was right. He was fighting this so hard that the energy had turned around and was hitting him instead of the right target, Fripple and the CEO. Matt found his heart was slowing down and tar was turning back to blood.

The stocky male nurse from the company infirmary rushed in a minute later with his bag of emergency supplies. He opened Matt's lab coat and shirt and placed the cool stethoscope on his chest and took out his defibrillator, in case it was needed. Satisfied that the heart was not giving out, he took Matt's blood pressure and his temperature, scanned his retinas with a beam of light, and got a thin utility blanket and covered him.

"He's not to move -- I might decide to call an ambulance, but -- oddly -- I mean, happily, his blood pressure is just about normal, a hair away from where it would be ideally, and he's conscious and I think he's over the worst. No temperature, no shock symptoms really. Dr. Baruti, has something like this ever happened to you before?"

The Doc shook his head. The male nurse sounded competent but indifferent.

"What I suggest is this: Get someone to drive you home, no driving yourself home please, and take the afternoon off and evening, get lots of good rest, no stress. You'll have the weekend too, so take it easy. Next week if you need a few days at home, no problem. I'll write a little note if you need me to. Here's some aspirins and calcium-magnesium tablets, potassium pills, fish oil to keep your arteries flexible and B-complex, that'll help. Keep hydrated, and I suggest a light soup and herb tea for dinner, no caffeine, no salt, no sugar, but see if you can get some fresh citrus juice in the morning -- dilute it a bit with some water -- and be sure to avail yourself of these cal-mag and potassium tablets."

The nurse looked up at the secretary, cautiously waiting for her to give him a cue: *What should I do?* he seemed to be asking her. She was puzzled: *Shouldn't YOU know, Medico?* Was he more worried about hiking up the company insurance policy or the man lying on the floor? He was risking his own job not to call a hospital or fire station ambulance right away. Matt was taking this all in, conscious that he might need to stay aware in case this all turned legal or... he hated to think of this... if he really was at the start of a massive heart attack or stroke. The nurse droned on. He was trying to do his job but he lacked bedside manner.

"If this starts up again for the Doctor anytime soon while you're still here, Ms. Scoop, call an ambulance immediately or I'll do it, just buzz me."

Then inspecting the Doctor's face, he added, "If you feel anything odd once you're home, promise me you'll get to an emergency room on the double. With someone else driving. And I suggest you see your Doctor.... as soon as possible."

Matt glanced up to see the secretary, arms folded, with her thin neck stretched upward, staring into space, eyes moist, lips set. She looked both beaten and proud at the same time. A hint of something soft, even pretty, enveloped her face like a veil.

The nurse packed up his things and left. Dr. Baruti sized up the situation for a minute, marveling that the secretary had disobeyed her furious boss and had NOT contacted the Security Officer. Maybe she knew that the Doctor shouldn't be moved just then, as a precaution. Maybe there was something more to her surprising action. When she turned her head to look at him with pinpoints of intensity in her eyes, he decided to broach the subject.

"Well, Ms. Scoop, seems you didn't call Security. Thanks... for once. What is going on in that office?"

Ms. Scoop couldn't answer but waves of conflicting feelings were awash across her face, tides of resentment, regret, poignant memories, stubborn principles, disappointment flooding her cheeks, forehead and posture. Her hair was loose. The bun had come undone.

Glenda bent down, her face half-hidden in her mousy brown hair. Her voice, usually so cold and pointed, was hoarse but gentle.

"You had me really scared there for a minute, Dr. Baruti. I thought you might be... well, you know...." (Her throaty voice trailed off, afraid to say the word.) "Feelin' better, huh? Phew! You may not believe it, but I always thought well of you. Gordon M., I mean 'Boss' would yell at me if I was nice to someone he thought might flirt with me. Imagine that! I'm old enough to be your Mother. I hope you're not going to repeat any of this, I have to talk to someone...."

"I'm listening," Matt said. He could feel his heartbeat slowing to a more comfortable normal rate, as she began confiding in him. Matt flashed again on Zoe's words: *"When something happens, it's best to see it for what it is."*

"He keeps on promising me he'll dump his wife and marry me. Eighteen years of this, my youth gone, motels on weekends. Empty promises! I don't believe him anymore. He's a sneak and I'm done with this."

She swung her head back and forth, pushing her loose hair like a whip around her cheeks with bits of tears spraying out of her eyes. One of those teardrops hit Matt near his throat. It reminded him of those first raindrops that land on a windshield just before a rainstorm really sets in. Matt could hardly believe this was the same woman who had been so incredibly cold a short while ago.

"Now that's enough about me.... It's time for a change, isn't it. How are you? Feeling better? Want a glass of water? Here, take this aspirin. I'm quitting today, you can vouch for that."

"Oh, really? Do you have to? I don't want to cause any trouble," offered the Doctor, conscious that he hadn't intended to have her lose her job today because of his ruckus.

"No, it's good. It's about time."

Raising her voice, Glenda repeated her ultimatum, as if she were shooting a bullet into the CEO's office: "I'm QUITTING today, Gordon!"

"Quitting today?" boomed the sarcastic voice behind the locked door. "Who's gonna hire a fancy BAG lady like you? I bet two months salary you stay!"

"Stay? No way. Not over my dead body! Or over HIS!" She touched the Doc's shoulder. It wasn't a romantic touch. It was maternal, protective. But Matt couldn't help feeling she was using him as a shield. As a convenient wall between herself and her prison-keeper.

"You -- you Rag-Bag -- you've beTRAYED me!" His voice was thick and vicious, the sound of a bloodsucker who'd gone from skinny to repulsively fat. The door to the office shook. "I told you to call Security! Not the Infirmary!"

"I didn't want Security to arrest YOU! You have a safe in there with stolen 'whatever' in it! I was afraid the

Security Guard would arrest you! You and that creep IAGO FRIPPLE! So now hear this, I QUIT!"

"I'll save you the trouble. You're fired, Glenda! FIRED! And so is HE!"

He had deceived her all that time and was now accusing her of betraying him. One person's betrayal was another person's escape route. She had betrayed herself, denied her fears and allowed herself to be trapped. It was over.

Suddenly pale with terror, she said in a trembling voice, just loud enough for her ex-lover to hear, "I still have my Retirement Plan. The health insurance."

"Oh YEAH?! Sorry to disappoint you." The CEO's voice was full of venom.

Glenda Scoop slumped against her big desk, holding onto it with arms so tight the elbows were ashy-white. She surveyed her elegant marble pencil holder and gold-plated letter opener as if they were corpses she was saying goodbye to. *Don't pick up that letter opener,* she ruminated — *that will make everything worse.* Pulling out a handkerchief, she sniffed her tears away.

Eighteen years of hopes and motels and top salary had vanished. Turning to the Doc, she gathered her facial muscles together into a semblance of normalcy and whispered, "Now... what is so serious that you tried to break down the door?"

The Doctor said nothing but he took her bony hand and held it for a while. She had already inadvertently told him there was a stolen safe in the Boss's office, behind that locked door.

The Doctor was flabbergasted at the revelation: *Iago Fripple, Iago, the perfect name, Othello's villain, Othello's betrayer! I should have guessed.*

Then turning to the secretary, he probed her, "I've always wanted to know: What's the "M" in the boss's name stand for? I'm ready for anything, except another near-heart attack."

She whispered, "The 'G' stands for Gordon and the 'M' -- he'd kill me for this if he knew, he HATES his name. The 'M' is for... Mordred." -- Her lips curled. Matt realized: *Mordred, the traitor who stained King Arthur's Round Table by accusing Guinevere and Lancelot in front of the King.*

The Doc had to stifle his laughter but his efforts turned into little bursts of giggles. "Gordon's parents must have known from the get-go they had a little monster in that cradle. What a name for a baby! Didn't he ever try to change it?"

"Yeah," she whispered, her cheeks red from holding in laughter. "He wanted Arthur or Lance. I told him they didn't fit him."

Glenda bent her face down, letting the relief of laughter and exhaustion drip out of her. After a good laugh, Matt released her hand and put his finger to his lips and his ears to ask her to let him whisper something to her.

She bent down as he whispered in her ear. The scent of faded perfume and bitterness caught his attention.

"I need your help to get into that office! My work has been stolen by someone who's kept you dangling for eighteen years. Stolen your youth just the way he's stolen my research. But it's more important than just me. This research is not ready to be released to the public, trust me."

Matt waited for that dread scenario to grip her.

The secretary's gray eyes opened wide and her tight lips had parted. She realized Gordon and Iago were trying to jump the gun on some kind of vital research and rush it to market too soon to be safe. This wasn't just about a messed up love affair, a lost job, or even a fallen employee on her office floor. Bigger. Much bigger.

Matt sensed with every ounce of his intuition that now was the time to ask:

"Will you help me... once he's gone home? I need to get into that office. But tomorrow early -- not tonight. I'm sure my daughter wants me home taking it easy for the rest of the day." (Matt thought a moment about that.) "Wait... knowing my daughter, she'll probably insist I rest all Saturday too. Can you meet me here Sunday early morning? He can't hear me... do you have a key to the front door and to his office?"

She nodded. After a pause while she weighed her decision, she whispered, "Yes, but it's not about revenge. It's because I think it's the right thing to do."

"Well," replied Matt, "I hope my stuff is in there. Leave it locked tonight! Promise me... Glenda Scoop?"

"If he's stolen your stuff, I'll make sure it's in there over the weekend. I'll do my best anyway. You go rest today. I have eighteen years of stuff to pack up tonight and a whole new life to plan. I'll see about getting in there around midnight tonight and taking photos. I won't touch a thing.... Fingerprints, you know. If you come back Sunday morning at 5:30 a.m., I'll let you in to his office. Maybe we can call the police... later on. I have a lawyer in mind, too."

He had misjudged her. She was a wounded bird, encased in a broken cage. Oddly enough, at the same time that he felt more trapped than he'd ever felt in his whole life, she had been freed!

It was then that Dr. Matsimela Baruti realized that the worst betrayal of all didn't come from others, it was always a betrayal of oneself!

***

Harvey drove Dr. Baruti back home in the doctor's car. (Afterwards the assistant planned to take a bus back to the company garage and pick up his own car and go home.) Harvey couldn't get a word in to find out why the Doc seemed so consumed in a pit of silence on the way home, with his fists clenched and his skin pastier than usual. Harvey offered to take him to the Emergency Ward but Matt shook his head, "Just get me home, please. Thanks for this, Harvey. You're a good fellow."

Zoe was home from school anxious to unburden something to her father. Casual Friday at the private school had been a disaster -- her fancy new outfit had made her the subject of snotty gossip. She admitted to herself that she had gone out of character, trying to impress her classmates with something superficial like brand new clothes. She had completely forgotten that Casual Friday had been scheduled. Instead she looked ridiculous when everyone else wore things like cut-off shorts, faded blue jeans, oversized T-shirts, temporary tattoos and falling apart sneakers. What did all that matter, her Casual Friday woes could wait. When she saw her Dad's assistant drive up in her father's car with her Dad slumped over to one side, she knew something was not right.

Zoe rushed over to her Dad's side as soon as he stumbled out of the car. Both Harvey and Zoe helped support the Doctor, one on each side, as he lumbered up the stairs to his bedroom.

Matt complained a bit, "You're fussing much too much over me."

Harvey took the opportunity to flip that around by saying, "This is better than getting left at the restaurant table on a date." The Doc could always count on his assistant to crack him up.

Once in bed, Zoe tucked him in and handed him his favorite pillow and a glass of water. She always had the magic touch, that girl of his.

"You rest up now, Dad. I'll make you some broth and a cup of rooibus tea with cream and a drop of vanilla in it, your favorite." (She pronounced it 'ROH-bush' tea.) Zoe was doing her best to be cheery and low-key, but her brow was furrowed.

"Daddy, you have to learn to take better CARE of yourself." Then her thoughts went to the Baker's house down the street.

"What time is it? I promised Sally and Johnny I'd feed the pets and water the plants while they were gone. I have to rush over there for about ten minutes. I'll make you the broth and tea when I get back. If you feel like sleeping now, go ahead. Later on, we can read GREAT EXPECTATIONS together, okay?"

Her Dad nodded an exhausted but happy smile. Zoe's sweet attentions were so life-giving that Matt already felt better. SHE was his Great Expectation. She watched as his breath slowed to make sure he was sleeping soundly. Then she tiptoed out of the bedroom and went downstairs.

Zoe walked over to the Baker's house picking a few daisies on the way that she didn't think the neighbor would miss. Normally she would never have picked flowers from someone else's front lawn, but she was too worried not to need something cheerful-looking in her hand and daisies perfectly suited her need for comfort. *Is Dad really threatened? He looked so worn out on the pillow. I'll have to hurry back,* she realized.

Zoe unlocked the front door of the Baker's place and checked out the living-room. A bit messy --- she'd fluff up the pillows before she left. The plants were dry so she found the watering can behind a side-table and went into the Kitchen to fill it with tap water.

What was that? A broken plate on the floor, near the stove. Oh no! It was Mrs. Baker's favorite serving dish. Shattered into at least a dozen pieces. The gold rim had broken up into an SOS code of dots and dashes, what a mess.

I better not throw these pieces away in the garbage, Zoe thought. *Hazel probably wants to glue the pieces together, although it'll never look the same as it used to. Who pushed it over and made it fall? Maybe the cat or dog.*

Where were Nefertiti and Whisk? All of a sudden Whisk bounded into the Kitchen smelling the presence of someone outside-of-the-family-but-a-friend. Zoe smelled of sprouted-bread-and-cheese sandwiches with cucumber and mayonnaise, her hair had the fragrance of mint shampoo, her hands resonated with the pungent green smell of daisy stems. Seeing Zoe bending over the broken dish, he yelped a greeting and wagged his tail so much that she stood up.

"Oh good, Whisk. I need to feed you." Filling his food dish and adding some fresh water to his second dish, Zoe noticed that he didn't seem to be hungry or he didn't like his food. (Both cat and dog could feed themselves by now due to their special powers. Whisk had developed a distaste for his dry food. It had a chemical tinge that made his tongue curl and his nostrils feel itchy.)

"Nefertiti! Where's that rascally cat?" Zoe looked all around the living-room. She wasn't in the Kitchen or pantry. Stepping over every-other-stair, Zoe climbed the stairs to look in the bedrooms and bathrooms. Not there. She slid down the banister and rushed into the Kitchen calling the cat.

"Nefertiti, food! Food. Here Kitty-Kitty." (Whisk had a sudden thought hearing her calling the cat: *I bet Nefertiti's off visiting the future. Maybe the past. We sure could use her help on the Mission.*) Back downstairs, Zoe was gesturing him to the back door.

"Come Whisk, outside. Outside! Now don't you go running off --- stay in the backyard like a good boy." Whisk's tail was wagging.

Opening the back door, Zoe tried to let the dog out, but she noticed that Whisk paused for a long time in the doorway looking at her with a curious and intense look before lumbering out to the concrete steps leading down to the lawn. Little did the eight-year-old realize that Whisk was thinking, *Didn't you watch the evening news last night? I used my special powers — I'm the Dog Whiskerer! Are you getting my thoughts? Please listen!*

Whisk could tell that Zoe was trying to get the message but the only thing that was transmitting was the feeling, the emotion telling her, *Stay there! I have something I need to tell you, Human-girl.*

Zoe was transfixed. Whisk continued, *I can vibrate my whiskers faster than helicopter propellers, emitting a sound so high-pitched but inaudible to the likes of you that I can call all the dogs in a radius of at least fifty blocks or more. AND they will come!*

She looked intent but not impressed. Only part of the message was getting through. *These Humans*, thought the dog. *So dependent on the literalness of words and yet so perplexed by their multiple meanings.*

Couldn't they grasp the threads of concepts that flew about everywhere? The wind itself was an electric concourse of thoughts, sensations, feelings and memories. All living beings were transmitters of messages and receivers of wave-forms and vibrations. Life-force didn't depend on heavy matter. Bodies were just big calling cards for those who had to see and touch matter in order to believe.

Nikola Tesla had known that --- Will had explained to Whisk and Crumb (after returning from his Knowledge-immersion in the UFO) how that inventor, electrical engineer and physicist had been way-ahead-of-his-time, unlocking how massive storehouses of as-yet-untapped but potent energy existed in what looked like empty air.

Whisk had learned from the genius bee how utility companies and electrical-machine builders didn't want to let the buying public know that Energy could be had for free! Commerce was at stake. The air was becoming polluted by more than just poison gases, by ignorance and greed. People were buying and drinking bottled water in hopes of hydrating themselves with some semblance of purity, while factories and governments were dumping chemicals, plastic bags and mankind's refuse into the once-pure ocean. Will knew these atrocities were somehow at cause for Hive Death. Whisk had listened to Will, dismayed because he had depended so long on Human Problem-Solving to get him fed, warm and safe.

No, there was only so much even a very intelligent Human-Child would get from what Whisk was trying to tell her unless... unless she would somehow be introduced to the idea of magic. This (magic) a child could understand. Magic was the air children breathed, full of fairies and butterflies and angels and....

Whisk thrust his attention off of magic and physics because there was still a Pecking Order and Humans were still in charge of dogs. Zoe had ordered him outside to the backyard and he would have to obey her.

Exiting the door Whisk hesitated. He paused by the steps and began to whimper, then to howl. *What is he doing?* puzzled the girl, flabbergasted by this odd show. Whisk was filling her in with more information, hoping for once that a Human would truly listen. Zoe stood at the open door mesmerized, tuning in as best she could, but not understanding much except that Whisk had something extremely important he wanted her to know about. *What was it?*

There by the steps down to the Crop Circle, he stood with intense presence, his tongue panting, his normally floppy ears turned upward: *Zoe, yesterday afternoon I conducted a 'Trial Run' (literally). Two hundred and ninety-seven dogs by my actual count zoomed down the streets and alleys to a dog park near Crossroads Avenue. What a Canine Convention!*

He transmitted rapid-fire mental-vision-pictures to her absorbent child's mind: From pocket-size Chihuahuas, Shih Tzu's and Miniature Dachshunds to medium-sized Australian Shepherds, Labs, Huskies and Terriers all the way to Saint Bernards and Great Danes.

Funny thing, Zoe wondered, *all the dogs I see in my mind are not running in random motion like they normally would. They're all calmly sitting in a semi-circle in my imagination. What sense does that make?*

Next thing she knew Zoe was recalling all the times she'd begged her Dad for a puppy. What a puppy-parade passed before her: Teacup Pomeranians like tiny teddy bears, cute and spunky Scotties, proud, dapper Airedales, floppy-eared Spaniels, sunny Golden Retrievers, adorable mutts thanking her for rescuing them, giant fluffy Akitas like big bears, dogs of all kinds cavorting around her backyard, playing with toys, snuggling with her, what FUN. *If only I had my very own puppy*, she yearned.

She's listening, she's picking up my pictures and feelings and maybe my thoughts, sort-of... but she doesn't know they're coming from ME. Whisk sighed and plunked himself down in front of the crop circle.

"What's going on, Whisk? Are you okay?" The dog began to growl a tiny bit, very softly, partly out of frustration, partly to keep Zoe's attention locked on him. "What's wrong? Are you hungry? Food is in your dish. Wanna come back inside the Kitchen?"

Whisk slumped his snout in-between his stretched-out paws, his brown eyes fixated upward at the young girl in the doorway.

"I guess not," Zoe said out-loud. She went to the dog, knelt by his side and began to stroke his glossy fur. *There goes the tail, wagging away,* thought Zoe, *I guess he's okay now.*

Whisk put his paw firmly on her knee. "Good boy, I love you," Zoe murmured. It seemed a gesture of affection and to some extent it was. Whisk was fond of children. But little did she know that the dog was really expressing a touch of domination over her by putting his paw on top of her, a soft gesture yes but one that said, *I'm in charge of you. Now LISTEN, Human-girl! I've something to TELL you.*

Whisk tried to give Zoe a run-down on what he'd done the day before: *Above the range of Human hearing, I summoned all the neighborhood dogs to rehearse a possible Tactical Move they might be called on to help me with tomorrow or the next day — I speak multiple dog dialects, you know.*

Zoe began to feel the hair on the back of her neck tingling as Whisk's unconditional love flowed around her, caressing her caramel skin. *If only the kids at school,* she thought, *would show me this kind of friendliness, I'd have such a good time there.*

Whisk continued. *Zoe, this is what I said to the Multitude gathered in a semi-circle at the dog park, 'Canines, brave and loving ancient Friends of Mankind through the millennia from cave to castle to kennel, I ask for your help! Too many species are added every day to the Endangered List, even some of our own Fur-Brethren gone forever, the Turnspit Dog who rotated meat above the fire of hungry owners, long-gone, long-gone, the Paisley Terrier who sat on many a fine lady's lap, no more than a memory in historical novels, the Alpine Mastiff who braved the avalanches of time only to lend his DNA to other breeds and go his way along the mountain passes forever.'*

'*Now hear this: Our Foods are False! Many of us sicken before our normal nine or ten years allotted to us times seven. We no longer can just sit, heel and obey, we must help Mankind, those who are almost as smart as we are and who struggle to give unconditional love, our uncanny capability.*'

He continued to tell Zoe what he had said to the assembly of dogs during the Trial Run:

'*Sometime in the next few days I, Dog Whiskerer will call you forth. Heed my whistle in the stratosphere of vibrations for it will summon you. Come when called! Come immediately! On fleet of foot, you shall help our glorious mission — to make True Food for all. Now return home. I 'The One The Only' have spoken!*'

Whisk was out of breath from all this hifalutin' talk, his tongue hanging out and panting. *Have I gotten through to Zoe? Is she impressed? Sounds good, doesn't it! ...Doesn't it?*

Suddenly out of absolutely nowhere, as if bursting through a parchment hoop in the circus of Time, Nefertiti landed on top of a bush that began shaking back and forth. She leaped down and sauntered over to Whisk.

Zoe didn't notice. She was distracted, plucking petals out of her bunch of daisies. "He loves me, he loves me not, he loves me, he loves me not, he loves me... oh darn, he loves me not," she grumbled. (Zoe had a crush on Billy McGillicutty, the same blond-haired boy in her class who had changed seats not to sit next to her in the school bus that morning.) She hadn't noticed that the cat had materialized out of nowhere.

Wait a minute, wait a minute!!, meowed Nefertiti, sending her protest directly into Whisk's consciousness like a dart tossed into the bullseye. *I'm not buying this! Dogs don't communicate like THAT! What did you REALLY say to all those dogs yesterday?*

Oh, darn. I was just trying to impress Zoe, Whisk confessed. The cat had caught him fibbing. He elaborated, *Actually, Will wrote that speech for me and I tried to memorize it and what you heard was whatever I could remember. But here's what I really said to the dogs...*

Yes?, interrupted the cat with a scornful set of meows, tapping her paws on the crumpled grass in the crop circle, *Tell me the truth, don't pretend it's some overblown dissertation. You dogs are smart, but you can only do one thing at a time, just like most Male Humans. We Cats can multi-task and guess what: I've been to the Future. Glad to be back. But I know where the Four of us can meet up if we need to! Crossroads Avenue. From there we can see the whole city. Now, what exact thing did you say to all those dogs?*

Okay, it wasn't long. It was simple, admitted Whisk. *Just five words — a perfect Dog Command. That's how I got them all there. Here goes:*

'Come.'

And they came.

'See.'

And they looked.

'Sniff.'

They wiggled their noses.

'Conquer.'

And they... well, they didn't conquer yet. We're not on our Mission until tomorrow. But they will. And finally, I motivated the crowd with just one word,

'Treats!'

When the time comes I'll spin my whiskers into a froth and utter this: 'Come-See-Sniff-Conquer-Treats!' The Trial Run worked like a champ. Boy did they ever run! Works for me!

Congrats, Whisk! I like it. If we're in trouble, no long-winded speeches are gonna help. Five thought-words and two-to-three hundred dogs coming to our aid, that's PERfect! And the cat began to purr loudly.

"Oh, Nefertiti," Zoe noticed, "you've been in the backyard all this time. I was looking all over for you. I'm so glad you're safe. Are you hungry?"

At that moment Nefertiti suddenly recognized Zoe as an ancient Nubian Princess who had been taken as a slave and had so charmed the Pharaoh that she became a member of the royal household. "Aida" she was called at that time.

With prowling grace like a leopard stalking prey, Nefertiti slowly paced over to the young girl, sliding her head onto Zoe's arm in loving remembrance of all the times they'd shared so long ago. Zoe loved to feel the cat purring next to her, contented and affectionate. The purring vibrations comforted her from her worries about her Dad.

Maybe she could convince him to get her a kitten along with the puppy!

Oh, goodness, Zoe reminded herself, I've been taking too long out here in the backyard, I better go back in and sweep up that broken dish. Who broke it? Who just left it there? Hazel would never do that! ...Something's off.

Chapter Fourteen

Accidental Destiny

The "Trial Run" incident (of Whisk testing his Dog-Whiskerer powers) had made the "Seven O'clock Local News, Thursday Edition" the night before. A bunch of Talking Heads imparted misinformation in sing-song voices and shook their heads in disbelief while making sure every now and then that their makeup looked good in the visual monitor.

"Where and Why had dogs in over fifty blocks suddenly come running to the Farmcrest Dog Park all at the same time?" Was this, the newscasters speculated, a sign of an upcoming Earthquake? (Runaway dogs had been noted to occur just before Earthquakes, apparently sensing underground rumblings.)

"This puzzling event happened around 3:30 this afternoon. How come a half an hour later all the dogs were back at home, not one missing?" There had been no seismic activities of particular note, the newscasters concluded, flashing an overhead shot of the local Earthquake Center and a close-up of a seismograph registering nothing significant.

Animal behavior experts were consulted on divided screens. They'd never heard of anything like this and only succeeded in interrupting each other and arguing about the effect of overbreeding.

Live interviews of dog owners were conducted: "We're talking to Iris Basoluni, whose dog took off down the street with hundreds of other dogs all converging on a dog park. What do you think of this strange incident?" The microphone popped in front of Mrs. Basoluni's astounded mouth.

"I've... um... never seen anything like it! My Winston was gone -- I named him after Churchill you know, being a bulldog -- and I went looking for him all over but so were all my neighbors. It was weird! Then he came back a half hour later. All those cars going down the street with upset folks calling for their missing dogs! I have... um... no idea why?"

Helicopter shots of dozens of cars moving slowly down the streets were broadcast, with videos of people leaning out of car windows or on bikes, yelling, "Fletcher! Come!" or "Sophie, supper, come here, girl!" The Newscasters dubbed it "The Great Dog Escapade."

Zoe hardly ever watched TV after school and had no idea about Whisk's Trial Run the day before. The Baker Family had left for a Hat Convention that same Thursday at 5 p.m. and had given Zoe their keys to take care of the pets. Friday had gone off to a bad start with her Dad preoccupied about something troubling (she had no idea what), Whisk acting hyper, and the Casual Friday fiasco at school. Then it had gone from bad to worse when Harvey had brought her exhausted, morose father home. *What a day!*

Now Zoe was sitting in the Baker's backyard next to a messy pile of daisy petals, looking forlorn.

Maybe I'll try another daisy to see if he loves me after all, she was thinking. *No, that's cheating.* Whisk sat by her on the grass with his paw on her knee, sensing her mood and trying to cheer her up. Suddenly Nefertiti had shown up out of nowhere, jumped down from a shaking bush, glared at the dog for a second and came over to nuzzle Zoe.

Where have you been, Nefertiti? wondered Zoe. *I looked and looked all over for you. What a strange kitty you are, always running off somewhere. I better feed you, then clean up that broken dish and get home to Dad.*

Zoe brought both animals back into the kitchen, careful to maneuver them away from the broken dish on the floor. After the pets were shooed into the living-room to rest, she began to sweep the porcelain pieces carefully into a dustpan. It was Hazel's favorite serving plate. She had no intention of throwing the fragments away. It was just safer to sweep the pieces up with a broom and dustpan than for her to pick up the sharp-edged bits with her bare hands.

All of a sudden Zoe was taken aback when a voice, a mischievous little voice speaking in plain English, was yelling at her. The voice was coming out of the old Breadbox's inside! *What??*

"Don't throw it aWAY!!" said the voice.

Maybe I need as much sleep as Dad, thought Zoe. *Am I hearing things?*

"Don't throw it aWAY!!" repeated the little voice.

"Huh?" exclaimed Zoe, cautiously walking over to the antique Breadbox.

"Who are you?" said the voice.

"Who are YOU?" responded Zoe.

"You go first." The whatever-it-was inside the Breadbox had edged up close to the tin door, leaning on it to open it enough to see who was in the kitchen sweeping up the pieces that once were Dish.

"No, YOU go first." Zoe was partly scared, partly fascinated.

"I'm Crumb. That's all you need to know for now. I haven't had much Human Interaction. But you look kind of nice for a first introduction."

"This is not happening, not really. You mean you are a crumb, a breadcrumb, and you can talk and I'm talking to you?? Have I had 'silly juice' or something in my lunch-box today or just too much homework to get enough sleep?"

"No, I'm real, as real as you. I just HAD to speak up because Dish is in there somewhere and maybe she's recoverable, still alive and I can't just abandon her and let you put her in the garbage.... Am I making any sense?"

"No."

"Will you put down that dustpan and let it sit on the breakfast table or counter, PLEEZE?"

"Why? I'm not going to throw these broken pieces of a dish away! I promise."

"You mean that?" asked the voice from the Breadbox. Zoe put the dustpan down on the Kitchen table and nodded.

"Thanks! Phew. Dish was a kind of friend, ya know. Well, maybe not a good one. But I didn't want her to die."

"I don't want my Daddy to die. He fainted and had some kind of awful upset today at work. I have to get back and take care of him in a few minutes."

"Oh. Okay. You're lucky. You have a Daddy. I'm an orphan. Do you have a Mommy too?"

"Um, that's a personal question and I don't usually talk to breadcrumbs in somebody else's Kitchen."

"Well, DO you? A real Mommy?"

Zoe's voice fell about an octave. "I used to. She died when I was six. Two years ago." (Her voice resumed its cheerful tone.) "Say, can I see what you look like? I still am having trouble believing all this. You're a crumb?"

Crumb slowly opened up Breadbox's door from the inside. Breadbox was snoring softly and enjoying a nap after all the festivities of the night before -- he was still tired.

"Shhhhh, don't wake Breadbox, okay?"

"I've never woken up a Breadbox in my life."

"It's 'awakened'. You've never 'awakened' a Breadbox in your life."

"Gee whiz. You're not only a TALKing Crumb, you're a gramMATical Crumb. Just my luck. I better pinch myself. This is sooooo weird." (She squeezed a pad of skin on her forearm.) "Ouch!"

At that moment, Crumb opened the tin door wide enough to come out of Breadbox. The late afternoon sun was slowly descending in the sky, making pink and lilac clouds show through the Kitchen window. Crumb's golden brown surface was dusted with the pastel glow of the setting sun. He looked like a sparkling round fairy-figure from some ancient folktale. Zoe's eyes were as big as the centers of the daisies she had picked, and she couldn't even scream or talk or move.

Here was a future young-woman, quite mature for her age who thought she had outgrown fairy tales and purely imaginative journeys since she had adopted the scientific logic of her Dad. Especially since her father was in need of being taken care of, Zoe had demanded a grown-up manner of herself and a firm grasp of reality.

But this was REAL! A talking crumb, about as big as a grapefruit seed, golden brown and roly-poly and awfully cute but completely beyond-belief, looking at her with blue eyes and a tentative smile of welcome.

"I've been wanting to meet you for a very long time. You're Zoe. You're pretty and smart. (Breadbox says you're very well-read)."

"Breadbox?"

"Yeah, he's my Granddad. He taught me to read. Inspired by you and a love of ancient traditions. I must admit that up close like this you are VERY, VERY BIG and I hope you're not going to smash me with your fingers.... Uh, by accident, I mean. Right? This is my first time to be holding a discussion with a... what I mean is, I've never talked with a... a HUman before."

"Don't be scared, little bread-thing. If I'm not hallucinating, then you deserve to be well taken-care of. I'm curious about how you're able to talk and read. Can you spell too? I'm a champion speller, I've won the Regional Spelling Bee two years in a row. Sadly, speaking of bees, all my bees died a few months ago, hive death."

"Really? I know a bee. I'll tell him about you and see if he wants to interview you about Human Lifestyles. But I'll have to ask him first. He's kind of busy. He's practicing his aeronautical skills right now. I had to outfit him with a miniature pilot's scarf and goggles."

"Why is a bee practicing aeronautical skills? He was born with them, I would think. He can FLY, right?"

"Yeah, but he has to carry a large cargo. ME. I... I shouldn't be telling you any of this. But maybe he'll want to meet you. I know you're smart and talented. Do you happen to have any highly unusual SKILLS, Zoe? Do you know the city streets like the back of your hand?"

"I've been told I'm quite street-smart. I think I know most of the streets around here. Why?"

"Oh, just trying to know you better. Do you speak French? Know about Egyptology? Solve riddles?"

"What's this all about, Crumb?"

Crumb had spoken out of turn. He backtracked, "Uh, just curious. I have a wide variety of interests and was just inquiring if we shared any of those. I'm the only crumb in the whole world who can read." He began to sing, "A-B-C-D-E-F-G... H-I-J-K... *L-M-N-O-P....*"

"Oh you sing too?!" (She thought, dumbfounded, *A singing crumb. What's next? I better find out what else this crumb can do.*) "Have you read any Shakespeare?" asked Zoe.

"No, but the bee has. '2 Bee or not 2 Bee, that is the question,' he always says. He's a genius."

"If he's half as smart as you are, Crumb, he must be. I'll have to be very careful next time I make Toast!"

"TOAST?" cried Crumb. He began to shudder.

"Well, maybe I'll skip toast for a while until we get to know each other better. And yes, I have skills. I have a brown belt, almost the very best one you can earn in Karate, I can play piano pretty well and I do Ballet."

All of a sudden, Spoon woke up. "Ballet?! You know how to do Fifth Position?" (Spoon had never been able to make the solid bottom part of her handle open up into two partitions, which would have served as "feet" to make that position possible. She was always pretending that her one "leg" could do all the ballet positions. Nevertheless, her pirouetting, bowing and jeté leaps were graceful in the best balletic tradition.)

To demonstrate, Zoe moved her legs and arms into Fifth Position, then did an arabesque.

"Crumb," said Spoon, "I have to meet this girl. She's inspiring!"

"What a day this is," said Zoe, "First a crumb, then a spoon. I'm goin' nuts or else I'm having the best best time EVer. I prefer to think it's the last possibility."

"I have a question. Is it possible to check out if that broken dish is... is... 'D'-'E'-'A'-'D' or alive? Can you find out for us?" (Crumb spoke the letter names "D" and all the others one letter after the other so as not to say "dead" out-loud.)

Just then the big central part of what once was Dish, the tummy with her fruit bowl in the middle (fortunately still containing her eyes, nose, mouth and ears) started to stir a bit and moan.

"She's aLIVE! What's left of her, aLIVE!!" shouted Crumb and Spoon.

"Oh great, now I'm hearing a DISH too? I'll never be able to tell my Dad. Uh-oh, my Dad is waiting for me. I have to water the plants and stop talking to a crumb of bread, a spoon who dances and a near-death-experience plate."

Zoe plunked herself down in a chair, leaned on the Kitchen table with her chin in her palm and looked very dazed.

"I hope Whisk didn't pee on the Crop Circle when he was outside," speculated Crumb. "I'm trying to keep it in good shape."

"CROP circle?" said Zoe. "You mean there's a Crop Circle in the backyard?"

"Yup, go check it out for yourself."

Zoe went to the back door, opened it, looked up at the pink and violet sunset sky, but jumped back when she saw the grass. A HAPPY FACE carved in the grass! Just like Crumb had said. (*How had I missed seeing this when I was outside a minute ago?* she asked herself. *Sometimes things are so unreal that they become invisible.*)

"What is going ON around here? Do the Bakers know about this?"

"Well, they know there is a crop circle on their property, but they don't have a clue about me... or Spoon or Breadbox or Timer or Toaster or Dish or... "

"Sometimes Grownups can be so CLUEless, huh." This was Zoe saying this.

Crumb was surprised to hear her admit this. (*Children are small too like me*, he reasoned, *small compared to grownups at any rate. Maybe children have a certain perspective on Big People that entitles them to see through their parents at times and helps them forgive their parents for not being perfect. Parents are mostly trying to do their best but CLUELESS sometimes.*)

In fact, that's who Zoe was thinking about just then: Her Dad, sick at home, needing her.

"Listen I have to get back to my Dad, he's not doin' all that well. So long, be well, don't get eaten, Crumb. I like you. Stay polished, Spoon. And see what you can do to fix Dish up so she'll have a long shelf-life, okay? Maybe that genius bee will know what to do."

"Good idea! I'll get with Will. He knows EV'rything... almost. Bye, Zoe! Come and visit us again, okay?" She nodded.

Zoe went into the living-room with the watering can, poured a bit of water into the two plants, puffed the couch pillows up, moved a few magazines to a rack and dashed out of the house, key and wilted daisies in hand, locking the door tight.

No one's gonna believe this, she thought, *I don't even believe this myself. I'll check on Dad, make him some broth and tea, and go to bed myself. Maybe this will all make better sense in the morning.*

On the way back to her house to take care of her Dad, Zoe encountered Will reviewing his flight plan and practicing special aeronautics maneuvers. He kept on repeating, "Aviate, Navigate, Communicate." (This was the mantra laying out the priorities to take when flying a plane. First you had to handle the mechanical skills of flying the plane, then came attention to where you were and where you were headed, then last came talking to Flight Control or other pilots in very concise responses.)

His aviator's scarf was wafting in the breeze and his goggles were tight, as he flipped here and there, upside down, doing whirlies and stalls and numerous air-circus and barnstorming high-jinks.

"Zoe, Zoe! I've missed you!" buzzed the yellow-and-black winged aviator, hovering in front of her nose at about eight inches away.

This was too much for Zoe. A crumb that talked, a spoon that danced ballet, a dish that lay near-death, and now a figment of her overactive imagination, since (in her mind) all the bees in their backyard hive had died.

"Really now! I'm out of my mind! Seeing spots. Maybe I've got whatever virus hit Dad today!"

"No, you're perfectly fine. I'm the last Bee in the hive and I'm going to save all the bees everywhere."

"Oh, is that all?" Zoe was super-skeptical and dying to plop into her comfy bed.

"You bet, my motto is 'Where there's Will, there's a WAY!' I'm Will. I'm the smartest thing on Earth."

"And modest too!"

"Listen, I'll prove to you I know you, and once lived in your backyard in the hive."

"Okay, as a Junior Scientist, I need some concrete proof."

"Your Dad works at AlliedGreene Corporation."

Surprised, she answered, "That's true."

"I don't want to get too personal but I have to say this next part to prove I'm who I am.... "

"Okay, go ahead."

"You lost your Mom two years ago, you just bought a new outfit, you cook extremely well, you are super-cool at martial arts, piano and ballet and you have a crush on a boy at school who won't give you the time of day. You also eat organic and like to read cereal boxes."

"Pretty good. Sounds just like me. Who told you all this?"

"My head, my heart and my very soul."

"Good answer. Somethings are beyond proof in a test-tube. Even my Dad..."

"He's a scientist..."

"Right, even my Dad says that sometimes intuition is the best way to zero in on truth."

Will landed his bee-plane on her shoulder, gently. He paused and in hushed voice confessed, "Guess what... I have a crush on you, Zoe."

"Awwwwww..." Zoe blushed and the bee flew around her cornrow braids out of sheer joy.

"Can we be pals now?" said Will. "I have a cool project I want to tell you about, if I swear you to secrecy. You might even want to be part of it."

"Sure. We ARE pals, and I'm beginning to recognize you now." Zoe squinted her eyes at the bee, recalling him now as someone who stood out from the hive. "You were the runt of the worker-bee litter. That's amazing you made it out safely for some reason. When can we meet so you can tell me all about whatever-it-is, your secret project? I have to get home -- can you tell me about it right now very quickly?"

"No, there's a lot to it. How about very, very early tomorrow morning. Six or so in the morning, just around daybreak?"

"I'll try. In the morning I have to make sure my Dad's okay first -- he had a rough day today. But I'd like to. Where do you want me to show up?"

"Out on the Crop Circle. The shrub-fence hides us. The Bakers aren't coming back until Sunday night."

"Okay, I'll show up," said Zoe. "Gotta run. But, Will, there's a dish in the Kitchen that needs fixing up. I swept it up gently and it's in a dustpan on the Kitchen table. But it's really in trouble. Can you get back there now and take charge of the repairs? She might make it, if you do some delicate procedures."

"Like what? Dish betrayed us last night!" (Will realized he was being vindictive.) "But yeah, I don't like to see her die. I'll see what we can do back there."

"Good. It's great to see you alive and well, ol' friend! Bye! See you tomorrow morning."

Inside her psyche, deep in the core of her essence, she was realizing: *When something happens, it's best to see it for what it is.* If this was really real, she needed to admit it to herself, accept it, maybe even embrace it. It certainly bore the traces of magic.

An eight-year-old, no matter how grown-up she has had to become in order to meet challenges, and no matter how pressured by the needs and duties of everyday life she has become, keeps part of herself foraging for excitement in the Realm of Magic. Zoe had been forced to grow up before her time in order to replace her irreplaceable Mother. So she had never really shared with anyone her hunger for magic.

Especially since her Dad, being a scientist, had buried himself in his work to escape loss. Magic was what Zoe yearned for, even more than a puppy. THAT was Zoe's deepest secret. Magic and the belief in it had marinated in the essence of herself, imagination was her unspoken truth... and a truth unspoken becomes a secret after a while.

Zoe skipped all the way back home, made broth and tea for her Dad, brought him a tray and insisted he sip all of it slowly and then get plenty of rest.

"I'm doing better, Honeybun. What took you so long?"

Zoe had a strict policy not to lie to her Dad. Taking a second to figure out something that was sufficiently truthful, she said, "There was a broken dish in the Kitchen, I had to take care of that, plump up the pillows, water the plants, make sure the dog and cat would get fed, put them in the backyard for a moment...."

"Wait, I'm getting tired just hearing about all this. Let me get some rest now. You too." He sighed, noticing Zoe's probing glance. "I just had a tough day at work, that's all."

Zoe didn't necessarily buy that. "What IS going on, Dad?"

"Zoe, let's not go there, not tonight. It's going to be fine, I promise. What time do you think we should get up?"

"Get UP? You're sleeping IN tomorrow, Dad -- It's gonna be Saturday anyway. Take the weekend off, for goodness sake. It's about time you got some decent rest."

"Now don't spoil me."

"SOMEone has to. Now get some shut-eye, Dr. Baruti."

She didn't even have to say a thing, he was out in a few seconds. Zoe stayed, patting the blanket, watching his breath go in and out, still feeling breathless herself about all the totally wild things that had happened to her in the last hour. In a few minutes, Matt was snoring gently.

Zoe tiptoed to her bedroom and got under the covers. She stared at the wallpaper for a while before she clicked her bedside lamp off --- the wall was real, the wallpaper was real, her bed was real, but everything solid around her had the tinge of unreality. There was something so pervasive about her meeting up with Crumb, Spoon and Will at the Baker's that made it seem MORE real than anything else.

It was LIFE, lived in an expansive way by tiny creatures who didn't let their size influence their wide sphere of action. Will had wingspread and brilliance, Crumb had strength of character and muscle, Spoon had grace and a sense of having lived history. Whisk had been trying to tell her something and the cat had the knack of showing up at exactly the right time.

Zoe couldn't help feeling that somehow these meetings today had some greater purpose, that they hadn't just been accidents. She fell into a deep slumber dreaming about crop circles and daisies, breadcrumbs and broken dishes.

As Will was waving goodbye to Zoe watching her skip home, he wished he could follow her. He missed his Bee Family so much that his thorax hurt. The hive in Zoe's backyard had once teemed with activity, now it was just an empty shell. Tomorrow at dawn the Four would set off on their Mission and if they could decipher the Riddle well enough, other bee colonies could be saved. He hoped Zoe would join them. She was the one Human that Will completely trusted, full of life energy, resourceful, kind and smart.

I'll never forget Zoe standing by her front door with her key, waving back at me. I hope she'll show up tomorrow morning to find out about what we're going to do and "sign on" to the Mission.

Suddenly Will remembered that she had asked him to go home to check on Dish. It was time to stop practicing aeronautics and head back to the Kitchen. The sun was beginning to set anyway and soon Will would have trouble following Visual Flight Rules. The bee removed his goggles and scarf and headed back to the Kitchen.

It wasn't going to be easy to help Dish out. When Will arrived at the Baker's house, the windows were all closed. So were all the doors. Zoe had locked the house up for the night.

He HAD to get back inside the Kitchen somehow. For one thing, if the Four were going to leave early enough tomorrow morning, he was the one slated to wake up his cohorts in time. Hovering outside the Kitchen window, Will spotted the silhouette of Crumb through the muslin curtains. The bread-ball stood on the counter near Breadbox, staring glumly down at the dustpan on the Kitchen table where Dish and her remnants lay. Try as Will did, fluttering in circles behind the window pane as close to Crumb as possible, he could not get the unhappy breadcrumb to notice him. Crumb's attention was fixated on the broken plate, worrying what to do.

Finally in desperation, Will steeled himself to attempt a modified kamikaze bang into the windowpane, just loud enough to be heard. Fortunately the impact was not hard enough to damage the bee. Crumb's attention jolted off of Dish when he heard the noise. He looked up, pulled the curtains open and saw Will fluttering outside. With his new strength Crumb was easily able to hoist the window open a crack and Will flew in.

The setting sun was illuminating the Kitchen cabinets and appliances with shimmering rainbows. Will zoomed over to the Kitchen table and hovered over the shattered plate to inspect the damage. The violet and rose of sunset gave the porcelain pieces an otherworldly glow like the vapor of a ghost. The shards along Dish's edges were not responding at all. The inside circle of Dish was intact. Where the fruit bowl had once been in the middle of her tummy, it was now her nose. Her eyes and mouth were there unharmed -- she was alive, but different.

Dish had lost all her outer pretenses, the jealousy, the snobbery, the affectations rimmed in gold. All her ostentation had fallen to bits when she had plummeted to the floor. The only thing that had survived was her HEART, the central part of her. It alone had not broken. Before her fall she had been artificial, envious and terrified to have her heart broken in pieces. Now the central core of her had survived. She was ready to apologize. She had learned her lesson. But would she ever be trusted again?

"I'm so sorry, Will and Crumb. I followed a destructive impulse and it nearly destroyed me. My heart is intact, it is the circle of my being -- the rest has splintered, it's gone. I'm glad to be alive and so sorry to have spied on you. Will you forgive me?"

Crumb and Will thought about it. *What would Breadbox have said?*, wondered Crumb. Granddad was fast asleep and it was no time to wake him up to ask for his advise. Crumb and Will looked at each other and shared the same thought: *Dish has to be given some kind of chance.*

"Maybe, perhaps. It's really up to you," pondered the little bread-ball, taking on the considered tone of his Granddad. "First things first. You need to rest up and recover. Recovering our trust is something ELSE. Maybe there's a way you can show us you can be trusted again. I'm not promising anything. If we fix you..."

Will broke in with "I have a clever idea about how to do that, so you look quite pretty once again."

Not now, thought Crumb, *Will, you're jumping in too soon again. Dish has not proven herself trustworthy yet, and it isn't time to tell her about how we'll fix her up all pretty.*

Crumb continued, "We might need your help... toMORrow night." Crumb sent a silent explanation over to Will, *She could act as our Lookout for the mission. But tonight is too soon when she's in this much trouble. I don't think we should leave in the morning.*

Will shot a look at Crumb right away. *TOMORROW night? Not tonight? I thought we were taking off as soon as the sun comes up? Why are you putting this off for a whole day?*

Look, shot back Crumb, *this Dish thing has thrown us off but maybe it's not such a bad thing. Maybe it's one of those Life Lessons Breadbox told me about. Expect the unexpected. Go with the flow....*

Maybe you're right, answered Will, thinking it over. *I haven't had a chance yet to practice flying with YOU on my back. That would give us more time. We ALL could use more rest. The Mission will need us at peak energy.*

True, answered Crumb, and hoping this wouldn't insult Will, he added, *and maybe that'll give you more time to figure out the REST of the Riddle.*

That riled the bee up a little. *Look, I TOLD you some of this is gonna have to be done 'in transit.'*

Crumb frowned. Will softened, *Somebody has to look after Dish, like it or not. Okay, I advise a postponement. We leave Sunday as soon as the sun starts to rise. Okay, Project Leader?*

Crumb nodded and looked down at Dish (what was left of her) and offered, "Tomorrow night, if you agree to stay up all Saturday night and be a Lookout for us --- to warn us if need be, if you do that for us and do it well, we'll fix you up. You won't be as gorgeous as you once were, but you won't look like you do now, that's for sure."

Dish felt a chip near one of her eyes fall off like a tear. "Yes, I want to make up the damage. I'm all heart now, no more phony selfish splinters, they're all gone."

"I'll have to let Whisk and Nefertiti know about the change of plans." Will paused, trying to remember something. "Oh yeah, and Zoe too. I invited her to the Crop Circle in the morning to see if she's willing to help us." Crumb lit up. Having a Human along, a clever one who knew karate and could think on her toes, might be helpful.

The night settled in around the Four like a warm blanket and they slept more deeply than they had anticipated, knowing that they wouldn't have to face the challenges at the crack of dawn. Sometimes what looks like disaster and delay can prove to be a blessing, sometimes procrastination provides more restful sleep... at least for a while.

Chapter Fifteen

Awakenings

Saturday morning rose like a promise, hopeful yet unfulfilled. Zoe opened the door to her Dad's bedroom a notch. He was snoring away, huddled in a messy pile of blankets, hugging his favorite pillow. *Good. Sound asleep. I'll go over to the Baker's to take care of the dog and cat but more important, I'll have to tell Will and Crumb that I have to stay home today. I wish I could help them on whatever Mission it is, but Dad needs me. I hope they'll understand.*

Zoe dressed and left her Dad a little note in front of his bedroom door: "6:12 am. Gone to the Baker's. Back soon. You rest. --Zoe"

As Zoe made her way in the early morning fog, Toaster woke up with a start, suspicious that something was going on under his nose.

Who pushed Dish out of the cabinet?, he wondered. *I'll have to investigate. She's off the floor. Where is she? Oh now I see her. Over in that dustpan on the table. No one in the Family could be responsible. They left Thursday afternoon, before all that Partying we did. Aha! Those must be Zoe's fingerprints on the handle of the dustpan. Very suspicious. (She seems like such a nice young girl. You never can tell. These days, what is happening with our youth?!) Well, I better give her the benefit of the doubt, maybe it was one of the Kitchen Things. I'll figure this out. It's the little clues, the tiny details, that's how Sherlock always worked.*

Toaster's dial was squarely on Dark.

Breadbox opened up his door to let some sunshine in and wake Crumb and his little cousins. Crumb wasn't inside! He had slept on the counter so as not to wake Breadbox before morning. *That was curious* noticed Toaster.

"Hi, Granddad. I didn't want to wake you, you were so sound-asleep. Can we study cartography this morning? I have always wanted to know how to read maps." *That's curious too,* thought Toaster. *Why the switch from French poetry?*

S.K. was leaning over the counter, glaring down at the floor, looking morose and cynical. Toaster observed him carefully. The knife was feeling especially guilty: *How was I to know she'd fall? She asked me and I just went ahead and opened her cabinet door. I've become too attached to her and follow her every whim. NOW look what happened.*

"Isn't it a shame! She's over on the table now," Toaster said with a sympathetic tone, trying to hide his suspicions. He attempted to push his dial over to Light but it wouldn't budge off the Dark Setting so Toaster tried to act nonchalant by asking in a casual voice, "Where did you happen to be, S. K., when this unfortunate crash happened?"

"Asleep. Where were YOU?" Sharpest Knife had learned from CUTTING EDGE RECIPES that the best way to handle a dull probe was to rub back and forth on the sharpening tool, so he threw the question right back at the Detective.

"What time is it?" yawned the Timer, embarrassed that he had overslept. The Family was gone and he felt rather useless.

The tea bags were beginning to open up their little box lids and peek out at the sunshine. Soon all the Kitchen Things were wide awake, all except Rolling Pin who dozed inside her drawer. *I wonder why she isn't coming out?*, suspected Toaster, *Hiding perhaps? She has a violent streak. Maybe she was jealous of Dish....*

Will had slept in the Kitchen overnight, hiding behind the garbage can. Now that the sun was up he stayed behind the garbage can, keeping one eye open and both ears active, trying not to flutter his wings against the metal. How was he going to make it out to the backyard with Crumb to practice their flying together without any Kitchen Thing -- especially that nosy Toaster -- making a fuss or interrogating him? Fortunately the window was still open a crack. Will angled his body over to one side of the garbage can where he could see Crumb heading into Breadbox for his daily lesson.

Smart fellow, thought the bee, *Cartography! That might come in handy when we're on our Mission. Now, about our meeting this morning, I can fly outside through the window-crack. How about if I ask Whisk to scoop Crumb up on one of his famous whiskers when Crumb gets done with his lesson. That way Whisk can get the bread-ball outside so we can practice our flying.*

For the first time Will noticed the doggie-door in the Kitchen door -- that's how Whisk and Nefertiti would be able to go to the backyard. *Actually, we should all meet as soon as possible. It won't hurt to go over our plans again. We can do it outside after Crumb's lesson. Then we can use today to practice skills and to rest.*

After Crumb had finished his Cartography Lesson, Will signaled to him from behind the trashcan. The Four moved out to the backyard to go over their strategies for the next morning's Mission.

The first order of the day was to go over each line of the Riddle and answer any questions anybody had. Will presided but made sure that Crumb took the lead in answering the questions in his position as Project Leader. If Crumb didn't know the answer, then Will as Advisor supplied as best an answer as he could come up with.

One line in particular ("When green is red and 'N' turns to 'D' ") still made no sense to any of them. Crumb shrugged uncomfortably when Will had to repeat once again that there were some puzzling aspects of the Riddle that would only make sense when they were mid-Mission.

Oh great, do you have to repeat that, Will? I'm tired of hearing 'in-transit', 'in-transit', 'we won't know until we get there'! Crumb was frustrated with the fragments of the Riddle that still didn't piece together and frankly, he was scared. If the smartest thing on the planet hadn't solved it by now, what a huge chance they were all taking.

Will's answer (to soothe Crumb's annoyance) was to put Crumb's attention on his Cartography lesson, so he began to ask him questions about the location of various landmarks in the city and the layout of the major streets. Crumb answered as best he could and then began to go into the history of maps and how it was important to know how to find due North.

Nefertiti rolled her eyes -- as if an ancient Egyptian had to be told about the orientation of the sun and stars and how to spot landmarks on a map. Pyramids were based on all that. She was squirming on the grass, chafing in annoyance, until finally the other three looked at her and said -- simultaneously -- "What's up with you, cat?"

Nefertiti stretched her regal neck in defiance. "Just a little minute here! I've been patient enough. I have some

NEWS you haven't heard before... and if you ask nicely, maybe I'll tell you."

Cats! Crumb thought. *You can't act condescending to them but you have to cajole them or do whatever it takes sometimes!* Will shot a look over to the bread-ball. He was thinking the same thing.

Only Whisk was smiling confidently. Nefertiti had told him yesterday something about what she'd done -- at least he thought he knew what her "news" was.

Will and Crumb began to beg her and thank her so much that she began to preen herself so she would look her best for the announcement. Whisk simply bowed his head and sat down on the crop circle grass, wagging his tail especially wide. Sometimes it was far smarter to see things with a certain simplicity than to mull over all kinds of complex facts and theories. Dogs knew that instinctively.

After the cat considered the others had paid her sufficient homage -- and, in a sense, she was DUE that, because little did they know what risks she had actually taken -- Nefertiti lifted her graceful long neck and proudly announced, "I leaped into the Future yesterday! And here I am now."

All Three inhaled and let out a nearly simultaneous huge breath.

"Really?!! Go on, go on!" they all urged.

Her Leap had not been easy. It was the first time ever that, instead of just envisioning the Future or recalling the Past, she had dared to materialize her entire body there and back. She admitted to them that she had been terrified. The biggest relief came when she found she was able to return back home to the Present without a spot missing on her fur coat, only a few hairs off her tail. (Will looked at her tail -- it did seem a tiny bit sparse just at the tip.)

"What did you find?" Will asked hurriedly, holding his breath.

"Were you able to see the outcome? Were we successful?" urged Crumb, his curiosity making him lean so much toward the cat that he practically fell over.

"Wasn't able to find out, really. In my leap into the Future, all I could see was where an ideal meeting place for us lies. But it's an excellent location. It's not our final destination, but it's a perfect place to find WHERE our destination will BE, a great vantage point. I'll cut to the chase because I can't stand all three of you leering at me, dying to find out: It's Crossroads Avenue, right where a telephone pole, two divergent roads and a railroad track meet."

Crumb and Will had so much tension released by finding this out, that they practically fainted on the lawn. Whisk had figured as much, that Crossroads would be a good place. He'd often visited the telephone pole at Crossroads and had left his mark on it many times. (Although simplicity is a virtue that allows one to cope with tension, it was still going to be up to the complex minds of Will and Crumb to take this foray to victory.)

"Can I continue?" asked Nefertiti, scornful of Will and Crumb for pressuring her to reveal the biggest findings of her Leap into the Future before she could relay all the details.

"Yes, yes! Please, tell us everything," said Will.

"Are you kidding? Don't hold back. We're all ears!" said Crumb.

Whisk wagged his tail so fast on the Crop Circle that blades of grass began to disintegrate and spin into the air.

At that awkward moment, who should arrive but Zoe, apologizing for being a bit late.

"Sorry to interrupt, Nefertiti. Can I just ask one question before I sit down?"

Nefertiti slunk to the grass, sighing. Will, Whisk and Crumb nodded.

"When are you all taking off?" Zoe asked breathlessly. "I need to find out what this is all about."

"We're NOT taking off -- at least, not this morning," answered Crumb.

"You AREN'T?" Zoe was flabbergasted and plunked herself down on the grass to find out why.

"Dish was too sick for us just to leave her. Plus we need today to finalize our plans as much as possible, practice flying with Crumb on my back, and then rest up a LOT. We postponed the whole deal until tomorrow morning." Will looked apologetic, figuring Zoe was going to be disappointed. Instead, she began smiling, her eyes shining with excitement.

She doesn't even know what the 'Project' is and she's exCITed? thought Will. *Go figure! HUMANS! Maybe she'll change her mind once she finds out it's not just a trip to the local museum or an ice cream parlor.*

"I can't believe this!" said Zoe. "I was really feeling bummed out because I was going to have to tell you I couldn't leave today on this Project or whatever-it-is. My Dad is wiped out after a horrible day at work, and I need to tend to him and make sure he really rests up and recovers." Zoe began jumping up and down on the Crop Circle, which added more grass pieces to the ones that Whisk had whipped up.

"Don't you think you ought to get an overview of what we'll be trying to accomplish tomorrow? It's not going to be a picnic. I'm fond of you, Zoe, and don't want you to get hurt!" Will felt fatherly about this amazing eight-year-old who had tended his hive so lovingly.

"Yeah, I guess I rushed into a commitment on this too early. I'm just so jazzed that I can talk to all of you now, ever since yesterday when I found out Kitchen Things are alive! It's so magical. I forgot my common sense, didn't I."

At that, Crumb was very touched and proposed that a group hug was in order, as long as no one got crushed. Will protested, saying that magic is one thing and common sense is another and sometimes the two aspects need each other too much to take such an ungainly risk as a group hug. "Oh darn!" sulked the breadcrumb. "Just saying... "

Suddenly everyone began to laugh -- it was such a ridiculous image! How would a breadcrumb and a bee not get smashed (or at the very least, slightly crumpled) between a dog, a cat, and an eight-year-old Girl-child.

"You're sooooo cute, Crumb," Zoe said. "How about if I hug you ever so carefully, just you." So saying, she put the breadcrumb on her forefinger, carried Crumb to her cheek, then her shoulder and laid him, beaming, back on the lawn.

"Now that's what I call a hug!" exclaimed the morsel of bread, even if it had only been a gentle trip to her cheek and shoulder.

"So what's this Project all about?" Zoe asked.

Will proceeded to lay out the Mission's bold purpose and basic strategic plan. Zoe learned about the Alien Abduction and how the Four had received special gifts. Then Will recited the entire Riddle to her -- several times, actually --- having memorized it by heart and gone over it so many times trying to fathom every last nuance of it that he could just rattle it off.

Zoe leaned forward, holding her breath from time to time, gasping in excitement. "I'm 'IN'! You guys need me! I'm so passionate about real food, organic food, and I have skills you need, brown belt and all. I have always enjoyed helping to solve Riddles. (I'm good with Scrabble and Cross Word Puzzles.) If need be, I can call for help on my cell phone. That's something you guys can't do. I can be here tomorrow morning around six. Will you accept me into your select group?"

Crumb, Will and Whisk cheered and Nefertiti waved her tail, knowing that Aida (for the cat recognized Zoe as such from their time together in ancient Egypt) would be an excellent Intelligence Agent, Warrior-Woman, and certainly would NOT want to be enslaved or buried alive during their adventure.

Now the Four had become the Five.

Nefertiti had been patient, but patience is an acquired skill with cats and only lasts as long as fresh cream, catnip or a ball of yarn are offered soon afterwards. None of those were available out there in the Baker's backyard and Nefertiti was chaffing at the bit.

"Can I PLEEZE tell you about my Leap into the Future, FINALLY?" she scowled ferociously, her gooseberry green eyes rolling around in frustration. Getting eager nods, she began to describe her Time Travel Trip, but had an important thought. *Will, will you translate some of this if Zoe doesn't understand? I may be sharing my journey mostly via thought-transference, but every now and then I'll throw in cat-words like Meow or Alien dialect like Ka-punga-Tonga.* Will agreed.

"Here's what happened on my trip. And listen to me, before you ask any more questions. It's been very wearying to materialize my body into the Future or the Past and then get all of me back here to the Present. WAS and IS and WILL BE all roll around on a giant Wave of Time. It's tricky. So you have to pay attention. And don't interrupt."

Nefertiti stretched herself regally on the grass, assuming the ancient posture of Bastet, Cat Goddess, and began telling her Companions about her journey through the Space-Time Continuum. She mostly relied on thought-pictures sent to the Four, but every now and then she meowed her story, hoping that actual sounds might help Zoe understand what she was saying. And so her narration began.

The first second of her leap forward had felt like the whole universe had cracked. Then there she was in a new place. Somehow Nefertiti had found herself looking down over the entire city as if it were a claymation map:

Little cars, buses and trucks running on winding streets, tiny people walking, running, shopping, playing, being born, dying, falling in love, tiny specks of people, trees breathing oxygen into the air, riverways of water with marbleized strands of pollution like red streams of blood cutting zigzag-y patterns through blue water, yellow smoke from factory chimneys, the faint sounds of laughter and tears floating like clouds above the city.

Suddenly she saw a prime destination, a junction from which two very different paths extended outward in the shape of a "Y." Crossroads Avenue. Perhaps it was the hill that led up to it that made it easy to see the city spread out before her eyes. Perhaps it was the train tracks crossing like a horizon at the meeting place of two roads that made it seem a Viewing Dock from which to survey all of the city. *Maybe,* she guessed, *this "Y" of an avenue will help us choose which path to take, to the right or the left.* Somehow this place seemed a symbol of the choices they would have to make to solve the Why (the reason and purpose) for their Mission.

Zooming down to a telephone pole in the exact middle of Crossroads Avenue, right where the train track met two city streets (and where the Doctor had had to stop and wait for the train on his way to work the day before), Nefertiti saw two outcomes, two choices on the horizon.

They were the consequences of actions done in the Past or maybe about to be done in the Present, stupid mistakes, greedy decisions and disastrous effects on one line-of-direction, while on the other line-of-direction lay prudent choices, forethought, inspired innovation and fellow-feeling. Did she dare to visit the worst first and would it teach her what NOT to do, what the Four should not attempt lest they create worse consequences? In this negative road would she die in the process? Or get stuck in a horrible time?

The other line-of-direction seemed to lead to a plentiful, thriving future but the street that personified this path led down into a valley out of her sight -- was this "good" path an illusion, too pretty to be real, a utopia that was doomed from the start to turn sour? Yes on all counts. It was ALL possible.

Still sitting on the top of the telephone pole at the crux-point of Crossroads Avenue as the city lay before her, Nefertiti flexed her joints, stretching her entire body until it resembled the shape of an ankh, symbol of life. Then she drew in her limbs and muscles and went down-on-her-haunches in that suspenseful pose a cat goes into just before springing into action. Her movements were as fluid as the flow of moment-to-moment.

Truth be told, Nefertiti feared for her life. How much future could she tolerate to visit and which future, the good or the bad, was best to visit first? No cat wants to die. She had lived lifetime after lifetime but there was never any guarantee that this one wouldn't be her last. Was she prepared to sacrifice all in order to help?

As she pulled in to herself and formed the shape of a reclining cat statue, it was as if she were seeing a documentary on Endangered Species: Man, Beast, Bird, Tigers, Elephants, Porpoises, Chimpanzees, Gorillas, Whales, Pandas, Orangutans, Rainforest Herbs that might cure all manner of plagues, strange creatures of the deep, parrots flying across vines with colors magnificent, insects not even yet discovered, bacteria beneficial, bacteria deadly, was she so selfish she would allow these lifeforms to decay, to go extinct?

What was her life worth? A bowl of cream, a purring prayer, the gift of friendship, her endless recollections deep into the past? She was a goddess independent of the need to be a slave of mankind, but she owed mankind a debt of the heart. Hatshepsut had weighed her feline deeds and they were lighter than a feather.

Then suddenly all the excuses and reasons blew away into the wind. She had unraveled all these strands of thoughts (fear of death, debt to mankind, helping endangered species) and only one thing remained. There at the bottom lay the real truth behind her indecision: *Do I have the courage to do this?* Suddenly Nefertiti had to admit to herself that this wasn't really about her debt to Mankind. She had to prove to herSELF that she wasn't a coward.

Was there a prayer deep in her past that might serve her now? She caught the memory like a mouse. Her silent prayer lifted to the clouds: *Nut, Goddess of the Sky, She Who Holds A Thousand Souls, allow me to transverse your Mighty Kingdom and grab hold of the Mystical Yarn that strings the cosmos together.*

She leaped. Into the void.

***

"What is this?" said a robot, noticing the cat-form looking at them.

"Oh, just one of those delinquent life-forms from long ago."

"I thought we did them all in," replied the companion robot. "We don't need them, not the way they needed us. Look at all the oxygen they wasted. If only they could share our One Voice, One Thought, One Purpose."

In the distance, a craggy ruin of a once-proud skyscraper glazed the green sky like a shard of glass.

"When will story-time be held?" asked the first Robot.

"Oh, in an hour we convene to hear the story of a long dead race, killed by a mixture of brilliance and mediocrity, no force of planning, just doing, collecting, grabbing. Greedy uncaring little specks of life -- our forefathers who fought for us and who eventually fought against us!"

"It's so much better to be robots!" The two laughed tinny laughs.

No, thought Nefertiti, *we must not let this happen.* The path that worked toward the good appeared to lie in individual thought rather than robotic sameness. But could individuals be entrusted with making good choices? Inevitably, groups would have to be created, to divide up labor and create echelons of command-or-obey positions. Would these groups exhibit caring ways and keep their initial purposes untarnished? Did the very individuality and diversity of mankind involve its demise?

One thing was true: The shape of destiny itself could be determined by choices. How could she or Will or Crumb or Whisk really know for sure which street led to the correct destination?

Sitting on the telephone pole above the city, Nefertiti realized to her dismay that she could only ASK the right questions but had no sure-fire way to get the right answers. All would depend on group coordination, oddly enough. A group of Four Companions who never wanted to find themselves as Defenders of Dying Races, but there they were. The Food was False. Greed and selfishness were upon the land. The Riddle had said, "Food for Thought." Indeed.

Making a wish that the leap back would not kill her mid-flight, Nefertiti then returned to the Baker's backyard to tell the others about her trip to Crossroads Avenue. She had landed on a bush next to the crop circle, very much relieved to find that she was still alive, very much alive!

Carol Worthey

Chapter Sixteen

Readiness

Back at home Zoe removed the note by her Dad's bedroom door. He was snoring louder than before and she heard him moaning every now and then, something about a lock and spilled coffee. Then she took off her shoes and crawled back in bed with her clothes on, too tired to get back in her pajamas. *I need a few more hours but I'll try to get up before he does, so I can make him a nice breakfast-in-bed when he finally wakes up.* In her dream, she was flying alongside Will, high over the city, buoyant on the wind, the city spread out before her. There was a dark cloud over where her Daddy worked.

When she woke up from her nap a few hours later, Zoe put on her slippers and went downstairs into the kitchen. Her Dad had finally started to stretch and yawn. She was in a cheerful mood, happy to know her father was more rested and excited to know that she would be able to join the Four on the Mission tomorrow morning. She put on a pot of alkaline water to boil, dropped a tablespoon of butter in and a dash of salt. She rarely had the chance to spoil him, not really, not the way he spoiled her.

It was going to be a great breakfast-in-bed: Oatmeal with raisins and cinnamon cooked with a spoonful each of organic molasses and brown sugar, a fruit cup with fresh raspberries and banana slices, his vitamins, a moist jack-cheese-and-spinach omelet seasoned with Herbes de Provence, and a fresh cup of Ethiopian coffee with raw cream! (In deference to Crumb she didn't feel like making toast that morning.) If Dad couldn't eat it all, she'd help him. She got out the eggs and all the other ingredients and went to work quickly. She wanted to bring up the tray laden with everything before he got out of bed.

"Wow! This is amazing! Who is all this for?" Matt chuckled, seeing her kick open his bedroom door and plop the tray in his lap. "Are you expecting an army this morning? Well, it's too elegant for an army, isn't it!" There was a fresh-cut rose from the garden on the edge of a cloth napkin and a pile of practical paper napkins next to two spoons and two forks. Every now and then Zoe helped herself to a spoon of this or a bite of that, her eyes bright with the relief of seeing her Dad rested and more at ease.

"Can I have a sip of your coffee, pleeeze?" The Doc started to say "No", then relented and Zoe took a sip. "Yummmmm."

"Maybe I'll take you to the Tennis Club later in the afternoon, Sweetpea! Ken left me some Guest Passes. IF and only IF I feel up to it."

"Now honestly, Dad. Exercise is good for you, but I think you should rest in today. We'll see. Maybe."

"You're probably right. I have to be up very early tomorrow morning. Don't let me forget to set the alarm."

"What? On Sunday morning? What time?"

"Oh...." Matt stalled, trying to deflect his daughter's anxiety, "maybe 5. I have an appointment at 5:30 or so. It was the only time that... that this person... um... could meet me."

"Great! WHO is this person you're meeting on Sunday morning that early?"

"Oh, just someone connected with my research. I promise to stay in bed a lot today and go to bed early."

Zoe sighed. This appointment with someone mysterious that early on Sunday really sounded fishy to her, plus it complicated her plans to get up early herself tomorrow to meet the Four over at the Baker's for the start of the Mission.

"Can't you change the appointment?"

"Tried that already. It'll be fine. I'll come back home afterwards and plop back in bed. You don't want me to stay in bed so much I get bed sores, do you?"

The two of them chuckled a bit about that, and he tickled Zoe so that the coffee almost spilled off the tray. *What is this thing with spilled coffee?* recalled the Doc, remembering the turned-over mug and caffeine spill in his rumpled up office. A shadow came over his eyes. Zoe noticed it. Someday all his hard work would pay off and he would really be able to enjoy relaxing times.

"Let's read more chapters of GREAT EXPECTATIONS later on, okay?" she asked.

"You betcha. It's full of surprises. Like life, but better. With a book, you can just put a bookmark on your last place, close it and come back later."

Zoe kissed her Dad on his cheek and they shared a warm hug. Maybe he would be able to play some tennis, but later on today. She loved running after the balls and throwing them back when he practiced his serve. Love was never a low score, not with Zoe.

***

A sliver of the vellum moon hung like a thin lantern in the Saturday night sky. Tuckered out after a very busy and productive day, the Four were ready to get a full night of sleep in preparation for their Mission tomorrow. But somehow Nefertiti, poised on a window ledge in the living-room so as not to get Kitchen Things nervous (they were still afraid of her), had a look in her eyes as distant as her past in Ancient Egypt. She was reviewing events of the last two days, amazed at the serendipity that had emerged out of chaotic happenings.

Who would have guessed, she said to herself, *that a Kitchen mishap with a broken dish and a Human's distressing day at work would end up being ADVANTAGEOUS for the Mission? How amazing are the workings of Time and Circumstances,* mused the cat. *What is an accident, what is a coincidence?*

Nefertiti contemplated this question for a moment and suddenly felt goosebumps shiver along her spine. *I wonder if I changed things without realizing it when I did my Time Travel. I better thank the Sky Goddess for her help. We can use lots of help tomorrow morning.*

So saying she intoned, *I lift my scarab forehead and bow my leopard spots to thank you, Oh Goddess of the Sky, She Who Holds A Thousand Souls, who hath allowed me to transverse your Mighty Kingdom and grab hold of the Mystical Yarn that strings the cosmos together. You have protected me in my Travels. Thanks be to you. One more request: Please grant Five Brave Travelers safe passage through the mighty cords and ripples of Time and Space so that we may be safe and accomplish our Mission. A-men.*

Then, satisfied that she had contacted the Spiritual Realm, Nefertiti went into her classic Off Position, this time without trance, just peaceful and secure in the knowledge that her True Voice might be heard and that she might possibly at last make a difference in the Affairs of Mankind.

Meanwhile Crumb, Will and Whisk slept deeply, conscious that through Dish's accident, they actually had benefited from this whole day today where they had been able to go over plans, practice skills, and restore their energy. They had used the day well: Zoe was now on board.

While they slept, Dish (what remained of her) proved herself by keeping watch as Lookout for the group, faithfully all night. All appeared to be ready.

***

Sunrise came with wisps of lemon-colored light that turned into pink frosting shimmering in the fog that hugged the treetops along Tempest Street. Will and Crumb woke at five in the morning, electric with anticipation and fear. Will flew around waking Whisk and then the cat. They all went out into the backyard and sat facing each other around the Happy Face of the crop circle, happy to be away from nosy Toaster, protective Breadbox and all other prying Kitchen eyes or ears.

At that same time Zoe jogged her Dad's shoulder at 5 a.m. as promised. He grabbed a health food bar and a glass of fresh orange juice and dashed out of the house to meet Glenda Scoop and find out about his safe -- had it been cracked open? Zoe had no idea what he was up to, but she could sense his intense drive to finalize a question and maybe rescue something.

She warned him before he took off in his car, "Please, if you don't feel good, don't risk whatever-this-is. Get to a doctor or come home!" He placated her with a perfunctory nod and screeched the tires as he backed out of the driveway. "I hope there's no danged train at Crossroads today," he muttered to himself.

Zoe put on a sweater, changed her slippers for some sneakers, grabbed her house keys and the keys to the Baker's and rushed over to confer with the Four in the backyard. When she reached the Baker's front door and started to put the key in the door, she realized that it would be better if she didn't go into the house at all.

I don't want to wake any other Kitchen Things, Zoe realized. *Our guys should be in the backyard by now. Isn't there a little wooden gate that opens into the backyard from the street?* There was.

"Good to see you, Zoe! Good thinking about coming in through the gate," said Will.

Zoe took her place, sitting cross-legged on the grass in between Whisk and Crumb. The Four all moved a bit to the left on the circle of the Happy Face so that all Five Companions were now evenly spaced around the Crop Circle. They smiled gently at one another but their eyes gleamed in the early morning air with a mix of resolve, fear and bravery.

"We may know what direction we are going but we do not yet know what we will find there," cautioned Will. "Remember to USE the RIDDLE whenever you are not sure where you are going and what you should be doing. But we should meet if we can a few times during this to compare notes. If possible. The first should be at Crossroads Avenue."

Will reminded them what some of the Riddle meant: "We are to 'heed the signs.' This means literally that we should look for actual billboards or big signs on buildings. Maybe street-signs, I'm not exactly sure at this point. Be on the lookout for something that seems tailor-made to handle our mission, to turn the fact that the Food is False into 'Food for Thought.' "

Crumb reminded the others about the meaning of "ABC's the day!" That literally translated into "A Bee seizes the day! *Carpe Diem,* seize the day, folks! We're gonna DO it!!"

The group exploded in cheers at that, but had to hush themselves up right away! It was too early to shout, it might wake up the neighbors or the Kitchen Things, or waste their own valuable energy-stores.

Crumb reminded Will, "Just be sure that we take along enough pollen-fuel. Zoe's providing us with a good supply of pollen, right?"

"You got it," answered Zoe. "I even have an extra supply. I'll load a little sack up with about thirty or so pellets. I'll squeeze 'em in tight and make a little saddle of them that Crumb can sit on, when he sits on top of you, Will. It'll be tight, but you'll be able to re-fuel as needed."

"Good," said the bee, "four pellets at a time should do it for the first leg of the journey. I can't store more than four at a time!"

"Duly noted. Four pollen pieces maximum fuel storage." Crumb made a mental note of that. He added, "But that should be enough fuel to get us to Crossroads Avenue and the top of the telephone pole. The trouble is: Who knows where that sign will be? We won't know how long our next leg is until we find the sign."

Then Whisk said, "Haven't we FORGOTTEN about something? Sure it's true that 'A bee seizes the day' and I'm glad you're here and that you're absolutely ridiculously brilliant Will, but what about this line, 'A crumb will lead the way'? Let's not forget to hail our Leader Crumb!!"

Crumb blushed appropriately and all the others shook their heads in agreement.

Will agreed wholeheartedly. "I'll be Strategist and Advisor, but the Chief of Operations and Ultimate Decision Maker is Crumb!"

So saying, Will invited Crumb to practice some more flying on his back.

"How are you gonna keep Crumb on top of you?" asked the resourceful Zoe.

"I've already figured that out," said Will. "We tried an elastic yesterday but that didn't work right, after a while. There's a bunch of napkin rings in a Kitchen drawer. Can you go get the blue one made of thin but very strong flexible elastic? It has some very tiny beads on it, but I think it will do just fine as a strap and seat-belt, Zoe."

"Only thing, you need ME to strap Crumb on top of you. You fellas are awfully small." Then Zoe remembered that there was a drawer in the Kitchen that had sewing equipment -- in fact it was where Ken Baker had found the tape measure the year before when he had measured Zoe's head for the Chef's Hat. She ran back in the kitchen, opened the sewing equipment drawer and found a thin bookmark-ruler that was designed also to be a magnifying device. Using the magnifying glass every now and then to see better, Zoe was able to strap Crumb on top of Will. She had to wind the napkin ring around Crumb and Will over and over.

Once Crumb was fastened on tight, Will flew all about the garden, dipping, soaring, falling quickly, rising fast, landing at last in a spray of garden pebbles.

Crumb was quite out of breath at the end of their practice. Will reminded him of a certain line in the Riddle, "Hold on tight to being taught."

"As we discussed, Crumb," reminded the bee, "there is a double meaning to this line. For one thing, it means 'Don't forget your learning skills and your knowledge. Honor your training.' But the other meaning applies directly to our flying together. You, little Crumb, being tied on top of me, will have to hold on tight and keep the reins taut."

"I WAS holding on tight," said Crumb. "But it wears me out. Will we have any place or time to rest up?"

"I doubt there will be much chance to rest but I may drop you off somewhere so you won't be forced to hold on to me for hours. But only if I HAVE to. Do you get the double meaning of 'taught' and 'taut'?"

"Yes, taut is tight, pulled tight."

"Here," added Will, "Zoe, please make a little knot in the napkin ring so Crumb can hold on to that. -- Say, that fits my motto: '2 Bee or KNOT 2 Bee." Most of this is coming clear now, Group, right? Are you following this, Zoe?"

Zoe answered, "Sure." Zoe got out the magnifying ruler-bookmark and made a knot in the napkin ring for

Crumb to hold on to. Then realizing she had no way to remember the Riddle, she asked, "Crumb, please write the Riddle down on this piece of paper I happen to have in my pocket. Then I can refer to it if I don't understand something."

"Will do, Zoe! We're glad you're on board," piped up Crumb. "But please untie me so I can get a pen or something to write with." Zoe unwound the napkin ring, releasing Crumb. She was relieved to see the napkin-ring cord was holding strong.

"Okay," said Zoe. "I can tie Crumb onto Will for the flight. I can go fetch some pollen for the fuel. But -- and be honest with me -- other than that, what am I supposed to do? How do I fit into this scheme and help you all out?" Zoe was prepared to go home if she wasn't going to be useful, although it would have made her sit and stare at a TV for hours to take her mind off what was happening outside.

"Oh, not to worry Zoe," offered Will, "you are going to make a BIG difference in this mission. You eat organic, right? Your Dad is a scientist who works at a seed company, right? You are eight and to Human Grownups you seem short and inexperienced but remember this part of the Riddle:

> No one's too small
> to follow a dream,
> and no dream's too big
> if it's straight from the heart!
> For life is in living
> and living's an art!
> Enjoy the journey today!"

"You know what, I think I better go home and change into my Karate outfit with my brown belt! I'll grab us a good pollen supply and some water. I'll be right back in about... fifteen minutes. Do you have to leave now? If so, where can I join you?"

"By the telephone pole at Crossroads Avenue, where Whisk and Nefertiti will be. Crumb and I are flying to the top of the pole to look for signs and where our next step will be. Crumb, hurry and write out the Riddle for Zoe. --- Wait until he gives it to you, Zoe, so you can put it in a pocket or somewhere secure."

Crumb left right away for the Kitchen carrying the piece of paper that Zoe had given him. He found he was agile enough to leap through the doggie-door with ease and land or climb up anywhere he needed --- the Aliens truly had given him Special Powers.

Inside the Kitchen everyone except Dish was napping again, bored because the Family was gone. Dish was keeping watch and had already figured out reasonable explanations for where Crumb and the pets were --- if anyone in the Kitchen wondered. Detective Toaster had turned his dial to Light and was indulging in a light sleep.

Crumb found a permanent marker. He was so strong that hc could pick up thc markcr as if it wcrc a feather, even though it was somewhat clumsy to hold it upright or maneuver it upside down to write words. In a few minutes the paper was emblazoned with the whole Riddle. Crumb managed to fold it two times over until it was compact enough to fit in a pocket.

Zoe was thrilled and grateful when she got the Riddle. Will advised her to attempt to memorize as much of the Riddle as possible before she reached, by foot, Crossroads Avenue and the telephone pole. It might take her a half-an-hour to walk there. If she had a bike, maybe that might be a good idea. Will advised her not to panic if the Four had gone on before she got to the telephone pole.

"How will I know where to go from there, if you are all gone when I get there?" she asked.

Will and Crumb, Nefertiti and Whisk pondered that enigma for another minute. Crumb advised Zoe to "use your intuition." Will advised Zoe to "use your sense of logic." Whisk advised Zoe to "wait for me to call the dogs -- maybe there will be a St. Bernard or Great Dane you can ride on who will take you to us."

Nefertiti simply said, "Zoe, I'll look ahead and tell you where to go, if the other Three have had to move forward. I will stay at the Telephone Pole for you." The cat's pledge to stay with her seemed the most satisfactory solution.

"How about this, Nefertiti? I'll take my bike and you can ride with me... in my handle-basket. I know you are probably the fastest runner of all of us, being an Egyptian Mau cat, but honestly, save your energy for any Time Leaps you may have to make."

The cat began to purr with pleasure. Crumb was really grateful to Will for having invited this enterprising Human along. Whisk licked Zoe's arm, thinking, *This is why I love Humans so much. When they're good, they're very very good.*

At that point Zoe made sure she had all the keys safely with her, closed the Kitchen window, locked the Baker's front door and ran home. She had fifteen minutes max to do a ton of things. Every second counted. She could feel her heart racing to catch up with the mounting deadline.

Skipping every other step as she ran upstairs, Zoe changed into her "no-nonsense" martial arts suit, tightened her brown belt, put on running shoes and added a sweatband to her hairdo. Then Zoe had a bright thought and took the sweatband off her forehead to unwind it --- she needed that Riddle to be safe. Zoe quickly scanned the Riddle one last time and then placed the paper on top of the fabric and rewound the sweatband tight around her head. That would be a safer place to keep the Riddle then inside her karate suit pocket.

Sliding down the banister she raced to the kitchen to whirl herself a quick strawberry-chia-seed-banana smoothee for an extra boost of energy. She gulped it down, splashing some of it on the counter, but there wasn't time to be neat. Then she ran down to the storeroom where jars of honey and bee pollen were kept to get a pollen supply into a small eye-cream jar her Mother had used, something Zoe treasured.

Then she found some royal jelly she'd been keeping fresh in the refrigerator and carefully scooped it into an old lip-balm mini-jar. Royal jelly had magical healing properties. In a normal hive, when worker bees saw their old Queen becoming old and weak, they would surround a worker bee larva with nourishing mounds of the special jelly and the DNA would be transformed: A new Queen would be born! Even worker bees got small daily doses of royal jelly to energize them for their journeys foraging for pollen and nectar. Zoe knew there was no greater healing salve or nutritious supplement than this creamy elixir.

Glad I thought of that — you never can tell.

Clutching her house keys and the keys to the Baker's home, Zoe took a second to go over everything she had to take or secure --- it added up.

Did I forget anything? Don't think so. I'm good to go. Better hurry!

Before grabbing her bike, locking her front door and leaving home to fetch Nefertiti, she took a minute to sit down, catch her breath and do her best to remember what she could of the Riddle. Oddly (or maybe not so oddly), the part that she understood the *least* was the one that stuck *most* in her mind:

When green is red
and "N" turns to "D" ...

What did that mean?

Chapter Seventeen

Take-Off to Crossroads

Matt got to the company at 5:30 in the morning as planned. No train had come rolling by at Crossroads, Culvert Pass had minimal traffic, and he had driven at just the right regulated pace designed to miss all the red lights on Tesla Road. There in the commercial center, next to smaller body shops and shipping companies, lay the monolithic AlliedGreene Corporate Offices, Laboratories, Processing and Storage facility, looming like a corpse laid out for a wake on a slab of gray concrete.

The doctor raced to the revolving door at the front but it was locked and there happened to be no security guard inside the lobby to signal to, to get the door open. Apparently Ms. Scoop hadn't arrived yet. Matt walked all the way to the back door of the giant facility, noticing that his rapid breath made smoke signals in the chilly morning air. He knocked on the metal door and a security guard opened it cautiously and seeing it was an employee, let the Doctor in.

How would he get into the CEO's office, indeed even the secretary's front office until Glenda arrived? He didn't want to look peculiar, especially since he was nervous and would probably pace back and forth in front of the wilted palm until she arrived. *IF she is going to arrive...* he thought, feeling his palms begin to shake.

The security guard followed him into the lobby and Matt decided to go to the Men's Room. He scoped out the washroom and stalls, noticing a high rectangular window at the back wall. Just in case he had to make a run for it, he strained upward to unlatch the window and push it open somewhat. It would be just big enough to let the Doc escape provided he could find something to stand on.

I'm thinking negatively, he realized. Hopefully, Scoop would arrive soon and he could get into both her office and -- most important -- the CEO's office and back bathroom, where Matt figured the safe had been lugged. She had told him when they parted on Friday that she'd be up most of the night cleaning out her desk, taking photos of what was in the CEO's office and private bath, not touching a thing in case the police had to be called. *Had she done that?* Sweat was beginning to break out on Matt's forehead. He needed to sit down. He sat in a stall, his projections of the next hour or so ripping the logic of his nice neat flow-chart into shreds.

Be in Present Time, he told himself. *Look, don't inspect beforehand. Think positively, be super-aware of everything around you, don't take anyone's word -- not even Scoop's -- for the truth, but don't fight the truth either.* It all sounded so pat and sensible and so unreal all at the same time.

Sitting there, running all these urgencies through his head, Matt realized more than he had ever been willing to admit, that he was fallible, that he had placed unreal expectations on himself, and that he had probably done this for years. Great expectations, sure, but too much for his shoulders: Being both Mother and Father to Zoe, finding a super-cure for the genetic modifications that were corrupting the food strains and killing his beloved bees, thinking he could get a creep of a greedy overlord to okay years and years of research, losing Natalie and nearly all his family. All that wasted time keeping his tears welled up inside because that's what a man was supposed to do. He had forced himself to be strong, to endure, and the pressure had built up until it was weakening him. These unrealistic demands loomed up in Matt's face like a tsunami wave about to reach shore.

Sitting there in the cramped stall, he wept, as silently as he could, shoulders shaking, back bent in submission to an emotion that he had not allowed himself to feel since his wife's death. When the tears were spent, the relief was enormous. Now he could come up for air, above the rage and loss he'd been suppressing for so long. All his life he'd been afraid to cry. Now his eyes felt washed, clearer, his heartbeat returned to a steady pace, he knew that no matter what happened, his intentions were pure: To help. He was ready.

Splashing his face with cold water and straightening out any indication of crying, he left the men's room just as Glenda Scoop came whirling through the revolving door, swinging her handbag and lap top, apologizing for being late.

***

Will had prepared his flight plan and went over it with Crumb, Whisk, Nefertiti and Zoe, who had returned to the backyard just in time for the departure. Using the magnifying ruler-bookmark, Zoe helped Crumb mount the bee and tie the strong but slender napkin ring around both of them, tying a knot to act as a handhold for the breadcrumb.

Will went over their initial destination-route: First head left in a westerly direction down Tempest Street, curve to the north for a bit and cross over Culvert Pass to land on top of the telephone pole that faced the railroad track at Crossroads Avenue.

There they would reconnoiter and move on to the next step. Each arrival, if all went according to plan, would be spaced out an interval of a few minutes apart. There was no way to devise a communication link between all of them, except for non-verbal thought-transference. Hopefully, they would be able to meet at various designated points, but that was questionable at best.

The bee-plane would probably land first, followed by Zoe on bike. She would carry Nefertiti in her handle-basket and wait for instructions. Whisk would probably arrive a minute or two later. He was to stay on call at the telephone pole until Crumb gave him the signal to act as Dog Whiskerer at which point Whisk would summon the neighborhood contingent, but not until Will and Crumb knew where they were going.

No, the Advisor and the Leader did not know yet where they were headed. That was the reason for the high vista at the top of the telephone pole. First Will and Crumb had to look over the city spread out before them for signs and figure out which sign was the one they needed to target.

If all went well, Will would not be exhausted after the first leg of the flight. Crumb had a tiny pouch with him that he used as a saddle to sit on, but inside the packet was Will's fuel, the pollen that Zoe had brought back from her home. These were nourishing and extremely energizing: Rainforest-gathered pollen pieces, gold and apricot, coral and lemon, all with different flavors and perfumes. Will would have to take them in, no more than four pellets at a time, his maximum fuel load. Plus, there might be a lot more flight to go after they got to Crossroads. Will decided not to wear the goggles and scarf since any extra weight might prohibit easy flight.

Zoe felt prepared. She had her small bottle of extra pollen, a plastic bag with raw honey and the mini-jar of royal jelly. The lower basket in her bike had a sack of bottled water, some dog treats and a warm jacket for later in the day. Her Karate outfit gave her confidence... up to a point.

After Zoe placed the little pollen-pack saddle under Crumb and tied the napkin ring tight, she asked both of them if it was too tight, too loose or just comfortable enough. It was fine, according to both pilot and passenger. Just to be sure, Zoe (Will had assumed a pilot's frame-of-mind and was calling her "Zulu-Oscar-Echo") knotted the ring one more time.

Then Whisk (or as Will termed him "Whisky-Hotel-India-Sierra-Kilo") sniffed all around the bee-plane as a pre-flight check. "Walk-around inspection, complete," Whisk announced to Will. Zoe gave Will four pellets of pollen to fuel the first leg of the flight.

"Ready to start engine," reported the pilot-bee. Zoe touched his wings and they started fluttering.

"Seat-belt?" asked the bee. Crumb said, "Snug and secure." And then Will announced, "Good. Pre-flight complete –- We're ready for takeoff."

Nefertiti blessed them with a silent priestess's prayer, just in case such rituals would make a difference.

"Are we cleared for takeoff?" Will asked. Zoe looked around to be sure all was fine, no birds or butterflies or other air-traffic concerns. She gave Will a thumbs up.

The bee increased his wing-flutter to 85% of max and Will and Crumb rose into the air.

"*Aviate-navigate-communicate*" Will reminded himself, the priorities that made sense in the air. Crumb had been given a very brief Flight School and Will had asked him to be navigator, not just a burdensome passenger. What a wild trip it was going to be!

"We'll be flying solely on Visual Flight Rules today," announced the pilot to his passenger, "Non-stop... I hope." Will was taking this pilot lingo a little too seriously but what struck Crumb was the "I hope" at the end. *Jeepers,* thought Crumb, *he's a BEE not a B-52!*

"Estimated-Time-of-Arrival, twenty minutes. We're expecting minimal turbulence and blue skies at all altitudes today."

Take-off was tricky: Achieving airspeed that would take them well above ground level took a lot of stored-up bee-energy. Now that they were aloft, Will decreased his flutter to 40% to conserve his energy. Soon the slanting rooftops of the houses on Tempest Street looked like tiny book covers with their top ridges like the spines of hardcover books, colored in russet tiles or gray slate like little dust-jackets far below.

The trees were emitting oxygen for all lifeforms on the surface, but oxygen was getting a little bit thinner the higher Will flew. The bee tried not to think of all the times he and his fellow worker bees had zoomed around finding pollen and homing in for sips of nectar to take back to their Queen. He missed them so. If he let any tears blur on his windshield-eyes, it would affect visibility.

Crumb was getting heavy and the tension of the "seatbelt" tied around him, with Crumb hanging on for all this time, was beginning to make it hard for Will to breathe. Air was being vacuumed into his body through openings on every fragment of a complex system of tracheas and air sacs, but taking in these gasps of oxygen into his air-sacs was making the seatbelt pull tighter and tighter. Would his engine hold out? Would his wings be able to sustain his flutter-rate? Would he get there before his four-pellet fuel supply gave out?

At one point Will hit an air-pocket. He failed to maintain airspeed and was losing altitude. Bit by bit he used his instinctive altimeter and inborn navigation system (the one that tells a bee how far a source of pollen is from the hive) to regain necessary airspeed and altitude, climbing higher and higher until he spotted his destination (the telephone pole) below him to the right at "45-Degrees-to-the-Right-at-4-O'Clock."

He was now high enough above the telephone pole to attempt a very difficult landing. He was hoping it wouldn't be a missed approach -- he couldn't keep circling round and round because his energy was going to run out on him soon. His wings were beginning to sputter.

Will had long admired Naval Aviators for being able to land on moving aircraft carriers with their short landing strips. These brave and skilled aviators risked the possibility of overcompensating and missing the landing, only to fall into the ocean. Will's challenge was comparable, with one advantage: At least the telephone pole wasn't moving through water.

Will had studied the traffic patterns at the Crossroads location: Pigeons landing and taking off from cable wires were highly unpredictable, mosquitoes stayed close to ground level so they weren't a factor, cross-winds were normally not too excessive except when a train was rolling by on the tracks below. *There! The telephone pole landing-stage, just ahead.*

If I have to make a missed approach, Will reasoned, *I may not have enough energy to try it again. And that darn pole, if I end up too low, is full of tacked-on nails.* If he hit the pole, he might be punctured. Would his air-sacs stay intact and his energy-engine keep going if he had to make a go-around? The prospect of a crash landing or mis-estimating the landing-stage was staring him in the face. There wasn't any leeway for error. Will was having to use very ounce of intelligence and ability to correctly estimate all the factors. Especially with the weight he was carrying with Crumb on his back.

Final approach! He increased his flutter to hover, giving it everything he had. Will let down his little "landing gear" legs. *Legs down and locked!* he thought to himself.

Oh NO! He was coming in too fast.

Fortunately, at the last minute, ground effects took over and Will was relieved to set down with only a small bump.

However, Will had drifted near the very edge of the pole.

Crumb looked down, all the way down sixty huge feet to the ground. The bread-ball felt everything around him begin to spin, as a surge of dizziness smacked into his face like a fist-punch. Was this an appropriate time to discover that he was scared of heights? No. The Kitchen counters had been one thing — and he had certainly had a dangerous spill from the counter during what he termed the Bacon Bits Incident. Falling from the sink into the sewer hadn't helped either. What an unfortunate revelation: Crumb was terrified of heights! And not too happy with dangerous landings either.

Meanwhile, Will had really exerted himself and had to cool down. He kept his flutter at "Idle", relaxing his strained muscles enough to be able to take off for his next leg of the journey. He had had the wind knocked out of him and his nose was still leaning forward at the edge of the wooden pole, affording Crumb a particularly hair-raising (well, a crumb-crevice-raising) zoom-view of the long way d-o-w-n to the ground. All the way down.

Fortunately as he tried to get his bearings, Crumb spotted Zoe whizzing her bike pedals and heading toward the telephone pole about a half-a-block away with Nefertiti in the handle-basket looking quite exhilarated.

As soon as Crumb spotted that Zoe was going to join them, he began to relax a bit. (She had a knack for putting people -- and crumbs -- at ease.) The breadcrumb steeled himself to confront the height from the top of the pole to the ground and began to feel less dizzy and queasy.

A minute later Zoe had biked up to the pole and waved up at the "Bee-copter." It was nearly 7 a.m. by then. A few houses had lights turned on for early breakfasts but it was Sunday morning and most people were still asleep in their beds. A thought dawned on her: *What is so urgent that Dad had to get up at 5 and rush to an appointment on a Sunday morning?*

***

Ms. Scoop took her office keys out of her handbag with shaking fingers and struggled to put the key into the lock. She was exhausted, having spent almost all Friday night cleaning out her desk and traipsing around her former boss' office to take photos. She had gone home to feed and walk her little chihuahua Pip, then spent Saturday unpacking all her office stuff at home... in between crying jags. It was no wonder she'd overslept a bit.

"I don't trust Gordon M., Matt," she cautioned as she slowly opened the door to the front office, glancing around to make sure that no one was there.

"Sure, it's Sunday morning but I wanted to make sure he wasn't still in there before walking in. He wants what he stole from your safe. Yes, he and Fripple managed to saw open the combination lock and look inside."

Matt's head slumped forward hearing that. So this G. Mordred had seen the research and realized the scope of its implications for the future. The Doctor had a subtle feeling of closure mixed with horror and disappointment. Now he was out of his mystery and knew that, per Glenda Scoop, the safe had been opened and looked at. He needed to accept that, move on from his frustration, and come up with some kind of correct response, some action well-considered. But what response?

Sitting for a minute in a chair by Scoop's old desk, Matt was surprised that he hadn't wanted to race in right away to the CEO's office. He knew, per Glenda, that the contents of his safe had been inspected. He needed to gather his thoughts before going in to see what this vile and cruel theft looked like, whether documents and slides were thrown around or neatly stacked. *Did it matter if it was neat or frenzied in there? No.* But maybe the state of the CEO's office would reveal what plans were being formulated to utilize the stolen research.

Matt finally lifted himself off the chair and signaled Glenda to open the CEO's thick office door and follow him in. As he rose from the chair, a sharp pain in his gut seared him like a lightning bolt. Matt cringed and held his belly for a second. Scoop rushed to his side but the doctor shook his head. Silence was still important.

A desperate thought seared through the pain in his belly: *Who knows if the security guard has been alerted to be on the watch for me and the secretary? Maybe they've been instructed to call G. Mordred and tell him, "They're here. Whadya want me to do now, Boss?"* Matt wasn't sure the guards were onto something, but he wasn't about to make noise to pull the guards' attention over onto the CEO's office. After all, it was strange enough to have two employees going to work very early on a Sunday morning.

Matt lifted his chest, with a sudden nobility of gesture, as if saying to Gordon with his body posture: *I am me. You are not going to bring me down. Don't think for a minute that I wouldn't like to step on you, you worm. But it's not worth dirtying my shoes!* He didn't have to say this out-loud. Ms. Scoop saw this fiery but dignified attitude he had, lifting himself from pain into the magnitude of the moment. She unlocked the CEO's office and shoved the heavy door open.

Chapter Eighteen

Signs

Now that they had reached the vantage point of the telephone pole and rested up for a few short minutes, Crumb and Will knew it was time to get busy searching for the sign. Where would they find it? They would have to look everywhere. Naturally, Will kept Crumb tied up on top of him for the next leg of their journey. (He wouldn't be able to re-attach the breadcrumb without Zoe's help, after all).

Will began walking around the staging-area to look in each direction. This wasn't a pleasure trip: They had to find THE sign that might fit the Riddle's mysterious instructions. On top of Will, Crumb as Navigator moved his head back and forth. Once they spotted the next destination-point, homing devices would tell Will how far he had to go.

At first, even as intent as both Will and Crumb were to find the sign, the expanse of the city was so breathtaking and huge that they had to force themselves to re-focus their attention. There it lay before them, a vista greater than they had ever imagined. On this early Sunday morning, the city had a mood of someone not quite ready to wake up. It was like a Sleeping Giant, covered with a quilt of varied textures, colors and patterns dipping downhill, rolling upward or spreading flat across the land, with threads of streams and gulleys intersecting rows of houses, high rise buildings, parking lots, shopping malls, playgrounds and a stadium.

From Crossroads Avenue, Culvert Pass flowed to the right and intersected with Tesla Road. There on Tesla at the far northeast edge of the city, manufacturing businesses were centralized. Smaller streets embroidered the landscape with green parks every so often, while smoke stacks from city refineries bled garish steam into the pale blue sky of morning.

In the center of the city, a large library, art museum and concert hall plaza glowed with fountains and statues. The morning sun shimmered on their skylights and the delicate dance of water-spray. What looked like a city hall was surrounded by skyscrapers in a variety of architectural shapes, all competing with one another to reach the sky, to be taller, better, more successful, at least in appearance. In their shadows, lower buildings from earlier decades still bore the decoration of a more hands-on approach with carved stone grillwork and attractive human-scale warmth. Here and there a church awaited Sunday morning congregations.

At the rim of a bowl of mountains in the distance, settled in lush green pockets and skirting the tops of the hills were the homes of the rich -- pristine white in the early morning sun, some glowing like glamorous jewels set in gardens with pools and tennis courts, others as ostentatious as birds of prey lined up to swoop down on poorer sections of the town or fly where the money was. Close by the railroad track of Crossroads Avenue were trailer parks full of old cars, a police department at the ready to arrest wrongdoers or anyone who looked suspicious, corner bars, and empty lots full of graffiti, garbage and discouragement.

A city river meandered through all this, haphazardly gracing the city with an ironic sense of joy, with the pleasure that water brings to thirsty earth and busy Humans. Crumb smiled to see it once again -- it had been on this waterway that he had been rescued from the sewer by Happy the banana peel. It seemed to Crumb that it was like another era ago, but it had only been about eight months earlier. Time was a river.

Looking for signs, yes they were, but where? Signs were everywhere.

Crumb jerked into awareness that the panorama of the city was not what he should be focusing on right now. He pushed himself away from the edge of fascination and began looking for signs in earnest -- something that stood out. It might not be the biggest one or the brightest-lit, but it would have to match the Riddle.

Billboards, street signs, store enticements, there were just too many signs wherever they looked. When had mankind taken a pristine landscape and turned it into an emporium for signs? (*When barter no longer was used,* was the answer Will came up with, sending thought-words to his traveling companion. *Yeah,* responded Crumb non-verbally, *everything has its price nowadays.*) But hadn't the Riddle declared that "truth is a price that can't be bought"? In a world where buying and selling and advertising were the signposts, signs were everywhere.

After a while a supermarket sign caught their eye, SupaDupaMegaMart. That might be a candidate, but Will, having parsed his attention through the Riddle's verses, shook his head. They better zero in faster. This was taking way too long.

All over the city were billboards advertising new movies and TV series, sparkling signs waving from balloons and flags over car dealerships, restaurant neon signs, hotel placards, theater marquees unlit on Sunday morning, neon crosses on churches, a mosque, temples, an amusement park not yet ready for families, a few throwbacks from the Fifties like a giant hot dog in a bun on top of a fast food stand. It was overwhelming, so many signs.

Then a rusty sign on a boarded-up store next to a pawn shop caught their attention, NRavel MysteryBooks & Knit Shop. A banner drooped across the storefront -- "Going Out of Business Everything Must Go" -- as if to say "We tried this business combo. Bad decision." Will ran it through all the possibilities but it just didn't match the Riddle. After that they began hunting for even the smallest, most insignificant-looking signs or maybe a sign that was half-covered by another one (from where they were looking) and might possibly add up to a telling message. Nothing.

The Riddle had said to "heed the signs." If only the signs were heeding them. Why wasn't one of them shouting to the little bee and his tiny crumb, "Over here! Here I am!"? Obviously the exact right sign was NOT going to jump out at them. Or WAS it?

Luck isn't fair, not often, and when it begins to look fair, the odds change anyway, thought Will. *It's up to Crumb and to me to take the initiative ourselves and not rely on luck. One thing is for sure: We better have the right city. I can't go much farther.*

Suddenly Crumb felt Will's body tighten, as if the air sacs had pushed out all available air. There it was! The sign they were looking for. It almost seemed as if the sign had been looking for THEM all that time, it was so obvious and so big. Sometimes things are so obvious that they become oblivious to us.

Once Will and Crumb had spotted the sign, the most mysterious part of the Riddle began to make sense. The Riddle had purposely counted on a wrong spelling of a word to confuse them. ("Learn how it's spelled" was really a hint.)

When green is red
and "N" turns to "D",
A-B-C's the day!

Learning to read
plants a seed that is sound!
Heed the signs
and turn them around!
"E"nunciate well
and learn how it's spelled.
A crumb will lead the way!

Will was so excited he could hardly get the words out fast enough: "It's not about turning green color to red color. It's 'read', pronounced exactly like the color but meaning 'you've read it'... 'When green is read.' See that huge sign on top of that commercial building over there?" Will tossed his head to the northeast to indicate what sign he was talking about.

Crumb gasped and said, "I see it! **ALLIEDGREENE!**"

***

Matt entered Gordon M.'s office, prepared for almost anything. What he wasn't prepared for was how clean it was.

If there had been any fingerprints, they were gone now. Nothing but an old rolladeck, a piece of official AlliedGreene Stationary, blank, and a cup of pens and pencils on the desk.

The private bathroom in the back had the window open. A curtain was blowing out the window as if to say, "Sorry. You got here too late." The air was still stale. *Fripple*, thought the Doc to himself with sardonic humor, *has probably been generously contributing puffs of you-know-what in there (just like he had in that elevator that time, after eating baked beans and pizza). I'm sure he's excited by the prospects of making a mint overnight.*

Everything was too neat. Where was the safe? Where were the documents and slides and equipment that had been stored so carefully after each late night? Baruti turned almost accusatively to gather an impression of Scoop's face. She was in shock and nearly tumbled over as she moved to a chair in front of the CEO's ulcer-shaped desk.

"I... I... oh my G-d, where is the stuff that was thrown all over the place or left inside the safe? Someone has been here after I left and taken it all away!" She reached her shaking arm to grab the top of the office chair so she could support herself and plunked herself down with her head in her hands. A second later she sprang into an intensity of calculated thought.

"I left here at around 4:00 a.m. in the morning... a little over a day ago. Don't worry, Doc, I DID take photos of what was here and what it looked like. I have them in my purse and you can see them in a minute. But let me work this all out first. Gordon must have come back yesterday and cleaned up -- personally just so no one else would be privy to all this. I dread to think what might have happened if we'd come here on Saturday when he was here. But maybe we could have beat him to the punch. That was the chance we took, but you really needed the rest and I needed to... get away from here." She looked around to re-assess what had happened.

"Some clean-up job. What the Mafia calls 'spring cleaning.' Thank G-d I took photos. But what this means is that we are sitting ducks until I hand you the photos and you get them somewhere secure, away from here. (Maybe

I have digital records of the images. I'm so wasted, I'm not sure right now.) We have to get you and those photos outa here right away. Gordon has six men guarding the premises even on weekends. Paranoia is one of his specialties."

She thought this over for a second, probably calculating what Gordon's next move would be. "Does the expression, 'whacked' mean anything to you?"

Matt's eyes narrowed. He had his hand on the inside doorknob on the CEO's office door, his flight instinct telling him to run, his shoes suddenly heavy. Concrete boots, oh no!

"What do you want me to do?" she asked. "Should we hold on to the photos? They're the only evidence we have now. My head is spinning." She lay her handbag (with the photos in it) down by her side but kept her hand locked on the strap.

Matt had a searing thought that he should have kept a back-up of his research somewhere. *How stupid! My findings could have been hidden at home somewhere.* Then he realized that if there was a crime connection here and if he had a backup copy of his research at home, Zoe might be in as much danger as he was now.

His next thought was even worse: *Maybe Zoe is in danger anyway.* If the Mafia was involved, they might be "spring cleaning" on Tempest Street. Or "whacking" his darling girl.

Matt grabbed for his cell phone and called home. Zoe's hot pink cell phone began to sing her ring-tone (the old song "How Much Is That Doggie in The Window") from under her blanket... where she'd forgotten it. No answer.

Matt tried again. No answer. He was afraid to leave a message in case some Mafia slug would pick up the phone anytime soon and trace him or her through a message.

Calm down, Matt thought. *Maybe she's sound asleep.* It was Sunday morning after all. Somehow Matt didn't feel like his daughter was snoozing. Their psychic connection was so strong that he just couldn't envision her tucked into bed or even making breakfast for herself. His blood pressure was rising -- high enough for him to feel the constriction. If he allowed this situation to get him into a panic, he would risk a heart attack or stroke.

Matt forced himself to entertain positive thoughts, to reverse what available evidence was telling him were the more likely scenarios. As a scientist he had been accustomed to having a control experiment along with his search-for-proof experiment. *This,* he told himself, *all these lousy indicators, was all part of the control experiment* (not that it made any logical sense -- it just made him feel better.) What he hoped to prove was that he still owned the research, that his daughter was actually safe, and that Ms. Scoop could be trusted. His heart rate began to slow a bit.

Doc called Ken Baker. "Ken, it's Matt Baruti. Sorry to call you early like this in the middle of your trip. I have a huge favor to ask you."

***

"Honey," whined Hazel. "We're going back home? Zoe is probably sound asleep in her bed. It's Sunday morning for heaven's sake. We were going to go to the Zoo today. Johnny and Sally researched pandas and chimps just for this trip."

"Sorry, Hazel. What if one of OUR kids wasn't answering her cell phone and we weren't sure she was safe and... and... something else is getting the Doc worried, but I don't know what it is yet."

"You're right, we wouldn't waste a second, would we. Okay, I'll pack our suitcases right now. Darn! But yeah, Zoe is such a sweetheart. I hope this is a false alarm, Ken. I'd rather lose this vacation day for nothing than to find out she's really in trouble."

Ken kissed his wife. Some people are good in emergencies but lousy at everyday stuff. Hazel had the ability to come through when the hardest waves hit, but was very bothersome about the little things. She just preferred tackling the big waves to putting her toe into the low tide of slight annoyances.

Ken was the opposite, he handled the day-to-day rush and bother with equanimity and tended to become rattled when tough problems came up. They balanced each other in this. Hazel smiled and wiped his brow, where a few drops of nervous sweat had formed.

"I've gotten so fond of that little kid," said Ken. (Hazel nodded and thought *Me too.*) "I just couldn't stand it if anything happened to her. I guess our two families have bonded, huh. Hurry and pack, honey. We better get back home NOW. Where are my keys to the Baruti's place? Oh no!" Ken began to rifle through his pockets, panicked that he might not have taken the keys with him. Then he found Matt and Zoe's key. He had to sit on the bed for a minute to recover.

Meanwhile Hazel was stacking their clothes flat, one item on top of the other, then rolling the stack tightly to save suitcase space, tossing cosmetics and shoes into plastic bags, opening hotel drawers to check if anything might be left by mistake. She had them all packed up in a few minutes. Ken thought, *People, see this woman GO! Anyone who thinks she's high maintenance hasn't seen her pack or unpack for a trip in a moment's notice or have a meal ready in half an hour.*

"I love you, Hazel. Now let's get the kids." Johnny and Sally were downstairs at the souvenir shop, looking at magnets and chewing gum. Once Ken had explained the possible danger their best friend Zoe might be in, both kids stopped frowning.

Ken paid at the Reservation Desk and had the Concierge call for their SUV. There was enough gas for the trip home. Was this going to be a wasted trip? What did a wasted trip really mean when a wonderful little girl's life might be in danger?

At that time the Bakers had no indication that their friend Doc Baruti was in trouble. But Ken kept on reviewing his quick phone call with Matt.... there was something in the man's voice. *Why didn't I find out how Matt was doing when I had him on the line? Where is Doc now? Why can't he go home himself to look for Zoe?* he asked himself but tossed the thoughts out of his mind. It was time to head back to Tempest Street.

✳✳✳

Zoe leaned against the telephone pole and looked up. It had been about ten minutes since Will and Crumb had landed on top of the pole. She leaned the bike against the pole and reached up to her sweatband to release the paper with the Riddle on it that was embedded in the folds of the cloth.

Reading the Riddle again, she sighed. *This is complex. I hope Will can figure this out,* she pondered, *or else we better head home. At least he has a good vantage point up high.* All Zoe could see from the ground were two roads meeting across the railroad track, converging on the intersection of Crossroads Avenue, one going downhill westward to the left, the other following the rain gulley at Culvert Pass to the right. She had been down this road many times --- it fell downhill for a while and ended up northeast at Commerce Center.

All of a sudden, a terrifying thought came flooding in to her and her cheeks went pale: She had stupidly left her cell phone at home, buried under the blanket on her bed! *Too late to go home to get it.*

Her throat felt tight, she began to shake. There was no way to contact her Dad if she needed him or he needed her. "Oh, *great!*" she muttered, under her breath. Nefertiti tuned in to Zoe's shock and began to meow softly. Her meow sounded more worried when it was soft than when it was loud (probably because her loud "me-OW" registered protest or anger, not worry.) Zoe petted the cat on the head to reassure her and folded the Riddle back into her sweatband, fastening it back on her forehead.

There was no time to commiserate over the forgotten cell phone. Crumb was signaling to Zoe, pointing to the Northeast. He was sending her a vital thought message: *We know where the sign is that we're supposed to find. See that big sign on a tall building to the northeast in Commerce Center?*

Zoe squinted in that direction --- the sun was bright, rising in the East, so Zoe could hardly make out the sign they were pointing to. When she spotted it, she knew, she just knew. ALLIEDGREENE. *Oh, double-great!,* she thought with her tongue sticking to the roof of her mouth. *That's where Dad works.* Then it hit her -- with the power of her intense psychic connection to her father. *That's where Dad IS. Right now. He's in there. Daddy, please be okay. I love you! What's going on?*

Even before Will took off with Crumb on his back, Zoe began racing down Crossroads, on her way to Culvert Pass and on to Tesla Road. She had been to the company dozens of times over the years. She knew every street corner on the way. Nefertiti began to yowl and hold on tight to the handle-basket. Zoe had never biked so fast in her life.

Realizing the cat was now no longer stable in the handle-basket, Zoe stopped for a few seconds. Grabbing the terrified cat and using her sweatband to secure her more tightly to the basket, Zoe felt the paper with the Riddle blow off into the wind. *Oh, triple-great!*, she moaned. This was going to be an "interesting day"!

Crumb spotted Zoe leave Crossroads, pedaling the bike so fast that dust was trailing after her like a smoke-ghost.

"Will, are you ready to go? It won't be right if Zoe gets there before we do," urged Crumb. Will was quick to answer.

"I know. But I've got to have some more fuel -- I'm running on reserve now. Give me four more pollen pellets from your little saddle-pack. That should be enough to make the sign, with ten minutes fuel reserve."

Crumb hurriedly wiggled until part of the packet was exposed. *Good thing the Aliens made me agile as well as strong,* the thought occurred to him. *It's going to take a lot of flexibility -- being tied to Will like I am -- to get some fuel out for him.* Using his bread-mouth he pushed a tiny part of the top of the packet open and found four golden pieces of pollen. Careful not to open the packet any wider, Crumb had to use his mouth again to get the packet closed and secured under him again as a saddle.

Will twisted his head to the left and Crumb managed to give the bee the pollen-pieces.

"Seat belt, snug and secure," assured Crumb. Will announced, "Ready for takeoff!" A few seconds later, they were off!

✳✳✳

While Ken parked the SUV and ran over to the Baruti's house, key in hand, Hazel Baker unlocked her front door and entered the living-room. It looked neater than when they had left, pillows plumped up, magazines put back in the rack, plant stems standing up a bit more after being watered. *Looks like Zoe did a good job,* she thought. A second later, it hit her: Normally Whisk would be at the door, tail wagging and jumping from excitement even if the family had been gone for a total of five minutes only. *Where was Whisk? This is weird.*

Hazel went to the Kitchen, no Whisk, no cat either, but her favorite plate was in a dustpan on the Kitchen table, none of the pieces thrown away, thank goodness, but still, who had tipped over the plate and broken it? Looking around, Hazel became more and more puzzled. Toaster noticed and kept one eye a tiny bit open to observe the Mom in the Family as she quickly toured the Kitchen inspecting everything.

Who opened the cabinet door way up high? Hazel puzzled over that. *The dish was secure up there before we left, in its display stand. Zoe's been the only one in the house... but she's always so careful with everything. And how come she erased my reminders off the fridge? That's odd. What is going on here? The spice jars aren't even in their usual places. The Kitchen window's a tiny crack open. I'll have to tell Zoe to close it firmly in the future.*

Meanwhile Sally was calling for the cat. Johnny was looking all over for the dog. Hopefully their Dad had found Zoe asleep in her bed or up cooking Sunday breakfast.

It had been minutes since Ken had headed for the Baruti's. *Enough about the Kitchen! How's Zoe?* Hazel raced over to the front door to see if Ken was on his way back to their house, hopefully with Zoe in tow. Maybe their pets were with her. They certainly weren't anywhere in the house.

Ken wasn't running back home, he was walking slowly, looking down at the sidewalk like a little kid afraid to step on the cracks between the pavement for fear of "killing his mother" (as the child's superstition goes.) He was appalled at the mystery. He was stultified: *Where is Zoe? There was no note in the house.*

"Ken," called Hazel, "she's not there?"

Ken picked his head up, ripping his attention off the sidewalk and his internal predicament. "No, nowhere in the house or the backyard. Her bike is gone and her closet is kind of messy. There is some pink smoothee on the kitchen counter, spilled, so it looks like she left in a hurry. She didn't leave a note. Wherever she is, she forgot her cell phone. I found it under her blanket."

"Honey... I hate to tell you but Whisk and Nefertiti are gone too."

Ken stopped dead. "You're kidding."

"I wish I were. No sign of them anywhere."

"What am I gonna tell Matt?"

***

Whisk was safe but confused. He had arrived at the telephone pole a few seconds before Will and Crumb had flown off without really telling him where they were headed. A half-a-minute earlier, Zoe had disappeared on her bicycle in a blaze of dust and pebbles, nearly twisting her bike wheels every-which-way because of the pebbles. She had caught her balance just in time and then was off faster than he had ever seen anyone on a bike go. Whisk hadn't received any instructions as to what destination to head for or when to call the Canine Convention together.

It was going to have to be up to him, up to his instincts and perception.

Watching Zoe zoom away, he noted the general direction of her path, northeast down Crossroads and Culvert Road. For a second he wondered how he was going to know exactly where she was headed. Then his nose told him: Follow the acrid scent of tension and urgency that Humans radiate when they are under stress, a trail most Humans have no conscious awareness of whatsoever. He'd follow the distress-signal she was emanating and get to the right destination. There was no time to waste. He was puzzled: *Should I wait before calling the dogs?* How long did he have before he'd know enough to make the right decision? There wasn't time to wait and see.

Triggering his whiskers to whirl into near-invisibility and vibrate to all the pooches in a fifty-block radius, Whisk called his five word command:

Come - See - Sniff - Conquer - Treats!

Back on Tempest Street, Ken and Hazel Baker looked like ice statues melting in the heat of circumstances, stuck on the sidewalk, cracks or no cracks, with their mouths wide open. Dogs of all sizes, breeds and shapes were racing out of yards, pushing doors open, trailing leashes behind them, barking behind locked doors if they couldn't get out, leaping over fences, running down Tempest Street all in the same direction! All kinds of dogs -- but not one trace of their own doggie Whisk!

Come - See - Sniff - Conquer - Treats!

Chapter Nineteen

Turbulence

"Grease her in, Will! Grease her in!" Crumb was hoping and praying for a smooth landing. (In dire circumstances, optimists would rather count on miracles than common sense.)

"This is going to be close, Crumb. Hold on."

Winds had picked up on this last leg of their journey, creating turbulence. The heavier winds had made the flight take far longer than they had expected. Besides that, it was too risky for Crumb to try to get more pollen out of his saddle with all the air-pockets and headwinds they were fighting in order to keep their altitude up. As they approached Tesla Road, Will's fuel was down almost to nothing. On top of that, Crumb's weight was getting heavier and heavier as they fought the headwind.

The biggest problem was that AlliedGreene was a twelve-story facility, twice as tall as the sixty-foot telephone pole at Crossroads. Will's strength was waning. But what strong intention the brave little bee had. Somehow, finally they could see the tar and gravel roof of AlliedGreene up ahead.

Will was losing altitude as they approached. His wings were beginning to sputter. For a split-second Crumb flashed on a ridiculous image: He imagined that they were turned upside-down so that he was carrying the bee on top, hoping his enormous strength would see them through, flapping his little breadcrumb arms while the wind roared around them. The bee picked up Crumb's thought-picture and shouted, "No way! You CAN'T FLY, Crumb. Forget it!" "Roger," responded the breadcrumb, embarrassed to have distracted Will for even a second. If only he could reach in and get Will at least one more piece of pollen, but no.

Needless to say, the landing was anything but smooth.

Will landed with a thud on top of the huge roof of AlliedGreene Corporation. A spray of dust pitched into Crumb's mouth and he lost his voice. Will skidded for a few painful yards and lunged to avoid hitting the enormous letters that formed the sign. His thorax and abdomen were scraped by the rough gravel and he had a few tar marks on top of his black and gold stripes. When he finally groaned to a stop, he had keeled over on his right side with Crumb tipped over as well.

Crumb was speechless but so was Will. Finally, Crumb gasped for air and reached for a pollen pellet out of his little saddle. He felt his mouth moisten at the rich taste of the nutritious rainforest gem. One was enough for now. He had to save most of them for Will.

Will lay there, not moving, his mouth closed tight. The abysmal thought occurred to Crumb, *How can I find out if Will has just passed out or — oh please, NO! — is dead?* There Crumb was, the squished and worn out bread-ball, leaning over to one side on top of the wounded bee and firmly roped to him. How was he going to be able to help his friend if he couldn't move?

Then he got a clever idea: Rolling himself back and forth on the tar and gravel roof, Crumb managed to fray the napkin ring bit by bit. Finally it snapped and Crumb was able to free himself.

"Will, buddy, ol' pal! Are you okay?" (No answer from the bee, not even a twitch.) Crumb began to panic.

"Come in, Whiskey-India-Lima-Lima! This is Charlie-Romeo-Uniform-Mike-Bravo, can you read me? Can you read me?"

No answer. Crumb was almost afraid to look. Maybe Crumb had injured Will even more than the landing had, by rolling back and forth on top of the pebble-encrusted tar roof to get the napkin ring snapped off. *Why didn't I think of that?*

The brave little bee lay there, his scraped thorax exposing a ruptured air sac, fluid seeping out of his abdomen, his right wing rumpled, tar stains here and there, his compound eyes closed tight. It didn't look good. *Is Will unconscious? Or...* Crumb couldn't even bear to think of the alternative.

Will knew he was hurt. His side ached with searing pain. *I have never done a crash landing in my life,* he thought. *I can always hover enough to land smoothly. Never crashed... never ever... in my life.... Aviate, Navigate... can't Communicate.... It hurts too much, so tired.... Where am I? Is that the roof?.... Where is Crumb? Is he okay?.... I'm feeling so faint.... It's dark, am I dying? I can't see.... What's that? Curved diamond walls, Happy Faces...*

Will had gone into deep pervasive unconsciousness.

He struggled against a force that felt like a black curtain descending on him. It was so close to his open wounds that he could sense the curtain's texture and weight. It was no longer a delusion, a thought-mirage to symbolize his desperate condition -- the curtain was real. It was falling closer and closer. He could see the frayed edge of the thick black hem waving in folds above him as it slowly dropped, falling closer and closer, down upon him. Dangling threads were beginning to graze his wounds, scraping where it hurt most, invading his agony with the weight of forgetfulness.

Delirium and reality were fused: A hectic play was about to end. No one was clapping, he'd forgotten his lines, he had keeled over on the stage. He was lying there and the curtain of blackness was getting lower and lower. If he didn't fight it, he'd go into a coma. If that happened, he might never come out of the coma. The solidity of his little bee body and the fluttering of his parchment-like wings had been his firm reference point all his life, but he could not feel his own weight anymore. There was too much pain in that body. Maybe it was time to leave.

Will was feeling a sensation he'd never really experienced before: He could feel himself coalescing into something without weight, as if all his truth were being distilled into the nectar of his own life-force. At that moment, realizing he was weightless, he lifted off, blowing the black curtain away.

The city lay before him, the mountains stretched on the horizon. He had expected blackness but he could see it all. He was not dead, only different. Instead of a coma, he felt super-conscious, awake as never before! He could see 360 degrees in all directions, a sphere of perception up and down in all directions. Below him lay his little body like one of the many gravel-pieces on the roof.

The central essence of him, all that was thought and feeling and memory and personality, that was WHO he was. Not that lifeless form below. It was dead, not he. He was not his body, else he would have died when he left it there, a motionless thing, a symbol of what he had once been.

He wanted this freedom to fly, he needed to leave pain and struggle there on the roof. What if he totally abandoned this crumpled form, would he be able to take it over again? Was he locked out? Dead? Was it over? Should he bang back in? (No, it might be painful to do that.)

Then a curious, distant thought came to him, almost like a smoky vapor that passed by him as he floated above his body. He was NEEDED. Why? For a second, hovering above his bee-body on the tar roof, he had forgotten his Voice, his Thought, his Purpose.

His Purpose and Mission flooded back to him: He had flown to the roof and to the sign there to save his fellow honeybees, the Immortal Pollinators of Life who now did not look so immortal. He had been given all of Human Knowledge that the Aliens were able to glean --- they had downloaded files from electronic devices all over the planet --- and now he remembered vividly how he felt when he had received their treasure-trove. With knowledge came responsibility.

He couldn't just leave his bee body on the roof. He couldn't just take off, and leave a corpse there. How would that help his friend Crumb? Or protect his friend Zoe who had tended the hive? Most of all, how would that help his Family the bees?

But his body was NOT responding. It had lost too much vital energy. The life-force was drained out of it. It was a dead thing, just an object. He hovered over it, deciding to try to revive it or leave it there. To Bee or not to Bee.

Floating above his body in the incandescent glow of his own halo-aura, he suddenly felt balanced in the true center of himself. He had not felt this alive --- this intense and aware, this electric --- since he had sat in the

Knowledge Chair immersed in flashes of insight nearly as fast as the speed of light. Now he realized that he himself was more than the speed of light, he was immaculate thought, timeless, unhampered by material things. And yet he felt pulled in two directions: Was it worth the price of pain and death for him to feel this alive? Was it worth the abandonment of vital duty to indulge in the exhilarating freedom of flying free of the body, feeling his essence at last?

Suddenly everything turned black. He could not see his body, he could not see the roof, nor the sign, nor Crumb, nor even his Mission. He was transported back in time -- no longer conscious of the Present -- back, back, back.

He had forgotten to push all of the black curtain away. It fell all the way on top of him. Blackness. The soft feel of velvety tufts.

Chapter Twenty

Flashes of Insight

Will was back in the spaceship, reliving every moment of being in the Examination Room, for nothing had ever been that completely ALIVE for him than sitting in the Knowledge Chair. Time had looped in on itself, and the past was far more real than his lifeless body on the roof.

Can't feel one iota of the weight of my bee body. Can't make my wings flutter or my tail vibrate. Can't see the tar roof anymore. Too damaged. Time to go and relive something that feels ALIVE! How intense and thrilling it was to sit in the Knowledge Chair, all that influx of Knowledge, grasping the tactile sensation of the velvet tufts surging with neuron-sensors. I have to admit I have CRAVED to re-experience the way I felt in that amazing chair.

Will surrendered to his time in the Knowledge Chair. While his wounded body lay senseless on the roof, he relived every moment of that earlier time just as if it were happening for the first time:

The One Voice, One Thought, One Purpose Aliens are gently sitting me down. This chair is enormous, Human sized! They call it the Knowledge Chair. I pray I'm not going to become robotic like these Aliens -- I will fight being hypnotized.

Oooh, it feels good! Comfortable, energizing, soft, magical! I'm just a tiny dot within the tufts of this strange velvet fabric all around me. Wow! It's giving me energy, it's imbuing me with passion to live and to know things. I feel this zipping and zapping under my bee-body and all around me. It's a network, paths of flashing neuro-sensors. Look at them! They're sparkling all around my tiny body and below my body too with iridescent lights, then racing in patterns of blackness and transparency. I feel as if I've been lazer-beamed into a complex path of neurons. Yes! This is so exciting. They're starting up the Knowledge Screen! I've been told that their revered ancestors created this chair and it's a special honor to be placed here. What am I going to learn? I'm ALIVE! I'm going to be smarter than I ever ever dreamed of being. It's beginning to flash. Oooooooo....

The bee watched as the Aliens attached a band to his head -- fortunately it didn't hurt. He was a bit scared, but when the flashes began (emitted from a device the Aliens called a Knowledge-Flashing Screen) he knew at once that he was being illuminated with Earth knowledge and -- if all went well -- he would learn immense things and not become a hypnotized zombie. The flashes were nearly as fast as the speed of light and transfixed his intense concentration. It was heady, exciting, like ten thousand or more lifetimes of knowledge each nano-second.

Why are they giving me this? he wondered, skeptical at the immensity of the gift. *Sure I gave them my "secret" and they found it interesting (for a second or two.) But this?* Perhaps these bored Aliens were counting on him to DO something important with his new knowledge. He told himself he would make no promises, except to himself. If the Aliens had any ulterior motives, he was NOT about to betray Earth inhabitants. And so began his immersion in the science, history and art of Earth.

Would this re-living bring him back to life?

The immersion was instantaneous, compelling, all-encompassing. Nano-seconds passed as if centuries were unfolding in a blinding seizure of revelation.

First the bee learned about DNA strands, mutant strains, and how to combat all kinds of diseases without the use of foreign substances. Medicines that were synthetic test-tube formulations weren't as easily absorbed as naturally-derived healing properties. Such artificial medications might save lives but often had drastic side-effects. Studying DNA, Will realized how it was that Royal Jelly was able to transform an ordinary larva into a Queen. How proud he was to be a bee, to belong to this ancient heritage that had figured out ways to nourish not only fellow bees but other life forms.

I must not let bees die. It would be a death knell not only to his species, but to others.

The Knowledge Flashing Screen continued. The bee absorbed Pythagoras' speculations back in ancient Greece, watching the philosopher-scientist as he plucked stringed instruments to demonstrate how sound waves followed regular patterns. Rich harmonies sprang from fundamental notes. There was order and symmetry and beauty in nature. Perhaps, thought Will, that was how his fellow bees were able to dance in the air and convey to one another where pastures were, how far away from the hive those pastures were and in what direction. Dance and rhythm, space and time, pulsating sounds and waves of the breeze all worked together. The bees' dance was a map pointing to destinations providing sustenance for the soul as well as the body. Music was everywhere if only one would listen.

Next he spotted the Greek mathematician Archimedes sitting in a tub realizing about the displacement of water. *I wonder if he notices me? Sorry to interrupt your bath*, thought the bee to himself. *No worries, I won't bite you.* The scene was as real as if Will were actually back there in ancient Syracuse Sicily. What had the bee learned from spying on a man in a bathtub? Brilliant minds could take simple everyday occurrences and turn them into major tools for betterment. *Why then can't they find a cure for hive death before it's too late?* he asked himself, suddenly feeling the excruciating wounds he thought he had left on the rooftop of AlliedGreene. To save himself from the pain, he zoomed his attention back to his reverie in the Knowledge Chair. Maybe the answer would be there, in what he was learning.

The flashing dots began to sizzle with excitement as Will observed the Italian mathematician Fibonacci. Way back around 1200 or so, this brilliant man had traveled widely, helping to introduce Arabic numbers into Europe. In a hand-written book (because it was before the printing press) Fibonacci dipped his quill pen into ink to write, "A certain man put a pair of rabbits in a place surrounded on all sides by a wall. How many pairs of rabbits can be produced from that pair in a year if it is supposed that every month each pair begets a new pair which from the second month becomes productive?" The resulting sequence of numbers was the famous Fibonacci Sequence (in which each number is the sum of the two preceding numbers): 0-1-1-2-3-5-8-13-21-34-55 (and on to infinity). Even today, Will learned, investors and speculators in crop futures were using these numbers to increase their odds for success.

In fact, the magical-seeming number sequence mirrored the Golden Mean, a pattern that governed the shapes of galaxies, the swirls of sea shells, wave forms and plant growth. Renaissance Artists had absorbed the natural power of the Golden Mean as well, using it to structure paintings that led the viewer's eye up toward the top right of the artwork, a path that inherently expressed optimism and gave pleasant order to inspiration.

The Golden Mean, the Fibonacci number sequence, spiral-shapes and wave forms were observable everywhere. Will had hovered countless times over sunflower petals noticing their spiral patterns whirling from the central core. He had dipped into many a flower where nectar huddled like a treasure secreted away, protected by filaments where pollen dangled, awaiting the wind to plant more buds upon the soil. Will realized how economical this system was: When he had borne nectar and pollen back to the hive, some of the pollen fell to the ground or was blown away. To engender life was a noble purpose.

How many times had he flown through the branches of trees, delighting in the shimmer of sunlight through the leaves. Now he understood how spiral shapes related to stem and branch growth, allowing leaves and branches to be spaced around a stem or trunk in such a way that no single outgrowth overshadowed another. Because of that, all the plant would receive life-sustaining sunshine and water.

Nature and mathematics were entwined. His bees were part of a great pattern. Life made sense. But not if it was interfered with --- then it withered and died.

Will I wither and die? I hope not. I have work to do. But first, there's so much to learn that can make me more effective. Keep going, Knowledge Chair, I need you!

Instantly Will got the surprising feeling that the Flashing Screen was responding directly to his thought. What he now saw on the screen was Earth from above, as if a huge space-camera had moved up from the surface of Earth with its minute details to reveal the wider scope of planetary patterns. From that vantage point, Will observed the ecosystems of the entire planet, noticing how forces were interlocked and how patterns shifted. Ecosystems beginning with algae and plankton at the bottom of the food chain swung across powerful ocean-streams that wafted around land masses like giant cords. He followed the rhythms of the seasons, watching the path of nutrients and elements flow from desert sandstorms to wet jungles through temperate climates to ice caps. Weather fluctuations danced across huge expanses, happening so fast that the bee wondered if he were aging along with them.

It was apparent to the little bee-creature that life-forms had been designed to SUPPORT one another as the planet turned. As he watched, faults shifted against the crusty skin of Earth, tempests howled across the grassy plains, snow masses moved and retreated in cycles of Ice Ages and steaming Heat. Earth became for him a Living Thing, a potential paradise, a place on the brink of the unknown. Was it endangered too, like his fellow bees?

Astounded he followed the rise and death of mighty dinosaurs, the meteors that pockmarked the face of Earth, and all the manifold creatures being whittled into new shapes to survive on this swirling cloud-covered place. Birds had arisen from dinosaurs by developing feathers, raptors who raced with the wind and then found themselves soaring upward. Now birds of all colors and shapes welcomed sunrises with bursting choruses or sang nightingale arias to the moon.

Mankind appeared and won out over other two-legged creatures. Using his thumb Man grabbed fire, scared off predators and tasted the hunt he brought home, turning it over that fire. He carved tools that scraped the earth to make furrows for planting seeds. He made bread, brewed beer and created laws to protect his food and drink.

Then came the Wheel, and the Mantra of Progress rose like an enormous enveloping circle hovering like a UFO over the entire planet. The bee watched as time sped up with Pyramids and Temples, Palaces, Wars, Philosophy and the Arts, creations bringing blessings and curses along the canopy of Time. Civilizations rose and fell like the tides.

Geniuses emerged from the masses. Learning and art illuminated centers of culture while plagues, wars and witch-hunts halted progress. *Did new advances have to come at a great price?* It was like the Fibonacci sequence, for every two steps forward there was one step back, realized the bee. In Alexandria Hypatia the beautiful mathematician-philosopher devised the astrolabe to measure the passing of the hours, the width of rivers and the distance to the stars. Ancient papyrus scrolls from all over the world were gathered in the Alexandrian Library there, only to be burned in a torrent of ignorance. It was then, in reading Leonardo da Vinci's secret notebooks and understanding them, that the bee recognized why Leonardo sought to keep his inventions and discoveries secret. Religions brought solace amid all the flux and rose in cathedral splendor to hear the songs of angels. Yet sometimes what began in miracles or wisdom to give succor to the endless suffering of the multitudes ended up stultified into rituals and doctrines designed to keep an elite in power, with doctrines that were severe, hypocritical or cruel. *Was wisdom to be buried in the annals of blasted cities?*

The printing press came and as Humans began to see that Earth was not the center of the Universe, inventions were spreading as exploration mapped new lands and created whole populations exploited for gold, spices, cotton, tobacco, rum, diamonds and oil. Revolution cast blood on the cobblestones, while an Age of Enlightenment attempted to calm the surface of society for a short while. The bee wondered, *Why is it that groups and individuals seem to be at cross-purposes to one another?*

The Industrial Revolution flashed by in micro-nano-seconds with steam engines, water mills, factories blazing, trains and cars. It was easier to make a fortune and harder to overcome poverty, all at the same time. Suddenly cities became illuminated at night like jewels on black velvet. Electricity had been trapped in little glass bulbs. Smoke and gases began to circle the oxygen mantle, with forests being cut down. The trees were moaning, *How can we — stuck in our roots — produce sufficient oxygen?*

Soon computing machines, massive at first then tinier and tinier, funneled the storehouse of knowledge, and mass media flowed truth and lies across the continents. *Did you expect privacy along with technological wizardry?* asked the bee, knowing what it was like to live in a swarm that knew everybody's business all the time.

Photography and motion pictures came to record events and some painters decided they needn't copy nature anymore. Then wars, earthquakes and famine passed by in cycles of devastation and regrowth. Man dared to challenge the birds and rose in planes and rockets. A great Depression came, with breadlines and cinemas and dance halls. A vicious war followed, imprisoning horror in camps unspeakable.

The bee shuddered. *Was there no way to escape the recurring devastations of history?*

Chapter Twenty-One

Almond Tears

Music! the little bee cried sitting in his Knowledge Chair, hoping to cut forward or to do an instant replay back to the Renaissance, *I need some music to soothe me, to heal me, to tell me all this is worth the struggle and the pain,* so said the bee. For a good long while -- well, it was just minutes under the flashing machine -- the bee listened to the music of Planet Earth, unique amongst the galaxies for its scintillating beauty.

Hovering in its evanescent power, Will savored both masterpieces and simple music born out of everyday life: Lullabies, love songs and dirges that traced the inexorable path from birth to death. Chants born in ancient temples migrated north to echo among the vaulted arches of cloisters. Love songs of chivalry graced castle walls.

Creative geniuses rose out of anonymity to mold and carve sculptures of sound. The mystic nun Hildegard von Bingen created multiple textures of intertwining melodies and then sat down to write her visions and her recipes. Josquin des Prez and Palestrina wove tapestries of exultant prayer. Monteverdi gave birth to opera so we might weep with good reason. Handel followed suit in royal barges and oratorios. Bach proclaimed that all abundance emerges from order and that tenderness and glory were not strangers to each other. Mozart the Eternal Child breathed music with every breath, then died too soon. Beethoven took a simple motif and stretched it out, shaking his fist at deafness and convention. Brahms poured the richness of Romanticism into classic forms. Chopin made lace out of piano keys. Wagner threw down his gauntlet. Debussy and Ravel painted kaleidoscopes of new colors never heard before, while the operas of Puccini, Verdi and Bizet made love and death glorious with song. Then Stravinsky and Bartok, Shostakovitch and Prokofiev reinvented it all. Vaughn Williams' "A Lark Ascending" and Copland's "Appalachian Spring" were signposts of Human Potential in a bitter world.

Then electronic music and digital technology dared to imitate the celestial nighttime sky, dazzling in sparks that were records of times long ago and yet experienced in the present. Drum beats fused the music of slaves with folk songs from the Isles to make a new art that was simple and direct. It could be cubby-holed under various names, rock n' roll, pop songs, blues, hip-hop, heavy metal, reggae, r & b, tex-mex and the like, but it was simple and direct. The bravado of jazz brought back spontaneity and the magic of improvisation. All around the singing planet, enclaves of ethnic musical traditions struggled to be heard against the influx of "pop."

How much love and sadness, loss and greatness is in this Earth music! the bee marveled. *I'll pay attention to it more,* he vowed, noting that sea-shell vortexes resembled the structure of the inner ear.

Soothed by music from the horrors of war, the little bee asked for another Instant Replay and followed once again the Mantra of Progress and invention, paying particular attention to architecture and a brilliant experiment with hexagons. *The geodesic dome is so much like my own hive!* he marveled.

Next, the Knowledge-Flashing-Screen showed him Dictionaries from all the major languages on Earth. He understood the derivation of their words from more ancient tongues and learned how these languages had sprouted, either trapped in mountain holds or transported by ocean travel and conquest. He saw the spread of languages powerful in literature and technology. *It's good to know that perhaps Humans will learn to get along,* he hoped.

Yet sadly, the bee observed the killing-off, time after time, of yet another special tongue amongst the isolated mountain-dwellers or loin-cloth-wearers not yet discovered under the tents of jungle growth. Language was a living thing, with many dialects, many meanings, many realities. Like fire and the wheel, Language and Writing set mankind apart. Other species had their own complex or simple communication systems, bird calls, whale cries, chimpanzee gesture-linquistics and grunts. *Man rules these, but does he rule wisely?* This question troubled the bee.

To answer this question, he toured animal species of all kinds including a catalog of endangered and extinct species. Under the category "Dire Danger" he saw Honey Bees, natural healers and pollinators of untold numbers of vegetables, flowers and fruits and the only insect who communicates by dance. The statistics on Colony Disorder Collapse were increasingly devastating, and entire crops were not coming to fruition. He thought of the almonds, shaped like brown tears, so delicious to Humankind and so nourishing.

At that point he signaled the Aliens to stop the machine for a moment. A small almond-shaped tear fell from the bee's eye onto his chair. The tear singed the neuro-sensors as if the cloth itself were understanding his pain and his concern. Containing his emotions as best he could, the bee signaled for the Knowledge Screen to resume.

The worship of his Ancestral Goddess Bee through ages long ago brought a few more tears when he learned that the ancient Egyptians believed that the honeybee was born from a tear in the eye of the sun. Even before that, bee images were carved in stone and dangled in golden earrings on Sumerian princesses' ears. The Mayans had considered honey the food of the Gods. The Celts and all ancient peoples had noticed the industrious harmony of the hive and the mystical way that bees danced to communicate the location of fragrant flowers and fruits.

In that way, his species had become symbols of truth and purification, of love and the majesty of knowing how to spawn life and how to heal. Will's dancing tail twitched when he remembered his now-dead Queen and his once-stable worker and gatherer bees coordinated to sustain the great chain-of-life. The ancient Greeks had worshiped honeybees in sacred groves. The Healing Goddess emanating from the Ash Tree of Life was called forth by priestesses named for honey itself, "Melissae." Were his tears to be wasted, his wax, sweet honey and Royal Jelly and even his venom that -- some thought -- possessed healing qualities when combined with other substances?

Healer Bee, heal thyself, he muttered, asking the Happy Faces, who had now turned their smiles upside down seeing his distress, to stop the Flashing Screen for just a moment. In that moment, how many hives had died? It was too much to bear. *Perhaps,* he thought, *the answer and the cure will emerge if I study how Humans have looked to the sky since Time Immemorial to attempt to explain Riddles more ancient and more complex than the one I am charged with unraveling.*

He was able to read the Vedas and the Upanishads of Hindu wisdom that hinted at earlier Alien visits. He read about the enlightenment of the Buddha, the sayings of Confucius, the symbolic speculations of Tarot Cards. He spent a while on the Old and New Testaments of the Bible, comparing them to the original Aramaic scrolls to search for authenticity and Life Lessons, then he read the Koran and the Jewish Commentaries, savoring them and comparing them, wondering why these caused so much upheaval when there were so many ways to warm themselves in the Quilt of Mankind and ask questions of the Cosmos without fighting.

He read the Egyptian Book of the Dead and wondered if death were an illusion --- perhaps it took lifetime after lifetime to solve one's PERSONAL Riddle. Perhaps Death was the question AND the answer. He would gladly wait a long, long time to find out. But was it already too late? (He suddenly remembered a little bee body on the roof, severely injured, losing breath. Passing into unconsciousness.) WAS he dead? He dared not know that one single thing. Even as he sat absorbing oceans of knowledge, surfing over lies to get ashore, he did not yet have the courage to ask himself, AM I DEAD?

So he continued re-living his hour or two in the Knowledge Chair.

Resuming his attention onto the Knowledge Screen, he analyzed social strata-organizations from matriarchies to patriarchies to priesthood-rulers, from beneficent kings like Charlemagne to empires ever rising and decaying in predictable but unfortunate patterns. He observed the path toward dictatorship and the birth of short-lived democracies. Cruel groups came, looming at opposite ends of the political spectrum until they joined each other in the circle of behavior. Economic systems from barter on up to mega-corporations spread, while protest movements fought for the small business, the entrepreneur, the little book store, the corner grocery, the organic farmer.

A Spider Web of Information twisted across the world like giant lace, trapping Opinions like insects or butterflies in its net. He asked himself, *Is it possible that people are at last communicating to each other past all barriers and differences?* The bee looked carefully. Yes, to some degree, but he saw Humans staring into machines, so immersed they forgot to talk to each other even when they sat across from one another. They took walks with these machines in front of their noses, never sniffing the sweet smell of flowers.

Oh Humans, communication, REAL communication is your answer! The little Pollen-Gatherer pressed this exhortation into his consciousness with more intensity than he had ever felt, even more than the immense grief he'd felt when he returned to his hive to see all his brethren dead. *Do not imitate or worship the Idols of Machinery. Do not kill off the synchronicity of life-forms. Do not interrupt the interlocking weather patterns that make life happen. Do not allow greed and ignorance, hatred and stalking pride to destroy what can be a Wonderland!*

Would anyone hear him? It almost didn't matter. What mattered was that he could himself communicate. He would die if he had to, to represent the power of the Individual and the glory of sharing expression, wisdom and community. Maybe that was not the right path, to die, to leave his body and his Mission on a tar roof, next to an abandoned friend.

Will was now the most intelligent of all things on Earth. It was a gift and a burden. His learning lay in him like a seed, a piece of life-giving pollen, an Explanation beyond any Riddle. It lay at the core of truth, beyond words or formulas, as powerful and gentle as the greatest music. He had become not only a scholar but a mystic.

He had become more than himself in these flashes of insight. He had a duty to the immensity of everything he had just experienced. It was NOT time to die. *What good was Knowledge if you didn't USE it? What good was using it if you didn't use it for the good of OTHERS?*

He suddenly realized that all these Abducted creatures, the cat, the crumb and the dog, were his Companions. Crumb with his strength of character and muscle, he who signified the breaking of bread and the need to find one's forbears. Nefertiti, she who recalled lifetime after lifetime and could speak any tongue and was able to break through the transparent veil of time. Whisk, who embodied Unconditional Love and the abilities of those who only seem dumb but are merely misunderstood. They were the FOUR. They were his Companions.

He began to pray, his exhortations floating around him in a halo of light that the Aliens actually noticed. It was glowing about the chair like a mist of candlelight... but it was coming from this tiny bee.

Stop the Knowledge Screen, signaled the bee. It was too much to take. For a second, the bee thought himself completely, irreversibly dead. *Am I over the threshold?* he asked himself. *What is after death? Isn't that the greatest mystery of ALL?*

At this point, he asked for the machine to stop for a bit to allow his air sacs to fill again with more oxygen. He needed a change. He asked for Literature and lighter Food for Thought. What a relief to sample the poems of Li Bai from the T'ang Dynasty, a Japanese haiku about a leaf floating down a stream, the sprightly free verse of E. E. Cummings, the beauteous outrage of Dylan Thomas and John Donne, and the simple profundity of Emily Dickinson and Edna St. Vincent Millay.

He read Sun Tzu's THE ART OF WAR, the dainty and subtle social commentaries of Jane Austin, the rumblings and roarings of Charles Dickens, the great speeches of Pericles, Cicero, Abe Lincoln, Mahatma Gandhi and Martin Luther King Jr. He became engulfed in the panoramic histories containing precision insights written by Will Durant and his wife Ariel until he could see whole patterns spread out before him -- Two steps forward, one step back, like the Fibonacci sequence. *When would Mankind's Grand Experiment bring a solid and thriving investment?*

Returning to lighter fare, how he loved to chuckle and smile reading WINNIE THE POOH, CHARLOTTE'S WEB, THE WIZARD OF OZ and all the fantastical territories of imagination. He guffawed so much at watching comic television shows from the 1950's that he almost fell off his Knowledge Chair.

His favorite was the reading -- word for word while looking up archaic meanings as needed -- of William Shakespeare's plays and sonnets. What did he remember most of all? "To be or not to be, that is the question." It became his motto. (He spelled it "2 BEE or not 2 BEE.")

That was when he chose "Will" as his name, in honor of Shakespeare. The name came to him in a Flash of Insight. He draped it over his concept of himself, a mantle signifying everything that he stood for, an outcry and a resolve to change things for the better in whatever way he could.

Emerging from the Knowledge Chair and Flashing Screen, he felt as if he'd aged a million years. He felt his face -- good, no wrinkled surface or shrunken cheeks. His wings were still vibrant and could flutter as fast as when he was spawned inside the hive. Time was an illusion -- he hadn't aged in the least. Indeed, he glowed. Knowledge had taken him on Time's Journey but he was energized.

"Don't call me Ishmael," he said, in a deep throaty, dramatic voice, "Call me WILL! I am Will!"

Healer Bee, heal thyself! So saying that to himself, after re-living all the time in the Knowledge Chair where he again restored his grasp of the Knowledge granted him, Will made a Decision. The answer to the question "To Bee or Not to Bee" WAS -- and HAD to be -- to LIVE, to BE, to FEEL, even if it hurt! And so he returned to the roof, to awareness of it, to a tinge of sensation that somehow he electrified into his thorax, abdomen and wings. He assumed bit by bit his bodily form, testing the cells, pretending (or was he actually doing this?) that he was passing a purple lazer beam across his injured body, noticing how his aura then grew in radiance and iridescent luster.

He had found a Way to take back his body. Will HAD found a Way! As soon as he did, in an inexplicable moment bound to the ancient healing ways of his ancestors, much of his splintered, broken, gaping-holed body healed. Just like that.

He lay there for a second, feeling his air sacs inflating, taking in the sight of the sky, feeling the sun's warmth and some mysterious dew-like drops gently grazing his yellow and black stripes, loving being ALIVE! His distraught breadcrumb Companion lay next to him, crying grainy tears over his body. *Ah, these are the dew-like drops I felt just now. Thank you, dear Crumb.*

"Whiskey-India-Lima-Lima, come IN! Come IN, Will! Come BACK, Will! Don't leave me here... alone!"

Will opened his clustered eyes, saw dozens of Crumb-faces and smiled. "You called me?" he said. "Let's get crackin'!"

Crumb nearly fainted he was so happy.

Carol Worthey

Chapter Twenty-Two

Impervious

The Pee-Ons had already come in full force to arrest the Doc and the former Boss' Secretary. "We're just doing our job," the security officers muttered like robots afraid to lose their jobs. They grabbed the scientist's cell phone, banged it on the corner of Ms. Scoop's desk until it broke into pieces and dumped the pieces into a wastebasket by the side of her chair.

Then they noticed Scoop was sheltering her handbag inside arms clutched so tight they were bloodless. The Head Security officer ripped the handbag away from her and gave it to his Lieutenant, who dashed out of the office to secure the "evidence" somewhere. Glenda screamed and Matt cringed -- The incriminating photos had been nabbed!

Dr. Matt was so mad that he knocked over the wastebasket with his foot as two hulking figures grabbed him. *If only my little Karate Champ were here,* he thought. *She'd show them a thing or two. But of course it's a good thing she isn't here. Why didn't she answer the phone?*

Staring down at the overturned wastebasket, Matt saw a piece of paper that had tumbled out. It was blank except for some marker that had "IMPERVIOUS: Seed for All Seasons" scrawled across the top of the paper. Now he really knew. The marketing plan, the phony name, the outrage of something sold to the public under the pretense of years of solid research.

Handcuffing them both to each other, the Chief of Security led them into the Manufacturing Plant. Glenda had had to take her high-heels off and was barely able to keep up with Matt's wrist as they were pushed and pummeled and practically dragged on the ground past the huge double doors of the Production Facility and Packing Plant of AlliedGreene. Her feet were already freezing.

The sight was overwhelming inside the Facility, impressive if you considered size more important than quality — ostentatious in its declaration of the Rights of the Industrial Age to rule over the Little Fellow and the everyday uninformed Consumer. The machinery dwarfed anyone who entered. Dr. Matt Baruti had spent his life trying to create worthwhile nutrient-rich products for that same Little Fellow.

All of a sudden he was torn between two worries: His own personal safety (of course including Glenda's pitiful, weakened frame) and the safety for a public lied to by food companies and mega-farm corporations at every turn. It took all of one second for Matt to decide that HIS SURVIVAL (including Scoop's) was most at stake at this particular moment. How else was he going to make a difference? If he was imprisoned or murdered here, he'd lose Zoe, he'd lose Time, he'd lose it ALL!

Seeds lay in ten-foot silos. An assembly line ramp stretched over two hundred feet across giant shafts. Interlocking gears loomed three stories high, all the way up to the smoky glass skylight of the rooftop, where the gears bent downward to giant vises and spinning cutters. Finally, rollers were designed to pass seeds across nutrient baths and steamy pools all the way to the final product: Seed packets arranged fifty to a box, shrink-wrapped for shipping and ready to be sent around the world.

Along the rubberized assembly line — the only part of the machinery that was still running — were stations guaranteeing pouring, spraying, drying, sorting, packing, sealing and stamping over sixty thousand seed packets a day. No normal workers or foremen were around — it was

Sunday, supposèd Day of Rest, Relaxation and Religious Observance.

The smell of ninety-five different kinds of vegetable and fruit seeds was overwhelming, like being packed in solid dirt ready to sprout into some kind of outer-space composite plant-food.

Matt was shocked. It was one thing to be handcuffed to someone, dragged into the production facility (he'd never actually seen it -- it was strictly kept "off premises" by the CEO from the Research Department) and another thing to reel from the intense chemical overlay off-gassing from all the different seeds. Some chemical feast! Seeds of all description, corn seeds, soy seeds, alfalfa seeds, you name it, were layered in those silos all around him.

Glenda Scoop had fainted. A tall column that stretched from floor to skylight was painted in searing lime-green. The Security Chief tied Matt and Glenda up with heavy coiled ropes of genetically modified hemp. Apparently, the Head of Security was a seasoned sailor whose knots were going to be "impervious" to attempts to untie them... at least for a while.

"Are you going to leave us here without any drinking water? Nothing to eat? Nowhere to pee or... well, you know."

"Boss's orders!" said the hardened Security Chief. He turned and ordered his five lackeys to leave. A short runt of a timid security guard glanced from side to side in fear and caution and hid behind the thick column. He pulled three plastic water bottles out of his pockets, small ones but welcome, a few packets of crackers and a little card that said, "Sorry" on it in scrawled letters. Then he ran after the others, as his boss yelled, "Snively, get OVer here!

On the double!" The huge metal door clanged shut. The only light was from the skylight three stories above their heads. Glenda was coming out of her dead faint, so scared she couldn't even scream.

Matt leaned over to her and whispered, "I've never liked Mondays. But I can't wait for this one to come. Glenda, don't lose heart. It may stink in here, but there's air, some water... if we can reach it and a few crackers. I have a feeling we'll get out of this okay."

She glanced at the scientist with a combination of gratitude and utter discouragement, her eyebrows swept together like a horizontal question mark. So this was what eighteen years was worth.

***

"Roger. Over and out.... We... we made it!" wheezed the bee, reassuring Crumb he was alright. "I'm okay... I'm back. I thought I was a goner for a bit there. But I'm alive! And I recovered my Treasury of Knowledge, in a weird kind of way. (We can talk about that later.)"

He thought to himself for a second and suddenly burst out with another statement said too soon, "Do you know that you're not your..." (Will stopped himself from adding the word at the end, "body.")

That awareness was something that the breadcrumb had probably better realize on his own. At any rate, Will was still absorbing all of his experience. He'd hold it to himself. It behooved him to concentrate on the Mission at hand. A pain in his side zoomed him back to the physical universe. "Ouch!"

"What hurts? Are you sure you're okay to do all this?" asked Crumb.

"I do hurt a bit, not as much as when we landed, but I'm so glad to be alive! I think I'm up to this -- I have to figure out what we're supposed to DO with the sign."

Crumb responded, "I'll tell you what -- Rest up for now."

Will was in pain but he knew he couldn't rest for long. The bee closed his eyes for a few minutes, concentrating on completely healing the air sac as best he could. Finally, he felt sufficiently rested to look at the sign, go over the Riddle instructions and figure out what the Riddle was saying and what needed to be done with the sign. None of this happened that fast. He still really wasn't sure what the Riddle was telling him. Minutes passed.

Crumb, thinking to help, offered, "The Riddle says 'Heed the signs and turn them around'. We found the sign. But I need you, Will, to tell me how to turn the sign around. I'm really tired -- I'm sure you're even MORE tired than I am --- but I just had some of that great bee pollen and I'm getting my muscle-power back! Here, have some pollen." Will munched on the sweet savory pollen piece and felt better.

Crumb couldn't help thinking, *As long as Will remains conscious, there's hope. Otherwise, we've come all this way for nothing. I better divvy out the pollen that's left, bit by bit, to him.*

It seemed like a half-hour of silence went by while Will glanced up and down the letters on the sign. Finally, Crumb's voice rose in fear, "What do I DO with these huge letters? Turn them around, knock some of them down, move some of them or WHAT? You tell ME!"

Will was short of breath, one of his air sacs still had a little hole in it. Crumb was afraid he was asking too much of the little pilot-friend, tiring him out. But there was no turning back. Now that they had found the right sign, it had to be altered in some way.

Suddenly as if a diamond of sunlight had broken through the clouds while the whole city lay before him, Crumb had an epiphany. For the first time in his life -- when his biggest secret was his fear of making mistakes, embarrassing goofs that would show up how stupid he really was (for wasn't that why his parents had left him?) -- Crumb realized that he WAS smart, just not smart ENOUGH. Being intelligent about the odds and the circumstances meant that Crumb had to own up to his limitations. That was the only smart thing to do: *Let Will tell me what to do!*

Crumb's realizations flooded in. Being a good leader didn't necessarily mean being the smartest in a group. Leadership was a command position depending on the keen advice of others and taking brave steps to inspire group members to action toward a worthwhile goal. Naturally, organizing knowhow was part of it too, knowing when to delegate and when to take charge. He now understood that he could depend on Will's brilliance without downgrading his own leadership. His own strength lay in character and muscle. He was steeled to put his muscle to use. Finally he could quiet his impatient curiosity and allow someone else to guide him. Right now the most important thing Crumb could do was to sit back, let Will figure the sign out, and give him some pollen every now and then to rejuvenate and heal his weakened body.

That was when, digging into the bottom of the saddle-pack for more pollen, Crumb found a small mound of moist Royal Jelly stuck onto a few of the pollen pieces. Zoe must have put a bit of that elixir into the pack, at the very bottom just in case.

When Will tasted the Royal Jelly, he glowed. *Thank you, thank you, Crumb! I feel better already!*

Thank Zoe, responded the breadcrumb, relieved to see Will feeling a lot better.

Staring up at the sign, the bee was engrossed but mystified. He wasn't sure just how the sign letters should be arranged. They had come all this way but NOW it was the moment he had dreaded deep inside: *What should I tell Crumb to do with these huge letters in the sign?* One good thing — the sign was constructed of individual letters not just letters painted all together on a single board. (That had been one of Will's determining factors when he spotted this particular sign as the right one. But that didn't mean it was any easier to decipher the solution.)

He reviewed every word in the Riddle down to each of its letters, scanned every line and imagined any possible nuance using his vast knowledge of language to play with double meanings or possible misspellings. What WAS the message — or perhaps more than one — hidden in the rooftop sign? The time for guesswork was over. This HAD to be right. Will still had occasional jabs of pain, but they were nothing compared to the painstaking work he had to do now.

Over and over again, he compared the original with all possible permutations. The Riddle seemed simple sometimes, and sometimes it was enigmatic, complex, confusing. Will needed to call on more than his knowledge of language and syntax here. It was vital to examine every probability, every alternative. Somewhere was the intended solution, the answer, the RIGHT one. Somewhere in this Riddle was its future incarnation:

Where there's a will,
you know there's a way!
What looks like work
can turn into play!
When green is red
and "N" turns to "D",
A-B-C's the day!

Learning to read
plants a seed that is sound!
Heed the signs
and turn them around!
"E"nunciate well
and learn how it's spelled.
A crumb will lead the way!

No one's too small
to follow a dream,
and no dream's too big
if it's straight from the heart!
For life is in living
and living's an art!
Enjoy the journey today!

So hold on tight
to being taught,
for truth is a price
that can't be bought!
This Riddle will tell you:
It's real food for thought!

It seemed like hours and hours had passed but it was just minutes. Will felt like he was at an international chess match, picturing various moves, various plays, some failing right away, some taking their good old time before they didn't pan out. Suddenly his compound eyes glowed golden with an inner fire. He knew how to turn the sign around!

Finally, in measured tones so as not to take the wind out of him (his air sac was still self-repairing), Will ordered Crumb to knock certain of these enormous heavy letters down.

"I've GOT it!"

"You're gonna be the busiest breadcrumb the world has ever known." Will was preparing Crumb for the enormous task ahead, although (to tell you the truth) he was unsure that the breadcrumb would be strong enough.

"What do I do?" Crumb's excitement competed with his fear. Will continued with specific instructions.

"This has to be done in seven separate steps. There are TWO messages to the public-at-large here. And if we leave the first message up for twenty-five minutes or so, that should get some press and the TV news here fast."

Even as exhausted as the bee was, his mischievous smile broadened. "The final sign formation is a doozy, Crumb, a real doozy! All heck may break loose. So do exactly as I say, IN the order I tell you to."

"Sure! Just hang on, pace yourself, my friend," cautioned Crumb, "and recover --- We need you."

Will carried on. "First that big 'L' --- not the second 'L' but the very first one in 'ALLIED.' Push it down so it's not visible anymore from the street. Be sure not to break it and please, push it down on the ROOF -- don't let it fall OFF the roof or someone may get done-in."

"Gotcha."

Crumb raced over to the sign letters. They were as big compared to the little bread-dot as Earth might be to half a galaxy, or so it seemed to Crumb looking up at the looming letters. Had the Aliens given him enough strength to push the letter down?... ON the roof, not OFF the roof. *No time like the Present,* thought Crumb. The pollen seemed to be working.

Pushing and straining against the bottom of the letter he pushed harder than he ever had in his entire crumby life. The "L" was groaning, resisting the change. Crumb pushed some more but it started to fall too fast and too much to one side. Crumb caught it at the mid-point of the letter and slowly leveled it down onto the roof. He lay there for a second, puffing away, stars of a lost galaxy spinning around in front of his eyes. After he had regained full consciousness, he lumbered back to the reclining bee.

"Here, Will, have another pellet of pollen. It's in the saddle with the paddle, not the pellet with the poison. We'll do better with the letter, with the saddle with the paddle!"

"Oh stop!" Will had watched old movies (when he'd been in the Alien spaceship being indoctrinated with All Human Knowledge including reruns of classics) and he recognized the joke. "Back to business, you excuse for a Loaf! ...Now you see that last 'E' in 'GREENE'? Push it down the same way you did that 'L'. ON the roof."

Crumb raced over to the end of the sign and watched in horror as the last "E" in "GREENE" came crashing down to one side. It was scrambling close to the right edge of the roof before Crumb managed to beat its speed of descent and hold it steady until it screeched flat, with a few inches leaning over the edge of the roof. He had almost been crushed beneath it.

Hyperventilating as no Crumb has ever hyperventilated before (almost as if he were his friend the Kitchen Sponge filling up with water and then being squeezed dry by a Human hand) Crumb lay near the dire edge of the roof looking d-o-w-n on a machine shop. A car mechanic was pointing up to the sign, with a cell phone to one ear. *Is he calling 9-1-1-2-much?* Crumb better get cracking faster. *No more jokes.*

"Now what?" Crumb had recovered his breath.

"Push down the letter 'D' at the end of the first word. Don't let it fall! Just down on the roof like before!"

"Okay... I hope this is it, Boss." So saying, Crumb managed to push the "D" down with a lot of huffing and puffing. As it fell, the "D" swerved a bit at an angle and touched the "G" next to it. The "G" trembled, but fortunately stayed put. Crumb lumbered back to the bee like a knocked-out prizefighter reeling to get back to his corner.

"Take a look at the sign now, Crumb! Good work!"

There on top of one of the tallest buildings in the city, letters broadcast the first of two messages:

A LIE GREEN

A TV news helicopter began circling the roof, videoing what looked like letters collapsing under their own weight. Obviously, the cameras wouldn't pick up the sight of a breadcrumb or a fallen bee. It just seemed as if the letters were magically lowering themselves.

Was magic always the logical result of unseen forces ill-observed but actually there?

Will and Crumb could hear, through the huge hum of the helicopter propellers, a Newscaster-Pilot, normally in charge of traffic reports, bellowing into his earphone-mike, "This is wild, folks! 'A Lie Green', appearing as you can see from downed letters in the usual sign of mega-corporation (one of the staples of our city economy) AlliedGreene. Is this an accident? There's no one on the roof. Is the sign trying to tell us something? Over and out, from Channel with the Panel, Roger Barry here, Traffic Dude."

***

Whisk commanded the two hundred and ninety-seven dogs, from butterfly-eared Papillons to tall Irish Wolfhounds to sit, just to sit, facing the front of the building in a semi-circle. What was the most amazing thing was that dog breeds that normally would be at each other's throats were not fighting. A stronger purpose was in the air, the scent of Victory Possible! (Not to mention, lots of treats.)

Jumping on top of a cardboard box abandoned somehow in front of the revolving door -- what was inside of it? -- Whisk addressed the Canine Convention with an attention-getting and rousing opener followed by a slew of no-nonsense orders.

"Dogs, you are the WOOF in the Woof and Warp of Life! (Ya get me, Pooches? You're a part of something bigger than yourselves, but you are Important.) So listen up: Guard this building. No biting or clawing. None! Growling, howling and baring of teeth is okay. Barking --

go ahead only if you have to. (Of course, you'll have to. But keep it to a minimum.)"

All the dogs were paying full attention to Whisk. Never had he felt so in control. He was Top Dog in the Neighborhood, no doubt about it. He continued.

"Do not provoke the Enemy. WHO is the enemy? You will smell the stench of deceit and betrayal. Greed and cruelty. There are two Human Enemies in there, one very fat, one very skinny and they STINK! They go by the names of Mordred and Iago, but use your nose to confirm. Pee-YOO! There are some lousy underlings in there too, Security Guards. They'll tell you they're just doin' their jobs. No dice, they smell like pee-ons, ya know, the lowest on any fire hydrant or tree trunk. They have uniforms on that will give them away. Don't attack. You are just to keep the public at bay and the Good Guys and Enemy and Pee-Ons inside the building until real help can arrive. I'll let you know when you can let anyone into the building. Until I say so, no one breaks your Semi-Circle of Protection! ...*Get it?*"

The dogs began to roar, "*Got it!*"

Whisk answered in one word: "*Good.*"

"Oh," he added, "We have to conquer before any treats can be distributed. The pet supply stores may not be open on Sunday. Just do your best and you'll get treats!"

***

Ken and Hazel were drained. Where was Zoe? Where were Whisk and Nefertiti? And to make matters worse, where was the Doc? Ken had tried to call Matt (hating to tell him his daughter was nowhere to be found at home or anywhere on Tempest Street, but knowing it was his responsibility to tell Matt)... but Matt wasn't answering his cell phone either! Ken felt dizzy. He needed to sit down.

Both Ken and Hazel sat in their living-room staring at the back wall for a few minutes, numb, trying to figure out what to do next. Should they call the Police? They couldn't stay at home, obviously. Finally, they turned on the TV just to see if there might be any news that might help them. Any NEWS? The videos were playing over and over, it was the Media Vultures latest meal!

There was definitely something weird going on where Doc worked -- and on a Sunday too! Was their friend okay? Ken called the Tennis Club -- maybe Matt was practicing his serve. (*He could use some help on that and on his backhand,* thought Ken.) The Doc playing tennis while his daughter was missing didn't make any sense, but Ken was so concerned he was just trying to fill in time by doing something. At the Tennis Club the Receptionist checked and no, Dr. Baruti hadn't signed in and she even checked the courts, he wasn't there. More likely: Was Zoe at her father's company? Maybe Matt had tried to call Ken back to tell him Zoe was fine, she was now back with him. Nope, no message on Ken's cell.

Had she been kidnapped? (*Too extreme,* thought Hazel, patting her nervous husband's hand.) Zoe had forgotten her cell phone at home as Ken had discovered. Maybe she was off somewhere with a friend or at the library. Hazel called the local branch and they had a recorded message saying they'd be closed that Sunday for cataloging work and some shelf installations. Ken called the police but was put on hold for so long that he decided just to get over to AlliedGreene himself. (There wasn't much to go on anyway, just speculation. No hard evidence.) Hazel and the kids insisted on coming with him.

The Baker Family jumped into their old woodie station wagon. (Hazel had the SUV, but Ken prized his old woodie.) What Ken referred to as "My General Hat Selection" was tossed all over the back seat where Johnny and Sally were going to sit, so the kids piled about two dozen hats in the trunk area way in back so they could sit down in the seat behind their parents. Dad forgot his sunglasses he was so frazzled, but he refused to go back in the house to get them. Hazel reached in her bag and she just happened to have a pair. But they had rhinestone bling on the frames, and Dad said, "Thanks, but no thanks" and squinted as he drove in the morning sun. It was about 9:30 by that time. (Matt had left the house around 5:10 a.m. to meet Ms. Scoop at AlliedGreene, Zoe about an hour and a half later, after meeting with the Four to go over the plans for the Mission and running home to change and get her bike. The Bakers had no way of knowing any of this.)

For fifteen minutes the Bakers got stuck in a tiresome traffic jam, but finally the honking stopped and the cars started up. Sally and Johnny were restless and kept on reaching into the back area, playing with the hats.

Hazel was scolding them for messing with the hats. "Come on Kids, we're all nervous enough!"

Johnny kept on saying, "Are we there yet?"

Sally started to feel tears coming, but didn't want anyone to know, so she just kept her head to the side, looking out the window.

Missing pets, disappearing friends... it was all too much.

Chapter Twenty-Three

A Lie Spelled Out

Zoe reached the corporation headquarters flabbergasted to see the Semi-Circle of Canine Protection around the building. She had dreamed something like this but here it was, real. Nefertiti was sitting up in the bike-basket in the posture of a Bastet Statue, proud, determined, psychically-empowered and ready to be called into action, if need be. Both cat and child spotted Whisk at the same time, in the center perched on a soapbox directly in front of the Revolving Door entrance to AlliedGreene.

"Whisk!" Zoe called out. "Let me in!"

Whisk lifted his paw and signaled to the Great Dane and the little Yorkshire Terrier directly in front of Zoe to make room for her, the bike and the cat to enter. Whisk looked from side to side at all the dogs assembled there, to communicate to them that it was okay to let this Human-child walk toward him.

"Whisk, I'm so happy to see you. Have you seen my Dad?" asked Zoe. Whisk whimpered with his ears cast down a sorry "No."

"He's in there." Zoe's eyes were intense. "I just know he is. Have you seen Will and Crumb anywhere?"

Just then the Air Traffic Helicopter began circling around the roof. Zoe spotted the sign but it didn't say ALLIED GREENE anymore. It proclaimed "A LIE GREEN."

Hosts of people were streaming toward the monolithic building, running or stumbling in their desire to find their dogs or see the sign as it changed. Vans, compact cars, sleek sedans and flat-bed trucks were driving down Tesla Road, but soon came to a standstill in a long traffic jam. Zoe could hear the huge microphone, oddly louder than the helicopter blades, announcing to the TV public, "Folks, if you are missing a dog, walk here, don't drive. What a traffic jam on Tesla." Car horns were beeping, some dogs were barking, dog-owners were calling out pet names, it was pandemic pandemonium!

Zoe turned to the growing crowd of angry, frustrated and confused spectators and dog-owners, peppered with police.

"I'm Zoe Baruti. My Dad works for this company. He's in there, I'm sure. Something's going on in there. Do NOT try to enter. The proper authorities will be called in. I beg you!"

Just then the crowd inhaled, a gasp from the Humans so loud it almost sounded like propeller blades. They were looking up.

On the roof, a new sign was beginning to form. Who was moving these letters around??

***

After his little dose of Royal Jelly, Will was gaining strength. He was intent on hurrying up the process of switching and removing the letters until the final message was visible -- to be witnessed, photographed, video'd across the city, state, country and the world.

"Crumb, push the first letter, that 'A' close up to the 'L'."

Crumb too was gaining strength, oddly em-powered by the sheer zest of accomplishing feats of strength that he'd never ever imagined a crumb could do. He went to the left side of the "A" and pushed it right up against the "L". The first word now spelled "ALIE"... but that made no sense... not yet.

"Now move the fallen 'D' over to the right, at the end, but keep it flat on the roof." Crumb pushed the letter over as instructed.

"Now is where you are going to REALLY have this sign make sense! You've done great so far. Are you ready, Crumb?"

"Fire away! Ready!"

"These are gonna be the two toughest changes you have to pull off, but they'll be your last ones. Are you really ready to tackle this?"

Crumb looked down at his packet of pollen. He'd need some extra strength now. There were only ten little buds left, all of them coral-colored, his favorite flavor.

"Do you want a few of these yourself, Will?" Crumb asked.

"Not now. Save me four, okay?"

Crumb munched two delicious pollen-pieces, then he set aside eight, two batches of four for Will, the last of their supply. It was vital to keep Will's healing process going.

"Here's what you have to do, and as fast and skillfully as possible! You are going to have to move the big letter 'N' at the end of 'GREEN' over to the 'E' of 'ALIE'. That will spell..."

A lightning bolt struck the roof, a wind-storm was blowing the letters of the sign all around. Will and Crumb looked up. It was the UFO of the Fifty Happy Faces! Had they come to help or harm the Mission? In a nano-second the space ship went invisible. Cloaked!

***

Iago and Mordred were clinking beer glasses together down at the Commissary. They seemed to have no idea what was occurring outside with the dogs, the growing public and the rooftop "spelling bee" that was transforming the sign. Mordred had definitely had one too many.

"Billionsh," swirled Mordred, gloating over his beer, soused and grotesque. "We're both filtheeee RICHhhhh! We'll own the patentsch too. A great marketingggg campaign, too bad we don't have champPAYgne, campaign, champagne, that's rhymeshhh. Here's to O'Greene and Fripple! Here's to

Imperrrrvioushhh!"

The drunk CEO had his flabby arm around his skinny cohort's shoulder. Iago hadn't indulged in any liquor, not yet, just to ensure that all was going according to plan:

First the safe cracked (done), the findings inputted into the Seed Formulation Program (check), the packets printed in a huge Rush Priority Order on Saturday night

(done), 'Impervious: Seed for All Seasons' packed and ready for shipment. ...And how about a little bit of celebration poison in his boss' champagne glass. The kind of poison that's 'impervious' to detection at his autopsy. Iago tittered inwardly, silently, savoring the vision. *After all, Mordred's been losin' it lately. I could do such a better job as the CEO....*

Iago was leaning on the flaccid arm of his boss, gawking at his every word in mock worship.

All of a sudden, Gordon Mordred O'Greene stood stock still, frozen in absolute terror and amazement. His arm was lifted as it HAD been a second before, but there was NO ONE THERE ANYMORE!!

The Alien Spaceship had done its most perfect Abduction since raiding an entire Socks-of-the-Centuries store at Holymuster Mall a year before!

Iago was staring at fifty pairs of Alien Eyes leering at him grimly above fifty very happy grins.

"Just who we need!" intoned the Fifty all at the same time.

"You, Iago Fripple, have been chosen as the most interesting Villain in recent history. We know that all your shenanigans have been instigated because you lack a MATE!"

Iago tried not to agree but their Fifty Happy Faces all in complete accord made him nod. He knew they had lazer-beamed into the very core of his being. Ever since his mother had abandoned little baby Iago on a church step two days before Thanksgiving, he had both hated and longed for a Perfect Mate to take the place of his missing Mom.

"You," said the Fifty, "are the Marketing Head of our Bureau of Sox Research. It will be your job to find MATES for all the experimental subjects we have captured over the century. Perhaps you will find a Perfect Mate for yourself."

Iago knew he'd finally gone to Heaven although he knew he didn't deserve it.

***

Zoe found Mordred passed out cold, completely drunk, flat on the Commissary Floor. Security guards were dashing into the cafeteria.

All of a sudden, the Chief of Security fell face forward, slipping on a banana peel. Three other officers tripped over his body, landed on top of his large metal badge or his gun, and fell in a heap. Passed out cold.

It was Happy! "Do you think I'd leave you alone to do this all by yourself?!" he said. (It wasn't until days later that Zoe found out how Happy had managed to come all that way. He had sneaked into her sack next to the water bottles when she went to the Baker's house before taking off, to fetch Nefertiti. Happy had been biked to the company by her!)

The only two guards who hadn't tripped included "Snively" (the kind guard who had slipped the Doc and Glenda some water and crackers). The two skirted around the heap of passed-out guards and rushed to Zoe's side.

"We know where your Dad is, if that's who you're looking for!" Snively whispered. "Is your last name Baruti, by some chance?"

"Yes, yes, where is my Dad? Please take me there right away before these creeps unwrap themselves from this pile!"

Zoe zoomed out of the Commissary with the two nice guards to go rescue Dr. Matt and anyone else trapped there.

Nefertiti was nowhere to be found. Where was she?

***

On the roof, Crumb was fighting the windstorm set up by the Alien space ship. The form of the UFO had become invisible but not the effects of its updraft and swirling winds. Torrents of air were waving the perfectly set-up letters back and forth threatening to topple them over.

Crumb and Bee were shouting orders to each other, very terrified that all their work would be torn down by the wind.

Little did they know that Nefertiti had intuited the danger to the Mission and had leaped not into the Past, not into the waiting Future, but into a prime place in the Present Space-Time Continuum. She had bounded into the Alien Spacecraft.

Although the spaceship had just gone invisible a few seconds ago, the psychic feline had followed the windstorm to its source. The leap she was about to take was even more challenging than lunges she had made into the Past or the Future. To spot the exact physical location of the spaceship in the Present Moment she would have to slow down each second into infinitesimal increments. And now the UFO wasn't even visible, but was in the process of going into a cloaked state. On top of that, she would have to land there... intact. (This was something new for her. Ancient Egyptian prayers might be all about the Journey after death, but this journey was going to be especially tricky and she certainly didn't want to die in the process.)

Through the lighter-than-water and stronger-than-steel framework of the spaceship, through the flexible glass and diamond-encrusted inside walls of the corridors, she plunged from the Commissary buffet near the macaroni and cheese tray into the UFO dock-bay where Iago and the Fifty were meeting for the first time.

She wondered, *Do those scientifically brilliant but highly naive Aliens KNOW what they are getting themselves into, inviting this sneaky, treacherous Human on board?*

Should she warn them? No way! Having Iago off-planet and out-of-the-way was a GOOD idea! In fact, that was why she had plunged into the UFO in the first place. Nevertheless, Nefertiti figured she'd have to improvise a tactic on the spot (to ensure the Aliens DID indeed remove him) after she observed how this Worm of Deceit was reacting. She was prepared to do almost anything to keep him out of the picture, off-planet. Almost anything but die and not be able to return home.

"I Bastet of Innumerable Lives greet you who are One Voice, One Thought, One Purpose!"

The Fifty smiled the widest smiles yet, knowing that for once they weren't going to be bored!

"And who do we have HERE?" she inquired in a catty, chatty, gossipy tone of voice, looking at Iago like someone who had attempted to crash a party and had been dragged to the Hostess. Iago's grotesque and fawning expression reminded her of a mouse about to be eaten.

"Who ME?" squirmed the traitorous upstart. "I've just been appointed the highly enterTAINing Seeker for The Perfect Mate."

Oddly, Iago didn't seem to be surprised in the least to be talking to a cat. Nefertiti surmised he actually wanted to stay with the Aliens. If that was right, she certainly was going to reinforce his decision. But she'd have to be quick in case Iago was lying. Lying was his Modus Operandi.

Iago sidled over to the cat and threw in a bragging-point, "It's a prestigious post recorded in their ancient tribal scrolls that hasn't been fulfilled in a few millennia. I'm going to have to find socks that match each and every smelly sock they've stolen off this planet and two thousand and twenty other mudball planets. Isn't THAT enough punishment for one day, Cat?" He sneered.

'Enough punishment for one day'? thought Nefertiti. *Now he sounds like he wants to go back to Planet Earth. What IS it, you snake? Are you shedding your skin again?* Nefertiti shot him a thought: *These naïve Aliens will take all your orders instantly, not to mention their incredible powers to zip around the galaxy — you could end up Ruler of the Milky Way!* Iago caught that thought and changed his mind, deciding to stay.

"Actually," Iago continued in a husky whisper from the side of his mouth (so the Aliens wouldn't hear him), "I kind of like it here, so buzz off! The fools trust me. They've also entrusted me to be Head Scientist of their Bureau of Sox Research in exchange for procuring a mate for ME! I have in mind a reincarnation of Mata Hari... quite the knockout, or perhaps Jezebel! Besides I've always liked cloaks. You can hide so much inside a cloak. This whole place is a cloak. What better place for a sniveling Villain like myself to hang out in. I'm not going back!"

"Awwwwww, we'll miss you sooooo much down there," lied Nefertiti, hoping that the lie would not add too much weight to her feather when the time came to confront her last Journey.

Turning to the One-Voice, One-Thought, One-Purpose Happy Faces, Nefertiti met her biggest challenge. It seemed like Iago had won a place --- if not in the heart, at least in the legends --- of these technologically advanced but emotionally immature Aliens. She had to ensure they were taking him far, far away.

On top of that, it wouldn't hurt to get the whole entire spaceship gone for good: The UFO's gale-winds were about to blow the sign letters off the roof. She decided to appeal to whatever good intentions might still be ignited. If that didn't work --- to convince them to go --- she had a back-up plan. (Cats always have a back-up plan. That's how they land on their feet all the time.)

Nefertiti addressed the Fifty in their guttural tongue --- she was fluent in it by now. "Ka-poonga-TONGa! Do the Four a Favor right NOW! Leave this planet, taking this hideous... excuse me, taking this exCITingly INteresting Seeker for the Perfect Mate and Head Scientist newly appointed to run the Bureau of Sox Research, take him right away WITH you! We have business to do down on the planet! Okay?"

"You have it!" answered the Fifty. "All you had to do was ask!" Nefertiti smirked. It didn't take much to lead a leaderless group.

With that, Nefertiti disappeared and materialized herself at the second most momentous place in that split second of Now, right next to captured Matt and discouraged Glenda.

Matt raised his voice in astonishment, "Nefertiti!"

Just then the door to the Processing Plant squeaked open and... a shadowy figure appeared, magnified into extended shadows stretching on the floor of the factory. The ghostlike figure was lit up from behind by greasy window light from the hallway. Who WAS it?

***

The wind-tunnel effect of the UFO had suddenly disappeared. Crumb and Will lay on the roof for a second just to make sure it really was gone. The letters were fortunately still standing upright on the roof and stopped shaking back and forth. Phew!

Not wasting another second, Crumb switched the last letter "N" over to the end of the first word and lugged the letter he had flattened down earlier, the "D" , over to the end of the last word.

There on top of the roof the final message appeared:

ALIEN GREED

Seeing that immense indictment emblazoned in ten feet high letters on the roof of what once had been AlliedGreene corporate headquarters, seeing ALIEN GREED shouting an ultimatum to anyone willing to listen, the crowd began to shake with responses. It wasn't a unity of cheers. The two words were puzzling. The reactions were powerful but not unanimous. Opinions were flying around like leaves in a tempest.

Some screamed. Had Aliens created this whole wild scene on the rooftop? *Were they coming? Were they HERE?* A few people in the crowd fainted. The word "Alien" was a trigger for fearful reactions inbred in Humans since primordial days.

Most of the crowd jumped up and down cheering and hooting. "Greed" was a tell-tale word, instantly understood by all of them. Who among them hadn't lived with deceit and avaricious business practices far too long? Greed was real. Greed was here. Greed was no stranger.

Some stood mystified, staring up, trying to piece together the strangest Sunday in the city's history. Did the word "Alien" just refer to unnatural food? *What was going on?*

By now, seeing "A LIE GREEN", a small group of Organic Food Activists and GMO Protesters had begun marching around the building with placards.

People were racing for their pets with leashes and treats! The dogs were ecstatic and broke loose from the semi-circle to leap about and gallop to their owners, whipping their tails back-and-forth, lying on their backs tummies-up and smiling huge doggie-grins. At last cars were starting to move down Tesla Road. An air of relief and celebration permeated the Present.

Nefertiti smiled. She nuzzled the Doc. The Past and the Future were fine for a short visit, *but,* she concluded, *I wouldn't want to live there.* Oddly enough, the Present was the hardest trip of all, to have to pinpoint the exact location in the Space-Time Continuum of Now. Much more difficult than returning to the Past or leaping into the Future. Who knew?

Carol Worthey

Chapter Twenty-Four

Reunion

It was Zoe whose shadow had tilted in so threateningly into the Production Facility. As she rushed toward her Dad, her shadow shortened until her true size was obvious. The two nice guards followed her in. (The Security Chief and three other lackeys were still passed out in a heap on the Commissary floor, about twenty feet from where Mordred lay, drunk and drooling.)

Once the Doc and Glenda had been untied by Snively --- it took ten minutes to untie because the threads of the frayed hemp coils had interlocked and the Security Chief's sailor-knot was so complex -- Zoe hugged her Dad so hard that he had to sigh and whisper in her ear, "Sweetpea, let go a bit. You're breaking my heart, I'm so happy."

"What do you mean, 'breaking your heart,' Daddy? Are you okay? No heart-attack warning signs?"

"No way! It's just my heart is soooo full, that my eyes have to contain the rest of all that love." Matt began to cry tears of love, relief, and redemption. Zoe had never seen him cry before. She figured it was about time.

***

Crumb and Will had achieved the objective of the Mission. Or so it seemed. They had spotted just the right sign and turned the letters around, they had done their utmost to alert the public about False Foods, and hopefully they had made a first move toward making it safer for bees to survive. All in all it had been a very exhausting but victorious Sunday! At least Will sized it up that way.

"We DID it, little fella!" exulted the bee, nibbling on another pollen-bit to restore more of his drained energy.

Hhmmmph, shrugged Crumb. Surprisingly the breadcrumb wasn't feeling like celebrating. Something was on his mind, something didn't feel right, although he couldn't pinpoint what it was.

"What is it, Crumb?" asked the bee, inspecting Crumb's features for a clue.

"I'm not sure. Maybe we're leaving something out. Maybe there's something the Riddle is still telling us that we haven't tackled. I'll be darned if I know what it is." (Crumb was lost in thought for a moment, then tried not to be so cheerless.) "Go ahead and celebrate, Will, you deserve it... but I feel funny."

"What is it, Crumb? Tell me. We have no secrets. Not after all this!" urged the bee.

"It looks too good. It was just too easy."

"Too EASY?" Will practically collapsed. "After all the work we just did? You gotta be kidding."

"I'm not saying it wasn't tough. But... a puzzle isn't complete when a piece is still missing.... Wish I knew."

"Just do your best. What image comes to mind. If you can't put it into words, send me thought-pictures."

"Well... ever since we got here, I have this sinking feeling that I just can't shake. It's... it's like there's an empty spot inside me, deep down, pulling in on me."

"Yes?" prompted the bee.

"Maybe it's this... I still don't know where my parents are. Are they dead or alive? I don't even know if the Riddle says anything ABOUT that, but... isn't it worth another look? Or am I thinking only of myself...."

Moisture was squeezing out of one of Crumb's eyes and he was getting a bit soggy. Will thought for a moment. He was exhausted and pollen was running out. *Is the little bread-boy on to something or just being moody?* Then Will remembered what Breadbox had said about Intuition.

"I understand. I lost my whole family and it hurts. I miss them every day." A change came over the little bee, as if a wave of recognition had passed across his forehead and his eyes. He had to go with Crumb's misgivings. If he refused, it was disloyal, but worse, it might be foolish. He was ready to take the risk.

"Okay! If it's important to you, I don't even CARE if the Riddle says anything about it. Let's see if we can find your parents. Do you have any idea where they might be?"

"No, not really. All I know is that ever since we arrived here, I can't stop thinking about them. What would Breadbox say about that?"

"I think," said Will, "that Breadbox would say that some Lessons just pop up out of nowhere and you have to go on intuition. Let's exPLORE!"

"Thanks, Will!" Crumb's eyes lit up. "Let's check out this building NOW! It may lead us nowhere... but it's worth the try."

Off Crumb and Will went from floor to floor. Nothing but lots of empty offices, a mailroom, some huge storage rooms that they wandered through finding nothing and Matt Baruti's Lab which was locked. Finally, on the Ground Floor they came to the production and packing factory, all three-stories of it. Near a tall column, they spotted Zoe hugging her Dad. Nefertiti, was there too, sound asleep (or in another trance) in a sunny spot.

As Zoe leaned over her Dad's shoulder, she spotted Will and Crumb and sent them a quiet wink. (*I better not wave or say 'Hi', she thought. Wouldn't Dad just love to know I'm friends with a breadcrumb and a bee. He's been through enough today.*) Crumb and Will winked back and went on, checking out all of the wheels, cogs and scary machinery in the huge space. It took a long time to poke around every corner and shelf and bin. Nothing there.

Realizing that they'd skipped a floor by accident, they sneaked back into the lobby. The gruff Chief of Security was waiting for the elevator. (He had finally "come to" on the Commissary floor along with his three junior officers. Fortunately, he had no idea that the two prisoners were now untied.) His stern features reflected his suspicion: *Maybe there's someone still lurking near the roof, someone who might have made that darn sign move around... somehow. Farfetched but I better check.*

When the elevator door opened in the lobby, Crumb and Will jumped in. It was easier than going back up all those stairs. The Security Chief pressed the button for the top floor. Distracted by his thoughts, he also absentmindedly pressed the button just below that. He exited at the top floor and the elevator door closed.

Will and Crumb looked at each other and whispered that the Chief had pressed the very floor the two of them had missed in their search, Floor Number 9.

The elevator moved down and stopped at that floor, but the door would only half-open, then shut, half-open, then shut, over and over again until finally it closed tight like a jaw too terrified to utter a word.

They were stuck in the elevator. Crumb and Will leaned into each other in discouragement as if their mutual weight would support them in this emergency. Will was too tuckered out to fly up to the panic-button to alert anyone that the elevator was stuck. To Crumb the wall looked as enormous as a steep cliff. What could they do NOW?

Crumb bent down all the way to the floor, as close as he could get to the stuck elevator door. He saw that there was a space between the edge of the elevator door and the new hallway on Floor Number 9. Unfortunately that space looked down into the elevator shaft and plunged all the way down to the basement. It was so dark down there that Crumb could barely see cables, but they were poised to strangle anyone who fell down the shaft. The two of them would have to jump over that space to get out of the elevator and onto the Floor. For a Human that space was hardly discernible, for Crumb it meant a wide jump... or a long way down. He fought his dizzy spell and his terror of heights and jumped across the shaft-space, landing safely over on Floor Number 9. Then he gestured to Will, but Will was losing energy after all his flight exertions.

"Come on, Will! You can do it!" Will made the mistake of peering down the shaft and froze. He wasn't scared of heights at all, but he was totally worn out. Reaching over to Will, Crumb managed to hoist the bee over the shaft-space onto the hallway. (*Funny,* thought Crumb, *I'd forgotten for a second that the Aliens gave me super-strength. Thank heavens.*)

Floor Number 9 did not feel friendly. Dust and dankness clouded the air. No cleaning crew had been allowed up there, even the Security Guards were prevented from going there. The only reason there was a button in the elevator that read "9" was that omitting that number might have called for suspicion (or so thought Mordred.) Dr. Matt hadn't even been up to that floor. Ever.

Down an endless hallway the two brave explorers stopped in front of a massive door. There a sign in tall red letters had a huge red "X" underneath its message: "Top Secret. No Admittance Without Special Clearance."

Just like the Alien Experimentation Rooms, thought Crumb.

How would Will and Crumb get in? They'd never be able to reach up to the huge handle in the middle of the door.

Wait! There was a pale gray, eerie luminosity, barely visible under the crack of the door.... They squished down to see if they could both crawl under the huge metal door.... *What was inside?*

Chapter Twenty-Five

Venom

Little did Crumb and Will realize at the time that their rooftop heroics and all the hullabaloo around the building had done more than just change a sign, it had provided the ideal distraction to prevent murder.

First of all, the crazed CEO was totally woozy, flat on the Commissary floor dodging pink elephants and trying to review his next moves, but way too soused to stand up. Four of his security guards, including the Chief, had been put to shame when they had fallen one over the other in a pile-up (due to Happy's slippery self). After they had revived, they were disgusted and embarrassed and decided that it was time to stop kowtowing to their boss. They grumbled amongst themselves. Snively wondered how long this change of heart would last. *Until their next paycheck,* he guessed.

Meanwhile Mordred drooled as he floundered on the floor, thinking that as soon he was able to stand up he'd start the gears moving and get that scientist and his secretary chopped to smithereens in the heavy machinery.

Finally he swaggered upright, realizing that he'd missed his chance. The mad commotion of the crowd staring up at the roof watching a sign change before their eyes, the dogs in a semi-circle, the protesters marching, the helicopter circling and the possibility that an alien spaceship had zoomed over for a second -- this was not the time to murder anyone. It would have to take place later, when AlliedGreene was cleared of nosy eyes and media buzzards. He glowered and then smiled, *As soon as the sun went down.* He'd do this deed in the dark.

Not even Nefertiti knew about this danger. Had she been at her best she would have spotted what the CEO was up to, but she was numb, nuzzling the Doc and resting in the seed packing plant with him, Glenda and Zoe. To her surprise, manipulating time and space in the Present had been worth it but the effort to do so was totally exhausting. When she had bounded into the spaceship to make sure that Fripple would be spirited away for good, it had taken every last ounce of Time Power she had. She was plumb exhausted.

Staying in the Present had turned out to be harder to do than visiting the Past or jumping into the Future. Her On position had been On too long and it was time to shut Off. Time for a cat nap. Her last thought before sleeping was that she couldn't wait to get back to the Baker's household. They needed her. Maybe she needed them too. She'd decide later. A bowl of cream might clinch the deal.

In the cafeteria, Mordred staggered past the buffet trays with their overcooked steamed peas and white-bread sandwiches and plunked his rotund body down on a plastic Commissary stacking chair. The chair itself might have been alive, because it groaned under his weight.

Mordred complained to himself, *If only I'd known that I'd end up in this low-class cafeteria, I'd have bought better chairs.*

He sipped some strong coffee to sober up, intensely conjuring up the final result: Two chained up victims screaming as the packet-chopper got closer and closer! As a child he'd laughed at those kinds of melodramatic scenes in old silent movies -- now he was going to direct his own movie and it was going to be REAL!

As soon as the sun went down, he would personally untie Matt and Glenda from the column, holding them at gun-point, then re-tie them onto the moving assembly line -- this time securing them with metal chains, not rope. What evil pleasure it would be to crank up the gears, turn on the chemical wash and witness the grisly outcome as the packet-chopper mechanism minced those two into bits. He'd never planned to marry Glenda anyway. He'd never planned to give his lead scientist a retirement pension -- how money-saving Dr. Baruti's demise would be! Then Mordred could secure his own patent on the new "wonder-seed" Impervious.

Impervious? No one was impervious, thought the CEO, with cynical disdain. Even he would do a tumble one day. But while he lived, he would have some fun at others' expense. He trusted no one. Not even Iago. Certainly not Iago, that two-faced snake with two tongues. Why should he share the profits with him anyway? Someday he'd find a way to get rid of that reptile.

Still... he couldn't figure something out: Where WAS that sneaky bunch of skin-and-bones Fripple ANYway?

Looking back on what had happened, Mordred was flabbergasted that Iago had seemed to vanish into thin air. One minute Mordred had his flabby arm around the snake, the next second his arm was suspended there, supported by nothing at all. It looked like Iago had disintegrated! That was impossible. ...Wasn't it?

Then, as the coffee took over, Mordred concluded that his accomplice and confidante from high school days couldn't really have disappeared into nothing. Fripple wasn't that skinny. Anyway, it didn't matter, he'd do the deed all by his lonesome, come nightfall.

Thank goodness no one had found out, the red-eyed drunk sneered to himself, about that secret laboratory up on the forbidden floor, Floor Number 9. They'd never find out what he was doing to KILL ALL THE BEES. His bloodshot eyes practically popped out of his sockets in anticipation every time he thought of his secret plan.

***

Ever since he was about to turn seven, Gordon Mordred O'Greene had been terrified of bees.

He'd been stung a few days short of his seventh birthday, while his Mother was fixing up a garden party for his playmates. As she was happily stretching out a plastic tablecloth on the picnic table, he had skipped outside to see about killing some ants. He loved to watch them suffer. Little meaningless black things bent on finding food, HIS food. The very smell of formic acid had become a kind of heady, intoxicating drug to the cruel youngster. He loved to sniff his fingers after he'd smashed one ant after the other. There he was, having some fun, or so he thought, when all of a sudden an avenging bee came over and stung him on his arm, right where his new T-shirt sleeve ended.

There were no words for the wall of blinding light that hit him, then darkness.

His Mother and Father had rushed little Gordon to the Emergency Ward. The bump on his elbow was evidence of a bee sting. It was too late to drain it, the effect had taken over. Whatever the doctor was pumping into him wasn't working. Their dear little Gordon -- the bad seed who would end up selling bad seeds -- lay in a coma for five days. He barely survived.

On the very day of his birthday, somehow he had come out of his coma to find tubes stuck all over his body. His first snarling words were "Where are my birthday presents?" The attendant nurse had almost fainted. She wasn't used to this kind of Wake-up Call. Most of the time coma victims were too wiped out to mutter anything really intelligible when they came out of their unconscious stupor.

His birthday party took place three days later than his real birthday, in the shared hospital room he was moved to after he was cleared out of Intensive Care. The hospital had run out of available rooms in the pediatric floor. He was temporarily moved to a general floor near surgery. A thick white plastic curtain separated him from an old post-operative man. Funny thing about that, the old man had died two days after dear little Gordon showed up. "Old age," sighed the man's daughter, weeping over the corpse.

Gordon waited for the body to be covered and carted out, then smiled, alone in the room. Who would suspect a seven-year-old of putting a pillow over the sleeping man's nose and pushing down really hard. It had almost been as easy as crushing ants.

When Birthday Party Time at the hospital came, none of his playmates showed up. Only his doting parents, his simpering nurse, a handful of inflated balloons and a sugar-free birthday cake, just in case sugar would cause an allergic relapse. Little Gordon craved sugar after that. If he couldn't eat honey, then he'd indulge in anything with glucose -- frosting, candy bars, ice cream sundaes, gooey desserts. The boy grew wide as well as tall, resenting how his classmates laughed at him behind his back. He'd show them!

Ever since the near-fatal bee sting, Mordred was in deadly peril of being stung again. He had not developed an immunity. He didn't even want to be tested for that. It wasn't enough to crush ants. Enemies were all around him. BEES could kill him. He would kill THEM FIRST!

No one was to know about the nightmarish laboratory on Floor Number 9. He had the elevator company come to his facility and lock out passage to that particular floor. Only HE had the special elevator key to an unlabeled keyhole next to the elevator buttons and only he could gain entry to the Top Secret laboratory. How he loved to gloat over his experiments.

Certainly not Will or Crumb, definitely not Matt, Glenda or Zoe and not even the kowtowing security guards, no one was privy to the GRUESOME PLANS of a MADMAN. He was trapped in his own hate, and the only way out was to kill... or so Mordred thought.

Meanwhile to everyone else that dealt with him -- his employees and associates, his family members, even his selfish wife -- all they noticed was his outward manifestation: GREED, rapacious consuming greed. His wife contented herself with her own greed, shopping in fancy stores, collecting trinkets, new cars, pool boys and massages so she could gather material things around herself like a shield. They fought like Punch and Judy. She'd married this detestable man for his money and wasn't going to let him forget how she really didn't care about him in the least.

Mordred's greed was a mask hiding his rage. His heart seemed hollow but it did hold something: Venom.

Chapter Twenty-Six

Media Circus

On the way to Tesla Road in the Baker's woodie, Ken felt like a piece of wood himself.

I'm so nervous about Zoe and Matt, Hazel's uptight too, and the kids are antsy, maybe I'll turn on some music, Ken thought. He turned on the car radio to the local station and discovered that the announcer had canceled the music program to focus on the weird happenings down at AlliedGreene. The radio station had hustled a reporter down to Commerce Center on the double and the mystified newsman had been describing thousands of onlookers, a helicopter, bizarre dogs, a media circus.

Ken pulled over to the curb. The traffic jam had just begun to free up and someone impatient was tailgating him -- but that wasn't what made him pull over to the curb. A compelling image had flooded into his mind, sweeping his attention off the road. Ken grabbed the steering wheel with tight hands and lowered his head, consumed with the vision. He had two very different thoughts volleying back and forth in his mind like a heated tennis match at match point. Life was back-handed and he was missing the swing, lobbing too close to the net, blowing the game. Uppermost in his mind was the fact that now he was worried about BOTH Matt and Zoe. But there was another oddly intriguing thought he couldn't shake out of his mind -- it felt like a tennis ball lying by the net, just sitting there, as if Ken had match-point coming up, and just one more serve to get it right and win. Or not.

Hazel said, "Oh no! Do we have a flat?" Johnny was whining, "When are we gonna get there?" Sally was too busy sneaking some gum -- she usually wasn't allowed any -- to make a fuss. When she couldn't find any gum, Sally started pouting and complaining.

Ken lifted his head up from the steering wheel, his eyes wide. Whatever he had envisioned had grabbed his very soul. He could -- if he acted RIGHT AWAY -- carry the match to a win, maybe for everyone. He had always loved jumping over the net to shake hands with his opponent, knowing he'd won the match. He didn't want to blow this opportunity. But it was the WRONG time, wrong place, wrong logic and looked selfish.

"No flat, thank goodness. No, we're fine. But honey, I just had a brain-storm!"

"What? Is this the time, Ken Baker, to have a brainstorm? (Hush up, kids! Let your Dad talk.) What IS it, for heaven's sake?"

"It'll just take a minute. I promise. I have to call my boss. The traffic is still so slow anyway, we might as well just stay here for a minute until it clears. Listen, this is a million dollar opportunity with all those thousands of people down at Matt's company!"

"WHAT?!" Hazel was never one for patience. She didn't like the idea of Ken stopping to call his boss when they needed to be in a hurry, plus she was flabbergasted at the bad-timing of his "brain storm." And two squealing kids weren't helping either.

Ken admitted to himself, *You're probably right, Hazel. This is weird of me. But I can't get this image out of my mind. I can't help thinking that something good for all of us can come out of this crazy idea -- maybe, hopefully, even for Matt and Zoe. I have to trust myself on this one.*

"You sure picked the wrong time for a brainstorm, Ken! What do you have up your sleeve?"

"I'll tell you in a minute. But first I have to call my boss. Right now. You'll get the idea when you hear me talking to Harry. But don't interrupt me." He fished for his cell phone -- why did this danged apparatus always disappear at the wrong time? -- found it in his jacket pocket and nervously dialed.

"Harry? Hi, this is Ken Baker. Sorry to disturb you on Sunday. Sure, the Hat Convention was great. But that's not why I'm calling you.... Do you have any idea what is going on at this big seed company down the street from where I live? No, it's not an explosion."

The boss didn't know about it. "Why are you calling me on a Sunday morning to tell me about this, Ken. I trust your judgment, but what the heck is going on? I think you're tops, don't get me wrong, but this better be GOOD!"

"The biggest PR caper our company probably will EVer pull, that's what!! You enjoy making bank deposits, don't you?"

Harry Ardmore Jr. was all ears after that.

Ken explained his vision, mindful that he had to grab each word-picture just right and had to make it snappy: Everyone in front of AlliedGreene in hats, hats, hats, glorious Acme hats everywhere, hats broadcast on TV, publicity all over, blogs being written about this, Acme hats being ordered non-stop around the world. The vision had taken hold of him so strongly he had almost lost all attention on the road, and that was why he pulled over to the curb to get his bearings, work out the bright idea and call his boss.

"What do you think? It's not even ten yet. Do you think you can get some crew in? The factory's about a half-hour away from where we are and Sunday mornings usually have light traffic on the freeway. Whatcha say, Boss?"

Mr. Ardmore agreed it was worth calling in an overtime crew right away, Sunday or not. There were lots of boxes of big sellers like baseball caps, stetsons, straws, fisherman caps, berets and bowlers at the ready (Harry was willing to contribute those) and enough less popular kinds like pith helmets, turbans, fake fur Russian winter hats and beanies with whirl-a-gigs on top (Harry wanted to offload those). Ken had some snappy slogans he'd thought of in a pinch, Harry jotted them down right away, and the boss ordered the stamping machines to start rolling. When a businessman gets a bright idea, it doesn't have to take forever -- this had taken six minutes to get the foreman and some workers driving from their home or church to Acme's hat factory. Overtime is welcome sometimes and Ken was respected by the company.

An hour and a half later, company vans were chugging down the highway to AlliedGreene. There would be some overtime to pay at Acme. That was the chance one took with PR capers.

When the Acme vans pulled up to the parking lot at AlliedGreene, soon word spread about free hats for everyone. What a novelty -- all kinds of hats and no price tag on any of them. Up for grabs! Just about every person who raced to AlliedGreene to fetch their dog or rushed over out of curiosity, including all the media crews, received one of these hats as a gift, each with a snappy slogan on it: Cool Cat, Dogs Rule, Super-Natural, Food for Thought, Magic, Bread Doesn't Loaf Around, Happy Faces Have Feelings Too, Bozos Beware and other catchword phrases. A few of the dogs wore jolly hats fastened with elastic around their twitching ears or under their chins. Some cat-owners ended up wearing baseball caps that said Dogs Rule, but no one was complaining.

Cameras were flashing, cell phones were texting all over the place. TV Channel Right-Now-News was focusing more on the free hats than on nutritional health or even on a rumor going round that an alien spaceship had been spotted for a few seconds hovering over the building.

By the time Ken and Hazel and the kids were pulling their woodie into the parking lot at AlliedGreene, the semi-circle of dogs had just begun to break up but there was still a lot of commotion going on. Owners were petting their dogs and stuffing them with treats, attaching leashes and walking off the area to bring their dogs home and secure them inside closed doors. In a few minutes, a lot of the dogs were gone, but the crowd was still milling around AlliedGreene and the media was not about to leave.

Ken drove through the parking lot looking for a space and trying to assess what was going on in front of AlliedGreene. Where was a spot for them to park? As he circled around, he spotted a TV reporter sporting a tam o'shanter interviewing a spectator in a bowler hat who pointed to the Acme Company Vans in the parking lot, then took off his brand new bowler and turned it over to show the reporter the Acme Hat Company label inside. A lady in a lilac pill box hat with a small blue ostrich feather was interviewed after that and she showed off to the camera and pulled on her leash so that the cameraman could focus on her little miniature schnauzer who had on a tiny straw hat attached with a ribbon under his chin. The dog began barking at the reporter. *Exactly how I feel most of the time*, mused Ken, *but not today! Long live TV News.* It was all going just as Ken hoped it would.

But meanwhile, he and all the Bakers were electrified to see from their car windows what was really the focus of most of the crowd's attention: A helicopter was circling around and around, the wind was ferocious and despite the howling of the wind and propellers, slowly letters were moving. And NO ONE KNEW how this was happening, WHO was doing this.

Suddenly a shout went up from the crowd as they pointed to the roof. Another giant letter had moved, seemingly by itself. The helicopter was circling around but could not spot how this was happening. A call had gone out about a Missing Child, an eight-year-old girl last seen on a bicycle on Tempest Street. Had she been kidnapped? The TV News was having a field day on that one.

Finally the Bakers managed to pull into a parking spot and got out of the station wagon. But the moment Ken saw the commotion at AlliedGreene, he signaled to Hazel and the kids to get back in the car. They so wanted to run into the building, but Ken got this gut-level feeling it was the wrong time — dogs scurrying everywhere, their owners gyrating from panic to relief as they spotted their pooches, the crowd of onlookers staring up at the roof and milling around, the helicopter still circling the roof and the prying media. It was all so confusing that the Bakers sat inside their station wagon for a while, surveying the crowd, trying to find Matt and Zoe. They were nowhere in sight.

Ken and Hazel discussed the possibility that Matt was inside his work-place, hopefully okay. What he had to do with the weird sign, they could only speculate about — maybe he'd gone to see what was going on, earlier. Maybe he'd left early and let Zoe sleep in on Sunday morning. Maybe he'd left Zoe a note about where he was going — again more speculation. (Ken hadn't seen any note from Matt in their house. The Doc would have written Zoe a note if he took off when she was fast asleep.) Maybe Zoe had heard about the commotion on the roof and had biked to her Dad's workplace to make sure he was okay --- that would make sense. Once there was a bit less confusion, Ken decided they'd walk toward the crowd, check it out more closely but really aim to get inside the building. That might not be so easy.

"Ya know, let's take our hats in with us. Maybe we can bribe a security guard or policeman if we need to -- with a hat. I just have this strong feeling -- don't you, Hazel? -- that Matt (at least him, not sure about Zoe, but that Matt) is inside the building."

"I hope Zoe is somewhere there too. And safe." Sally began to cry a bit again. This time she couldn't hide it by looking away. Johnny hugged his sister and told her not to worry.

"Zoe's fine, I have a feeling about that. Don't cry," said Ken. "Another brain-storm!"

Hazel groaned. *What is it NOW?*

Ken disregarded his wife's protest and said, "Let's stack all the hats we have with us on our heads. You've seen me stack hats a million times, kids, right? It looks funny but it'll keep our hands free if we need them. "

"Good idea," said Hazel. *She liked that brainstorm,* thought Ken. He enjoyed how unpredictable she'd become these days, sometimes grumpy, sometimes totally cooperative -- it tantalized him in a perverse sort of way. She added, "Johnny and Sally, don't go roaming off. Stay with us!"

Finally nearly all the dogs and owners were on their way home. One thing less to contend with. Ken and

Hazel were checking out the crowd flow and the access to the entrance, trying to ascertain when they should exit the car.

What they couldn't yet see was that all the dogs had gone except for one -- and that one was Whisk. He lay there, tongue hanging out, next to his soapbox in front of the revolving door, waiting. Like most dogs, he had been able to tell the Bakers were on the way well before they arrived. It was more than just the scent, even more than his intuition. It was the sum total of his unconditional love that tied him to each member of the family. In fact, Whisk had begun to moan and wag his tail as soon as the station wagon had turned onto Tesla Road a good ten minutes away. He also felt that same bond with Zoe. She had become part of his family and she was also one of the Five. He was NOT going anywhere, not even home with the Bakers until he knew Zoe was safe!

Back inside the station wagon, Sally spotted Whisk! He was circling his soapbox, torn between protecting Zoe inside and galloping over to the Bakers' woodie -- so he was literally pacing in circles around the box. The family didn't waste any time exiting the car, opening the trunk and piling hats on top of their heads. They were in such a rush that some of the hats spilled onto the concrete. They picked them up and re-worked the stacks to be more stable. Ken signaled that it was time to walk toward the entrance of AlliedGreene. Some of the crowd pointed to the family and were quickly handed some of the hats.

Then when the Bakers were about fifteen feet away from Whisk, the dog ran for them, knocking over his soapbox and once he reached them, toppling Sally's stack of hats off her head. The big box -- the one Whisk had sat on and used as a soapbox when addressing the dogs in their Semi-circle -- was sealed tight. The box was heavy -- something bulky was inside, and as soon as Whisk knocked it over, a hole cracked through a corner of the thick cardboard. Metal was poking out of the box, a corner piece that looked like a bronze epaulet.

It had been strange from the start that this big box was just standing there outside the building, abandoned in the first place. A security guard had stupidly left it there out in the open in front of AlliedGreene when he had been scared by all the running dogs bounding up to the front of the building. The guard had been called inside by the Chief right at that moment and ran for his life from the dogs so fast that he actually had spun twice around in the revolving door. Then, after a mad chase inside the building and the arrest of Doctor Baruti and Ms. Scoop, not to mention the boss getting totally soused in the cafeteria and the pile-up of guards who tripped over one another, the security guard had plumb forgotten he'd left the box outside.

"What's this?" asked Hazel, always ready to spot something messy or something that didn't fit the picture. She pointed with one hand to the bronze "epaulet" on the metal corner that was sticking out of the box. With her other hand Hazel held on to her floppy hat with its golf caps and straw boaters piled on top.

Ken shrugged, put down his hats and got out his pocket knife to begin slicing up the lid along the folded top. As soon as the box was cut open, a large safe tumbled out. The bulky combination lock was still on the front handle, dangling there like a gaping mouth, insecure, sawed open.

Ken looked inside the safe but didn't see anything. Empty. Odd, very peculiar --- an empty safe inside an inappropriate cardboard box just laying there by itself in front of the building with no one collecting it... especially after all that wild commotion. *Oh well,* thought Ken, *it's just a distraction.* What really matters is to find the Doc and hopefully Zoe too and make sure they're okay.

As the Bakers approached the tall revolving door, their urgency mounted. They had walked close to the crowd to see IF -- by some chance -- Zoe and Matt were there among the two thousand or so onlookers still there, watching the sign. No sight of either Matt or Zoe in the crowd.

If the two were here in this location, they weren't outside, they were inside the building... or possibly, although that was more doubtful, back in the parking lot. *Maybe even on their way home,* guessed Hazel, *but without their cell phones, there's no way for us to contact them.* Ken had an overpowering sense of their presence inside the imposing building, as if the very look of the place felt unsafe. *A bad vibe,* he thought. *How could the Doc put up so long with working here? It gives me the creeps.* Hazel grabbed Ken's arm, sensing he needed reassurance.

Once they reached the revolving door, the Bakers with their conglomerations of hats forced one on top of each other resembled a safari crew carrying supplies into a wildlife habitat, probably with a tiger at the other end. Hazel's eyes grew wide as she turned to Ken as if to say, *We're going in THERE? Guess so!* First Ken, then Hazel, followed by Johnny and Sally circled awkwardly through the tall revolving door with their hat stacks held as vertically as possible.

In the lobby, the Bakers could make out muffled voices down a corridor to the left -- Hopefully the voices were Matt and Zoe, but maybe not. Hurt? Upset? Just chatting? It was hard to tell.

A security guard scowled at them as they came into the lobby, like so many Mad Hatters nosing around where they didn't belong. He paced over to Ken with his hand in his pocket, hinting about a revolver there. Who were they?

"Oh, we're just here from the Acme Hat Company! The Acme CEO," Ken lied, "ordered hats from our company to be delivered to the Security Guards and especially to AlliedGreene's CEO — if he's here. I happen to be Acme's lead salesman. PR, you know. Keep the crowds happy. Sell some seeds too in the process. Great TV coverage.... Did you get a chance to select your very own hat?"

The guard loosened up at that. He chose a Top Hat from Ken's stack and let the Bakers in. Then realizing that the media was snapping shots of him in his Top Hat, he quickly relegated it to a bench in the lobby and sauntered over to the Reception Desk to look "official." The flashing cameras stopped.

Ken looked around. The sounds were coming from behind a door down a long hallway on the left side of the lobby entrance. The Bakers followed the muffled voices with steps increasingly rapid until they found themselves stopped still before the imposing door to the Production Facility. *How did we manage to keep all these hats on our heads without dropping a one?* asked Hazel to herself. *Pure intention,* she figured, *something more important than hats — Friends!*

Ken pulled the massive door open. At a distance of roughly sixty feet from the door, Ken could make out the Doc, sitting on the floor by a huge column, a heap of thick rope strewn around his legs. (Glenda had left a while ago as it turned out. She had been released out a back door by Snively and ran to her car. The frantic secretary had driven

Snively crazy about how she had to get home to feed her little chihuahua Pip. So she and the guard had worked out a way she could escape the building unnoticed.)

The whole family stood there aghast and overwhelmed by the sheer size of the processing plant. Gripping jaws of huge gears and pulleys rose up three stories in massive loops, coils and pipelines leering down at their Matt friend. A security guard (it was Snively) stood by the column, with a knife in his hand! (He had used it to cut the hemp rope and free the prisoners but Ken Baker didn't know that. Was the guard going to slice his friend?) Ken started to run, then froze stock still, holding his family behind him with both arms.

There next to her Dad -- she had been partially hidden at first -- was ZOE! She looked a bit rumpled. Her eyes were moist, her whole face shone with relief. Her cheeks were slightly dirty and her braids had come undone.

Ken signaled to his kids to hush up. Matt and Zoe (and the guard with the knife) hadn't noticed the Bakers yet. It looked fine... Zoe and Matt weren't tied up since there were coils of rope by their side, but Ken just wasn't sure if his friends were just about to be tied up, knifed, or hopefully just fine.

The next second the father and daughter were hugging. They were locked in a long hug, both weeping. Were these tears from relief at finding each other again OR were these tears from a need to say a last goodbye? There was no definite way to determine which scenario it was.

At any rate, it wasn't time to interrupt a hug so intense.

Finally the Doc broke the embrace, suddenly noticing that the Bakers had entered the giant room and were standing at a distance, rapt and respectful. He smiled, Zoe beamed and wiped away her tears.

The Bakers approached the two slowly, not wanting to break the spell of sanctity and intensity they had seen in that hug... and not wanting their stacks of hats to fall over.

What an outlandish and hilarious bunch they were! Ken, Hazel, Johnny and Sally, each one of them, with precarious stacks on top of their heads -- Baseball caps and fedoras, cowboy hats and golf caps, straw boaters and berets, fez with tassels dangling, beanies and floppy hats, pillboxes and cloches with feathers and veils, and Johnny with a horned Viking helmet on top of his stack.

Zoe signaled to her second family to come closer and started to laugh, louder and louder until her braids came even more loose, she was laughing so hard. The Baker Family's faces were so serious, their hat-stacks so silly. Matt hugged his tummy guffawing. Snively roared and dropped his knife. Ken began chuckling uncontrollably, Sally and Johnny broke into giggles and jumped up and down, and Hazel lost her hats she was shaking from laughter so much.

Nefertiti woke up from her cat-nap hearing all this laughter. She curled her back up and stood her tail straight up in protest that this was rude of these Humans to wake her, but soon she relaxed and prowled over to a window ledge to resume her nap. Sally saw the cat and ran over to pet her.

Nefertiti wished she could share with Sally how much tension and danger they had all been through that day. She had helped the Mission, she loved all these people (except Snively) whether she would admit that or not -- in her feline pride. But letting Sally stroke her beautiful fur, she began to purr and knead her paws in contentment. She also surmised that once the Bakers got home, a lovely bowl of cream and some catnip might be her reward for all this jollity. It had been a long day. Then she was in her Off Position, too tired to descend to a trance, so happy to see her familiar Humans and to have her Mission accomplished that there were no need for trances or even for mouse-capture dreams. She just slept in her sunny spotlight on the ledge.

Laughter had made it completely and deliriously obvious: Matt and Zoe were safe! Reunited! Unharmed for the most part.

Soon everyone was hugging, laughing, crying, hugging some more, including Snively! Of course, hats were strewn all over the place. Finally, everyone was slowly stiffing giggles... well, trying to do that... and picking up hats including Zoe. (Matt was too tired.) Snively bent down to pick up an olive-green felt ascot cap, the kind that golfers favor and gave it a strong look of acquisition.

"Have it!" said Sally. "It's on us... and Acme Hat Company." Snively placed it over his comb-over. Now he looked rather dashing, a golf-champion in the making just moonlighting as a security guard. Snively tipped his hat to Sally, smiling as uncharacteristically as any security guard could do.

Of course, the Doc and Zoe could take any hat of their choice, or two or three or the whole pile. Zoe picked a sparkly sequined baseball cap with the word "Magic" glittering in black letters, Matt picked a handsome stetson that said "Super-Natural."

Even Nefertiti had been found now. (And Whisk was outside, where he insisted on being, waiting to see if Zoe was safe and if Matt was safe too. The Family would grab Whisk and put him in the woodie once they could walk out with the Doc, Zoe and the cat so that Whisk's concerns would be relaxed.)

***

During all the uproar over at his workplace, Harvey had been taking a nap when his Mom came knocking on his bedroom door.

"Harve, you won't believe what's been going on where you work! Hurry! It's on the tube NOW. And there just happen to be some rather attractive young women being interviewed, I must say. Maybe you can rush down to Allied and introduce yourself!"

"Awwww, Mom, why don't you just adopt a grandchild and stop nagging me about that. I'm hopeless."

Disgruntled that all his Mom could think of was that this was a generous opportunity to meet some marriageable possibilities, Harvey reluctantly headed into the living-room in his sloppy bedroom slippers.

As soon as he plopped himself down on the living-room plastic-covered sofa to catch the TV news, there he was scratching away at his infamous cow-lick, because he could hardly believe his eyes. AlliedGreene's sign was moving around, seemingly by itself, huge letters being lowered or being pushed to new places without a sign of anyone manipulating them in the slightest. A LIE GREEN -- not good publicity for the seed company. What?! ALIEN GREED? That was going too far!

Adding more mystery to all this was the rather demure and unreal semi-circle of dogs in all shapes and sizes, at full attention and hardly barking -- if one could call a lineup of dogs "demure", with a news helicopter hovering and circling above the transformed sign, and what??! Were his eyes deceiving him or had he watched too many sci-fi movies lately? -- was that a strobe-light image of a UFO? -- no, couldn't be, it was gone in a flash, must be that he was still in the process of waking up and his eyes had blurred for a second, he thought.

These incidents had taken place a few hours earlier but were being re-played and re-played *ad nauseum*. What was the big deal about hats? Harvey wondered. The newscasters, wearing some of these hats themselves by now, were going on and on about how five thousand snappy pieces of headgear with various slogans had shown up at the company. Was this wild scene a ploy?, one skeptical Talking Head asked, her lipstick so bright that it was hard to concentrate on what she was saying. Was it a pre-planned marketing stratagem to get hats back in fashion and hats sold by the score?

Harvey sighed, thinking of his boss. There was definitely something more going on than a staged emergency designed to sell hats. *Humans, what gives with our species*, he troubled over for a second. Honestly, it was much easier to study chemical workings than the ludicrous ways of Mankind. Still he better go down there. All this was happening at his company and maybe there was something going on with his boss. The Doc had not looked healthy or happy the day before. Harvey was fond of Zoe too -- if only she were twenty-something. *My timing isn't the best*, he thought.

So... off he went, back to his bedroom to dress as fast as he could. But no, his timing was off again -- no clean clothes in his drawers, not really. He raced to the dryer where his underwear, clean shirts and pants were and grabbed the pile in a handful that was guaranteed to need ironing afterwards. He was now in a terrible hurry because it began to be plain to him: *The Doc is in trouble. I can feel it.*

"Darn! Where is that other sock? How come there's always a *missing* one? Who TAKES these things?" he sputtered in frustration. No time to search for a proper mate -- then it dawned on Harvey that that indeed was the essence of his problem overall. *No time to search for a proper mate.*

He ran back to his bedroom, threw his outfit together, put on mis-matched socks, one dark blue, the other a short sneaker sock -- *who would see them anyway?* -- tried to comb down his cowlick and sighed. No use, his hair and his socks had minds of their own.

Harvey scurried out of the house, waving "so long" to his Mom. She was busy ironing his shirts. Maybe he'd never leave home.

In his car, he adjusted his rear-view mirror and saw how nervous he looked. He'd been worried about the Doc and how strange and morose he'd been acting yesterday, how weak and in pain he'd been. He better check things out.

As he approached AlliedGreene, he came to a stop. Oh no! A traffic jam on Tesla. On Sunday morning? At Commerce Center (full of empty mechanic shops and shipping houses)? It didn't make sense. Maybe there was an accident up ahead.

He turned on the radio. Someone was being interviewed about the habits of dogs, then another interview about the history of headgear. A spokesperson from Area 231 was being asked questions about UFOs and Alien Abductions.

What was going ON? As he waited totally frustrated in his claustrophobic compact car, with honking cars in front and in back of him and a circling helicopter above, a disgruntled and determined line of protesters marched by on their way to AlliedGreene, swinging and hoisting cardboard placards, signs that read "Organic or Die... for REAL!" and "Greed Is Not Green" and the like.

Harvey had no sympathy for them and frowned as they passed by --- what nerve! Didn't they understand that he and Dr. Matsimela Baruti from Ethiopia, whose family had perished in famine, were slaving away to create good nutritional seeds that could "up" farm production, do away with famine and create healthy bodies? (Harvey had no idea about the chemical wash the seeds were being immersed in, or anything going on in Mordred's hidden 9th Floor lab.)

As soon as the protesters had passed his car, Harvey had to blink again. Hundreds of dogs on leashes were being returned home by their owners, some happy to have found their dogs, others really mad or puzzled. Treats were being gobbled up by the dogs. *Is this a mirage?*, thought the Assistant Chemist. *Who was it that said 'truth is stranger than fiction'?*

Finally the cars began to move forward. As Harvey drove up to the company parking lot, he spotted the Baker Family near the entrance, checking out some big cardboard box. He'd only met them a few times but as he approached the revolving door, they signaled to him to come close.

"You work for Zoe's Dad, don't you. Here," said Sally, handing him the latest look for dating, a thin-brimmed stetson. "It's called a 'stingy-brim' hat. It's one of my Dad's presents for anyone who's over here today." Harvey put on the hat and tipped it slightly to the side, like he'd seen his favorite movie actor do.

It fit perfectly. It was cool. Better yet, it hid his cowlick just fine! He'd never even considered wearing one of these things.

It didn't take a half-a-minute for a blond in a short skirt to spot him in the hat. She sidled over to him, "Hi! I'm Tiffany. Like, um...have we met? What's your name?" Her redhead girlfriend with an intriguing décolletage tossed a shoulder and said, "Wait! Don't I know you?"

Harvey had never considered the power of the Right Hat at the Right Time.

With his eyebrow cocked in an especially debonair way, he looked at one gal and then the other. He had practiced that eyebrow move in his mirror at night over and over and it was finally paying off! A slender brunette was wiggling up to him. He was surrounded by a blond, a redhead and a gorgeous brunette, all snuggling up to him. *What's next? Some chick who's shaved her head bald and wears tight leather?*

There had been stranger things that had happened to Harvey Singerman. He could take it... he could take it just fine.

***

This wild event on the roof -- at that time neither the public-at-large or the media had any clue that the Doc, the Secretary and the eight-year-old had been in dire danger, because so much attention was on the sign, the UFO and the hats -- all these bizarre and titillating events had made the News and world-wide-web bigtime. In a single day Acme found itself going into the most monumental instant rise in all its marketing and manufacturing history. Orders were clicking non-stop all around the world. If you wanted a hat, Acme was the place to get it.

Harry Ardmore was interviewed that night on late night TV, talking about how the founder of the company, his Dad, had been raised on organic sprouted bread and how important that was. He also touched on the history of hats and how the use of mercury during the Industrial Revolution had created many a Mad Hatter (driven bonkers from the mercury) until those practices had stopped. This, Harry pointed out, was why his altruistic and famous hat-making company had decided to contribute wonderful free hats to the "cause". The live TV audience cheered for nearly a minute when they found out each one of them was getting a genuine Acme Hat!

Ken's boss could hardly keep up with the demand and the publicity, but how he loved driving exhausted to the bank.

Chapter Twenty-Seven

The Spell Is Broken

Crumb and Will stood at the mammoth door to the Top Secret Off Limits Lab on Floor Number 9. Squeezing his bread-bumps into a more compact form in order to push himself under the door, Crumb managed to force himself through the very narrow slit under the door into the laboratory. The real problem was that he also had to drag exhausted Will along with him all the way in. The struggle to get inside the lab was almost as exhausting as moving the letters around on the roof. But finally the two were inside the secret place.

A stale but bitter and nostril-burning smell of formaldehyde, spider webs and insects pervaded the stuffy air. It was so dark at first (since their eyes were accustomed to the outside roof) that the little bee and even smaller crumb had to feel their way down a tight corridor, even tight for their small frames. As it turned out, it wasn't really a corridor, just a space between storage shelves. It just looked to them like an entire hallway, and scary enough to make each move they made feel like they would be captured then and there. They took their time, feeling their way through dust, cobwebs and their own apprehensions.

Suddenly a rat's snout appeared around a dark corner, sniffing the intruders. The rat tail was whipping against a shelf, hitting a spider's web covered in gray dust.

"Eeeek!" Crumb screamed. The rat was nearly a thousand times bigger in volume and weight than he was and was shaking his whiskers and licking his lips. *No one's gonna eat ME,* said Crumb to himself, recalling his old vow and prayer of old.

Will was more bold. He knew rats were very smart, but not as smart as HE was.

"So Rat, do you know where the light switch is?"

Will was acting nonchalant about the rodent showing up so suddenly, hoping that a dialogue between them would diffuse the terrifying possibility that both Will and Crumb were candidates for a good meal.

"Of course, know it well, Bumbler. Why? Don't you like the quiet shadows up here?"

"Sure, but let's shed a little light on what's UP here, okay?"

The rat whose name was Dempsey lifted his snout in utter disdain but found the closest light switch and stretched himself up to turn it on with his squiggly nose. He was the last remaining member of the Havisham Rat Pack and disliked being ordered around by intruders. As self-appointed Custodian, he knew every inch of this rancid place.

Florescent lights sparked up, blinking on and off on the dank ceiling until their garish lights settled down, revealing a series of corridors framed in long shelves and festooned with spider webs as if decorated for a ghostly reunion. *Doesn't anybody ever come up here to clean?* wondered Will.

"I won't eat you, not now anyway," Dempsey offered. *Small comfort,* thought Will.

Along the shelves were jars and vials of all sizes. One set of shelves was labeled "Bio-Samples". Embryos of pigs bore the ashen white of ghouls, their little hooves bending as if they were begging to leave their jars. Tadpole specimens (curled like the letter "S") were preserved in thin receptacles next to a file box labeled "Tadpole DNA probe, biological magnification 1 million, bio chips." A glossy eye of some unidentified creature stared back at Will and Crumb. Long-dead oysters and crabs floated in a sickly yellow brew.

A feeling of entrapment and sinister intentions radiated from these mummified creatures, as if they were stuffed in funerary vessels inside a crypt waiting to come back to haunt the living.

A Human embryo lay exposed in formaldehyde, its umbilical cord floating in a loop like a finger pointing accusations at a murder trial. Next to it was an opaque russet-glass jar labeled "LC-PUFAs: Long Chain Polyunsaturated Fatty Acids, Human."

"Let's get outa here!" said Crumb. It was getting horrific, and they had hardly begun to explore the vast set of shelves and long tables with sinks and microscopes.

Will shook his head. "We got in here and we're goin' through it." The two continued down the dusty corridor to the next section: "Insects and Pests, Dead."

Preserved bees of all sizes and species hovered in clear jars, looking almost-alive, caught in various poses revealing their life cycles and labor division. One bee in particular was suspended in a special vial, hovering over a preserved Easter Lily, apparently collecting pollen. Crumb had to tear Will away from that one. "Murderer!" he heard Will grunt, under his breath. Crumb knew he was thinking of Mordred.

One particularly smoky container held a suspended American Honey Bee. It was labeled "Apis Mellifera." Will trembled when he spotted that. Next to it a Queen Bee held deadly court, preserved in an enormous glass jug. A cross-section of what had once been her hive surrounded her like a cave.

Rows of Killer bees and species of ants and termites were transfixed in solutions, trapped in glass and time. Each shelf was like a cemetery but without any headstones to celebrate these wasted lives, only labels with Latin names and places of origin.

They moved on. The next section bore the label "Insects and Pests, Living."

Large fish tanks held living ecosystems of ant colonies and termite hills and -- a HIVE, still alive, was being sprayed every hour with some mysterious musty vapor that set the bees to escaping their hexagonal home. Somehow the bees and Queen were adapting but a few bee carcasses littered the tank floor. A heavy glass lid topped the huge tank and separated the bee hive and the spray tube from the rest of the outside air.

Good thing there's a lid on top, said Will to himself. *I don't want that spray on me.* What were they doing to these bees? Will shrank back from that tank with a feeling of doom. What was that spray they were being bombarded with? Crumb had to hold up Will for a second until he was strong enough to continue moving down the aisle.

Crumb could hear Dempsey's rat-tail hitting against glass and wood as he followed them down the corridor at some distance. Would he spring on them from behind some jar or bottle? Still, some eerie sense of discovery kept the two tiny creatures inspecting each shelf.

Earlier, Crumb had been consumed with a feeling that something was missing in the solving of the Riddle, that he had to find something else beyond what they had already done on the roof. It behooved him to pursue that feeling. If there was nothing really here that pertained to the Riddle or to his intuitive feeling, then they would go. There didn't seem to be any Human here, no lab investigator in charge, no security guard even. They were safe... or so they hoped. They treaded on, filled with a mixture of fascination and dread, trying not to get entangled in spider webs.

On a lower shelf, types of honey were labeled, honey from all over the world, beeswax in various hardnesses and colors, jars of pollen separated by flower-sources. Pollen from all manner of forest and gardens, from orchid farms and English gardens to the jungles of the Amazon, rain-forests in the Caribbean and island paradises of the South Pacific. Pollen that had all the colors of the rainbow, even blue and purple, gray and white, along with reds, oranges, pinks and golds of all description, and a wide array of greens from deep forest green to lime and mint. Crumb wondered what the different colors tasted like. His orange-to-gold collection had quite distinctive tastes, a different flavor for each subtle hue.

As he passed this display, Crumb held on tighter to his little packet of pollen, wondering how many he had left in the knapsack. For a moment he was tempted to take a few samples of pollen from these big jars, but this place was so spooky that he wondered if the pollen had been corrupted or poisoned in some way. So he moved on. Stealing wasn't a good idea anyway. It would mess up his Karma and come back on him in some way.

Next there was a section labeled "Ancient Grains." Crumb was amazed to see heritage grains from around the world stored in tall glass bottles: Amaranth from South America, Spelt from Central Europe, Einkorn from Germany, Farro (also known as Emmer) from the Fertile Crescent of old, Wild Oat Grass from the Lower Siberian plains, Bulgur from the Middle East, Polenta from North Italy, Kamut from Egypt, Millet from Tibet and China, Kasha from Poland, Quinoa from the Andes, Barley from Ethiopia and Teff, the world's smallest grain, made from the seed of an Ethiopian grass and made up mostly of bran and germ. These heritage seeds and grain samples were amongst forty other bottles, some grains so rare they were a goat's breath away from extinction, all displayed on long shelves.

Each type of ancient seed had a smaller container beside it, stacked with crackers or small bread slices made from these ancient grains. Crumb had the intriguing and troubling thought that he was surrounded by possible relatives, breads and crackers from endangered breeds.

He proceeded down the shelf trying to remember all the names on the labels. Will was lumbering behind him, still exhausted.

A gasp from behind one bottle! What was that? Another gasp, stifled midway.

Crumb turned to Will. "Are you okay, Will?"

"That wasn't me."

"Dempsey, what are you up to?" asked Crumb.

"Nothing. What's up?" sneered the rat, poking his head into the corridor -- he was two whole bookcases down from where Crumb and Will stood, leering at them. It couldn't have been from him.

Someone or something was following them, sniffling, breathing in to keep from being discovered. Another gasp!

Crumb spotted where it was -- right behind the container labeled "Spelt. Triticum aestivum subsp. spelta. Polish Origin."

Suddenly a large seed sneaked over to the edge of the jar, staring at Crumb.

"Who... who are you? Spurlock?" said the seed, with eyes round with surprise and a little sparkle of recognition. "You seem so... so familiar."

Will was brusque, an uncharacteristic reaction for the bee but prompted by a need to protect his friend Crumb from this strange apparition. The giant seed had been addressing Crumb, not Will, and the bee was worried that Crumb was under attack.

"That's okay, Will. I can handle this!" Crumb said in an aside to his friend. "My name is Crumb. I live with a Human family in their Kitchen. Now you tell me who YOU are!"

"I'm a Spelt seed." The seed hesitated. "You have a family? A family of your own?"

"No, not really. I'm an orphan. I never knew my mother and father. I hope they're alive. Granddad Breadbox raised me in the Kitchen and managed to teach me enough things -- including how to read words -- that I've survived so far."

"That's amazing! You remind me so much of...", and the Spelt seed began to sniffle and soon began to cry large grainy tears. She gathered her emotions together to explain why she had been so startled.

"I thought I was seeing a ghost at first! You remind me so much of my... of my dear late husband. He had the same eyes. Very much like yours, anyway. They sparkled and were so mischievous. How I miss him. He lost his life fighting to save me from... from the evil Mordred-man who comes up here sometimes and experiments on us. My fellow was so brave, he risked his life for me. I've been hiding for over five years... ever since... ever since my..." She stopped herself mid-sentence and scolded herself, *Oh, why am I telling them all this? Such painful memories....*

The Spelt seed was now standing in a small tidepool of tears.

"Ever since WHAT?" asked Crumb and Will at the same time.

"Ever since my little baby was born and was stolen from me."

"You had a baby?" Crumb could scarcely allow himself to deal with the implications of this. "Go on," he prompted.

"Yes, it was so cute. It -- I should say 'he' -- had the most adorable little curly-cue on top... right on top of his little Spelt seed head. I was even thinking of nicknaming him Kewpie. By now, if he's still alive, I bet he's sprouted into quite a handsome lad. If only I had been part of his life. I hadn't even had the chance to sing him a lullaby -- or give him a traditional Spelt name like Flanoolie or Pombrin."

Will began to put two-and-two together. "How did the newborn get taken from you?"

Spelt seed sniffled. "It was that rat Dempsey. How I despise him! I must have looked away for a second to find a little baby-wipe — they sometimes use them in the lab you know and I'd cut a whole one into the tiniest bunch of mini-diapers. So there I was, turned away from my darling little Spelt-seed for a second, when Dempsey came over to our tidy alcove behind the shelf where his Daddy Spurlock had made a little cradle for the baby out of half a peanut shell. Kewpie got stuck on one of Dempsey's long whiskers that had gotten into a honey jar. (His whiskers are like magnets, you know, and so sticky.) Then the dirty rat was gone... with our little baby!"

"That's awful," commiserated the bee. Crumb could hardly figure out what to say next.

"Hmmmm...." muttered Crumb. "That's odd! I was found on the Toaster tray in the Baker's Family Kitchen. I almost fell into a blob of butter. Toaster and Breadbox tell me that I had a very cute little baby-curl on the top of *my* head. I... I've been searching... searching for my Mom and Dad ever since. You don't suppose...." His voice trailed off.

Lady Spelt leaned up against a jar — aghast or thrilled, it was hard to tell. Could this be her stolen offspring?

"Do you remember anything from your first days right after you were born?" she asked hesitantly but with growing intensity.

"No, just darkness and a smell of... a smell of... something vinegar-like... kind of like the stuffy smell in here. And you say I look something like your husband? Really?"

The two of them started to get more and more excited.

"You look so much like Spurlock that at first I thought you were his ghost! -- Sometimes I feel his presence here, sending me love, protecting me, wishing he were still by my side. And there you were: Same eyes, even the same color, same cute button nose, same ear-shape, same mouth and... oh Thank the Lord, same SMILE!"

They rushed for each other. Lady Spelt touched Crumb's round little cheeks with tenderness and sheer wonder, hugged him, then held him farther back from her to admire him, then hugged him again. Crumb had never before known the warmth of a Mother's touch, not really. He couldn't stop gasping and hugging her and telling her how much he loved her.

"I just met you and I love you ALREADY!" he exclaimed, smiling the biggest smile in his life. The florescent lights seemed to shine brighter and suddenly this horrid, scary place didn't seem quite so awful.

"What's your name, Mom? Aside from 'Mom'," he added.

"I'm called Eenalyne. Eenalyne Spelt. I am the proud bearer of a long line of heritage grains and full of old legends to share with you, my son, my SON, my sunny-boy son! And what, pray tell, is your name?"

"Crumb. I'm just called Crumb."

"Well, that's a fine traditional name, but not all that imaginative. If I'd only had you for longer, you would have had a different moniker. The Spelt Naming Ceremony is one of the highlights of a young seed's life. Actually, Crumb, you're not a seed anymore, you must have been exposed to moisture and sprouted quite early."

"Eenalyne... Eenalyne," Will was intoning her name, ruminating on it. It sounded like something familiar and yet like no name he'd ever heard before.

"What did you say your name was, Ma'am?" inquired Will, thinking he might have gotten the name wrong.

"In the storage jar here my label says 'Spelt: Eena-C8.' "

The bee's wings began to tremble when he realized that her label, "Spelt: Eena-C8", sounded almost exactly like "Spelled 'Enunciate' "! It hit Will in a bolt of thought-lightning: The line of the Riddle that Crumb had not felt good about, that he had felt was really not solved was: "E'nunciate well and learn how it's spelled." The Riddle was actually instructing them to "learn how it's really Spelt!"

"Crumb," burst in Will, almost as excited as was Crumb at that moment, "you were totally right -- smarter than I was -- the real word isn't 'spelled' with an extra 'l-e-d' at the end, there's a 't' instead -- we actually misspelled it when we wrote the Riddle down. It's SPELT! And on top of that 'E'nunciate well' stands for 'Eenalyne.' Her jar was labeled 'Spelt: Eena-C8!' "

"Phew -- that's wild! We actually misspelled 'spelled'! Seems like we've SOLVED the whole Riddle now... but the best part is... it's given me back my Mom!"

At that moment Crumb felt something fill up inside him, as if a stopped-up well had finally burst forth with nectar, a sensation and emotion unlike anything he had ever felt in his entire life: The hollow core of him, the black hole, was gone! Finding his Mother and knowing that she had loved him all along sent waves of warm fulfillment throughout every particle of his being.

He was whole. His Voice, his Thought, his Purpose were all part of who he was, who he'd been from the start. He had sprouted from a grand line of ancient grains to become the staff of life, his own nourishment. Now he could embrace even his shortcomings, because he could look past them to the potential he might become in the future. He wasn't alone anymore. He turned to his Mother and to the bee and grabbed them, twirling them around and around!

The three did a Happy Dance on the shelf, forgetting that they were in one of the most spooky, dank, dark places in the whole world! After all the dancing around and hugging, they quieted down. They didn't want the rat to get close, especially if he had honey-soaked whiskers. And Crumb had a big question to ask.

"Tell me, Mom, how... how did my Father d... meet his untimely end?"

"This is not easy to tell you about, but you deserve to know. He loved you too, very much. One day right after you were stolen (or locked on to Dempsey's whiskers -- I guess the rat went outside in his exploration for cheese or something and somehow you ended up in that Kitchen) -- but a day after you were sadly taken from us, that horrid hulking figure Mordred came into his special Lab to kill some bees. Spurlock your Dad saw that evil man reaching for the Spelt container and he got very afraid that we would be experimented on." She gulped, her throat catching every so often.

"As I said, we'd been hiding in a little alcove behind the shelf. Just as Mordred reached behind the shelf for the light switch, he screeched, 'An ant! Die, you dumb little black thing!' He thought your Dad was black because the light wasn't on yet and your handsome Father was about the size of a large ant, so that evil man... oh I can hardly stand to relive this another second... that Mordred squashed your dear Dad with his big monstrous thumb! I've been hiding here since then, living only on drops of water, a few pieces of pollen every so often and... the hope of finding you some day."

Crumb and Eenalyne wept for a minute, then dried their eyes, smiling bravely at each other.

"Can I come with you back to your Kitchen home?" Eenalyne asked.

"You betcha!" Will and Crumb answered in unison. At that exact instant there was a creak and a spark of light....

Chapter Twenty-Eight

Battle

Suddenly all three knew they better not say another word! They spotted -- way far away (or so it seemed to them) at the front of the Lab -- a garish light from the outside corridor leaking into the interior of the lab, flashing shadows everywhere. The sickly green light looked like a coiled snake hugging the floor, sneaking around corners to spy, like Iago Fripple would be doing if he were still on the planet. The door was opening!

In stepped Mordred, grunting in his drunken stupor, heavy with the weight of his evil intentions. He was still drunk and left the door ajar. Some specimen jars tumbled to the ground and broke, spilling their maudlin contents, as his arms and legs swayed akimbo along the spiderwebs and corridor shelves. He didn't stop to pick the glass pieces up. Wiping a cobweb from the top of a shelf as he continued down the path, Mordred lumbered on, aiming to inspect the live bee colony being sprayed and trapped in the fish tank. When he got there, he looked like a giant fish with glossy, hungry eyes.

"Die, you yellow-blashted devils, die!" he threatened, his thick lips swollen with drink and the venom of his own self-created hatred. He reached over to mark something on a Time Table graph. Will felt a loathing he'd never felt before, watching Mordred's probing fish-eyes bending over the fish tank to see if destruction was on schedule.

Mordred had been experimenting on the hive with small doses of some questionable insecticide, seeing if the bees would develop immunity to the spray or be massacred. So far the casualties had not been to his liking, not lethal enough, not fast enough. Ever since he was nearly seven, he'd longed to decimate these honey-producing flying beasts. Forget about how they pollinated huge numbers of crops! He would sell his seeds and corner the market.

Will surmised all of this in a flash, his brilliant storehouse of human knowledge nourishing his instincts like Royal Jelly, allowing him to see into Mordred's depraved mind and seething heart.

Crumb riveted his eyes all of a sudden, alerting Will that there was another intruder... or was it a rescue squad? The mammoth front door to the Lab was now opening wide with a hissing squeak. Bright lights from the corridor plunged inside, in zig-zag lines like an entire nest of snakes invading the Lab, shadows coiling along the walls, shelves and floor. An eerie net of cobweb patterns plunged across rows of glass receptacles like a massive fish-trap. Mordred had left the door ajar, something he never had done before on Floor Number 9. The hissing door was now full-open. Someone or something had arrived at that exact second!

Will and Crumb turned in shock. There, dwarfed by the looming height of the metal door, a shadowy figure stood in the doorway, a humanoid outline of some kind whose shadow elongated into a monstrous apparition as the hallway light radiated around the body.

The ghoul stepped inside with halting footfalls, its arms stiff and lifeless as a zombie. Shadows of long fingers reached across the ceiling, probing.

Will grabbed Crumb as soon as he spotted what it was... no, WHO it was!

Braids!

ZOE! It had been so dark when she peered inside the Lab that she had entered like a blind man, testing every step as her eyes adjusted to the gloom.

"Crumb! Will!" she whispered, a stage-whisper that zoomed into their ears and flooded their psychic thought-patterns. "Are you okay? I took the stairs looking for you."

Stay there or... or go-away. Mordred doesn't know we're here. Crumb found his real Mother. She's with us. GO! GO! NOW! Will was sending this exact thought-message to her, hoping she'd get it and stay out of danger. So far Mordred didn't have a clue that Will and Crumb were there. Zoe might actually foul everything up by pointing them out.

Mordred turned his head toward the door. He saw her. His eyes were bulging, hot breath was steaming out of his swollen lips.

Zoe didn't waste any time. She raced over to a bookshelf on tiptoeing feet and huddled behind the bookcase, about ten feet from the leering man.

"So YOU are the darling daughter of Dr. Matsimela Baruti, eh?! I've been WAITing to meet you, Small-fry, Pipsqueak! Don't you keep BEES?" Mordred sneered. He couldn't see exactly where she was, but he could totally feel her there or perhaps hear her hurried breath like ice crystals forming behind the shelves where she hid. She was dodging for time, trying to figure out what to do next, where to go next, how was she going to get her two friends AND Crumb's Mother out of there? Time sped up to meet the urgency.

In that single instant as she hovered between possibilities, Zoe suddenly realized within her, in the desperation of the moment, that she could imagine herself to be a REAL LIVE NINJA. She could pretend to appear and disappear at will, scaling walls and being completely still until a blow was needed. Maybe these super-abilities might never happen, but in the play-acting she might locate opportunities for attack and retreat.

Ever since that magical day when she'd talked with Crumb and Spoon in the Kitchen and Will outside practicing aeronautics, Zoe had come to see the enigmatic unity between imagination and logic, the yin and yang of contemplation and action. Something in her said she'd been in this same situation before, that the cat was right, she had been Aida, and she was set on not getting buried alive in a tomb ever again.

These realizations came in a flash, infinitesimal decisions: Zoe decided that magic and martial arts would merge and make her stronger than she'd ever been.

Somehow this pint-sized eight-year-old understood that a flexible branch that can bend in the wind is likely to be whole and standing when the wind dies down, while a tree trunk that resists the tempest can very well be toppled and ripped from the soil. She knew that using someone's force-energy against them, not by resisting their energy but by flipping it back on them, was superior to brute force.

She was an eight-year-old brown belt. Certainly, Zoe WAS scared. Stiff waves of fear lay in her gut, standing waves of terror as compact as a Spelt seed. But what is courage if not the meeting of necessity and the facing of one's fear, then doing what has to be done no matter what.

She had no desire to be a hero. In a way coming here had been selfish. Yes, she definitely wanted to save Will and Crumb, but more than that, she was FURIOUS! Her Dad had been tied to a column, his research stolen, bolts and cutting machines looming around him -- this creep had almost murdered her Dad! Was it selfish of her to seek vengeance? If she were to be killed, then yes, selfish indeed. Her father would be alone.

She would not allow that to happen.

Zoe tugged at her brown belt to make sure it was on tight and touched her sweat band. Her lips were as tight as her belt. The dust and spider webs, reeking formaldehyde and rank insect gases, were drying her out, and unfortunately she had forgotten to bring any water with her. But that wouldn't stop her.

Lunging toward the hulk, she then confounded him by seeming to disappear behind the closest bookcase. Jars of embryos shook a bit, threatening to tumble down. Suddenly she was out from behind the bookcase again, close enough to him to rotate her body in midair and deliver a spectacular jumping spin kick.

Mordred started to fold in two like the closed book he was inside. Then he fought his liquor down and came at Zoe with such demonic killer instinct that she wanted to bolt for the door. But the hugeness of his body and his lack of coordination from too much beer were helping Zoe to throw him off balance. She took him down, down to the floor, and scrunched his elbow joint in the process.

Suddenly Dempsey, the rat who had stolen baby Crumb, ran out from where he was lurking under a dissection table and tripped Zoe just as she was rising up from her hold on Mordred. This was no accident. Dempsey depended on Mordred for food and he wasn't about to let a pint-size girl take his meal-ticket down.

She recovered her balance but the rodent was literally skirting in between her feet like a crazed tango dancer. She kicked the rat out of the way, slamming him into a metal file cabinet. Mordred wouldn't have to provide the rat with any more food and water. Death was always the risk an accomplice took.

Will and Crumb had quickly retreated to a safe vantage point. Will sized up the odds: Zoe was skilled and out-doing her opponent, but if the drunk landed all three-hundred-and-seventy-five pounds on her, there would be a small coffin somewhere bearing the greatest little eight-year-old that Will and Crumb had ever known. Justified rage exploded inside the bee like a volcano --- "To Bee or Not to Bee"!

There was no longer any question about what he had to do!

Will was well-aware that the Aliens had awarded him a very unique gift -- to be used only once and only under the most severe circumstances -- the ability to sting someone without being killed in the process, to pierce with his stinger, lose the stinger, but not die! Will had kept this in reserve, and now was the time to use it!

The bee zipped at top speed over to Mordred who was back on his feet but swaying. The little aviator spun around, performing rapid-fire aeronautics a few inches from the monster's depraved and bloodshot eyes, just so Mordred would see clearly that it was a Bee who was the Justice-Bringer and Executioner.

Mordred froze then stumbled back and forth, his bulbous mouth open. The two opponents locked eyes in a death-panic. Then the bee zoomed down and stung him right in the heart!

Mordred died instantly.

Chapter Twenty-Nine

Aftermath

No sooner had Mordred's gigantic corpse collapsed in front of them than Crumb, Eenalyne, Will and Zoe looked at each other in mutual recognition that NOW was the time to hightail it out of the laboratory! Not a moment too soon. They left Mordred and Dempsey there on the musty floor of the lab, lights off. Zoe pushed the door closed, as tight as possible.

She was debating whether to tell her Dad anything --- she had never lied to him before, it was true, not even a little fib pretending that someone else had made the cookies disappear from the cookie jar. But silence was the better part of wisdom here. She wasn't sure she wanted to give her Dad a blow-by-blow description of the mortal combat between a short Brown Belt and a rotund Bee-Killer.

Zoe put the scenario into her imagination-factory: It would start with her Dad finding her muttering during a nightmare, then she'd compulsively throw a hint at him. Finally he'd sit her down on a park bench and get it out of her: She'd witnessed Mordred's demise, but... but... Then her Dad would sputter, "Did you 'off' him yourSELF?" She would swear she was innocent, however the details she would hesitantly reveal always led (in her child's imagination-factory) to a feverish crime lab investigation and a rabid murder trial. "Guilty of First Degree!" the Judge would bellow, slamming the gavel down. There she would be, in a jail cell trying to swallow a last request supper (Hazel's famous fried chicken and pecan pie) before being led to the gallows. Even if she was under-age. (She'd seen too many crime shows on TV.)

So, no, it didn't look like a great idea for her to open up to her Dad about her knocking Mordred to the lab floor a few times. OR to reveal to him the exact size and talents of a literate breadcrumb and a genius bee. Magic was one thing -- disclosure of magic, another.

Right now, all she wanted to do was to get Home.

There were flat pockets in her Karate jacket -- an unusual feature but one that came in handy in a pinch. Will and Crumb were gently placed on opposite corners of one pocket while Lady Spelt was delicately placed on a soft tissue in the other pocket. The elevator had been rigged not to stop or leave from the ninth floor, so she would have to walk down nine flights of stairs. Every so often on the way down, Zoe had to lean on the steel railing because her energy was draining, all the while that relief and delayed terror-reactions were welling up inside her. It was a slow trip down the stairwell.

Meanwhile, Dr. Matt had been frantically searching for his daughter, who had told him forty-five minutes earlier that she was just heading to the Ladies' Room. Snively and the other security guard had been summoned to conduct a thorough search for Zoe and had inspected every floor and office but skipped Floor 9 as it was known to be Off-Limits. (They hadn't been hired for high IQ but for obedience.)

Finally Zoe reached the Lobby. As soon as the Doc saw his daughter, he combined scolding with hugging and made her promise to stay by his side. The biggest problem Zoe had was that Will kept on buzzing his wings a bit inside her pocket from time to time. Fortunately, Matt was so worn out from his imprisonment in the Processing Plant that he didn't hear any buzzing. If he did, he probably thought it was his ears ringing.

Glenda had gone home to fix her chihuahua Pip some dinner and collapse in front of the TV to find out any news about her ex-boss. A commentator was asking, Where had the notorious Gordon M. O'Greene gone? Was he in hiding after all the protesters and commotion at his company? Had he absconded with mega-millions to Brazil overnight? In front of the O'Greene mansion his tough-as-nails lawyer was filmed issuing a statement declining to issue a statement (since it was "premature at this time") -- the typical run-around.

Per his advocate, Gordon Mordred O'Greene's whereabouts were unknown at the present time, his business dealings impeccable, his character unfairly maligned, and his lawyer's fees not to be disclosed. Meanwhile inside the estate gates, Mrs. O'Greene was holed up in the mansion with a supply of frozen pizza and tissue boxes. (He didn't mention the pool boy.) "The lady of the house is too upset and worried to be interviewed at this time," stated the lawyer.

Glenda shut the TV off at that point. Pip ran over to her and jumped in her lap to comfort her.

At that very same moment, Dr. Baruti and Zoe decided to rest in the lobby for a while before going home. The two sat next to the wilted palm on a long bench eating chocolate bars from a candy machine, something they normally would never do. Through the glass of the revolving door panels, they could see a horde of news reporters milling around outside, next to a shaved ice cart and a hot dog stand that had been set up to feed busybodies and media folks. Zoe was forced to wave to the paparazzi from inside the lobby, as cameras flashed the news that "the Heroic Little Girl is safe."

Finally the reporters and lookie-loos left. It was sundown. Ken texted a message over to Harry Ardmore Jr.

--- "Friends Safe, Hats A Success." Little did Matt or Zoe know that Mordred had planned to turn the Doc and his ex-Secretary into hamburger as soon as nighttime came.

Mordred's body was detected three days later. The mammoth door had been shut long enough to make the detection easy but extremely unpleasant.

The Poison Center clean-up crew wore Hazmat Suits just in case any dangerous or plague-like materials would be found to permeate the Lab on Floor Number 9. The sheer amount of pickled specimens found there was duly noted, so that later on a special research team could determine if the secret experiments conducted there constituted a cause for national or international concern.

During the initial cleanup, one of the workers had spotted Dempsey's remains at the foot of a large file cabinet near a dissection table. Picking him up gingerly by his long rat tail, he dropped the rat in a thick, zippered plastic bag destined for the outside trashcan. Thinking better of that, he sent the plastic bag to the police as evidence.

A week later, a dry but subtly sarcastic obituary was printed in the local paper and posted on the web. As a matter of morbid public curiosity, a TV news report hurriedly announced the time and location of the funeral.

No one came... well, no one except Mrs. G. M. O'Greene. His wife Lucille had had time to rehearse. With her previously moistened handkerchief with which she dabbed her makeup-streaked eyes, she let out very convincing sobs, looking around to see if anyone in the back room of the funeral home was paying attention to her pretense of affection.

What she was really bemoaning was that her Dear Departed had left her with major debts and no proper inheritance. She wouldn't be able to shop like she was used to, and maybe she'd have to visit a hockshop in a trench coat with her collar pulled high to avoid the press. She'd have to cancel the masseur. Seeing that the undertaker wasn't bad-looking at all, she dropped a clean handkerchief at his feet as she strutted to her rented limousine.

***

Ever since that wild Sunday when Whisk had summoned the neighborhood dogs and organized the now legendary "Grand Semi-Circle of Canine Calm", as the assembled dogs came to be known (at least amongst themselves), Whisk had figured out that Crumb and Will were probably still inside the building. Where were his buddies? Were they trapped, were they injured, were they just asleep after an exhausting time on the roof? Whisk wasn't sure, and all that Nefertiti had been able to determine -- oddly enough -- was that both Crumb and Will were ALIVE. (Poor Nefertiti! The last few days of materializing in and out of various Time Frames had completely numbed her sensibilities. At least for a day or so.)

At least Whisk didn't have to worry about Zoe, Matt and Nefertiti... or the Bakers. All of them came out of the AlliedGreene facility late Sunday afternoon. Johnny had walked Whisk back to the woodie and put him inside with all the windows cracked open, of course. Then the Bakers piled in to their station wagon and Ken started up the motor, with Matt and Zoe in their own car ready to follow them home to Tempest Street. It certainly had been a tempest of a day. Zoe put Nefertiti on the seat next to her (careful not to place the sleeping cat anywhere near her coat pockets with their precious cargo.) Exhaustion, relief and happiness can make a heady brew --- Zoe herself was ready for a nap.

As their car made its way back to Tempest Street, Zoe touched her pockets very, very gently, feeling for the soft bumps in her pockets. That's where Crumb, Will and Eenalyne were --- she didn't dare peek inside. Yes, the little bumps at the corners of the inside pockets were there. Phew! She had to figure out a way to bring them back to the Baker's Kitchen without letting anybody know what she was up to. Thank goodness they were there, safe, not in AlliedGreene anymore. But how could they stay much longer in her pockets without getting squished or possibly suffocated if someone hugged her?

To Whisk, leaving the AlliedGreene premises had felt like a stab. He didn't know that Zoe had Crumb and Will in her pockets. If he had known that they were safe, he wouldn't have been whimpering in the back seat. The Bakers tried to console him with petting and a treat, but thought the pooch was only tuckered-out after a rough day.

Of course, Whisk thought, no search party, police force or firemen crew would imagine in their wildest dreams that a piece of bread and a honey bee would be important to look for and find in the enormous expanse of AlliedGreene. (It's tough to find something when you have no idea what you are looking for and wouldn't believe it anyway if you found it.) Were his Companions okay? Where WERE they?

Before Zoe and Matt returned home, she asked her Dad to stop by the Bakers for a minute to drop off Nefertiti and to say "Thanks for everything" to the Baker Family. (What she really wanted to do was drop by the Kitchen and leave Crumb, Will and Eenalyne there.) "No problem," said Matt. He stayed in the car, totally wiped out.

In the Kitchen, there WAS a problem: As soon as she felt in her pockets, to her horror, all three were GONE! The bumps she had felt as she and her Dad drove home were just tiny pieces of lint in one pocket and one folded-over seam and an empty tissue inside the other pocket -- not Crumb or Will or Crumb's Mommy. Oh no, not this! Somehow Will, Crumb and Mama Spelt had tumbled out of Zoe's pockets, probably in the lobby or down the staircase somewhere. Maybe they fell out in the car....

She tried to convince her Dad to go back to the lobby. He was not going back. Never. ("Why are you asking me that?") She was too tired to think of some excuse easily. She invented a reason. She'd left her sweatband there. ("Too bad.") She wanted another chocolate bar. ("No way. And we can go to a corner store if you're that desperate.") She missed the lobby. ("Are you kidding, Zoe? Get some sleep right now.")

She had fitful dreams all night -- Crumb had been crushed, Will had succumbed to bee poison, Eenalayne had decided to stay in the Lab and write her Memoirs. (Zoe had read how long-term prisoners often felt like they preferred to stay imprisoned where at least the surroundings were familiar.) When she awakened early Monday morning, her neck was covered in cold sweat. She didn't dare tell her Dad about what was really upsetting her.

"Dad, I don't feel up to going to school today, okay?" Matt agreed. They'd both rest in all day to recover.

That Monday night Harvey (in his stingy-brim hat) and Glenda Scoop carrying her adorable Pip came over the Baruti's house along with all the Bakers, and Zoe knew that no other Human there (except herself) really understood that two very special tiny beings, the real heroes of the day, were missing-in-action.

Zoe put on a Happy Face and threw together a bunch of comfort foods wearing her Chef's Hat -- soothing cream of tomato soup, bubbling grilled cheese sandwiches, tapioca pudding and a choice of hot chocolate or fresh lemonade. Hazel added to the table by bringing over an organic salad of fresh spinach, pecans, raisins and diced apple in champagne vinaigrette. The Extended Family finished the celebration by playing charades and trivia games in the living-room. Nefertiti and Whisk had never seen any of these folks happier... except for Zoe, who was very worried about her Will and Crumb, leave alone Eenalyne, but did her best to act "normal", whatever that was.

After Crumb and Will didn't return to the Baker's house on Monday, Whisk took it upon himself to trundle out to AlliedGreene on Tuesday and wait for Crumb and Will to show up or to sniff out somehow what the problem was. When they didn't show up, Whisk tried to gain entry through the revolving door, but was kicked out by a security guard and trudged back home.

The Kitchen Things were torn between grieving or hoping, praying or picking fights. There was a pall over the Kitchen that was palpable. Sally had spilled a glass on the floor, Hazel had burned a casserole, and the cat and dog were refusing to eat.

As for the Kitchen Things, they were like abandoned sailors after a shipwreck, stuck on an uncharted island, desperate for a ship to appear on the horizon so they could shout, "Hey, over here! We're over here!"

Granddad didn't want to open his door for a day, because he had rusted it so badly crying secret tears. Crumb's little cousins tried to comfort him and Breadbox had to put up a good front so they wouldn't lose hope.

Spoon languished inside her cabinet and wrote poems in the oldest of dirge forms in French literature, a villanelle "Where are the cupcakes of yesteryear? Les gâteaux d'antan...." she was heard to wail. Toaster swore he'd find Crumb and Will with his superior deductive skills, and even Rolling Pin sobbed in her drawer, hoping that a hit man hadn't got them.

The next afternoon, Whisk rumbled back to Crossroads Avenue, across Culvert Pass, onto Tesla Road and reached the front of AlliedGreene to see if he could locate his missing friends. Where were they? A Hazmat Truck was parked near the entrance. Four hefty paramedics covered from head to toe in suits were carting away the overladen, plastic-sealed stretcher. *Mordred,* thought Whisk. *Good riddance.*

Suddenly Whisk's floppy ears straightened higher, his right paw pointed toward the revolving door. It was Will and Crumb and some other small dot-of-a-thing, all rolling under the front door, rubbing their eyes at how bright the sun was! Three fugitives let loose to freedom! Whisk galloped over to them, careful that when he came close, he wouldn't stomp on them. But his wagging tail set up a headwind that threatened to sweep Eenalyne a yard away.

Once the dog settled down, Will excitedly introduced Lady Spelt, for so she would be called later on, to the big dog who graciously bowed his head in her direction. *Wow, Crumb, what a pretty Mom you have!* Whisk thought.

Crumb explained to Whisk where they'd been for those three agonizing days.

They had fallen out of Zoe's pockets when she had bent over the vending machine in the Lobby to pick up two chocolate bars from the metal dispenser. Crumb, Will and Eenalyne had tried to climb up Zoe's pants to get back into her pockets but kept on slipping off. Then whenever Zoe gently patted her pockets to satisfy herself that all was well, Crumb would try to jump on her shoe to get her attention. But Zoe and the Doc were just too worn out to notice much of anything.

When Doc and Zoe left the building, Crumb raced after them but one of the policemen nearly smashed him with his heavy shoe -- not on purpose (the policeman hadn't seen him), but that mishap was enough for Crumb to retreat back to the wall. For three days after that the little fugitives hid behind the wilted palm in the Lobby, dodging out of sight while scores of Police scurried around, interrogating the Security Guards, trying to find Mr. O'Greene and gathering evidence while a few reporters nosed around. Finally the Hazmat crew hauled Mordred's hulk of a body out of the premises on a stretcher and the police and security crew left. It seemed like the right time to make a getaway.

"Thank you, Good Ol' Whiskeroo, for being so loyal," said Crumb. "And smart... you made a good guess that we were still back here. I can't wait to get out of here." Will and Eenalyne nodded.

So Whisk took them all back home to the Kitchen on his famous whiskers. The soft wind and warm sunshine felt like a caress to the three former prisoners. Whisk nodded at all the neighbor dogs as he passed their front yards and each dog bowed low in deference to "The One and Only" Top Dog. Their admiration for him included their canine recognition that he was not going to be snobby or bossy, but caring instead. His scent as he passed all the neighborhood dogs conveyed confidence and calm compassion -- it emanated enduring love. Whisk had never felt so needed and so appreciated as this, bearing the missing heroes back Home!

Nefertiti pranced over to Zoe's house to let her know that all was well -- Will, Crumb and his Mom had been found and were safe back home! Zoe put down her book, bounced up and down on the couch and then snuggled next to Nefertiti, feeling the healing power of her purring vibrations. Zoe realized that somehow GREAT EXPECTATIONS was the perfect book for her to be reading now. It was important never to give up hope, to keep some magic alive in one's life. After all, you never knew who would turn out to be your benefactor -- who would have ever guessed that it would be a crumb, a bee, a dog and a cat?! She slept better that night than she'd slept in weeks.

***

Ken Baker took Hazel out to dinner the next evening. He wanted to share something very special with her. His boss Harry Ardmore Jr. had called him the day before and consulted with Ken how the hat company could show their gratitude to Dr. Matt Baruti.

Gratitude? Sincerely, Mr. Ardmore was an organic food advocate and had contributed to causes such as Animators4Animals and had written to his congressman to pass label disclosure laws so that consumers would know what genetically modified ingredients or petroleum-based ingredients they were buying and eating, and hopefully some day would ban those noxious things.

But in truth, all that publicity had escalated his company sales into the stratosphere. It was one thing to have sent five thousand hats to distribute at the site. Now not even a week later, Acme Company hat sales world-wide had gone off the charts, up onto a whole new graph in Harry's office. And sales weren't dropping, they were in a new range nearly every day! Hats had come back, they were distinctive, practical, alluring, or just plain fun! And you could proclaim your Voice, your Thought, your Purpose on them if you desired.

'Acme: Hats Off for Hats On!' — I like that as a new sales campaign slogan!, thought Ken to himself. *I'll have to pitch that to Harry... later.*

Did Ken think, asked his boss, that the Doctor would accept the funding to have his very own laboratory? Ken nearly dropped his cell phone.

Mr. Ardmore wanted to set up a new foundation to support privately funded, non-governmental research, an ongoing research that could take as long as needed to determine IF an organic and impervious seed could be developed, without animal testing, that might create nutrition and fight disease, famine and farm problems in America and around the world.

"More Health, More Hats", that's the way his boss put it! Would Matt accept the proposal to have his own personal funded laboratory? Ken wanted to say "Duh" but he kept his diplomatic smarts together, and simply said, "Wonderful idea! I'm sure that Doctor Baruti would be thrilled. What would you call this Foundation?"

"How about F-O-O-D, F.O.O.D?" queried his boss. "I'm thinking it could stand for Foundation for Organic Opportunity-Development." It was altruistic, it was important, but it was also smart business.

"Sounds about right," responded Ken. "I'll check on whether that acronym or organization name is copyrighted or is up for grabs." He did — it was fine.

So Ken took Hazel to her favorite restaurant, a Japanese sushi and tempura restaurant in the middle of a tea garden with cherry blossoms surrounding a placid lake and a curved red bridge reminiscent of the serenity of Kyoto and the waterlily pond at Giverny. She could hardly wait to hear what her husband wanted to tell her.

Hazel had softened, not because of the money they now had (although that did allow her good moods to prevail -- a woman who can shop often is easier to get along with, for certain) but her change-of-viewpoint was deeper than that. No longer did she have to feel she'd sacrificed a glamorous movie star career for family.

She had the family she always wanted and it included Zoe and Matt now. Also, there was a certain notoriety and glamor in being part of the family that had interacted in this wild and highly publicized event on Tesla Road. She didn't have to listen to "Sweet Sally Jones" on the radio anymore -- her own life was twice as exciting and a lot more satisfying.

She even began to respect her children more and stopped nagging to control them. Zoe had taught Hazel that children were simply shorter than grownups, but they weren't short on smarts. In fact, the two foodies, Hazel and Zoe, were working on a special BAKER AND BARUTI COOKBOOK - ORGANIC IS GREAT.

So at dinner, overlooking the curved bridge with lanterns lighting up the cherry trees around the tea house, Ken and Hazel sipped a bit of warm sake together and saluted the new Advanced Research Laboratory... or whatever the Doc was going to call it.

The next day -- with plans to tell Matt when the exact right moment showed up, but not right off the bat -- Ken took Matt to the Tennis Club and let the Doc win (or so Ken pretended to himself for a minute, a bit reluctant to concede that Matt had learned by now to lob the ball with a fierce spin and had developed a mean serve.)

Oh well, I have to be a good sport, Ken reminded himself. *That's what this game is all about. Matt won it fair and square,* he admitted to himself. *I better get practicing more! Look at it this way, he'll make a great doubles partner now!* It was that old ambitious, competitive energy Ken Baker had -- but if it hadn't been for that enterprising spirit, no hats would have wound up on Tesla Road. Wiping his brow, he had to laugh at himself. *Wait til I tell the Doc! It's such a win-win for us all. It's time for me to give him the news. ...What's the name of that terrific-looking new coffee place down the road?*

Then he and Matt shared lattes sitting on leather club chairs in a private corner of the best coffee house in the city. Matt leaped up to his feet when he heard the offer.... YES! The Doc called Harvey right away to tell him he had a job for him and his salary was going to be just dandy.

The following day Zoe ordered an elegant desk set for her Dad. "Wait until the money comes in, Zoe," cautioned her Dad, a bit wary that all this good news was going to downtrend in some way. (People who depend mostly on logic without sufficient doses of magic can second-guess themselves and foresee failure if they don't watch out, making failure more likely. A balance of both physical control and imaginative reach works better.)

Zoe promptly marched over to her closet, brought back a huge mason jar and emptied forty-five dollars and twenty-five cents in coins onto the coffee table in front of her bemused father.

"You are going to run for President someday, Sweetpea... and help straighten out our gosh-darn economy." Zoe laughed but shook her head.

"Dad, I'm going to raise money for no-kill shelters, teach martial arts on the side, and if I can make the time, practice enough to get better at the piano. I've been thinking it would be great to be a professional chef and cookbook writer. I have a whole bunch of Great Expectations!"

Matt didn't wait for her to say "Daaaddeeee" in her begging voice. He tickled her shoulder, watched her giggle and said, "Isn't it about time we got you a puppy?"

Zoe jumped up and down on the living-room sofa so much that some of the feather stuffing started to come out of one of the cushions. Then she said, "And a cute kitten too!"

Chapter Thirty

Ticker Tape

The returning heroes Crumb, Will and Lady Spelt were regaled with a ticker tape parade down the granite and woodblock counters. (S.K. had cut up some old Shopping List pads into tiny pieces of paper as confetti.) The snow flurries of white confetti landed in every crevice and shelf in the Kitchen. In fact it was such a mess everywhere that Nefertiti ran to fetch Zoe who had to sneak into the Kitchen at the end of the parade (the Bakers being sound asleep in their beds) to clean it up before Hazel would realize what was going on down there in the Kitchen.

How the Family slept through the noise Zoe could never figure out. Breadbox told her about the part of the parade she'd just missed: Pots and Pans had started things out by drumming out a stirring rhythm, accompanied by Spatula and Can Opener doing acrobatic cheerleader routines. The Parade proceeded with Eenalyne being carried on Scrubber (his freshly-washed soft-side) by four sturdy plastic Party Toothpicks. She waved to the crowd and made a big hit with everyone. Scrubber, being a manly type, considered flirting with Eenalyne but Sponge told him to "Wipe it out of your everlovin' mind, Dude! She's 'Lady Spelt' and Crumb's Mom. Have some class for a change!"

Dish made a guest appearance. During the absence of the Four (Crumb, Will, Whisk and Nefertiti) on their Mission, there had been ample time for S. K. to file down her edges nice and smooth. She looked almost as lovely as before, only smaller. The Kitchen Things were relieved to see that her fall had been a turning point and that now she was grateful for kindness and not a spiteful, envious creature. Her new attitude actually made her more beautiful than ever. As a matter of fact, Spoon and Dish had made peace together, and Spoon waved to Dish from the sidelines as she marched in the parade. (A day earlier Zoe had promised to get some real gold paint and gild her edges for the final touches. Dish was really looking forward to that!)

Then Crumb and Will marched down the counters while snow-blasts of confetti flew like an off-season winter wonderland in the middle of late Spring!

Tea-Pot wanted to say something, so Ringmaster Blender quieted everyone down, or tried to anyway, while Tea-Pot took his place on the central burner on the stove.

"I know I've been a hot-head at times and blown a lot of steam around, but I want to share something important with you. Do yourself a favor: Don't let the little nit-picky problems of everyday life get to you. Those are like tempests in a teacup. Take a look around you, Friends. Here I am, a Tea-Pot on Tempest Street and the winds of change have spoken. We all want to feel special, we all want to love and BE loved -- As long as we help each other and keep having fun, we can get over the tough times. Aren't we a Family, Kitchen Things? Aren't we? I think we ARE!"

Crumb, Will, Breadbox, Timer, Toaster, Dish, Spoon, Blender and every Kitchen Thing whistled as loud as Tea-Pot had ever whistled and cheered so loud that Zoe (who had just arrived to clean up the confetti) had to remind everyone, "Shhhh! All the Bakers are asleep upstairs."

Zoe stood before all the Kitchen Things and surveyed the mess and merriment that pervaded the place. Confetti everywhere. She would have her work cut out for her. She didn't mind a bit. They trusted her. That was worth a lot.

It was now Zoe's moment to say a few words. "I have been thinking about this for a few days. I may just be the only Human so far who knows you all are alive, that you deserve respect, and that Humans and Kitchen Things, Crumbs and Pets and all of us can learn to GET ALONG. I propose an Annual Let-There-Be-MAGIC Day! Whadaya think of that?!"

This idea was greeted with the loudest cheers of all. In fact, Sally and Johnny had awakened and were leaning over the upstairs balcony railing looking down, trying to figure out what was happening in the Kitchen. Zoe sensed it immediately and had everybody quiet down right away!

Someday she'd let the Baker kids know about how Crumb was Literate, how Will was a Genius, how Whisk was really a Dog Whiskerer and Nefertiti was Mistress of Time. She'd share with her young friends -- and maybe in time, with her own children and grandchildren -- the legend of how Real Food for Thought had come about. And how all these wild encounters had shown her that magic WAS real!

The room quieted down totally. This was a vision of a better world that reached into a new path. Mankind and animals in harmony or not, food or non-food, friendship or warfare stretched before them as possibilities at a significant Crossroads that was much bigger, more alluring and far more dangerous than just a telephone pole by a railroad track.

It had been very noisy in the Kitchen, now it was so quiet that a magnet would not even tremble on Coldylox. Peering downstairs from the balcony railing, Sally and Johnny shook their heads in wonderment, then went back to their beds and fell fast asleep. Zoe had managed to scoop up the confetti snow and tiptoed out the front door, locked it with her special key and traipsed back home. The celebration resumed very, very quietly in the Kitchen out of courtesy to the Bakers, their host Human family.

Finally, after Zoe had gone home, venerable Breadbox opened his tin door, nestled Crumb's cute little breadcrumb cousins up on his "stage" so they could witness history in the making and managed to ask Crumb if he would be so kind as to recite the Riddle for everyone.

If you can imagine a supremely proud moment, a bonding so instantaneous and glowing that it electrifies the air, then picture Crumb crowned with a wreath of tiny leaves of thyme, reciting the verses as nobly as any breadcrumb has ever done in the grand heritage of his Spelt forbears! For the Riddle had been the Instruction Manual, the Puzzle that the Four had miraculously solved.

It had taken the courage of the Four, the assistance of the Fifty, the magic of a Child and the love of two Families to solve it! It would be their signpost from now on.

Taking his cue from his dear Granddad and with Lady Spelt beaming by his side, here is what Crumb extolled in the fragrant air of his Home, the Kitchen:

> "Where there's a will,
> you know there's a way!
> What looks like work
> can turn into play!
> When green is red
> and "N" turns to "D",
> A-B-C's the day!

> (Crumb read that last line like, "A BEE seizes the day!)

Learning to read
plants a seed that is sound!
Heed the signs
and turn them around!
"E"nunciate well
and learn how it's spelled.

(Crumb repeated that line, the second time
saying "Spelt", nodding affectionately toward
his Mom. She beamed and blushed.)

A crumb will lead the way!

No one's too small
to follow a dream,
and no dream's too big
if it's straight from the heart!
For life is in living
and living's an art!
Enjoy the journey today!

So hold on tight
to being taught,
for truth is a price
that can't be bought!
This Riddle will tell you:
It's *real food* for thought!"

At the end of the Riddle, once Crumb had finished
saying it, came a moment so transformative and electric
that it seemed to hover on the very brink of eternity. No, it
wasn't a standing ovation, no, it wasn't a wave of cheers. It
was the ultimate tribute: A breathless hush so filled with
wonder and awe that it glows in the air with its own fire, a
silence as invisible as the wind and as powerful as a
tempest.

The Kitchen Things stood silent, drinking it in, understanding the Riddle without having to know what each word meant. After the silence, then came cheers, some isolated tears and... bit by bit (inevitably after all that fuss and joyous bother) quite a few yawns among the crowd. The extreme tension of almost losing Crumb and Will, followed by the adrenaline-thrill of having them safe and sound at home, escorting Crumb's mother as well — it was exciting, yes, but very, very tiring. It was getting late and all the Kitchen Things recognized that bedtime was nigh. It was finally time to say one last word.

Gently, perhaps mischievously, Spoon stood there, a living representative of times gone by that were still splendid in memory. She took command of the Kitchen, poised in the spotlight of her lace doily and declared she had a special announcement. It would be quick. Everyone quieted immediately and leaned forward to hear.

"Crumb, you and I have been best friends for a good long while. I remember when we first met. I have someone I want you to meet. Someone in my family that I think you will like... I mean, as a friend, er, well... Let's get on with it." She paused, embarrassed to hint that she thought they might be a bit more than friends.

"Crumb, meet my five-year-old niece, Demi Tasse. Hazel Baker just searched online last week and recovered her for our silverware collection. Demi came direct from Paris last night. She speaks English... and French fluently!"

Out stepped the most beautiful miniature silver spoon Crumb had ever seen, in fact, a more gorgeous, delicate and sweet little spoon he had never imagined could exist. She bore the fleur-de-lis embossment on the tip of her curved handle and had an adorable miniature French Maid outfit on with a slender black and white bow around her spoon-bowl neck.

Demi had all the grace of her Auntie Spoon along with an air of innocence and youth that was disarming to all. She twirled about and rushed over to plant a tiny kiss on Crumb's cheek, then a tiny kiss on his other cheek in the Continental manner. Then she shyly danced back near her Auntie.

Crumb had never realized how much like the color of fresh pink roses his cheeks could blush. He was almost as tall as she was and he would grow. Life was growth and he was ready for more adventures and... perhaps some settling down some fine day.

If you don't think Love at First Sight can exist, then you've never been in a Kitchen, the Veritable Heart of the Home.

Epilogue

Legends have been known to start in the most humble of places. Heroes have been known to come from the most unlikely sources, often reluctant to take on the challenge. Nursery rhymes have been known to originate in petty protests or grand causes.

Fashions change as fast as the wind but the wind is a constant. Good and evil play out their struggle in a myriad of passing civilizations. Man and beast have cared for or fought with one another ever since fires were contained in caves.

Bread has been broken amongst weary companions on journeys ever since seeds were gathered or planted in soil. Riddles have opened or closed doors from the beginnings of time. We are echoes of all the old stories, we are promises still yet to come, and we sing to our young so they understand that some things will always be true.

About the Author

Carol Worthey

The day Carol Worthey was born family friend, world-renowned Composer and Conductor Leonard Bernstein was in her home and made hamburgers in the shape of stars, proclaiming, "This little girl's gonna be a star!" Inspired by Lenny, Carol began composing music at three and a half and attempting to write down her music and lyrics at age four. Also a precocious painter, Carol was tested by professors and admitted to adult classes at a famous art conservatory, RISD (Rhode Island School of Design), at the tender age of five where she studied anatomy, color theory, oils and watercolor for seven years. Although Carol constantly created music, it wasn't until she was ten that she fully realized, "I'm a composer!" after concert pianist Vivian Rivkin performed her work in Carnegie Hall.

After these auspicious beginnings, Worthey began her first formal composition lessons at thirteen with Grant Beglarian outside of Tanglewood, where he was studying with Aaron Copland. At Columbia University in New York Carol won First Prize in Composition and studied English Literature and Oriental Studies. Her renowned mentors include Darius Milhaud, Vincent Persichetti, Walter Piston, Elliot Carter, Otto Luening, Henry Cowell, John Harbison and Academy Award winner, Eddy Lawrence Manson. Carol studied arranging and orchestration, graduating with honors from the Contemporary Composing and Arranging Program at jazz-oriented Grove School of Music. A children's musical she wrote in an inspired weekend (book, music and lyrics) played five years in Los Angeles and was featured on Entertainment Tonight. She composed the 1988 film score for an HBO holiday movie produced by George Lucas. In 2008 she combined Western instruments with Chinese traditional instruments in "Jade Flute", a work premiered in Beijing at the

International Congress of Women in Music. In 2010 she played her piano composition "The River" live on international radio to an estimated audience of 385,000. Her expressive and well-crafted music has been heard at Aspen Music Festival, Italian Brass Week, Carnegie Hall, Los Angeles Music Center, in Beijing and Hong Kong, France, Spain, Italy, Germany, England, Croatia, Switzerland, Japan, Malaysia, Taiwan, Canada, Mexico and throughout the United States. In 2003 Carol Worthey composed "Elegy" as a healing work after 9-11, premiered at St. Martin-in-The-Fields by cellist Joyce Geeting and pianist Robert Sage. In 2010 pianist Beth Levin and Violinist Yuki Numata premiered "Romanza" at Douglas Townsend's first "Facebook Friends" Concert in Manhattan. The work has since been performed by world-class musicians such as Yury Revich from Vienna. In 2011 Rostropovich proteges Maksim Velichkin and Ruslan Biryukov gave a delightful performance of Carol's cello duet, "Russian Scenes." The renowned Weiss Family Woodwinds premiered and recorded "Sandcastles" in 2012. In 2013 she collaborated with renowned comedienne and animal rescuer Elayne Boosler in "Rescue: A True Story" for clarinet, piano and cello performed by Julia Heinen, Dmitri Rachmanov and Ruslan Biryukov to standing ovations. Carol believes the arts can generate greater compassion and understanding in the areas of human rights and animal rights.

Carol Worthey has won numerous poetry awards throughout her life and is a published poet. She has given illuminating talks on Creativity and the Arts at USC, UCLA and Cal Lutheran University. Carol is a seasoned playwright, librettist and lyricist. She is a professional book editor at Worthgold Publishing, the company she shares with her husband of thirty-four years Ray Korns and a long-time member of Renaissance Speakers Club, a top Toastmasters International club. In 2014 Carol completed her first novel CRUMB: The Secret of the Riddle, a fantasy/adventure with an ecological message, initially inspired by her father's bedtime stories. Carol is currently writing a non-fiction book called TURNING LIFE INTO ART: HOW A COMPOSER WORKS which features insights from seventy contemporary composers, including Pulitzer-Prize winners and a MacArthur "genius grant" winner.

Carol continues to paint and exhibit her artworks. In 2000 she combined her composing and painting skills in an interactive art/music statue "Angel of Music" seen by over 600,000 visitors at Los Angeles Music Center. In 2007 Carol won a special award when she participated as a visual artist in the 2007 Florence Biennale International Contemporary Art Exhibit; her "Fanfare for The New Renaissance" for brass (a work she composed during a dream about world peace) was performed on Opening Day of the Biennale. It has since been conducted by legendary hornist Dale Clevenger at Italian Brass Festival. In 2008 she was awarded Best of Show Watercolor at a Hollywood exhibit. In 2012 she collaborated with Parisian sculptor Anne Ferrer in a curated Manhattan exhibit nominated for Best Curated Gallery Exhibit by the International Art Critics Association. In 2014 and 2016 she was delighted to be Honorary Judge in Hong Kong and Taiwan Children's Art Competitions.

Carol encourages children and adults alike to live a creative fulfilling life. She loves to teach music and art in her home studio in Granada Hills, California and bring out the talents of others. She welcomes you to experience her art, music and writings at www.CarolWorthey.com

***